IF SHE WAKES

Also by Michael Koryta

How It Happened
Rise the Dark
Last Words
Those Who Wish Me Dead
The Prophet
The Ridge
The Cypress House
So Cold the River
The Silent Hour
Envy the Night
A Welcome Grave
Sorrow's Anthem
Tonight I Said Goodbye

IF SHE WAKES

MICHAEL KORYTA

LITTLE, BROWN AND COMPANY

NEW YORK BOSTON LONDON

Little, Brown and Company
Hachette Book Group
1290 Avenue of the Americas, New York, NY 10104
littlebrown.com

First Edition: May 2019

Little, Brown and Company is a division of Hachette Book Group, Inc. The Little, Brown name and logo are trademarks of Hachette Book Group, Inc.

The publisher is not responsible for websites (or their content) that are not owned by the publisher.

The Hachette Speakers Bureau provides a wide range of authors for speaking events. To find out more, go to hachettespeakersbureau.com or call (866) 376-6591.

ISBN 978-0-316-29400-3 (hc) / 978-0-316-45414-8 (large print)
LCCN 2018956909

10 9 8 7 6 5 4 3 2 1

LSC-C

Printed in the United States of America

For Pete Yonkman,
who gave me the book that gave me the book.
Many thanks for your support, motivation, and friendship.

Part One

IGNITION

I

Nineteen minutes before her brain and her body parted ways, Tara Beckley's concern was the cold.

First night of October, but as the sun set and the wind picked up, it felt like midwinter, and Tara could see her breath fogging the air. That would have been crisp New England charm on another night, but not this one, when she wore only a thin sweater over a summer-weight dress. Granted, she hadn't expected to be standing in the cold, but she had a commitment to deliver one Professor Amandi Oltamu from dinner to his keynote presentation, and the professor was pacing the parking lot of the restaurant they'd just left, alternately staring into the darkness and playing with his phone.

Tara tried to stay patient, shivering in that North Atlantic night wind that swept leaves off the trees. She needed to get moving, and not just because of the cold. Oltamu had to arrive at 7:45, and *precisely* 7:45, because the Hammel College conference was coordinated by a pleasant woman named Christine whose eyes turned into dark daggers if the schedule went awry. And Professor Oltamu—sorry, *Dr.* Oltamu, he was one of those prigs who insisted on the title even though he wasn't a medical doctor, just another PhD—occupied the very first position in the program of Christine with the Dagger Eyes, and thus he was worthy of more daggers. It was, after all, opening night of the whole silly academic show.

"We have to go, sir," Tara called to the good doctor. He lifted a hand, asking for another minute, and studied the blackness. Pre-speech jitters? Couldn't he at least have those indoors?

Conference coordinator Christine and every other faculty member and student who'd attended the kickoff dinner for Hammel's imitation TED Talks were already long gone, leaving Tara alone with Dr. Oltamu in the restaurant parking lot. He was an odd man who seemed like a collection of mismatched parts—his voice was steady but his posture was tense, and his eyes were nervous, flicking around the parking lot as if he were confused by it.

"I don't mean to rush you, but we really—"

"Of course," he said and walked briskly to the car. She'd expected him to ride shotgun, but instead he pushed aside her yoga mat and a stack of books and settled into the back. Good enough. At least she could turn on the heater.

She got behind the wheel, started the car, and glanced in the mirror. "All set, Dr. Oltamu?" she asked with a smile intended to suggest that she knew who he was and what he did when in truth she hadn't the faintest idea.

"All set" came the answer in the chipper, slightly accented, but perfectly articulated English of this man who was originally from…Sudan, was it? Nigeria? She couldn't recall. She'd seen his bio, of course—Christine made sure that the student escorts were equipped with head shots and full bios of the distinguished speakers they'd be picking up throughout this week of grandeur, when Hammel College sought to bring some of the world's finest minds to its campus. The small but tony liberal arts school in southern Maine was just close enough to Boston to snag some of the Harvard or MIT speakers looking for extra paid gigs, and that looked great in the brochures to donors and prospective students alike. You needed to get the big names, and Hammel managed to, but Dr. Oltamu wasn't one of them. There was a reason he was batting leadoff instead of cleanup.

This was Tara's second year serving on the student welcoming committee, but it was also her last, because she was close to an exit. She'd taken extra classes in the summers and was set to jet in December, although she could attend the official graduation day in May. She hoped to be immersed in bigger and better things by May, but who knew, maybe by then she would want to return. That wasn't hard to imagine. In fact, she was already nostalgic about Hammel, because she knew this was her last taste of it. Last autumn in Maine, last parties, last midterms, last of a lot of things.

"We are good on time, yes?" Dr. Oltamu said. He checked an impressive gold watch on his left wrist, a complement to his fine suit, if only the fine suit had actually fit him. It seemed he'd ignored tailoring, and as a result he would be presenting his speech in the sartorial equivalent of an expensive hand-me-down from a taller, leaner brother.

Presenting his speech about…

Damn all, what does he do?

"We'll be just fine," she said. "And I can't wait to hear your presentation tonight."

Presentation on…

She'd been hoping for a little help, but he twisted away and stared out the back window.

"There is a planned route?" he said.

"What do you mean?"

"From the restaurant to the theater. Everyone would drive the same way?"

"Uh, yeah. I mean, as far as I know."

"Can we go a different way?"

She frowned. "Pardon?"

"Give me the Tara tour," he said, turning back around and offering a smile that seemed forced. "I'd like to see your favorite places in the community."

"Um…well, I need to get you there on time, but…sure." The request was bizarre, but playing tour guide wouldn't slow her down. In fact, she knew exactly where she would take him—down to the old railroad bridge where she ran almost every morning and where, if she timed it right, she could feel as if she were racing the train itself. That bridge over the Willow River was one of her favorite places on earth.

"It is very beautiful here," Oltamu said as she drove.

Indeed it was. While Tara had applied exclusively to southern schools for her graduate program in a concerted effort to bust out of Maine before another February snagged her in its bleak grasp, she would miss the town. The campus was small but appealing, with the right blend of ancient academic limestone towers and contemporary labs; the faculty was good, the setting idyllic. Tonight they'd gone to a fine restaurant on a high plateau above town, and as she followed the winding roads back toward the sea, she was struck by her affection for this town of tidy Colonial homes on large, sloping lawns backed up against forested mountains that provided some of the best hiking you could ever hope to find. The fall chill was in the air, and that meant that woodstoves and fireplaces were going. This blend of colored leaves against a sunset yielding to darkness redolent with woodsmoke was what she loved about New England—the best time of day at the best time of year. She left her window cracked as she drove, not wanting to seal out that perfect autumn scent.

Dr. Oltamu had turned around and was staring behind them again, as if the rear window were the only one with a view. He'd been respectful but reserved at dinner, which was one of the reasons she couldn't remember what in the world he was there to speak about.

Oil? Energy crisis? No…

They wound down the mountain and into town. There was the North Woods Brewing Company on the left, a weekend staple for her, and there was the store where she'd bought her first skis, which had led to her first set of crutches, and there, down the hill and past the Catholic church and closer to the harbor, was

Garriner's, which had been serving the best greasy-spoon breakfast in town for sixty years. Down farther was the harbor itself, the water the color of ink now but a stunning cobalt at sunrise. Along this stretch were the few bars that Hammel could claim as its nightlife, though to most people they were nothing but pregame venues—the serious drinking was done at house parties. It wasn't a big school, and it wasn't a big town, but it was pleasant and peaceful, absolutely no traffic tonight as she drove toward the auditorium where Dr. Oltamu would address the crowd about...

Climate change?

"Lovely place," Oltamu said, facing forward again. "So charming."

"It was the perfect college town for me," she said, and she realized with some surprise that she wasn't just delivering the student-tour-guide shtick. She meant it. She could see the area just as he did: bucolic, quaint. A town designed for a college, a place for young adults to bump up against the real world, every experience there for the taking but with a kinder, gentler feel than some of the large campuses she'd visited.

"It is truly excellent when one finds where one belongs," Dr. Oltamu said as Tara drove away from the harbor. The car climbed and then descended into the valley, where the campus waited across the Willow River.

Oltamu was gazing behind them again.

"I'm looking forward to your talk tonight," she tried once more. *Your talk about...artificial intelligence?*

"I appreciate that, but I'm afraid I'll surely bore you," he said with a small laugh.

Come on, gimme some help here, Doc. "What's the most exciting part of your work in *your* opinion, then?" she asked. A pathetic attempt, but now she was determined to win the war. She would figure out what he did without stooping to ask him flat-out.

He paused, then said, "Well, the Black Lake is certainly intriguing. I've just come from there, actually. A fascinating trip.

But I doubt there are many creative-writing majors who are fascinated by batteries."

There it was! Batteries! He designed some sort of solar panels and batteries that were supposed to save fuel consumption and, thus, the earth. You know, trivial shit.

Tara was embarrassed that she hadn't been able to remember this on her own, especially since he'd somehow remembered her major from the chaotic introductions at the restaurant. Then again, he had a point—batteries were not an area of particular fascination for her. But you never knew. There was, as her favorite writing professor always said, a story around every corner.

"Where is Black Lake?" she asked, but he'd shifted away yet again and was staring intently out the back window. A vehicle had appeared in her rearview mirror in a sudden glare of lights and advanced quickly, riding right up along her bumper, its headlights shining down into the CRV, and she pumped the brake, annoyed. The taller vehicle—a truck or a van—backed off.

Tara drove beneath a sugar maple that was shedding its leaves, a cascade of crimson whispering across the hood, bloodred and brittle. No matter what warm and beautiful beach was within walking distance of wherever she was next year, she would miss autumn here. She understood that it was supposed to be a somber season, of course, that autumn leaves meant the end of something, but so far in her life, it had marked only beginnings; each fall brought another birthday, a new teacher and classmates, sometimes new schools, new friends, new boyfriends. She loved fall precisely for the way it underscored that sense of change. Change, for Tara Beckley, twenty-two years old as of a week ago, had always been a good thing.

She crested the hill, made the steep descent down Knowlton Street, and turned onto Ames Road, a residential stretch. The headlights behind them vanished, and Dr. Oltamu faced forward again.

She was just about to repeat her question—*Where is Black Lake?*—when he spoke.

"Why so dark?"

"Pardon?"

"The street is very dark."

He wasn't wrong. Ames Road was unusually dark.

"There was some fight with the property owners over light pollution," she said, a vague memory of the article in the student newspaper coming back to her. "They put in new street lamps, but they had to be dim."

She flicked on her high beams, illuminating another swirl of rust-colored leaves stirring in the road.

"I see. Now, Hammel is a walking campus, I understand? Things are close together?"

"Yes. In fact, we're coming up to a place where I run every morning. *Almost* every morning at least, unless there's a big exam or…something." Something like a hangover, but she didn't want to mention that to the good doctor. "There's an old bridge down here that crosses from campus into town, and it's for pedestrians and cyclists only. There's a railroad bridge next to it. In the morning, if I get up early enough, I can run with the train. I race it." She gave a self-conscious laugh.

In the darkness below, the old railroad bridge threw spindly shadows across the Willow River. Beside it, separated by maybe twenty feet, was the new pedestrian and cycling bridge, part of a pathway system that wound through the campus and town. Tara started to turn left at the last intersection above the bridge, but Oltamu spoke up.

"May we stop and walk?" he said.

It was such an odd and abrupt request that it took her a moment to respond. "I can show you around after your talk, but they'll kill me if I get you there late."

"I would very much like to walk," he said, and his voice now matched his tense posture. "It's my knee. Stiffens up and then I'm in terrible pain. Distracting pain."

"Um…" She glanced at the clock, doing the math and trying to imagine how she might explain this to Christine.

"Please," he said. In the mirror, the whites of his eyes stood out starkly against his dark face. "You said the bridge goes to campus, correct?"

"Yes, but we'd really be pushing it for time. I can't get you there late."

He leaned forward. "I would very much like to walk," he said again. "I would like to see the bridge. I will make it clear to anyone involved that this was my delay. But I walk quickly."

Even with that bad knee? "Sure," she said, because she was now more alarmed by the strange urgency in his request than by the specter of an angry Christine. "We can walk."

She eased the car down the hill, toward the old railroad bridge and the new footbridge. A dozen angled parking spaces waited beside a pillar with a plaque identifying the railroad bridge's historical significance. The spots were all empty now, but in the morning you'd see people piling out of their cars with dogs on leashes, or removing bikes from racks.

She pulled into one of the angled spaces, and Dr. Oltamu was out of the car almost before it was parked. He stood with his back to the river and the campus and stared up the hill. Everything there was lost to darkness. He'd wanted to see the bridge; now he faced the other way. He'd been worried about time; now he wanted to walk. He had a bad knee; now he craved exercise.

"Why don't we head across the bridge, sir," she said. But he ignored her, took his cell phone from his pocket, and beckoned for her.

"May we take a picture together? I've been asked to use social media. You know…for a broader reach. I am told photos are best for engagement. So may I? You are my Hammel escort, after all."

She didn't love the way he said *escort,* but she also wasn't going to be shy about putting an elbow into his windpipe if he tried to grab her ass or something, so she said, "Sure," and then leaned awkwardly toward him for the photo—head close, ass away—and watched their image fill the screen of his iPhone. The phone seemed identical to hers, but the camera function was different; the screen was broken into a grid of squares. He tilted the phone in a way that centered Tara in the frame, and her smile grew more pained and she started to pull away as he snapped the photo. He didn't touch her, though, didn't say anything remotely lewd, just a polite "Thank you very much," and then he turned his attention to the screen, tapping away as if he intended to crop, edit, and post the photo immediately.

"Sir, we really do need to get going."

"Yes. One moment." Head down, tapping away. Then he said, "Did you ever have a nickname?"

"Pardon?"

He looked up and smiled. "You know, something only a good friend calls you, something like that? Or were you always just Tara?"

She started to say, *Just Tara, thanks, and now let's get a move on,* but reflex took over and she blurted out, "Twitch."

"Twitch?"

"My sister, Shannon, called me that because I was a jumpy kid. I spooked easily, I guess. Scary movies, in particular—I always jumped."

When Tara was little, the nickname was just Shannon picking on her. But later on, it became affectionate. Shannon liked how much Tara cared about fictional characters, how emotionally invested she became in their stories.

"We really should be—"

There was a rustling sound behind them, and they whirled at the same time, Tara with a startled jerk that offered a live-action demonstration of the childhood nickname. Her response was still more composed than Oltamu's, though. He gave a strangled cry, stepped back, and lifted his hands as if surrendering.

Then Tara saw the dog in the bushes and smiled. "That's just Hobo."

"What?" Oltamu backed farther away.

"He's a stray. Always around the bridge. And he *always* comes out to bark at the morning train. That's how I spotted him. If you come by often enough, he'll get to know you. But he doesn't let you catch him. I've certainly tried." She knelt, extended her hand, and made a soft sound with her tongue on the roof of her mouth. Her rush to get Oltamu to the venue was forgotten in her instinct to show affection to the old stray, her companion on so many morning runs. He slunk out of the darkness, keeping low, and let Tara touch the side of his head. Only the side; never the top. If you reached for him, he'd bolt. Not far, at least not with her, but out of grasping distance. He was a blend of unknown breeds, with the high carriage and startling speed of a greyhound, the floppy ears of a beagle, and the coat of a terrier.

"He's been here for a long time," she said. "Every year people try to catch him and get him to a rescue, but nobody ever succeeds. So we just give up and feed him."

She scratched the dog's soft, floppy ears, one of which had a few tears along the edge, and then straightened.

"Okay," she said. "We've got to hurry now. I can't get you there late. So let's—"

"Hobo?" Oltamu was staring at the dog as if he'd never encountered such an animal.

"It's just what I call him. He likes to chase the train. Anyhow, we have to—"

"Stay there, please. I'd like a picture of him." He knelt. "Can you get him to look at me?" he asked as he extended his phone.

I'll tell Christine to look at his phone, Tara thought. *I have exculpatory evidence now. "Do you see, Christine? He made me stop to take pictures of a stray dog!"*

"His attention?" Oltamu said. "Please? Toward the camera?"

Tara raised her eyebrows and pursed her lips. *Oookay.* Then she turned back to Hobo and made the soft clucking sound again. He looked at her but didn't move. Oltamu was a stranger, and Hobo didn't approach strangers.

"Very good," Oltamu whispered, as entranced as if he were on a safari and had encountered a rare species. "Excellent."

The camera clicked, a flash illuminated the dog in stark white light, and Hobo growled.

"It's okay," Tara told him, but he gave a final growl, gazed up the hill at the dark street beyond, then slipped back into the trees.

"All right," Tara said, rising again. "We really *have to*—"

"I need you to do me a favor. It is very important. Crucial."

"Please, Doctor. They're waiting on you at the auditorium, so—"

"Crucial," he said, his accent heavier, the word loaded with emotion.

She looked at his earnest face and then across the river at the lights of the campus. Suddenly she felt far away from where she belonged, and very alone. "What's the favor?"

He moved toward her, and she stepped back, bumping into one of the bike racks. Pain shot through her hip. He reached out, and she recoiled, fearing his hand, but then she saw that he was extending the phone to her.

"Please put this in your car. Somewhere secure. Can you lock the glove compartment?"

She wanted to object, or at least ask him for a reason, but his face was so intense, so worried, that all she did was nod.

"Put it there, then. Please. I'm going to walk across the bridge myself. I'll find my way."

What is happening here? What in the world is he doing?

"Please," he repeated, and Tara took the phone from his hand, walked hurriedly past him, and opened the passenger door. She leaned in and put the phone in the glove box. It took her two tries to lock it, because her hand was trembling. She heard him move behind her, and she spun, hands rising, ready to fend him off, but he was just watching to see that she'd done what he'd asked.

"Thank you," he said. "I don't mean to frighten you, but that phone is very important." He looked up the hill, then back to her. "I will walk from here alone. You should drive."

She hadn't spoken throughout this, and she didn't now. She just wanted to get away from him. Driving off and leaving him here was fine by her.

"Thank you, Tara," he said. "It is important. I am sorry you are afraid."

She stood motionless, hands still raised, watching him as warily as Hobo had.

"Please go now," he said. "Take the car and go. I will walk across the bridge when you are gone."

She moved. Going around the front of the car would have been quicker, but she would have passed closer to him, so she made her way around the back. She'd just reached the driver's door when she heard the engine behind her.

She glanced in the direction of the noise with relief, glad that she was no longer alone with this bizarre man, expecting to see headlights coming on. Instead, there was just the dark street. The engine grew louder, and with it came the sound of motion, but she saw nothing, so she just stood there dumbly, her hand on the car door. Oltamu had also turned to face the sound. They were both staring into the darkness when Tara finally saw the black van.

It was running with no trace of light. It came on down the road like something supernatural, quiet and dark but also remarkably fast.

She had only an instant to move. Her guiding thought was that she wanted to be away from the car, even if that meant going into the river. Down there, she thought she might have a chance.

She was scrambling away from the CRV when the van hit it squarely in the rear passenger door, pinning Oltamu against the side of the car, and then the CRV hit her, and though she got her wish of making it into the river, she never knew it. She was airborne when the front of her skull connected with the concrete pillar that marked the railroad bridge as a historical site, and by the time she entered the water, she wasn't aware of anything at all.

2

When the flight from Portland to Detroit arrived and her asset didn't walk off the plane, Lisa Boone moved from the gate to the Delta Sky Club and ordered a Johnnie Walker Blue.

"Rocks?" the bartender asked.

"No."

"Water back?"

"No."

An overweight businessman in an off-the-rack suit with a hideously mismatched tie and pocket square turned on his bar stool and smiled a greasy, lecherous smile.

"The lady knows how to order her scotch."

Boone didn't look at him. "The lady does," she said and put cash on the bar.

"Have a seat." He moved his laptop bag off the stool beside him. The laptop bag had not one but two tags identifying him as a Diamond Medallion member. Wouldn't want your Sky Club status to slip under the radar.

"I'm fine."

"Oh, come on."

"I'm fine," Boone repeated, but already she knew this guy wasn't going to give up so easily. One didn't become a Diamond Medallion member without some dedication.

"Humor a fellow traveler," he said and patted the leather-topped stool. "I've been drinking Budweiser, but I like your style—scotch it is. Have a seat, and put your money away. I'll buy the drinks."

Boone didn't say anything. She breathed through her nose and waited for the bartender to break the fifty she'd put on the bar, and she thought of Iraq and the first fat man she'd killed. You weren't supposed to admit such a thing, but she'd always taken a little extra pleasure in killing fat men.

"I hope this doesn't seem too forward," Diamond Medallion Man said, leaning toward her and deepening his voice, "but you are absolutely stunning."

The bartender put her change down, and Boone picked up most of the bills, leaving a five behind, and turned to Diamond Medallion Man. He gave what was undoubtedly his winningest smile.

"I hope this doesn't seem too forward," Boone said, "but do you know the difference between Bud and Bud Light?"

His smile wavered. "What?"

She reached out, grasped the flesh under his chin, and pinched it hard between her thumb and index finger. "*That* is the difference," she said and released him as he went red-faced and wide-eyed. "You might consider switching it up."

She picked up her scotch and walked away from the bar, chastising herself. The fat man and the bartender were both staring, and that meant at least two people would remember her now, the polar opposite of her goal today. She'd known better, of course, should've just shrugged the lech off, but her temper could get away from her when she was forced to be passive.

All she could do right now was sit and wait and hope that her man had taken a later flight.

She went to the monitors and studied the arrival times. Maybe it wasn't trouble yet. Maybe he'd just gotten delayed or had overslept. There was not supposed to be any contact today, so even if he'd missed his flight, he wouldn't have reached out. She had no choice but to wait. The next flight in from Portland was in three hours. Then there was a final flight at nine p.m. If he wasn't on either one, it would be a very bad sign.

Of course, his last messages had been a bad sign. Cryptic and scared.

Am I being followed? If so, tell them to back off.

Nobody was following him. Nobody should have been, at least. That was by his own insistence too. He was out in the cold, unprotected, going through his last week of free movements as had long been agreed upon. He could not attract attention, and he thought that canceling an established speaking tour would launch a signal flare into the blackness.

Or what they hoped was blackness.

She wasn't allowed to call him, wasn't allowed to make contact. Just pick him up in Detroit and go from there. All week long, she'd waited as he went from stop to stop, and she'd wanted protection on him the whole time, but it had been refused. The last stop had seemed the safest, though. A small town in Maine, an hour of speaking at some overpriced liberal arts school for kids with Ivy League trust funds but SEC brains. Hardly hostile territory. One night in a hotel on campus, a drive to the Portland International Jetport that morning, then a flight bound for Los Angeles with a layover in Detroit, and in Detroit he would disappear.

But the magic trick wouldn't work if he never stepped onstage. A man who never appeared couldn't disappear.

Boone left the flight monitors and walked through the lounge, past the sitting area with the crackling electric fire and the dark paneled wood that strove for the feel of an elegant home library in a place where every minute you spent was one more than you wanted to spend, and on out to a row of chairs facing the glass walls that overlooked the concourse. She sat, crossed her legs, sipped her scotch, and stared at the crowds hurrying for the tram.

Two more flights. Two more chances.

If he didn't walk off one of those planes, she'd have to call it in. If he didn't walk off one of those planes, there were going to be big problems.

Come on, Doc, she thought. *Don't let me down now. Not so close to the finish line.*

She withdrew her secure phone from her purse, pulled up his last message, and read it again, as if it might tell her something she'd missed before.

ASK THE GIRL.

What girl? Ask her *what?*

Boone put the phone away, swirled her scotch, and silently begged the next flight from Portland to deliver her man.

3

On the day before negligent-vehicular-manslaughter charges were filed against him in Maine, Carlos Ramirez bought a plane ticket to Caracas under a name for which he had both a driver's license and passport and waited for the kid to pick him up and take him to the airport.

The kid was late, and Carlos had a feeling that was intentional. The kid looked barely old enough to buy cigarettes, and he didn't say much, but he always had this faint smile that suggested he was laughing at you, the kind of smile that made you want to check to see if your fly was unzipped or if there was food stuck in your teeth. That was annoying shit from anybody, but from a child, it was begging for an ass-beating.

Carlos didn't think he was supposed to touch the kid, though. In fact, he had a feeling that would be a terrible mistake. He didn't know why the kid was so protected, but it was clear that he was, and so Carlos dealt with that bullshit smile and the mocking eyes. He'd have to do it only once more. If the kid ever showed up in Venezuela, it would be a different story.

Twenty minutes after he was supposed to be picked up and just as he was beginning to worry that he'd miss his flight and everything would be fucked, Carlos stepped outside to have a cigarette and stare up the street, as if he could will the car into appearing.

The car was already at the curb.

He stared at it, shook his head, and muttered, "Can't you come up and knock on the damned door," under his breath.

The kid spoke from behind him.

"I was told to meet you on the porch."

He was sitting in a plastic lawn chair with his back against the house, one foot hooked over his knee, looking for all the world like an old man relaxing and watching the neighborhood pass by.

"The hell are you doing?" Carlos snapped. "How long you been here?"

The kid took his cell phone out. Studied it. "Twenty-six minutes."

"You fucking kidding me? You just sat there?"

"I was told to meet you on the porch," he repeated, unbothered, and pocketed the phone. All of his movements were slow, but there was a quality to his slender muscles that promised he could move fast if he was so inclined. He had a couple inches on Carlos and a longer reach, but Carlos would have liked nothing more than to step inside that reach and lay some good shots on his body, let the little prick understand that respect was not unimportant in this business.

Just get to the airport. Stay cool long enough to get your cash and get on the plane.

The cash was at the airport, and the kid was the ride. These were the rules.

Carlos said, "Let's get moving, you…" He stopped himself before saying *little asshole*. "Let's go."

"You?" The kid raised his eyebrows with patient curiosity, as if he weren't offended, merely intrigued. "You…what?"

"Nothing. Let's get moving. I can't miss this flight, man. You know that."

The kid didn't stand. He still had his foot resting on his knee, his posture relaxed, in total contrast to his pale blue eyes. They danced around until they locked on you, and once they did that, you wished they hadn't. It was an empty stare. Vacant. It reminded Carlos of men he'd fought in dingy gyms in Miami. They were always the guys who didn't seem to mind being hit.

The kid adjusted the bill of his baseball cap, bending it slightly with both hands. He always had that damn hat, which was jet-black with no logo and a line of metallic thread tracing the front seam. That was no doubt supposed to add flair, but instead it seemed to provide a target for anyone who wanted to stitch a line of bullets through his skull. Carlos would have happily volunteered for that task.

"I hate unfinished sentences," the kid said. "People do that all the time. Leave a thought floating in the air, and then you've got to guess at what it was going to be." He lowered his hands and his eyes flicked to Carlos and held on him in that creepy way he had, like he was deciphering something written in a foreign language. "That can cause misunderstandings."

Carlos beckoned to him with his right hand, because his right hand had risen despite himself, and now he needed to do something with it that didn't involve smacking the shit out of the kid.

"Come on. Get up. This is serious."

The kid didn't move. "Finish your thought."

"Excuse me?"

"Otherwise I'll keep guessing at what it was going to be. Then I'll be distracted on the drive. That's not safe. You, of all people, should be familiar with the risks of distracted drivers."

"You're a piece of work, man."

"Is that what you were going to say? 'Let's get moving, you piece of work'?"

"Sure."

The kid made a show of pondering this with a thoughtful frown, and then he mouthed the sentence without giving voice to the words and shook his head. "That doesn't sound right."

"How about 'you little asshole'?" Carlos said, finally losing his temper. "Does that sound better?"

The kid went back to the thoughtful frown, and then he mouthed this one too: *Let's get moving, you little asshole.* He snapped his fingers and pointed at Carlos.

"Yes," he said, smiling. "That's it. I can buy that one."

Carlos took a breath, ready to tell him to stand up or to *make* him stand up—this thing was going one way or the other—but the kid finally moved. Still with that practiced laziness, every motion slow, uncrossing his foot from his knee, standing, brushing off his pants, stretching, adjusting the ball cap. But at least he was moving.

"Let's get you out of here, sir," he said, formal as any suit-and-cap chauffeur.

"Yeah. Let's." Carlos went inside, grabbed the duffel bag that held the only belongings he was leaving the country with, and slammed the door for the last time. He was ready to be out of this shithole. Say what you wanted about Venezuela; he'd take any corner of that country over the Boston winters.

They walked down the porch steps and across the street to the kid's car. It was a rust-colored Camaro with dark-tinted windows that looked like an unmarked cop car. Or an asshole kid's car. Carlos opened the back door, threw the duffel bag in, then went around to the passenger side. The kid had the big engine growling by the time Carlos was in the passenger seat. The car was immaculate inside, absolutely devoid of personal effects except for an energy drink sitting in the cup holder, something called Bang, the word written in red on a black can. Music was playing, a high, tinkling keyboard riff over a thumping bass line that rattled the energy drink can against the cup holder. It sounded like the opening of a shitty rap song, dance-floor hip-hop, but nobody ever came on with a verse.

The kid drove them out of the neighborhood while the song played. He sipped the energy drink and set it down and it resumed rattling against the cup holder in tempo with the bass line from the song.

Bang.

When Carlos picked up the can, it was more to stop the rattling than anything else. The metallic jangle was getting in his head, bouncing around like a troublesome pinball determined to jostle every rage nerve it could find. "I bet this tastes like shit."

The kid didn't answer. He was smiling and bobbing his head to the music with a little right-to-left shimmy in his shoulders, and Carlos wanted to smash the aluminum can into his teeth. He forced himself to look down at it instead, fighting for calm.

"'Bang,'" he read from the label. "'Potent brain and body fuel.' What did you pay for this, six bucks? Potent brain and body fuel, my ass."

"Try it."

"I'd rather drink my own piss."

"Not in my car, please."

Carlos set the can down and watched it vibrate with each thumping shake of the speakers, the same riff still playing on loop.

"What is this bullshit music? Anybody ever gonna throw a verse?"

"You can if you want. I won't laugh."

"Oh, it's just the beat, eh? So you're a rapper? Cool, little man! Let me hear something. I bet you're good. Like Eminem…nah, more like Macklemore, right?"

Carlos was obviously screwing with him, but the kid didn't react, didn't lose his smile. There was a strange quality to him that didn't just unsettle Carlos; it reminded him of someone. He couldn't place it.

"What's your name, anyhow?" he said. It had honestly never occurred to him to ask. Their transactions hadn't been of the let's-get-to-know-each-other type.

"Dax."

"Dax. The hell kind of name is that?"

"Serbian. It means 'little asshole.'" He said it calmly and quietly and never looked at Carlos.

"Hilarious," Carlos said, worrying that he'd pissed the kid off and hating himself for worrying. The kid couldn't be more than nineteen, and Carlos had been in the game for twenty years and had killed fourteen men and two women and he was not about to be intimidated by some child with a weird smile.

But you are. He bothers you. He scares you.

"I don't like saying *Dax*," Carlos said, because talking made him feel better than just riding. "*Dax*. Makes me feel like I'm gagging."

"I'm sorry it doesn't roll off your tongue like *Carlos*."

"Sure doesn't. What's your last name? I'll call you that."

For the first time in their limited relationship, the kid seemed to hesitate. It was quick, just a little hitch, but it was there. It was exactly what you looked for in the ring, and when you saw it, you threw the knockout punch.

"Blackwell," the kid said then, and Carlos's knockout punch was forgotten, all his confidence sapped by this unanticipated jab.

That's it. Holy shit, that is it, he's just like them.

"Which one?" Carlos asked. He felt a cold tension along his spine.

"Pardon?"

"Which one of them are you related to?"

"Which one of who?"

"Don't be a dick. Which one of those brothers that got killed in Montana are you related to, Jack or Patrick?"

The kid glanced at him, amused. "That's a strange question."

"Why?"

"If they were brothers, and I was related to one, I'd have to be related to both. Do you follow that, Carlos? We'd all be part of the same family then. That's the way it works."

Again the urge to smack him rose, but this time it was easier to grip the armrest. The body count that Carlos had amassed would not have meant anything to Jack and Patrick Blackwell.

"I didn't know either of them had a son," Carlos said. "They didn't seem like—"

He managed to stop himself.

The kid said, "Want to finish that thought, Carlos? Or do you want me to guess?"

His eyes were on the road, and his right hand was looped over the steering wheel and he seemed perfectly relaxed, but Carlos did not like the sound of that question, so he decided to answer it without fucking around.

"They didn't seem like the family type," he said.

"Oh. All about their work, you mean?"

"I guess."

"Well, everyone has a personal life. Does that surprise you? That they would have had lives of their own and that they would have been private about those things?" He looked at Carlos, and Carlos struggled to meet his eyes, then chose instead to stare over the kid's shoulder at the construction site they were passing, the gutted remains of an old strip mall that stood waiting for bulldozers to raze it. Then he looked down at the vibrating aluminum can. *Bang. Potent brain and body fuel.* He released the armrest so that both hands were free. Suddenly, it seemed very important to have his hands free.

"No," he said. "It doesn't surprise me, and I don't really give a shit. I was just curious, that's all. I should've figured it out earlier. You remind me of them."

They'd pulled up to a stop sign. The kid smiled at him again.

"I hear that a lot," he said, and then he fired two shots from a suppressed handgun that was inside his jacket pocket. He shot left-handed, firing under his right arm without ever removing his right hand from the steering wheel, that confident in his aim, and he never lost the smile.

Then he turned the corner, pulled the Camaro to the curb, and put it in park. He left the key in the ignition and the engine running, the music still playing, those high piano notes over the low bass with no lyrics, but he took the energy drink. He sipped it while he shut the door on the music and the corpse, adjusted his baseball cap with the other hand, and walked away.

Part Two

LOCKED IN

4

The case was so simple that Abby Kaplan decided to stop for a beer on her way to the scene.

This wasn't encouraged protocol—drinking on the job could get her fired, of course—but there wasn't much pressure today. The cops had already gotten one of the drivers to admit guilt. They had a signed statement and a recorded statement. Not much for Abby to do but review their report, take her own photos, and agree with their assessment. Cut and dried.

Besides, Hammel was a forty-minute drive from the Biddeford office of Coastal Claims and Investigations, and Abby, well... Abby got a little nervous driving these days. A beer could help that. Contrary to what most people—and, certainly, the police—believed, a beer before driving could make her safer for society. It settled twitching hands and a jumpy mind, kept her both relaxed and focused. Abby had no doubt that she drove better with a six-pack in her bloodstream than most people did stone-cold sober. She was damn sure safer than most drivers, with their eyes on their cell phones and their heads up their asses.

This wasn't an argument you'd win in court, but that didn't mean it wasn't the truth.

She stopped at a brewpub not far from the Portland jetport, a place busy enough that she wouldn't stand out, and she paid cash so there would be no credit card transaction to haunt her if something went wrong. Not that anything *would* go wrong, but she'd seen the ways it could. She also made a point of tearing the receipt into bits, because cash could help you only so much; there were different kinds of paper trails. She'd worked one case where the driver had been dumb enough to leave a receipt on the console recording the five margaritas he'd knocked back just before getting behind the wheel and blowing through a stop sign. It wasn't that abnormal, really. You stopped by the body shop to take pictures of a cracked-up car and found damning evidence just sitting there in the cup holder, a tiny slip of paper with a time-and-date stamp that blew up any possible defense. Amazing. Abby had been on the fringes of the PI game for only a few months, but already she understood what sustained the profession: people lied, and people were stupid.

Oh, and one more: People sued. People *loved* to sue.

That was precisely what worried the good folks in the risk-mitigation office of Hammel College, her current client. When a world-renowned engineer was killed on your campus while in the care of a student escort, you didn't have to be paranoid to imagine the lawsuit.

Abby sat at the bar, sipped her beer, and reviewed the case file. She didn't see much for the college to worry about. The girl who'd been escorting the engineer around town had had clean blood-work—a relief to the college, since it meant no DUI claim, but not much help to the girl, because she was still lights-out, five days in a coma now. And even though she had a negative drug screen, she could still have been negligent or at fault, which could turn into an expensive wrongful-death suit, but—good news for the Hammel Hurricanes—the second driver involved had taken responsibility on the scene!

He'd given a full statement to the police that was the accident-report equivalent of tying a hangman's noose and sticking his own head through it: He'd been using his cell phone, trying to get his bearings through the phone's map application, and when he looked up, he realized that what he'd thought was a road bridge was in fact a pedestrian bridge. He swerved to avoid it—and ended up in a hell of a lot of trouble.

Mr. Carlos Ramirez of Brighton, Massachusetts, was now into the realm of criminal courts, because one person was dead and another was a vegetable and Ramirez had eliminated any compelling argument for even a shared-fault case, what was known in Maine as modified comparative negligence. A good investigator paired with a good attorney could almost always find a weasel's way into a modified-comparative-negligence ruling, but Carlos Ramirez was going to make it tough on his team.

It was Abby's job to imagine what that team was considering, though, and in this case, it would be Tara Beckley's location at the time of the accident. She was supposed to deliver her charge to an auditorium that was nowhere near where she'd parked. Some enterprising attorney might wonder whether her failure to follow the plan for the evening's keynote speaker might qualify as negligence and, if so, whether the college might be responsible for that.

After Tara had parked her CRV beside a bridge that led to the Hammel College campus, Carlos Ramirez smashed into the car, killing Amandi Oltamu and knocking Tara Beckley into the cold waters of the Willow River. A bystander on the opposite side of the river had heard the crash but hadn't seen it, and he managed to pull her out in a heroic but ultimately futile effort, because Tara Beckley was in a coma from which she was unlikely to emerge.

That left one dead man, one silent woman, and no witnesses.

I need to get my hands on her cell phone, Abby thought. Cell phones could either save you or hang you in almost any accident investigation. The beautiful simplicity of the case against Ramirez could be destroyed by something like a text message from Tara Beckley saying that her car had run out of gas or that she had a migraine and couldn't see well enough to drive. You just never knew. Dozens of apps kept tracking information that most users were blissfully unaware of; it was entirely possible that the precise timing of the accident could be established from a cell phone. And if Tara Beckley had been using the phone while she was behind the wheel, Oltamu's family might take a renewed interest in suing the college and their selected escort. Any whiff of negligence had to be considered.

Only problem: her phone seemed to be missing.

So it went into the river with her, Abby thought. *She came up, and the phone didn't.*

She drained her beer and frowned, flipping back and forth through the pages of the report. Explaining Tara Beckley's missing phone didn't seem to be difficult, but Amandi Oltamu's phone could also contain evidence, and Abby didn't see where that was either. The police report included the items removed from the car, and the coroner's report had a list of personal effects removed from the body, ranging from a wallet to a Rolex.

No phone, though.

The lead investigator was a guy with the state police named David Meredith. Abby wasn't eager to speak to police these days, considering that there were two cops in California still urging a prosecutor to press charges against her for an accident that had made her more of a celebrity than she'd ever desired to be.

The concern conjured the memory, as it always did. Luke's empty eyes, his limp hand, the soft whistle and hiss of the machines that kept him breathing. Synthetic life. And the photographers waiting outside the hospital for a shot of the woman responsible for it all: Abby Kaplan, the woman who'd killed Luke London, cut down a rising star in his prime. James Dean and Luke London, joined in immortality, young stars killed in car crashes. The only difference was that Luke hadn't been driving the car.

That was a fun little secret about his movies. He never drove the car.

Never felt any shame over that either. Luke was completely

comfortable in his own skin, happy to hand the keys over to a woman who barely came up to his shoulder, to smile that magazine-cover smile and say, "One day you'll teach me how to do it myself."

And I was going to. That was the idea, you see. It was his idea, not mine, I just happened to have the wheel, and my hands were steady, my hands were...

She shook her head, the gesture violent enough to draw a curious glance from the bartender, and Abby tried to recover by pointing at her now-empty glass, as if she'd been intending to attract attention.

One more, sure. One more couldn't hurt.

She took out her phone to call David Meredith. He was safe. Most people here were. This was why she'd come back to Maine. David Meredith knew Abby only as Hank Bauer's employee, nothing more. Hank was the closest thing Abby had to family, and he wasn't telling any tales about her return to Maine. She owed him good work in exchange, even if that meant speaking with police.

She found Meredith's number, called, and explained what she was working on.

"You guys caught that one?" Meredith said. "Good for Hank. It's easy money."

"Sure looks that way," Abby agreed. "But I'm heading out to take some pictures at the scene and see if there was anything that might be trouble for the college."

"There isn't. Tell the lawyers they can sleep easy."

"I'm curious about the phones, actually. Where are they?"

"We've got his."

"Ramirez's, you mean?"

"Yeah."

"What about hers? Or Oltamu's?"

David Meredith paused. "I'm assuming hers is in the water."

33

"Sure. But his?"

"The coroner's office, probably."

"The report doesn't account for it. His wallet and watch and keys and even a comb were mentioned. But there was no phone."

"So he didn't have one. Some people don't. His doesn't matter, anyhow. Now hers, I could see what you're worried about there. Was she texting or whatever. But…she was parked and out of the car. Hard to imagine a scenario where she gets blamed."

"She wasn't where she was supposed to be. That's my only worry."

"I can't help you on that one. But like you said, the wreck is simple, and Ramirez is going to be formally charged tomorrow. That'll help you. I've got to talk to the girl's family today. I'll ask about the phone, see if I can figure out who the last person to hear from her was."

"Great." Abby thanked Meredith and hung up, glad that her client was the university, faceless and emotionless, and not the family of that girl in the coma. Five days she'd been in there, alive but unresponsive. Abby didn't like to imagine that, let alone see it. That was precisely the kind of shit that could get in her head and take her back…

"I'll have one more," she told the bartender.

One more wouldn't kill her. It just might save her, in fact. Thinking about the girl in the hospital and wondering if her eyes were open or closed was not the sort of image Abby needed in her head before she got behind the wheel. Another beer would help. People didn't understand that, but another beer would *help*.

Abby was five foot three and a hundred and fifteen pounds, and two pints of Sebago Runabout Red would bring her blood alcohol content up to, oh, 0.4. Maybe 0.5, tops. Still legal. And steadier.

A whiskey for the spine and a beer for the shooting hand, her dad used to say. Abby had no idea where he'd picked up that phrase, but it had always made her laugh. He also liked to say *One more and then we'll all go,* which was even funnier because he was usually drinking alone. Jake Kaplan had been one funny guy. Maybe not in the mornings, but, hell, who was funny in the morning?

Abby sipped the pint and held her slim right hand out level above the bar.

Steady as a rock.

She turned back to the case file and flipped through it to see where the cars were impounded. Tara Beckley's CRV and the cargo van rented by Carlos Ramirez had both been hauled off by an outfit with the exquisite name of Savage Sam's Salvage.

Abby called. The phone was answered almost immediately with one curt word: "Sam."

Savage Sam? Abby almost asked, but she managed to hold that one back and explained who she was and why she was calling.

"Ayuh, I got 'em both, the van and the Honda," Sam acknowledged without much interest. "Both of 'em beat to shit, but the Honda took it worse. Those are little SUVs, but they're stout, so it must've taken a pretty good pop."

Abby thought of the photos of the bloodstained pavement and of Tara Beckley in her hospital bed, body running on tubes and machines, eyes wide open and staring at Abby.

"Yes," she said. "It did take a good pop. I'll need to see the vehicles, but I'm also interested in what you might have found in the car."

"I don't steal shit out of cars, honey."

That was an interesting reaction.

"My name is Abby, not honey, and I didn't mean to imply that you stole anything," she said. "It's just that I'm looking for a phone that seems to have gone missing and that might still be in the car."

There was a long pause before he said, "I can check it again, maybe."

First the adamant claim that he didn't steal things out of cars, now the willingness to check it again. Perhaps Savage Sam was uptight for a reason. Abby had a hunch that he was going to discover the phone—and maybe a few other valuables. She suspected this wasn't the first time he'd swept through a wrecked car in his impound lot.

"I'd appreciate that," Abby said. "Because that phone is going to be pretty important to the case, and we've got one dead and one in a coma. You know what that'll lead to—trial, lawyers, cops, all that happy crap."

She said it casually but made sure to emphasize the police and lawyers. It did not seem to be lost on Savage Sam, who said in a more agreeable tone of voice, "It's possible I overlooked somethin'."

Abby smiled. "Can happen to anyone. If you don't mind checking, that would be great. And I can keep the cops out of your hair. If they come by, they'll waste more of your time than I will, you know?"

"I'll check it, sure," Savage Sam said, now seeming positively enthusiastic about the prospect.

"Just give me a call back if you find anything."

Five minutes, she thought when she hung up. That was how long it would take Savage Sam to call back with news of the discovery of a cell phone. He probably already had it in his desk drawer, waiting on a buyer from Craigslist or eBay.

She was wrong—it took nine minutes.

"It turns out there *was* one in there," Savage Sam informed her with a level of shock more appropriate for the discovery of a live iguana in one's toilet. "Jammed down by the gas pedal and wedged just between it and the floor mat. Crazy—I *never* would've seen it unless I'd been looking for it."

Abby grinned. "I bet. Well, I'm sure glad you checked again for me."

"Yeah, happy to help."

"You're positive there was just one?" Abby said.

"Positive. What do you want me to do with it?"

"I can pick it up today, or I can have the police do it?"

"Why don't you grab it," Sam said. "I don't need to get in the middle of things."

Abby wondered just how much swag this guy sold. "I can be there just before five, if that works for you?"

"That works."

Abby paid the tab. Three beers—when had the third one snuck in there? Oh, well, she was still legal. One for the spine, one for the shooting hand, and one for the memories she'd rather not let into her head while she was behind the wheel. Clarity could be a bitch sometimes.

5

S he won't quit," Shannon Beckley insists.

Her face is hovering just inches from Tara's, but she's squinting like someone peering through a microscope, searching for something. Her voice carries conviction, but her eyes lack it. Her eyes think the search might be hopeless.

"Trust me," Shannon says.

I always trust you, Tara answers, but no sound comes out. Why isn't there a sound? Strange. She starts to speak again but Shannon interrupts. Not unusual with Shannon.

"Trust me," Shannon repeats, "this girl…will…not…quit." Shannon's green eyes are searing; her auburn hair is falling across her face, and her expression is as severe as any boot-camp drill sergeant's. Tara can smell Shannon's Aveda moisturizer, with its hint of juniper, and feel her breath warm on her cheek. She's that close, and yet Shannon's eyes suggest that she feels far away, unable to see whatever she's looking at. That's confusing, because she's looking at Tara.

Good for her if she will not quit, Tara tells her sister, and again there is no sound, but that concern is replaced by confusion. Hang on—*who* will not quit? And what is it that she's not going to quit?

Shannon is always forceful, but her face and words carry heightened intensity as she makes these stark but meaningless assertions about the girl who will not quit.

Not her eyes, though, Tara thinks. *Her eyes are not nearly so sure about things.*

Shannon leans away then, and the light that floods into Tara's face is harsh and white. At first she can't see anything because of that brightness, but then it dulls, as if someone has dialed back a dimmer switch, and she sees her mother. Her mother is crying. Rick is rubbing her shoulders. Good old Rick. Always the man with a hand for the shoulder and a comforting word. Usually the words don't mean much, silly platitudes, bits of recycled wisdom. But Tara's mother needs a steady diet of encouragement. The supportive touches and comforting words do the job she used to let the pills do.

But what is today's crisis? Tara watches her mother cry and watches Rick rub her back with a slow, circular motion that feels nearly hypnotic, and she tries to determine what the problem is, why everyone is so scared, so sad.

Oh, yeah—someone won't quit, that's the problem.

Tara's mouth is dry and her head aches and she is very tired. Too tired to deal with her mother's anxiety yet again. Let Rick deal with it. And Shannon. Shannon is here, ready to take charge, as always. Why is Shannon here? She's in her last year of law school at Stanford, and Shannon doesn't miss classes. Ever. But here she is…

Where is here? Where am I?

She knows this should matter, and yet it doesn't seem to. Between Rick's soothing and Shannon's shouting, it will all work out. Tara isn't needed for this one. She's too tired for this one.

What is this one?

The girl who won't quit. That girl is the problem. Who exactly she is and what exactly she is up to, Tara doesn't know, but the girl who won't quit is clearly causing the trouble here. Tara is too tired to join them all in their concern, though. The whole scene exhausts her and makes her strangely angry. Whoever the girl is, she needs to back the hell off and leave everyone alone. Look at them. Just look at their faces. See those tears, that fatigue, that sorrow? Back off, bitch. Back off and leave them alone.

Just go away.

Tara decides she will sleep again. Maybe while she sleeps, this relentless problem girl will finally abandon her confusing quest.

All Tara understands with certainty is that it will be better for everyone when that girl finally quits.

6

Savage Sam might've been sixty or a hundred. Either one seemed reasonable. He stood well over six feet, even with his stooped stance, and that natural forward lean paired with his unusually long arms gave the impression that he could have untied his boots without changing posture.

"I might not have been completely clear about the phone when we talked," he said when he greeted Abby at the front gate. He was carrying a shoe box.

"You don't have it?"

"Oh, no, I think I've got it."

Abby frowned. "I don't follow. Either you have it or you don't."

"Not necessarily," the old man said, and then he took the lid off the shoe box. Inside were at least a dozen cell phones as well as a heap of chargers and three GPS navigators.

"Now, before you get to thinkin' somethin' that isn't true," Sam cautioned, "I want you to know that I always hang on to them for thirty days before I sell them. A firm policy. Otherwise it'd be stealing."

"The state law is thirty days?"

Savage Sam blinked and squinted. He had bifocals tucked into the pocket of his flannel shirt but chose to squint instead, as if the glasses were a prop or he'd forgotten he had them. Or perhaps he'd swiped them out of a car and was intending to sell them later.

"It's awful close to thirty days, even if it isn't exactly that," he said. "They might've changed it."

Abby didn't think they'd changed the law regarding the presumption that whatever was in a wrecked car belonged to the car's owner, but she wasn't interested in debating the point. "That many people leave their phones?" she asked, peering into the bulging box. "Most people these days would rather cut off their hands than walk away from their phones."

"A lot of times it's probably an old phone or a backup or something. People give phones to their parents or grandparents, and the old-timers have no use for them, so they just pitch them into the glove compartment and forget about them. And you'd be surprised how many I find that are still in the boxes they came in."

It made some sense. She stared at the contents of the shoe box.

"You don't know which one came from the Honda, then?"

"Well...no. I mean, I just picked it up and threw it in there. Didn't think about it. Now, I recall it was one of the nicer ones. Probably an iPhone." His wizened thumb jammed into the box and shifted an iPhone forward, then another, and then a third. "But I don't know exactly which one. And with you saying there's police involved, and a man's been killed and all...it would probably be easier if you sorted it out."

He offered the box. Abby took it, contents shifting, and put the lid back on. If she just got them charged up and called numbers for Oltamu and Tara Beckley, the winner would ring.

"I've been here forty years and my brother's had a pawnshop for thirty-nine," Savage Sam said. "It works pretty well, you know?"

"I'd imagine so," Abby said, thinking that keeping crime in the family often did.

"I guess we were always the pack-rat kind. Hell, even the sign required a bit of scavenging."

He gestured above them, and the sign was indeed a sight to behold—a massive, old-fashioned neon marquee that would have been appropriate for a drive-in movie theater. *Savage Sam's Salvage* was lit up like the Fourth of July, even though the property didn't seem to consist of much more than an old man and a tow truck.

"It is an impressive sign," Abby acknowledged. "Mind if I ask about the name? Savage Sam?"

Sam leaned back, which brought him nearly to an upright posture, and grinned. For an instant Abby had a glimpse of what he must've looked like as a kid, one of those hell-raisers who charmed teachers and parents and then set the town on fire when the adults turned their backs.

"They misspelled it," he said, and laughed. "Was supposed to read *Sam's Salvage*. Simple. But then the sign came, two pieces, one said *Sam's,* the other said *Savage*. They forgot the *L*! I was *pissed* at first. Because the sign wasn't cheap. So I called the guy who sold it to me and gave him hell, asking what kind of idiot could screw up a sign with only two damned words. Dumb as he was, I guess I should've been grateful he got *Sam's* right. Anyhow, he sent me a replacement sign that had the mysterious missing *L,* but he didn't ask for the other one back. Shit, why should he? So I had the three of 'em, and I got to looking them over and I thought, *Why waste it?*"

Now Abby was laughing too. "So you just hung them all up?"

"Sure. I thought it was kind of catchy. By then, I was starting to like it. You know how there are always those kids with nicknames and you never had one? Or did you have one?"

Abby had earned plenty of nicknames on the speedway, some more kind than others. Even the kinder ones, like Danica, had usually been offered with a sneer.

"I'm just Abby," she told Sam, though she was remembering the Wiscasset Speedway; she'd become the first woman to win there. Someone had spray-painted *White Trash Rocket* on the driver's door before the race.

"Well, I'd always been just plain old Sam Jones, no nickname coming out of that, but then that idiot screwed up the sign and I've been Savage Sam about ever since." He laughed again. "But, hell, no reason to waste it. Like I said, my family's always been pack rats."

He seemed so happy staring at the old misspelled sign that Abby almost hated to interrupt his reverie. But she did. "The phone was in the Honda, right? Not the van?"

Sam blinked, jogged out of the past and into the present. "Yup, the Honda. I'm telling you, I never could've seen it down there if you hadn't asked me to look. You don't know which phone it is?"

"I don't. I'll have to charge them and call them, I guess. That'll take a while."

"Keep 'em all overnight, then. Just bring the rest back."

We wouldn't want those falling into the wrong hands before they hit the pawnshop, would we? Abby thought. "You're good with that?" she said. "You want to take an inventory of them or anything? A photo?"

It seemed like there should be some record of the transfer of evidence between two people who were not police, but the question apparently struck Savage Sam as an odd one. He thought it over and said, "You got a card or something?"

"Um…yeah." Abby fumbled through her purse and withdrew a business card. It had Hank Bauer's name on it; Abby had declined cards of her own on at least a half a dozen occasions because any formality suggested that this job might last for more than a few weeks. Never mind that she'd already been at it a few months. The gig was temporary, and she'd be West Coast–bound again soon, or back to Europe, maybe, or possibly Tokyo. Sure. Any day now. And until then, she had Hank Bauer's cards to hand over.

"You don't want to write down what all I'm taking?" she asked.

"This'll do." Sam pocketed the card. "Either you're gonna steal 'em or you're not." He shrugged.

With that official police business having been concluded with no police, no signatures, and the exchange of a shoe box, Abby decided to push ahead.

"You still have the cars?" she asked.

Savage Sam nodded. "Right out back. You want a look?"

"Please."

Despite his odd posture and nearsighted squint, Sam moved quickly, stepping nimbly around the piles of junk—hubcaps, a massive bag of bottles, a stack of what appeared to be truck fenders covered by a tarp—and out to the cars.

Tara Beckley's green Honda CRV was all too familiar to Abby from the photos; there was scarcely any part of the car left undamaged except for the driver's seat. Tara would have been better off if she'd stayed behind the wheel. Abby leaned down and looked at the floor mat there—it was khaki-colored, clean, and dry. The phone would've surely stood out against it. There was no trace of blood on the fabric.

The same couldn't be said for the backseat. She got only a glance at the crimson stains across the ripped upholstery before she felt dizzy, and she straightened up fast.

"He must've been driving to beat hell when he hit her," Sam said conversationally, running his long, knobby-knuckled fingers over the crumpled metal. "See the frame damage you got here? That doesn't happen at low speed. He must've been—"

"Where's the van?" Abby cut in. She hadn't intended to be rude; she simply wanted an excuse to look away from the bloodstained Honda.

"Right over here," Sam said without reproach. His interest in the Honda's former occupants and their blood was minimal.

The van was a cargo hauler with a heavy bumper that was crushed back into the hood. Damaged, yes, but nothing significant compared to the Honda.

"Those vans are big, heavy bastards," Sam said with admiration. "Wasn't even carrying a load, but it probably goes four thousand pounds empty. And as tall as it is, shit, that little car didn't have much of a chance. I heard he was using his phone or something.

Ain't surprising. You drive down the road any day of the week and pay attention, you'll see how many of these jackasses are driving with their heads down, not giving a damn about anybody on the road but... what are you looking at?"

Abby was on her knees in the gravel, one hand braced on the van. "The tires."

"They're still worth selling," Sam acknowledged. They'd probably be on their way to his brother's pawnshop before long.

And he wasn't wrong about the tires. They were certainly worth selling; the tread didn't look worn. The daylight was dying, and in the shadows, Abby couldn't find a wear-indicator bar on the tires, so she set the shoe box down and searched her purse for a coin. Sam's gnarled fingers appeared in her face, a penny held between them.

"Thanks." Abby rotated the penny so Abe Lincoln's head was pointed down and inserted the coin between the tire's tread grooves. Lincoln's head sank below the black rubber and vanished up to the shoulders. Sam was right; the tires were nearly new.

Abby sat back on her heels and stared first at the van, then at the Honda.

"I might need to come back and take some pictures," she said. "Tomorrow morning, when I return the phones?"

"I guess," Sam said. He sounded resigned to trouble. "Hell, I ought to stop taking cop tows. They ain't worth the hassle."

"I'll try to keep it from becoming a hassle for you," Abby said, no longer caring much if the old man had intended to sell the stolen phone. He'd turned it over, at least. Savage Sam of the misspelled neon signs wasn't such a bad guy. "I'll get in and out, quick and painless, I promise."

"That's what they told me the last time I had a colonoscopy," Sam said.

7

G hosts are real.
     Tara knows this because she is one.

When clarity first returns, she sees her mother, her stepfather, and her sister. She sees them and she hears Shannon's voice and thinks: *The dream is done.*

She thinks, slower and more carefully, because it is so important: *I am alive.*

There is relief with that realization, but it is a temporary relief, because she soon determines that she is invisible.

Shannon is arguing with Rick and Mom, but she is arguing on Tara's behalf, and Rick and Mom are facing Tara, staring right at her but not seeing her.

"She wouldn't quit on us, and so I am not going to listen to anyone say one word about what we must *consider*," Shannon snaps. "Because what you're *considering* is quitting on your own daughter!"

Tara looks into her mother's eyes and waits for recognition, awareness, something. *Notice me, speak to me, touch me.* But her mother just stares blankly, her eyes bloodshot and ringed by dark circles. She doesn't seem to see Tara. Rick looks at Tara as well, his bearded face doing a poor job of hiding his annoyance with Shannon. He doesn't see Tara either. She's used to being ignored by Rick—and to ignoring him—but this is different. He's looking right at her and yet for all the world he seems to be staring at a wall.

I'm invisible. Maybe I'm not alive. Maybe I'm dead, and this is what it's like?

She is a ghost. The realization is sudden and certain. It is the only explanation for her condition.

How did I die?

"It's too early to talk like this," Shannon says, and Rick closes his eyes with fatigue. Mom just keeps staring. Shannon starts to speak again, then thinks better of it, shakes her head furiously, and stalks to the window. Everyone is quiet then. Tara wants to speak but her tongue is heavy and rigid and uncooperative in her mouth, and so she lies there and tries to gather her voice.

It is then that understanding begins to come, agonizingly slowly, like filling a glass one drop of water at a time.

Mom. Rick. Shannon. A television turned to CNN, but muted. A bed with a pair of feet resting on it. Wait—those are her feet. She is in the bed. The bed is not her own. The room is not her own. Her confusingly thick tongue is not a tongue at all—it is a tube. There are more tubes in other places, and she's aware of them now, first with pain and then some shame. There are wires too, a seemingly endless amount of wires.

Hospital.

Yes, that is it. She is in a hospital, and she is not a ghost. Not just yet. What is she, though?

"Every coma is different," Shannon says without turning, her voice trembling with barely subdued anger, and in that sentence, in that single word—*coma*—Tara has her answer.

She has been in a coma. This makes sense; it's a better explanation than anything she's come up with on her own. But she is out of the coma now, because she is awake and alert and she can see and hear. Why don't they notice this? Why don't they see that she is awake?

Because you haven't said anything, dummy. Tell them!

Hello, Tara says.

No one reacts. Shannon doesn't turn; Mom's stare doesn't break; Rick's slumped shoulders don't tense.

Panic rises then, a terrible, claustrophobic panic, and this time Tara screams, determined to be heard.

I'm right here!

Nothing. Shannon stares out the window, Mom bows her head, Rick stands slumped and weary.

This time, Tara understands, though. She didn't make a sound. Her scream had produced...nothing.

Had she even parted her lips? Surely she had. She'd screamed at the top of her lungs, screamed in terror and confusion, and no one had reacted. How is this possible? Maybe there is a wall between them, some sort of glass partition, the kind with a mirror on their side like in the cop shows so she can see them but they can't see her.

This thought brings logic back to an insane world, and the terror subsides. She tells herself to sit up and figure out the two-way mirror, find that glass panel and rap on it and get their attention, let them know that she is here, she is back, awake again.

Sit up.

She thinks the words, visualizes the motion, and waits. Nothing happens. She's still lying down, and she should be upright. Just...sit up.

But she can't.

The terror is back now.

She tries again but makes no progress, and, worse, she realizes there's no sense of resistance, nothing holding her down, no weight or strap or anything that would block this simple command to her body. Even if she is injured—and she's in a hospital with tubes and IVs in her, so of course she has been injured—she should be able to fight upward.

She can issue the command, but her body can't obey it.

Paralyzed. Oh no, not that...

She starts to cry then. To cry and shake.

No tears come. No sounds.

Shannon turns and looks down at her, right into her eyes, and

49

Tara stares back into her older sister's loving face and pleads for help.

Shannon looks away.

"I don't want to hear any of the spiritual shit, Rick," she says. "I do not want to hear it yet."

"I'm sorry that *shit* bothers you, Shannon, but I think it's worth talking about!" Rick answers, taking a step toward her. "You need to begin to ask yourself who this is for, your sister or her body. You need to begin to consider that there is a *difference*."

"I am not *considering* a damn thing until we've seen a neurologist," Shannon says.

"Everyone says if we just keep our faith..." Mom tries timidly, but Shannon isn't having it.

"Everyone on your *Facebook page* says that. While you're making Team Tara posts and people are offering advice from their phones between bites of their bagels, I'm suggesting we consult an actual expert."

Mom winces, Rick sighs, and Shannon lifts her hands in regret. "Sorry. I'm not trying to be a bitch, Mom, I'm really not. The Facebook page is important. I get that. But I don't want us to begin premature conversations."

"Our job will be to imagine her quality of life," Rick says softly, "and you can't even reach that point until you know whether there *is* a life."

"She's breathing!" Shannon shouts. "Her heart is beating! Her eyes are open, she's *watching* us!"

Rick points at Tara, a beaded bracelet jangling on his right wrist. He is looking directly at her but seems to see only an empty bed.

"Her body is doing those things, yes. But where is Tara?" he asks in that pastoral whisper he uses so often to calm their mother. "Look into her eyes, Shannon, and then tell me. Where is *Tara* right now?"

I am right fucking here! Tara shouts.

They all turn toward her then, and for a moment she thinks she's made contact. Then she realizes they are just following Rick's outstretched hand and considering his question.

"Tell me, Shannon," he whispers, moving his hand to rub his graying beard. "Where...is...she?"

When Shannon says, "I don't know," the tears overwhelm Tara again.

No one in the room knows that she's right there, and no one in the room knows that she's crying.

8

The place where Amandi Oltamu had died was beautiful and peaceful. Crisp orange leaves glowed in the fading sunlight as they swirled across the pavement, and beneath them were glittering bits of pebbled glass that the cleanup effort had missed. The blood had been hosed off the pavement.

Abby stepped out of her car, looked at that bright, too-clean patch of asphalt, and tried to ignore the steady accelerating of her heartbeat.

Exposure therapy, that's what this job of studying car wrecks was supposed to be. You kept things from taking up damaging residence in your brain by meeting them on your own terms in small, planned doses, building up a tolerance. The mind was no different than the body—it could become immune to a bad memory just like it could to a virus.

This was what a therapist in California had told her. Granted, the therapist hadn't recommended changing careers, let alone moving back to Maine. She'd encouraged Abby to look at some pictures, that was all. And Abby had tried. But…

But the therapist hadn't killed her boyfriend in a car wreck, and once you've done that, well, those pictures can become harder to look at than most people would believe.

The job Abby had now was an almost ludicrous outgrowth of a technique she'd been asked to embrace in California, but she was the only person who understood the bridge between the two. Nobody on the West Coast knew what she was doing now, and she hadn't volunteered any of her stories to Hank or anyone else in Maine. She'd had absolutely no desire to.

Until today, at least. When Hank had given her the overview of the wreck in Hammel, Abby had almost broken and told him the details of her horror story, told him about the way Luke's hand had closed on her arm just before they left the road, told him that *maybe* his last words hadn't been *Faster, Abby,* but rather *Slow down,* told him how his eyes had seemed to track hers in the hospital even after the doctors said there was absolutely no indication of awareness. For an instant, she'd been ready to tell Hank that under no circumstances could she investigate an accident that had put someone in a coma.

She hadn't said a word, though. In the end, she'd just taken the file and headed out to do her job—with that quick stop for a beer on the way. Because the past was the past, Luke was nothing but a memory, and Abby couldn't afford to spend any more of her life with her eyes on the rearview mirror.

But now, standing here in the cold fall air with the sun setting behind the wooded hills and the smell of the sea riding the wind, she couldn't bring herself to look at the wreck photos. They would make her think of the miles of roads that lurked between here and home. Intersections and stoplights, sharp curves and banked slopes, all of those challenges so simply handled by basic instinct, and challenges that could be turned into creative triumphs if your mind was fast and your hands were steady. It was a bitch if that basic instinct ever wavered on you, but if you'd once had a fast mind and steady hands and a hundred and twenty miles per hour felt like fifty? In that case, it was worse. Deeper and darker. In that case, you began to feel like you didn't really know yourself anymore.

Focus, damn it. Focus on the job and then get out of here.

She stood at the base of the hill and looked out at the two-lane bridge that crossed the river and led to the college campus. There was a concrete pillar on the sidewalk identifying the bridge's place in the state's history. This was what Tara Beckley's CRV had struck after Carlos Ramirez, his head down and cell phone glowing, drove his van into the car.

Lives ended from mere moments of distraction. Happened all too often.

Doesn't require distraction, though. There are variations on the lost-lives theme. Stunt drivers taking famous actors out for a spin, for example. Those trips can end badly too.

Again, Abby could see Luke's hand reaching for hers.

She shook her head, then walked up the hill to put herself in the position the van's driver had been in. She took out her camera and pivoted slowly, shooting a 360-degree view. The sun was sinking fast and lights were visible on both sides of the bridge. The campus was on the western side of the river, and atop the steep hill on the east, everything was residential. If Ramirez hadn't already fallen on his sword, there might have been some mitigation from the lighting. The streetlights were toned-down replicas of old gas lamps, designed more for aesthetics than illumination.

Abby was about 280 degrees through her 360-degree turn when she lowered the camera and frowned, thinking of the massive amount of destruction done to Tara Beckley's Honda CRV. Carlos Ramirez had to have been hauling ass when he hit them to inflict that sort of damage. Down a steep hill and into those angled parking spaces…

She paced up the hill a few steps and turned to look back at the parking spots.

The wind that gusted and stirred the brittle leaves was getting colder. Abby zipped up her fleece and paced back down to the edge of the bridge and looked up at the hill, and now her old instincts were alive. This insurance investigator—could there be a less glamorous occupation?—had once been the fabled Professional Driver on a Closed Course, and while that was an adrenaline-jockey business, it was also a science-based business.

Abby Kaplan didn't need to run a calculation to know what was troubling her—the police photos didn't do justice to the hill.

That hill was much steeper than Abby had imagined. The road crested and then seemed to dive toward the river. The police had probably viewed that as a contributing factor to the wreck. Carlos Ramirez had been driving an unfamiliar cargo van, he'd been going fast, he'd been distracted, and he'd been on a dangerous slope. Check, check, check, check. All of that played well on paper. But…

How come he didn't roll it?

Abby chewed her lip and stared at that steep hill rising from the river and thought about the nearly new tires she'd seen on the van.

There were two types of rollovers, tripped and untripped. Most rollover accidents were tripped, which meant that some external object—a curb, a ditch, a guardrail—upset the vehicle's balance. The rarer untripped rollovers were the result of the battle among three cornering forces: centripetal (tire friction), inertial (vehicle mass), and good old gravity.

Untripped rollovers were caused or avoided by the driver's ability (or lack thereof) to understand and control the car. The driver was alone in that critical moment, tethered to the world by nothing but four points of rubber and her own skill.

Abby could remember standing on a course in Germany waiting to drive a Mercedes prototype while an engineer droned on about this; she kept wishing she could just get behind the wheel and *go* because her hands and eyes already understood everything the guy was babbling about.

Back then they had, at least.

He'd been talking about the CSV, or critical sliding velocity. She had started to pay more attention at that point, because he'd uttered the word that owned Abby's heart: *velocity*. The CSV formula determined the minimum lateral speed at which the vehicle would roll.

When he'd killed Amandi Oltamu and knocked Tara Beckley into a coma, Carlos Ramirez had been executing a fishhook maneuver. On test runs, that meant you followed a fishhook-shaped curve: You went straight, then turned sharply in one direction—as you'd do to avoid something in the road—then overcorrected in the other. On each run, you widened your path, steering at sharper and sharper angles, testing it until the tires howled and threatened to lift off the pavement—or until they did lift off.

Abby had executed maybe two thousand fishhook runs. She didn't need an engineering degree to see the problem with the scenario on the bridge across from Hammel College. The slope was too steep and the fishhook turn was too narrow.

He'd have rolled first. He might have hit Beckley's car, but he'd have had his van on its side by the time he did. The cargo van was too tall, its center of mass too high, to handle such abrupt cornering and remain upright.

Unless he'd never tried to turn. Unless he'd been coming straight at them, targeting them.

Abby didn't hesitate to look at the photos this time. Her curiosity had overridden her apprehension, and she was able to see past the blood on the pavement and focus on the vehicle positions.

The cargo van was upright, the CRV was upright, the damage was catastrophic, and all of that made sense until you stood down here and looked up the hill and thought about the angles.

Her phone rang, a shrill shattering of the quiet, and she closed the accident report and looked at the phone. Hank Bauer, her boss and friend and onetime sponsor, a man who'd paid the fees to get a teenage Abby Kaplan into stock-car races in Wiscasset, Scarborough, and Oxford.

"Hey, Hank."

"How's it going, Abs?"

"Fine. Actually … well, it's a little messed up."

"Whaddya mean?"

"Something's wrong in that report. What Ramirez said happened is impossible. It might be what he *thinks* happened, but it isn't right."

Hank's voice dropped an octave. "He smashed directly into a parked car. How wrong can he be about *that?*"

"He would have tipped that van," Abby said. "Hank, I'm telling you, there's no way he could have hit the passenger side of her car that hard if he'd swerved the way he said he did. He'd have rolled it into the river first."

"Let the police worry about Ramirez," Hank said. "I just want our girl Tara to be clean as a whistle. Okay?"

"Right," Abby said, but she didn't like it because she wanted someone who could talk on her level about this problem. She changed tack instead. "I might have good news there. I think I've got her phone."

"How'd you do that?"

Abby told him about the trip to the salvage yard, and Hank began to laugh before she was done.

"Only thing surprising about that is Sam hadn't sold it yet."

"Well, I've got a box of phones now and I don't know which is hers. I'll charge them up tonight and test them."

"Save yourself the trouble—you can ask her sister tomorrow."

"What?"

"She wants to know what you're doing, I guess. Wants to meet you. Wants to meet anyone and everyone who's involved."

"She's coming up here?"

"No, you're going down there, to the hospital in Massachusetts. Bring your treasure chest from Savage Sam along."

"The hospital? Why?" Abby felt a cold fist tighten in her gut. She did not want to go to the hospital. She most sincerely did not want to see that girl in the coma. "I'll call the sister. I don't need to go to Boston to see her in the hospital."

"You think I don't know that? I already called her. The sister is a law-school student but apparently believes she's already passed the bar and been appointed district attorney. I'm glad it's you and not me who gets the treat of meeting her in person."

"I'm not wasting a day in Boston just to explain what I'm doing."

"Like hell you're not. Billable hours! Abby, do you have any idea how much I can soak that college for? If the family wants to see you at the hospital, you go to the friggin' hospital. You can show her the phones. That won't be a waste of time. And you can take the Challenger!"

His enthusiasm made Abby close her eyes. "I'm good with the Chrysler, thanks."

"Aw, c'mon, Abs." Sorrowful now. "I bought the damned thing."

"Nobody told you to."

"Just drive it, would you? Get a taste again. See what it does for you."

"I'll think about it," Abby said, and then she hung up.

What Hank wanted her driving was a Dodge Challenger Hellcat with 707 horsepower growling under a black-on-red hood. He'd bought it for well under value after it was repossessed by a friend of his who sold cars in New Hampshire. Because Hank still believed Abby craved speed, he'd purchased the Challenger and offered it to her as a temporary "company car."

It could do zero to sixty in under four seconds, was outfitted with Pirelli racing tires, and was generally everything one could want in a modern American muscle car.

Abby hadn't had it over sixty miles an hour yet.

On a couple of occasions, Abby pretended that she'd put the car through its paces on the back roads and been duly impressed. One part of that wasn't a lie—she *did* keep it on the back roads. That was because she could avoid the anxiety of driving in traffic and at higher speeds, though, not so she could test those beautiful Pirellis on a double-S curve.

Hank wasn't wrong. Abby should have been driving it. Exposure therapy. Stare the fear down, in small doses.

Soon, she told herself.

Any day now.

She pocketed the phone and walked toward her Chrysler 300, a pleasant if somewhat staid sedan. Nothing threatening about it. Not like the Challenger Hellcat.

As she crossed the road, her right ankle throbbed, a souvenir from an early crack-up at the Oxford Plains Speedway in western Maine. She looked down and watched the way her hiking shoes flexed across the top as she walked sideways across the steep slope. The leather uppers pulled right, toward the river, while the rubber soles fought them and tugged left, biting into the pavement.

It would have rolled, she thought. *That van would have rolled.*

9

When she was a child, Tara was terrified of a house at the end of the road: 1804 London Street. It was a once-grand Victorian built by a family who'd made a small fortune in the days when Cleveland had been a manufacturing boomtown, money later tied up in a bitter feud among the siblings who'd inherited it upon their mother's death. When Tara first saw the house, it had been vacant for at least ten years, the beautiful wood trim rotting beneath peeling paint, the stonework around the gardens and the patio lost to weeds and untamed hedges. For the older kids in the neighborhood, it inspired ghost stories and fevered claims of a woman in white who appeared in the attic window. They would run onto the porch and knock on the door, just like the children in Tara's favorite book, *To Kill a Mockingbird,* and it was probably this association that gave her the bravery to finally join in the fun.

Boo Radley's home had held no terrors. Boo was simply misunderstood, and because all Tara wanted to do in life was be Scout Finch and because she liked to imagine her late father had been like Atticus Finch, she carried out a summer of replication, leaving notes and small treasures tucked in trees and under eaves on the property. However, because this was not a fictional southern town in the 1930s but a Cleveland suburb in the early 2000s, her notes were not replaced with intricate handmade delights. Instead, someone who saw her leaving the notes responded by filling her favorite hidey-hole with condom wrappers.

She stopped trying to re-create her Scout-and-Boo fantasy after that.

But still, she didn't fear the house as she once had. That was the power of imagination, the power of the mind—she'd taken ownership of the place, trading scary stories for warm ones, and with her fantasy vision, she erased the fear. The kids who mocked her might be able to replace her charm bracelets with condom wrappers, but they couldn't replace her new vision of the once-frightening abandoned house.

In her thirteenth summer, she used that power of imagination to win twenty dollars. That summer, when Mom was doing better and Shannon was distracted by the acquisition of her driver's license, a neighborhood boy named Jaylen dared Tara to go into the house alone and appear in a window on each floor, including the turret window of the supposed woman in white. If she did, he said, he'd give her twenty dollars and something she pretended she wanted nothing to do with: a kiss.

"Just the money, creep," she'd told him, but he was tall and handsome and had impossibly beautiful brown eyes and played on the basketball team, and, highly appealing to Tara, he told the most creative of the dumb scary stories about 1804 London Street. He was also black, and to Tara this seemed both exotic and undeniably Scout Finch–approved. If there was anything not to like about Jaylen, Tara hadn't yet discovered it.

He'd forced the front door open with a screwdriver, and then they'd both run away, sure there was an alarm, and hid behind a tree up the street. A few minutes went by and nothing happened, but he told her to wait awhile longer.

"It's probably a silent alarm, like they have in banks," Jaylen said, and Tara found that very wise.

No police came, though, and eventually Jaylen decided that the silent alarm must have been deactivated, probably because they weren't paying the bill, just like nobody paid to keep the lawn mowed. The house was fair game, and the dare was still on.

"You don't have to," he said when they reached the porch. His voice was soft and serious, and Tara realized that now that it had progressed from talk to possibility, he thought it was a bad idea and wanted out, the classic game of chicken that had gone too far. Facing the cracked porch steps and the tall weeds and the filthy windows with crude phrases written in the dust, Tara felt a surge of fear rise up, but she fought it down. She was Scout Finch, after all, and she could not only play with the boys but beat them at their own games. And take their money.

And, maybe, get a kiss.

"I'll wave to you from the windows," she said, and she pushed through the door and into the musty foyer. Stairs rose to the left, ascending into shadows, and in front of her a wide hallway led to what had to be the living room. To the right was a formal parlor or sitting room, old-fashioned chairs positioned around a china hutch that was filled with blue-and-white dishes and crystal glasses. In the center of the room was a puddle, and above it the ceiling sagged around a massive water stain.

The floorboards creaked like trees in a windstorm, but they held, and she reached the first window, looked outside, and saw Jaylen staring apprehensively up at the house. He appeared gravely concerned, more scared than Tara, and this gave her confidence. She grinned at him and waved. Relieved, he waved back, and then hollered that she could come out.

"You don't need to do 'em all! You win! Come back out!"

He wants that kiss, she thought.

Her confidence grew, and she shouted back that she was going to do them all, and then she walked confidently to the stairs.

The problem was the lack of light. A lot of the windows were shuttered and those that weren't were covered with years of filth, so only the dimmest light filtered in, and since she didn't know the house, each step into the darkness was a journey into unfamiliar territory. That built confusion, and confusion fed fear.

She was no longer smiling when she reached the second-floor window, and if Jaylen had yelled at her to come down again, she might have listened. But by now he seemed resigned to her determination not to quit, so he just waved back, silent and seeming very far away.

It took her some time to find the turret window. She was moving too fast, and she took wrong turns, and with each wrong turn, she felt her panic escalate. She was breathing raggedly and she was sweating even though it was cool in the house, and there was a terrible smell coming from behind one of the closed doors, and it took all of her imagination and willpower to fend off the images of a rotting corpse. She stopped, took a deep breath, and said, "Pass the damn ham, please," a Scout Finch quote that delighted her endlessly, particularly when she used it in situations where it made no sense to anyone else.

The line was a reminder of the power of imagination. There was no ghost in 1804 London Street, nothing worse in here than the lingering smell of old cigar smoke, which Tara hated because it reminded her of Mom's cigarette days. The house was as harmless as Boo Radley's home in Maycomb, Alabama, and she was as brave as Scout Finch.

She walked on down the hall through the darkness. When she finally found the turret window, she saw Jaylen pacing the yard nervously, and she had to rap on the glass with her knuckles to get his attention.

This time, instead of waving at her, he beckoned urgently, the message clear: *Get out of there!*

She was ready to go. More than ready; she'd held the panic off for as long as she could, but now the dark and the smells and all those images of what might lurk behind each closed door were piling up, gleefully crowding the space in her mind, a race to see which one would break her.

She was concentrating on staying calm and watching where she put her feet, sure that there would be rusty nails or a piece of broken glass or an ax matted with hair and blood—*Stop that, Tara, stop that!*—and in the intensity of her focus, she completely over-shot the main staircase and found herself on an unfamiliar one, tighter and steeper.

For a second, she hesitated, considering going back. Then her hand brushed a cobweb and that made her give a little cry and a jerk, and the steps creaked ominously underfoot, and now she was running, but she ran down, following instinct—the front door was below her, so down was the right direction.

She'd never been in a house with two staircases, and so the idea that it might not lead to the same place as the main stairs never occurred to her. Even when she reached a landing and the staircase bent in an unexpected direction, she trusted it. She had to go down to get out, and down she went, rushing and gasping for breath and feeling her way along the wall with her hand because it was nearly full dark here, and she couldn't see anything beyond the next step.

When she arrived in the cold room that smelled of damp stone, she realized her mistake. She'd bypassed everything and gone straight from the third floor to the cellar. Something rustled in the darkness to her right, and she scampered away and smacked into the wall, then ran right into a cobweb. She screamed, tearing at the sticky threads with both hands. She was no longer Scout Finch; she was Tara Beckley, known as Twitch to her sister, and she was earning the nickname now.

She backed up; her foot skidded on something wet and slick, and then the rustling sound came again, and she whirled and shouted.

That was when she saw daylight.

There was only a faint line of it—it looked as if someone had drawn it with yellow chalk on the dark stone wall—but it was there. She stared at it, gasping and crying, and thought about her options. She could run back the way she'd come and hope to find her way out, or she could cross the darkness and trust that light, however faint.

She trusted the light.

She fell twice crossing the cellar, banging her shin painfully into something hard and metal and then scraping her forearm on a rusted pipe that seemed to be a floor support, but she made it to the other side, and there she saw that the daylight was no illusion. There was a door here. Two of them, actually, heavy steel doors that might once have met squarely in the center but no longer did, offering just enough of a gap to let the light filter through.

She found the handles and pushed, then pulled. Rust flaked off and bit into her palms, and the doors grated over the rough concrete floor, a menacing, grinding sound like the time Shannon had broken the garbage disposal by filling it with Mom's pill bottles. Her hands ached and her shoulders throbbed, but the space between the doors widened slightly, more daylight flooded in, and she felt warm air on her face, and though there was no way she could slip through and escape, she thought the gap was wide enough that she might at least be heard.

She put her face close to the door and shouted for Jaylen over and over.

No one came. She could hear birds and the faint sound of a passing car, but no one answered her.

I'm trapped, she thought. *I will be here forever, somehow I found a staircase that no one else will find, they can search the whole house but they will never find me because the staircase won't be there, it was a trap, and I—*

"Damn it, Tara, what the *hell* were you thinking?"

Her sister's voice came through the doors. Then Shannon's face was in the two-inch gap Tara had opened between the monstrous old doors, and she was staring at Tara with anger and concern.

"Are you okay?" Shannon said. "Are you hurt?"

Tara sniffled out that no, she wasn't hurt, and yes, she was probably okay, she was just scared and she wanted *out*.

"I'll get you out," Shannon said. "Let me get your dumb boyfriend. I think he's scared of me."

With the help of an aluminum baseball bat, Jaylen and Shannon were able to pry the doors far enough apart for Tara to wedge herself through and back to freedom. She was covered in cobwebs and dirt and her shin and arm were bleeding, but she was safe again.

Shannon hauled her home, lecturing her the whole way; Jaylen said good-bye and started to offer Tara a whispered apology but Shannon shot him a look, which accelerated his exit. Once the sisters got back, Shannon told their mother that the car was making a weird noise, which drew her out of the house and into the driveway and let Tara sneak in the back and get herself cleaned up before Mom saw any evidence of her bloody adventure. When she got off the pills, Mom always wanted to play the good-mother role, but by then Shannon had claimed it. Discipline was handled by big sister, period. The same with protection.

Apparently, Shannon thought the scare had been enough for Tara, because she let it drop after extracting a promise from her: *never again* would she enter that house.

Two days later, Jaylen approached Tara cautiously in the yard, glanced left and right, then said, "Your sister isn't here, is she?" When Shannon's absence was confirmed, Tara finally got the twenty dollars and the kiss. A few of the latter, in fact. It turned into a good summer, one of the better ones of Tara's childhood, and she kept her promise to Shannon. She'd never entered 1804 London Street again.

Until now.

She was locked in again, and she didn't know the way out, and all around her was fear and shadow. She was on the dark staircase that she hadn't anticipated, hadn't even known existed, and this time she didn't have the option of turning around and going back the way she'd come.

Propped up in her hospital bed, tubes running up her nose and down her throat, machines humming at her side, and her family sitting around her with no idea where she was, Tara realized that her worst fear from the cellar of 1804 had come true. She was trapped, and they would never find her.

This time, there was no thin line of light for her to chase through the blackness.

10

The neurologist's name was Dr. Pine. His house in Marblehead was everything a prestigious New England doctor's home should be—three stories painted an appropriately coastal gray-blue with gleaming white trim and plenty of windows, exquisite brickwork on the driveway and sidewalks, massive brass light fixtures styled to look like old gas lamps. Lisa Boone waited an hour before he finally arrived, pulling up to the house in an equally appropriate Range Rover. He parked in the garage and put the overhead door down behind him, so Boone walked up the brick path that ran to the door on the side of the garage and waited for him to emerge. When he saw her, he stopped short, startled, and took a step back before determining that she posed no threat—an attractive white woman, thank goodness, no danger here.

"May I help you?" he said. His voice was deeper than his stature would suggest.

"Probably not," Boone said, "but I have to try."

"Pardon?"

"You have a patient named Tara Beckley. I need to speak with you about her."

He frowned and studied her, wary now.

"I can't talk about my patients," he said, "and I'm curious why you're at my home."

"Because the United States government needs you to understand that your patient might have been a casualty of—and, if she lives, potentially a witness to—an execution killing."

His jaw didn't quite drop. His mouth parted and then closed.

He took a breath, then gave a little shake of his head and a half laugh. "I expect to encounter new things every day," he said, "but this one is really something. What branch of the U.S. government needs me to understand this?"

"May we go inside, Doctor?"

"What branch?"

"Department of Energy." She smiled. "Surprised you twice, didn't I?"

"Yes," he said. "Come on in."

She followed him up the back steps and into a kitchen with thick wooden counters and a massive center island. He pulled a stool up to the island, offered one to her, then unbuttoned his cuffs and rolled up his shirtsleeves slowly and precisely. He seemed to be moving methodically to gather his thoughts, and Boone was pleased by his demeanor. She'd expected a flood of questions, but what she needed was someone who could listen.

When he looked up again, he said, "I don't want to seem foolish or paranoid, but it would probably be prudent to ask you for some identification."

Wise man. She showed him her ID card, and he studied it with care, even tilting it so that the hologram caught the light.

"'Office of Intelligence and Counterintelligence,'" he read. "I'll admit I didn't know the DOE had their own investigations division. I'd have guessed they'd farm that out."

"Sometimes. Not always."

"So what brings the DOE intelligence division into the game?"

Boone knew he was testing her, asking a question that achieved multiple things at once. He wanted to learn how legitimate she was and how much information she'd share, and he wanted to buy himself time to consider the situation while he listened.

"The office protects vital national security information and technologies that represent intellectual property of incalculable value," Boone said in her best public-speaker-introducing-a-bullshit-politician-at-a-ribbon-cutting voice. "Our distinctive contribution to national security is the ability to leverage the Energy Department's unmatched scientific and technological expertise in support of policy makers as well as national security missions in defense, homeland security, cybersecurity, intelligence, and energy security."

"Are you required to memorize that or is it your unique sense of humor?"

"It's on the website." She shrugged.

"Nicely done. Not exactly what I was hoping for, though. Would you give me an example of your work?"

Killing a man in a hotel room in Tokyo with a garrote, Boone thought, but the first example to come to mind wasn't usually the one you should share. She said, "Serving on a joint task force with the FBI and CIA using legal vulnerabilities to motivate employees of a chemical corporation to reveal the covert sharing of patent secrets with the Chinese military." She paused. "Hypothetically. Of course."

"Of course," he said, never looking away from her.

"Do you need another?"

"I'm not sure that I do." He gave a wan smile. "'Using legal vulnerabilities to motivate,' you said? That's quite a phrase. Distill it and one might say it means *blackmailing* employees."

"One might," Boone acknowledged. "But one would be wrong."

"Sure." He nodded, studying her, and then said, "Tara Beckley was a student escort. A creative-writing major. Neither she nor her family seems to have any expertise that would interest the Department of Energy. I know far less about her charge, simply that he was a guest speaker and that he was killed. Your belief, then, is that this man was assassinated—is that the idea?"

"I wouldn't use that term, but that's the gist."

"A killing with political intent isn't an assassination?"

"You'll note that I've said nothing about politics, sir. Pardon me, *Doctor*."

He waved that off. "No assassination, then. Fine. My understanding was that it was a car accident, and a driver admitted guilt. Rather unusual way to commit a professional execution. He even called the police himself, I believe."

"Do you know that he's dead?" Boone asked.

That stopped him.

"Police in Brighton just found his body in a car," Boone told him. "Shot twice in the head. This unfortunate development paired with his uniquely cooperative admission at the scene means there will be no investigation into the death of Amandi Oltamu now, no trial. Do you see?"

After a lengthy pause, the doctor said, "And who is Amandi Oltamu to you? What value did he have that you were hoping to use legal vulnerabilities to motivate?"

Boone smiled. "This is where we get to the unpleasant part. You have questions, I have answers, but I can't share them. And the less you know, the better for you."

His eyes narrowed. "For my safety?"

"Yes."

"So you want me to violate patient confidentiality—which means breaking the law, you know, not to mention the Hippocratic oath—and in exchange I get...nothing? Because of your deep concern for my safety, of course."

"That's the idea."

He gave that little disbelieving half laugh again, then stood up. "Mind if I pour myself a glass of wine?"

"By all means."

"Join me?"

"No, thank you."

He poured from an opened bottle of pinot noir on the counter, took a drink, then looked at the clock on the microwave. "My wife will be home in about fifteen minutes," he said. "If there is any chance that what you intend to tell me will put me in danger, well, such is life. The same philosophy does not apply to my family, though."

"I understand."

He turned back to her but didn't return to the island, just leaned against the counter.

"You don't have a witness," he said. "I can tell you that much, because you'll be able to find it out from other sources, and I can spare you that trouble, and we can spare ourselves the back-and-forth bullshit about the greater good in service of my country. That's what I'd get if I tried to hold out, right?"

Now it was Boone's turn to laugh. "Pretty much."

"Thought so."

"So there's no chance she'll regain consciousness?" Boone asked. "No chance of recovery?"

"Oh, I certainly intend to see that she has every chance at recovery. But at the moment, she is not going to offer you any help. If she has memories that could be of use to you, they're sealed up tight."

Boone nodded. "That was my understanding, but I had to try. What I need you to know is that if she wakes, she'll be not only a potential asset to me, but also likely in harm's way. I don't intend to ask you to break any laws or oaths, Doctor. What I want from you is your assurance that if anything changes with Tara Beckley, I'll be notified immediately."

"Why not ask that of her family? Why me?"

"Because I don't want to terrify them," Boone said. "And because the stakes on this require the poise of professionals. What I've heard about you suggests that you'd be good under pressure."

He tried not to look flattered, but he was. Everyone liked an ego stroke. Doctors too.

"It's beyond unorthodox," he said. "This shouldn't be my role."

Boone removed a business card from her purse and slid it across the gleaming hardwood surface of the island. "Just a phone call," she said. "If there's a change in Tara Beckley's condition, I need to know. *Tara* will need me to know. At that point, I'll deal with the family. Not until then. I wasn't fully honest with you a moment ago, Dr. Pine. I said I was holding off on contact with them because I didn't want to scare them. That's true, but it's not everything. I also can't afford too much conversation about this. You are, as you've already made clear, a man who understands the need for confidentiality, for professional silence. You know what breaking that silence can cost people."

He picked up the card and slid it into his shirt pocket. "What if there's no change in her condition?"

"Then you don't need to worry about me."

"That's not my point. If there's no change, when do you deal with the family? When do you let them know the truth about what happened to Tara?"

Boone didn't answer. She just gazed back at him, and he nodded.

"Right," he said. "That's where we'll reach the bullshit about the greater good, isn't it?"

Boone got to her feet. "You're asking questions above my pay grade, and I think you know that. What you decide to do here is up to you. But be aware that you've got something more than a patient in Tara Beckley. You might have the key to some vital intelligence."

"I have a human life. She's no different than any patient."

"Wrong. Tara is very different."

"I can't look at it that way."

"You'll need to." Boone bit her lower lip, looked at the floor for a moment, then back at him. "I'll give you this much perspective: Billions of dollars at stake, and dozens of lives. Maybe hundreds of lives. Still think she's no different than the rest?"

"What she saw is worth *that?*"

"Potentially," Boone said.

He didn't have a response.

Boone thanked him for his time and consideration and let herself out the back door. If she drove fast, she could make it to the airport and catch the last flight back to DC. Her asset was dead, the witness was unresponsive, and the Brighton cops were clueless about Carlos Ramirez. That meant that unless something changed, Lisa Boone was on to her next assignment. She'd spent nearly a year on Amandi Oltamu, but sometimes this was how it went. There was always more work, and you couldn't brood over lost causes.

But she wanted to know what he had. All this time, all this careful recruiting and secrecy, and she still didn't know what he'd been able to produce. She'd heard only his guarantees.

Still a chance, though, she thought as she pulled away from Dr. Pine's home. *If that man is one hell of a neurologist, I suppose there's still a chance.*

I I

Shannon has been in the room with Tara most of the afternoon, but she leaves when Mom and Rick return, saying she needs to answer some e-mails and study. This is no doubt true—Shannon is missing crucial days of law school—but Tara knows there are also other reasons why Shannon prefers to check her e-mail elsewhere. Shannon doesn't want to be with them because they have different opinions on what should happen to Tara.

The truth of it is obvious: Tara's mother and stepfather want to kill her.

They don't think about it this way, of course. They're wandering around the outside of 1804 London Street, calling her name and shining lights in through the filthy windows, but even if they could get through the locked doors and inside the house, they wouldn't find the staircase that leads into darkness.

No one can follow her down there.

They don't know that she's still in the house, and so they hate the house for what it represents: The house killed their daughter. It needs to be condemned, torn down, and the foundation scraped clean.

The problem with that is that Tara's body *is* the awful house.

She's listened to their halting, tearful exchanges already. The word *dignity* is Rick's mantra. They must think of her dignity. They'll be preserving her dignity by ending the feeding tubes and diapers. They have no idea that she's still here, watching them, listening to them. They have no idea what their hopelessness takes from her.

What am I taking from them, though? she thinks as she watches them. They seem so tired all the time. So beaten. All because of her.

Tell me if there's any hope, she wants to say. She begs them through her silence and her stillness to just look her in the eye and state the cold hard truth. Is Shannon delusional, or has a doctor told them that Tara might come out of this? Is there any hope that she can convey her awareness to anyone outside of her own skull? Because if not…

If not, then do it.

Their focus isn't even on her, though. No one wants to look her in the eye. Mom is usually on her iPad. She posts constantly on Facebook, updating friends, responding to well-wishers, and begging for help. She's corresponding with three doctors, two ministers, and at least one psychic—maybe more, but she shut down disclosures on that pretty quickly after Shannon's response to it. She sometimes stops and stares at Tara, but the rest of the time, she's tapping away on the iPad. She doesn't put on any makeup or do much more with her hair than run a brush through it. It hurts Tara to watch her. To feel responsible for it all.

Rick just gazes at Tara with a horrible detachment. He doesn't accept the possibility that she can see him, and he's unhappy about the time he is required to sit here and talk to her.

He will make the call, she thinks. *In the end, he will convince Mom that it's best, and then Shannon will be overruled. She doesn't get a vote, anyhow. All she can do is argue. From a legal standpoint, isn't my mother in charge of deciding to end my life?*

These are issues that the three of them surely discuss, but they never do it in front of her. And yet, as terrible as it might be to hear, she wants them to explain the situation to her. She needs to understand.

There's a soft knock. Rick stands and says, "Yes?" and the door opens.

Please be a doctor, Tara thinks. She hasn't seen the doctor since she returned to awareness, only heard her family talk about doctors.

It's not a doctor, though, or even a nurse.

It is a boy with a bouquet of flowers in hand. He's younger than her, maybe not even out of high school yet. Average height and build, but he seems carved out of something very hard, not earned muscle so much as a natural quality; his angular face is all rigid edges and crisp lines. He's dressed in old jeans and a black hoodie and a black baseball cap with a line of silver stitching down the front.

"Can I help you?" Rick says.

"Is this…" The stranger glances Tara's way. "Yeah, it's Tara's room." He says her name softly, almost reverently, and she is very confused. She has no idea who he is.

"Yes," Rick says. "And you are?"

"A friend," he says, and Tara thinks, *What? A friend? I've never seen you before.*

"Oh. Well, we've asked for some privacy from visitors, because it's very—"

"I know, and I'm sorry. I just…I had to see her. I wanted to drop these off and…I'll get out of your hair. I'm so sorry. I just had to see her."

Who are you?

"It's fine," Mom says. "That's very sweet. What's your name?"

"Justin Loveless."

Tara stares at him. No, he is not Justin Loveless. She hasn't seen Justin in months, but he doesn't look even remotely like this kid.

Is this a symptom of something? Is that really Justin? Why can't I tell that?

While she fights a rising hysteria over this disconnect, he steps farther into the room and sets the flowers down on a table already crowded with them. He turns to her then and stares into her face and she feels a deep, cold fear and thinks, *He is lying,* with a sudden certainty. *He is pretending to be Justin, and he is lying. Why is he here? Who is he?*

Unlike most visitors, he isn't avoiding her eyes but looking directly into them the way Shannon does, seeking some sign of connection, of awareness. It doesn't feel affectionate, though. They are a hunter's eyes.

"Hi, Tara," he whispers.

She holds her breath. It's the first time she's realized that she can do this—the first clear connection between brain command and body response—but any joy over the discovery is drowned by the fear she feels as he studies her.

Without taking his eyes off hers, he says, "She's not responding at all? No blinks or hand squeezes or anything?"

"Not yet," Rick says. "But we're hopeful."

"Yes," the stranger answers. "Everyone is. She's so strong. She'll make it back. Are the tests encouraging, at least? I know the scans can sometimes show—"

"We're dealing with all of that as a family and with the doctors," Rick says, cutting him off. The stranger nods, accepting that, and Mom seems embarrassed.

"How do you know her, Justin?" she asks. "Do you go to Hammel?"

He straightens and looks at Mom. "I do. We were in the same a cappella group."

It is true that Justin Loveless goes to Hammel College and that Tara sang with him during her brief flirtation with the music department as a freshman, when she had visions of Broadway that were quickly crushed. But...this is not Justin Loveless.

"It's very nice of you to come," Rick says, "but we really do need to ask you to respect the family's request."

If this were a real friend, Tara would be furious at Rick's coldness, but instead she thinks, *Yes, get him, Rick, get him out of here!*

"Of course. I shouldn't have come. I just wanted to see her and tell her that I know she can make it back to us. I'm sorry to intrude, though. I really am."

"It's okay, hon," Mom says.

He gives a little nod, then says, "I'll leave now. I really appreciate you letting me say hello, though. A lot of people are thinking of her. I hope you know that."

"We do. Thank you. Hey!" Mom's face brightens. "Have you joined the Team Tara page?"

"Team Tara," he echoes. "What's that?"

"We're on Facebook, Instagram, and Twitter. I'm trying to keep everyone updated because we can't, obviously, let everyone in to visit. But we know how many kind people like you are out there, and we don't want to take that for granted."

"Team Tara. I like that. I'll sign up. I am definitely on Team Tara."

Rick clears his throat, and the stranger nods with understanding, then turns back to Tara. He leans down and puts his hand on hers. The overwhelming, irrational fear returns, amplified now by his touch. His eyes search hers.

"When you come back, Tara," he says, "I'll be here."

12

It was a two-hour drive from Biddeford, Maine, to Boston, and Abby could have driven down, talked to the sister, and been back by early afternoon, but she took the train.

Not because she couldn't handle I-95, with that press of traffic, cars squeezing you from all sides, like being caught in a tightening fist—of course she could handle that. A simple drive in traffic was no problem, but...well, maybe it was better not to rush things.

She tried not to consider how many months she'd been using that excuse. Tried not to consider that she'd come back to Maine promising herself she would be there just two weeks, that she would clear her head, get away from the tabloid photographers who wanted to run her picture beside images of gorgeous Luke London in his hospital bed, and then go back to LA.

No, she certainly wasn't rushing things.

The Downeaster left Portland at 8:15 and arrived in Boston's North Station shortly before noon, and the train gave her a way to relax after a largely sleepless night. Train travel was underrated, she thought. Sure, going by Amtrak took longer than driving, the stations weren't pristine, and you ran the risk of sitting beside a talkative stranger, but wasn't that all part of the romance of the rails? Simpler times, as Abby's dad always said during reruns of black-and-white TV shows.

It was raining when she got to Boston, and she was soaked by the time she caught a taxi driven by a man who smelled like he would have benefited from a few minutes in the downpour, perhaps with a little shampoo mixed in. But, hey, simpler times. She reached the hospital a little after one—five hours to get here for a ten-minute conversation that she could have had over the phone. The shoe box was wet now, the cardboard starting to soften and peel, but the phones inside were dry. She wished she'd thought to put them in a briefcase or something more formal.

Tara Beckley could be seen by visitors if the family and doctor approved it, but Abby made it clear to the receptionist that she did not want to see Tara.

"I'm here for her sister," she said. "Shannon Beckley. I'll wait here for her."

She sat in a vinyl-covered chair and jittered her right palm off a closed left fist as if drumming along to a song and she tried not to think of the hospital in Los Angeles where Luke had died. Abby had done a good job of making visits there. At first. Maybe not so good of a job later. But what was the point? Luke's eyes were empty, and his family's eyes were not. His mother stared at Abby with hate, his father stared at her with a naked question of *Why couldn't it have been you?*, and Hollywood magazines featuring the story piled up on the bedside table. The reporters called endlessly, and everyone advised Abby to say nothing.

She was the only one who *could* say something, though. Luke couldn't say a damn thing, couldn't defend Abby.

Would he have defended you? Sure, he would have. He'd have understood. He wanted to see how far you could push it. That was for him, not you. He loved risk, and he cast no blame.

And, yet…had he yelled at her to slow down just before the last curve? He'd said it so many times, but he'd been laughing, and it wasn't a command or even a request, just the delight of a kid on a roller coaster saying, *Slow down, slow down,* but not really meaning it. That was how it had gone. His tone hadn't shifted when Abby pegged the needle at 145. No way. That was her revisionist memory seeking to take blame, but it wasn't reality.

Slow down! His hand on her arm, tightening, his nails biting into her skin.

In a hospital three thousand miles away from that scene, the receptionist cleared her throat loudly, and Abby realized how she'd picked up the speed and volume of the drumming of her open right palm off her closed left fist. She looked like a drug addict in need of a fix. Looked like a...

Speed freak.

She flattened her hands and pressed them together as if in prayer, giving a weak smile of apology to the receptionist.

I'm not a speed freak, ma'am. If you'd watched me driving around lately, you'd know I was anything but that.

The doors between the waiting room and the long hallway opened and a tall young woman with red-brown hair and very green eyes, bright enough to stand out above the puffy purple crescents of fatigue, strode through the doorway like a marshal summoned to a fight in a saloon.

"You're the investigator?" the woman said.

"Yes. Abby Kaplan." She rose and offered her hand. The woman seemed to consider rejecting it but then shook it grudgingly. Her fingers were long and slender and strong, like a piano player's. Or like the Boston Strangler's, judging from her grip.

"What's this crap about her phone?" she said. "What does her phone have to do with anything?"

Abby saw the receptionist give a tired little shake of her head, as if she were all too familiar with this woman.

"Uh, I was just hoping to meet with the family and introduce myself and then we can get into any questions you all might have," Abby began, because she knew there was more to the family than this woman, and she figured she might find more friendliness in that group. Or in a rattlesnake den.

"You don't need to bother meeting the family," Shannon Beckley said. "I'm the family's legal representative."

"You're a lawyer?"

"I'm the closest thing they have right now," Shannon said. Contrasted against the dark red hair, her green eyes seemed aflame. "And in point of fact, I *will* be a lawyer." She paused, and her voice was softer when she said, "Maybe a little later than I'd expected now. Stanford doesn't stop. Not even for tragedy."

She gave a cold smile that made Abby pity whoever would have to face this woman in the courtroom in the years to come.

"So I'll lose a semester maybe." She shrugged, but it was forced indifference. "Whatever it takes, fine. Because that girl in there?" Shannon pointed to the closed double doors. "She and I have been through..." She caught herself, and Abby had the distinct feeling she was walling off a rise of emotion, brick by brick. She wouldn't allow herself to fall apart. Not in front of Abby, at least.

"So," she said when she'd composed herself, "tell me what you're doing, please, and why her phone matters."

Yes, the emotion was gone now, and cold steel was back in its place.

"Her mother—your mother—is here, correct?" Abby asked, not because she had any desire to speak to the mother but because she wanted to counter this woman somehow, however politely, and show that she had at least a little power in this situation.

"My mother is glued to Facebook, where she posts updates every ten minutes on a Team Tara page that my stepfather created so she'd have something to do, something that calmed her down that did not involve a tranquilizer. Do you really need to interrupt that?"

Abby remembered Luke's Facebook fan page, the blog, the Twitter account, all the endless updates fading from hopeful to resigned. She shook her head. "No. I don't need to interrupt that. I'm just trying to answer your questions, and I was told you needed to see me in person to address them."

"That's right. But your boss said you wanted to show me her phone. What's on the phone?"

"I don't know. I'm not even sure if I have it." Abby lifted the wet shoe box, feeling like a fool, and pulled back the lid. "The guy at the salvage yard gave me this. He's pulled them all out of cars. I was wondering if one of them belonged to your sister."

Shannon Beckley's eyes narrowed and she reached in the box and sorted through the phones quickly with those long, elegant fingers.

"No."

"You're sure?"

"Positive. Hers was a rose-gold iPhone in a case."

"Okay. Well, maybe one of them belonged to her passenger, then. The guy who towed the car was positive that he found one of these inside."

"What does it matter when you've got a driver whose guilt is already established?"

"I'm just trying to find out whether the phones survived the wreck," she said, and then she regretted that phrasing—*survived* was not the right word for a phone. "If one did, it might contain something useful."

"Useful to whom?"

"To…I mean, to everyone. It could provide clarification on a few points of—"

"Are you trying to get out of a claim? Is that the idea? Because I promise you, if you guys pull any bullshit to make this more expensive to my family than it already is, I will get that story on the front page of the *New York Times*." She looked Abby up and down and then added, "Or on Fox News. Whatever hits your company harder."

"That would actually be the *Portland Press Herald,* then."

"This is funny to you?"

She was leaning in, and Abby almost stepped back but then decided not to give her the satisfaction. "No. But before you start shouting threats, you might want to remember that I'm working on her behalf."

"Oh, that is such crap. The college hired you to find out if they had any risk. That's the truth."

She wasn't wrong, of course. Abby started to offer a pat reply about how the college intended to work hand in hand with the family, but something about Shannon Beckley's heated eyes made her dispense with the bullshit. "They're going to have someone do it," Abby said. "It'll be me or it'll be somebody else, but they will have someone ask questions."

Shannon studied Abby for a moment and then said, "Come see her."

"What?"

"If you're working on her behalf, I'd like you to come see her with me. We can talk with her, right?"

Abby blinked at her. "I thought...I was told that..." Shannon waited, eyebrows raised, and Abby felt she was talking her way into a trap. "That she's nonresponsive," she finished finally. "Was I misinformed?"

"We're not sure." Shannon Beckley softened her tone. "Maybe she's hearing it all, maybe she's not. We just don't know. At first it was a medically induced coma to try to limit the swelling in the brain, but now they're bringing her back out of it, and..." She cleared her throat. "And we're waiting on more tests."

"I understand," Abby said. "And I'm sorry. I can't imagine what that's like."

Bullshit, Abby. Why lie?

For an instant, she almost corrected herself. Almost told the truth to this sleep-deprived stranger with the searing stare, almost told her that she knew the situation all too well.

All she got out, though, was a question: "Has she had an fMRI yet?"

"No, but it's scheduled."

Abby nodded. "They usually start there. Then other scans. There are lots of ways to try to determine if she's...aware of things. Different doctors have different ideas."

"Too many ideas. I've been reading about all of them, and it's exhausting. There's a university hospital nearby where they have the patient watch a movie while undergoing an MRI, and they scan the brain for an emotional response. They've had good results with that."

"Like that Hitchcock film," Abby said. Shannon Beckley looked offended, and Abby realized she thought that Abby was comparing Tara's situation to a movie and headed her off. "Some researchers use an episode called 'Bang, You're Dead' from Alfred Hitchcock's old black-and-white TV series. A kid picks up a loaded gun, and the audience knows it's loaded, but the kid doesn't know. So the audience reacts emotionally as he goes from place to place carrying what he thinks is harmless and what the audience knows is deadly. That activates different areas in the brain of someone watching it. It shows awareness."

"Tara hates anything in black-and-white. If she's not in a vegetative state now, the sight of a black-and-white TV show might put her into one." She forced a laugh that choked at the end, like an engine running out of gas, and then she looked away and tried to gather herself. Abby didn't want to offer any canned condolences or well wishes, knowing exactly how exhausting and hollow those grew, and so she tried to follow the attempt at humor.

"Tell the doctors she's got to see a favorite movie of hers, then, because you want to know if her memory is activated. That sounds legitimate."

She was kidding, but Shannon Beckley said, "You know, that's not a bad idea."

"Actually, it probably is a bad idea. The doctors have their protocols for a reason. They tend not to like input from an insurance investigator."

"I'll find a more credible source, don't worry." Shannon regarded Abby curiously. "So you've dealt with a case like hers before?"

"Not a case." Now Abby regretted telling her anything. This woman, who was just a few years younger than Abby's thirty-one, was clearly not in the Luke London fan club, because she hadn't reacted to Abby's name. But she would Google it at some point, and then she'd have new questions.

"You spend that much time reading about coma patients? It's a hobby?"

"I get a lot of newsletters, trade magazines, crap like that."

"Your *trade magazines* deal with advanced coma protocols?"

"They've got to fill space," Abby said. "Listen, let me just introduce myself and explain what we are—"

"Let's go into her room for all this talk."

The way she said it made Abby feel as if Shannon were baiting her, as if she sensed fear. "It's not my job, I mean, it's not my place to be in there."

"Actually, it's anyone's place. The doctors have encouraged us to talk to her. That's what I'm supposed to be doing right now. So join me. Who knows—maybe she'll respond to you."

Luke? Luke, baby, if you're in there...do something. Speak, blink, squeeze my hand, slap me, just do something so I know!

"Okay," Abby said, her mouth dry. "Sure."

She followed Shannon Beckley through the double doors that parted automatically as if hurrying out of her way.

13

The nurses think Tara is brain-dead.

They treat her as an empty shell. They adjust her in the bed to prevent sores from forming, turn her and spread her legs and clean her, unaware of the horrifying humiliation, handling her roughly and without interest, talking around her and above her. They don't bother to speak to her, to introduce themselves. She can't even be certain they're nurses. Therapists of some sort, maybe? How do you know what they are doing when they don't bother to explain it? If they have any hope for her future, they don't indicate it. All she picks up from them is apathy; all she feels is pain and shame.

A young blond woman wipes Tara's ass and complains to a gray-haired black woman about the amount of time her fiancé spends with his friends smoking cigars in the garage right below their bedroom, which fills her clothes with the awful smell.

"He just doesn't get it," she says, and then she rolls Tara back over without so much as a glance at her face, holding a soiled diaper with her free hand.

"A phase, maybe?" the black woman suggests. "Something he'll get out of his system now, and after the wedding it will be different?"

"I'd *love* to believe that. But I'm not sure that I do."

The blonde discards the diaper, peels off her gloves, and looks down at Tara without any interest, then she consults a clipboard and makes a note. Is there a box you check when you wipe someone's ass? If so, can they add that you're required to do it discreetly and with apology or compassion? Or tell the patient your damn name, at least?

The nurses finish with her, add a few more checks to the clipboard beside her bed, and then the black woman hesitates and looks down into Tara's eyes for the first time.

"This one is supposed to be on the move tomorrow."

"Yes," the blonde agrees without looking over, and then they are out of sight, crossing the room and vanishing out the door and into the hallway.

This one.

A body, nothing more. That's what Tara is to them.

Also a body that is supposed to be on the move tomorrow. Where are they taking her? And why?

Of all the agonies of her condition, none is worse than the lack of explanations. She reentered a world that has moved on without her, and because no one is aware that she's back in it, no one slows down to clarify anything. Even her most basic questions—*How long have I been here? What happened to put me in here? Is there a diagnosis? Is there a plan? Is there hope?*—are unanswered, because everyone around her has already had these conversations, probably countless times. Why go backward, then? Instead, they move forward, following a course that was charted while Tara was lost to the blackness. She doesn't know where it began, let alone where it will end.

An accident? An attack? An illness?

She has no idea. The coma she understands, but its cause remains a mystery. Was she felled by a club or a clot? Her lack of memory in this regard is terrifying. She knows who she is, where she lives, what she does, likes, hates, loves; everything related to her identity is clear. What brought her here, though…she can't even begin to retrace the steps. She remembers getting out of the shower and checking the clock, which was important because she couldn't be late for…

For what?

She has no idea. Something important and time-sensitive. Time was her primary concern.

Did they find me there in the bathroom, naked on the floor, steam still on the mirror?

Every now and then, flickers of images will rise and then sink, like leaves carried in a swift stream, but she believes those images aren't memories, just pieces of the awful nightmare she'd endured prior to waking. A stranger, a cold wind, and a wolf.

The door opens again. She feels Shannon's presence before she actually sees her. This is how it has always been with Shannon. She buzzes with a different energy than most people, moving through the world with a swirling, nearly chaotic force. It is a force that Tara clings to now, because she can feel the hope draining away from her mother and Rick. They aren't as bad as the nurses yet, and she expects they never could regard her with such indifference, but…they are drifting that way.

Shannon is with an unfamiliar young woman with short, dark blond hair and blue eyes. She is lean and slim-hipped, an almost boyish figure, though her eyes and athlete's grace would stand out if she weren't shuffling in so unhappily, like a child dragged into the principal's office. She glances at Tara only briefly, and while Tara is growing used to cursory glances, this one feels different. It isn't that the new woman sees no point in making eye contact with her; it's that she's afraid.

"Tara, I've found a new friend," Shannon says with false cheer. Shannon keeps up a steady stream of conversation most of the time she is here, and when she does finally fall silent, she usually leaves soon after. It reminds Tara of the years when they shared a bedroom—when Shannon stopped talking, it meant she'd fallen asleep.

Now Shannon rests her hand on Tara's arm. The touch is warm and kind. Tara wonders what her skin feels like to Shannon—the same healthy human warmth or the clamminess of sickness? Or something worse?

"Abby's an investigator," Shannon says. "She tells me she's working on your behalf."

Abby is holding an old, wet shoe box. She clears her throat and says, "Hello, Tara. It's good to meet you."

Tell me why you're here, Tara screams silently. Abby doesn't, but why would you tell a piece of furniture what your purpose in the room is?

Abby's attention is back on Shannon when she says, "Have the police asked you any questions about the accident?"

The accident. This is interesting. This is the first time anyone has spoken of what led her to this terrible, trapped place.

"Sure," Shannon says. "But nobody talked about her phone until your boss called me. The police said it was clear who was at fault. The driver *admitted* that at the scene. And then he repeated it, on the record."

The driver. So it was a car accident. This resonates in a way that is both exciting and troubling; it sets off a tingle of memory, but no images come forth, just a feeling of dread.

"I know that. And now he's going to hire an attorney who will find any way possible to mitigate the driver's responsibility. It's not right, but it's what happens. My job is to get out in front of that." Abby pauses, then says, "His story has some issues too."

"Do not tell me you're questioning his version of things." There's a warning in Shannon's voice.

"I'm not questioning that he was at fault."

"Good."

"But—"

"Oh, boy. Here we go."

"*But* I do not like his facts. It's clear that he hit her car, that her car was stationary, and that she was out of the vehicle. Of course he's at fault. But he's also mistaken about the details, and I don't understand why."

I was out of the vehicle. Tara feels that tingle again, stronger now, and she wants to grab Abby's hand and squeeze, wants to tell her to say more, paint a better picture, because she is close to remembering, she is very close, this woman can help Tara bridge the void.

"He's probably confused because he was staring at his damn phone," Shannon says.

Abby Kaplan shakes her head, and a muscle in her jaw flexes, as if she's grinding her teeth.

"The angles are wrong," she says softly. "The angles and the speed. He was driving terribly, yes, and he was negligent, but if he swerved like he says he did, then he should have flipped that van before he hit her."

"The police can probably explain that to you," Shannon says curtly.

Abby shakes her head, eyes distant, as if she is envisioning the scene.

Say what you're thinking! Tara screams, but of course Abby doesn't hear her.

"No, they actually can't," she tells Shannon. "They haven't driven the right kind of cars at the right kind of speeds to know what is possible and what isn't."

"And I suppose you have."

The short, slender girl looks at Shannon then, and there's a spark to her when she says, "Yes. I have." She takes a breath and the spark fades and she seems sad. "Anyhow, you don't need to worry about me messing up any claims. It wasn't your sister's fault. But…it also didn't happen the way Carlos Ramirez said it did."

"So Ramirez was confused."

"Maybe." Abby Kaplan turns to face Tara, and this time she lets her stare linger. Her eyes are on Tara's when she says, "I'm confident she would have a different memory of the way it happened."

Tara stares back at her from within her corporeal shell, trying somehow to convey how desperately she needs the facts. If someone can just walk her through it, then maybe she can remember.

"Have you talked to the other victim's family?" Shannon asks. "Oltamu's?"

"Not yet." Abby turns away from Tara.

Oltamu. Shannon says the name so casually, but it's a cataclysmic moment for Tara.

Dr. Oltamu. A visiting speaker. She was driving him from dinner to the auditorium. She was driving him and then...

A block in her memory rises again, and she has a distinct vision of a wolf with its ears pinned back and its hackles raised.

Hobo. The wolf's name is Hobo.

Why would a wolf have a name? But Oltamu is a name that registers; he is the black man with the nice smile and the expensive watch. Memories are returning now, scattered snapshots.

His name was Amandi Oltamu, and I was driving him. But who is he? Why was I driving him, and where? And what did he do to me?

Tara's mind is whirling now, trying to capture each crucial detail, knowing that she must catch them all before they escape into the blackness like fireflies and disappear for good.

"Think his family will sue the college?" Shannon asks.

"Maybe. But I don't see their case yet. The only thing that's odd is why she parked where she did."

Because he told me to, damn it, Tara thinks without hesitation. *He wanted the Tara tour.* This element is strangely vivid amid the fog of all the memories she's lost—Oltamu asked her to get out of the car. She sees the two of them walking toward a bridge and she knows that this is true. *We were both out of the car. We were both out because he wanted to walk, and I was worried about that because of the time, time was tight. But he told me that he wanted to walk, so we started to walk down to the bridge and then the wolf got us. The wolf came out of the darkness and got us.*

She knows this is madness, and it scares her that it seems so logical, so clear.

I am not just paralyzed, I am insane.

"Nobody can answer that but her," Abby Kaplan says, studying Tara's face, and again Tara feels that strange electric sense of connection just beyond her grasp, like a castaway watching a plane pass overhead. "Do you know anyone who was with her at that dinner?" Abby asks Shannon.

"A few people have reached out."

"I wonder if anyone would remember whether Oltamu had a phone on him."

"Why?"

"Because he's dead, and she can't talk," Abby says, running a hand through her hair as if to tamp down frustration. "People are on their phones all the time. He could have been using it right up until the end. And one of these"—she lifts the shoe box—"belongs to him. Unless the salvage guy kept it or sold it already. Neither would surprise me."

He took pictures with his phone, Tara tells them silently. *A selfie with me, because he needed to increase his social media presence. That was what worried him right before he died and I was erased from my own life. The last time I ever smiled, it was for a selfie with a stranger so he could improve his social media profile. If not for that, I'd have been across the bridge.*

The lucidity of this is exciting, but she knows it's still not complete. She is circling the memory like someone fumbling through a dark house searching for a light switch.

"I've wondered about *her* phone," Shannon says hesitantly, as if she isn't sure she should make this admission.

"Why?"

"Because when she drove, she put it on one of those magnet things on the dash. It wasn't there, and it wasn't in her purse. She was wearing a dress and a thin sweater with no pockets. So if it went into the river, that means she got out with the phone in her hand, as if she was using it."

Shannon pauses then, which is wonderful, because Tara is frantically snatching at all these fireflies—*phone, dress, sweater, river*—trying to capture them before they escape into the darkness.

Abby Kaplan clears her throat and says, "I hope she comes back to you soon. For her sake and yours, of course, but also because I'd like to hear what she remembers." She gives Shannon a business card, tells her to be in touch with any questions, and wishes her well, as if Shannon is alone in this struggle.

She does not look at Tara again before she leaves.

14

The untimely death of Carlos Ramirez was supposed to bring an end to a problem that should have been resolved easily, but this situation seemed determined to keep turning up like the proverbial bad penny.

Gerry Connors had dealt with such problems before, though, and he wasn't worried by this one. Not just yet, at least. The potential for concern was floating out there, simply because of the price tag on this job. The price tag, and the German's reputation. He had never met the German, but he'd heard of him, and when he did meet him, he certainly didn't want to be delivering bad news.

For this, Gerry had Dax Blackwell, and he needed him to be as good as his bloodline promised he'd be.

Gerry Connors had first made his way into organized crime in the 1990s in his hometown of Belfast, working with the IRA at a time when work was easy to come by for a man who didn't mind killings and bombings. Gerry felt no fierce loyalty to either church or state, and he hadn't met many like him in that struggle until the Blackwell brothers arrived. Two freelancers from Australia who looked like sweet lads, blond-haired and blue-eyed and innocent-faced as altar boys, they'd entered a room filled with hardened IRA men, outlined their plan, and didn't blink in the face of all the hostility and all the bloody history. Men had shouted at them, men had threatened them, and the brothers had calmly named their price and said take it or leave it.

Eventually, the boys in Belfast took it. A week after that, three members of the constabulary had been buried, the nation was in an uproar, and the Blackwells were wealthy—and long gone from the country.

They'd come back, of course. When the money was right, they returned, and during the 1990s, Jack and Patrick found plenty of work in Ireland. So did Gerry. He'd moved to America and gone into contract work, providing papers and identification for those who needed them. Soon he was providing more than papers—cars, guns, and, inevitably, it seemed, killers.

Jack and Patrick had come back around often then.

It was just after 9/11, and the business was experiencing fresh risks when Jack Blackwell requested multiple sets of identification for his newborn son. Gerry was reluctant to take on the task in those days, but he was even more reluctant to disappoint Jack Blackwell. He produced the requested birth certificates, which came from fifteen different states in America, as well as four sets of international papers, Australian, British, Dutch, and Swiss. Each was in a different name, and Jack provided all of the names, which led Gerry to wonder if they meant something to him, if they indicated something from his past life—or perhaps indicated lives he'd ended.

Gerry had no idea what the boy's real name was, but the first time he'd met him, Jack had called him Dax, and so that was what Gerry went with, even though there was no paperwork for that name. Or at least, none that Gerry had created. Knowing Jack, Gerry figured he'd likely sourced identification from more than one person.

More than a dozen years later, when Gerry had need of Jack and Patrick's services again, Jack told him they themselves were unavailable, but his son could handle the task. Gerry's first response was to laugh—a very dangerous response when one was around the Blackwells, but Gerry knew the boy wasn't even old enough to drive yet.

Jack Blackwell hadn't laughed. He'd waited until Gerry said,

"You're not serious," and then the faintest of smiles had crossed his face, and he nodded exactly once.

That was enough.

Nine days later, Dax Blackwell completed his first professional killing. Or at least, his first professional killing for Gerry Connors.

Over the years that followed, Gerry had been in touch with the boy fairly often. He had no idea where he lived or where he'd gone to school—or if he had gone to school, although he was certainly well educated, almost preternaturally bright. He also had no idea how much time the boy actually spent with his father and uncle, but based on his mannerisms and his skills, Gerry suspected that he was with them more often than not. After hearing word of Jack's and Patrick's deaths in Montana, Gerry considered offering his condolences to the boy, but he hadn't. Instead, he offered him work, and the boy accepted the job and completed it. Small-time stuff, mostly, no high-dollar work, no international work. Gerry viewed it as an internship.

The pupil flourished.

They never spoke of Dax's father and uncle formally, but they each mentioned them in passing and never referred to their deaths. Gerry followed the boy's lead in keeping discussions of them in the present tense, as if they were still there, ghosts in the room, just waiting for the call to summon them back.

And in fact, when Gerry sent for Dax, that was exactly how it felt. As the boy grew, Gerry saw more and more of those two Aussie lads who'd walked so calmly into the room of hardened IRA killers.

Yes, he felt very much like he was calling on a ghost when he sent for Dax Blackwell.

Today the ghost arrived. He entered Gerry's office in Boston's North End expecting a paycheck for a completed job, having no clue yet as to the trouble that had occurred. Carlos Ramirez had needed to kill one man and steal one phone. Somehow, Carlos

Ramirez had managed to steal the wrong fucking phone. Gerry understood this because the German had told him not to worry about a trace on the phone because it wasn't active and had no signal. The phones in Gerry's desk drawer had signals. Both of them had been ringing, and that was a problem. That was, maybe, an enormous problem, as the German was due to arrive by the weekend to pick up something for which he had already paid handsomely but that was not in Gerry's possession. The German did not travel internationally to pick up things in person that could be mailed unless the items were of the utmost importance. Based on Gerry's understanding of the German, he felt that this in-person disappointment was not the sort of thing one would want to experience firsthand.

Enter Dax Blackwell.

"The job's not done," Gerry told him as soon as the door was closed behind him.

"Not done? Did Carlos walk out of the morgue?" the kid asked as he sat down. Make no mistake, Dax carried his family's blood. Which was to say that he was empty and cold in all the right ways, but he also carried his father's smirk and his uncle's deadpan delivery. Gerry had never been a fan of those qualities.

The only thing Gerry hated more than Dax's attitude was his wardrobe. Jeans and hoodies, tennis shoes and a baseball cap. Always the fucking baseball cap. Whatever happened to gangsters with class? When did people decide they could come see him without shining their damn shoes, maybe putting on some cuff links?

But Dax wasn't a gangster, of course. You had to be patient with the young ones. When young shooters became old killers, then you could demand more from them. If they made it that far, they'd probably figured it out on their own. Right now he was an Australian version of what the cartels called a wolf boy—a teenage killer, an apprentice assassin. Wolf boys were valuable in the border towns. Why couldn't they be useful on a larger scale too?

Dax Blackwell, the Aussie lobo, descendant of ghosts.

"We are missing a phone," Gerry said, leaning back and propping his feet up on the glass-topped coffee table so the kid could get a good look at his hand-stitched, calfskin Moreschi wingtips. Put style in front of his face, maybe it'd seep through his skull.

"He gave me two. You have them."

"Neither is right. One is hers, and one is his, but neither one is right."

"Carlos's house was clean. So was his bag."

"What about his pockets?"

The kid looked nonplussed. Dax Blackwell didn't like to be asked questions for which he didn't have ready answers.

"Didn't check," he said eventually. "I hadn't been asked to. You told me get two phones; I got two phones. But I also don't think he'd have kept one unless he knew its value. Did he?"

This was both more attitude and more inquiry than Gerry wanted from the kid, but he wasn't wrong to ask the question. Carlos had no idea what the phone was worth. *Gerry* didn't know anything about the phone other than that he was supposed to hand it to the German.

One thing Gerry had learned over the years was not to ask too many questions about what went on above your pay grade—hell, not to *think* too many questions about it—and he surely did not want to begin thinking about what the German needed from this cell phone. What he *was* willing to extend his personal curiosity to, however, was what would happen if he disappointed people above his pay grade, and he didn't have to work too hard to imagine the outcome.

He needed that phone.

"Police found Carlos's body," Gerry said. "If he had the phone, it'll be in evidence lockup, and I'll get it. But I don't think he had it."

"I don't either. If he was going to make a mistake like that, he'd have done it a long time ago."

Again, more confidence than Gerry wanted to hear, more swagger, but also, again, not wrong.

"Probably. Which means it's missing somewhere between here and there."

Dax Blackwell thought about this, nodded, and then said, "He needed two phones, so he grabbed Oltamu's and grabbed the girl's. Dumb mistake, but that's probably what he did, and he didn't pause to check properly, so he missed the third. By the time they'd cleaned the scene and I picked them up by the river, the phone you needed was gone with the cars."

Now he sounded just like his old man. Jack Blackwell always got right to it, but he never showed impatience, and he never rushed.

"That phone is imperative," Gerry said. "I need it fast, and Carlos is no longer able to assist."

"I heard he was…deported, yes."

Now this was his uncle's personality, everything about it pure Patrick—no twitch of a smile, and yet you knew he'd amused himself with the comment.

"Unless you want an expedited trip to the same place, spare me the wit," Gerry said. The kid didn't so much as blink. Gerry wasn't sure whether he liked the kid's response or if it infuriated him. Composure was appropriate. But fearlessness in front of Gerry? Less appropriate.

"I'll get the phone, then," Dax said. "You should have just let me take the whole job from the start."

Gerry looked at him over the gleaming toe of the Moreschis, considered his response, and let silence ride. If it bothered the kid, he didn't show it.

"It was supposed to look like an accident, and it was time-sensitive," Dax said. "There were many better ways to do that than what he chose. He brought a brawler's touch to a finesse job."

"Just go find that fucking phone, and maybe I'll have more patience for your input in the future," Gerry said, frustration getting the better of him now, partly because the kid wasn't wrong and partly because he didn't understand one crucial element of the deal—Gerry had spared Dax's life. The German had been very clear that anyone involved with hitting Oltamu needed to be expendable. Carlos, already a risk to Gerry on other matters, had thus been ideal for the job. But Dax could've gone too. Should have, in fact, by the terms of the deal.

But he was too promising.

If I can own one of them, Gerry thought, visions of the Blackwell brothers coming back to him, *it will be worth it. If he grows into one of their kind, and he is all mine, loyal to the throne and not just the checkbook, then he will certainly be worth the trouble.*

The kid stood without being told they were done. For a moment, Gerry thought about ordering him to sit his ass back down, but what was the point?

"Go on," he said, and he waved at the door. "Get me the phone. It's an iPhone, but it has no signal. That's all I know. If the phone puts out a signal, it's the wrong one."

Dax Blackwell didn't move right away. Instead, he stood there looking at Gerry, and then he said, "The phone is one problem Carlos left behind. There might be another. Do you have an opinion on that yet?"

He meant the girl, of course.

"She's as good as gone, is my understanding."

"That's enough?"

"She's brain-dead. And even if she wakes up, what's she gonna say?"

"You don't know," Dax said. "That would be precisely my concern."

Gerry flushed and swung his feet down.

"I understand my fucking liabilities, son. I don't need your assistance with the big picture. I need you to bring me the phone. Now get out of here and do it."

He didn't like the way the kid studied him and then nodded and turned away as if he'd seen something in Gerry's anger that interested him.

No, it was more than interest, Gerry thought as he stared at the closed door, Dax Blackwell's footsteps reverberating across the tiled floor on the other side. That expression hadn't been one of intrigue or curiosity but something deeper, something darker.

Like whatever he'd seen in his boss had made him hungry.

"He's just a kid," Gerry said aloud. The words echoed in the empty room, and when they bounced back at him, they weren't reassuring. He sounded nervous, sitting in his own office and talking about his own employee. What in the hell was that about?

About the kid's old man and his uncle, of course. Jack and Patrick were long gone, yes, but they cast long shadows too, a pair of dark smiling ghosts.

The best hitters you ever saw. So trust the kid, Gerry thought. At least a little longer. He was a beta-Blackwell. But if he bloomed? Well, then.

Wouldn't that be something.

15

Dax had spent an hour the previous night listening to the idle chatter in Tara Beckley's hospital room, enough time to confirm both that they'd kept his flowers and that she remained mute, but each day had the potential for new blessings, as the Team Tara Facebook page reminded him that morning, and so he checked back in after leaving Gerry Connors's office.

The recorder he'd placed in the flower vase was of excellent microphone quality but he was disappointed with its computer interface and mobile options. He had to use the web browser to log in, and then he had to sort through multiple files that captured dialogue exchanges of longer than two minutes. He wished he'd used a better system, but Tara Beckley was only of value-added potential for Dax; she wasn't a threat. With threats, you spared no expense. The microphones he had planted in Gerry's office, for example, were cutting-edge, and he'd paid accordingly.

He sat in his car and updated himself on *A Day in the Semi-Life of Tara Beckley*. He listened to her mother talk endlessly and aimlessly, scrolled past that, found the same with the sister, and then some nurses chattering, and then...

What was this?

"Abby's an investigator. She tells me she's working on your behalf."

That was the sister talking. The investigator, when she spoke, sounded nervous. Well, no surprise there—Tara's empty-eyed stare and those tubes could be unsettling to some. Dax doubted many people had given her the kind of deep eye contact that he'd offered.

The investigator blathered on awkwardly, not saying much of

interest, but then the sister said something that made Dax sit up straight.

"Nobody talked about her phone until your boss called."

Her phone? Well, now. The investigator might be more interesting than Dax had thought.

He listened through more chatter, the investigator agreeing that Carlos Ramirez was at fault—apparently she didn't yet know that Carlos was also in the morgue—and then carrying on about how she didn't like Carlos's story. Dax had to give her some credit for this because she seemed to understand the physics of it all in a way the police hadn't, and thus she got what a colossal disaster Carlos Ramirez had been. Time-sensitive, make-it-an-undeniable-accident instructions be damned; Carlos had picked an awfully dumb way to go about the hit. Perhaps he hadn't cared because he knew he'd be out of the country by the time anyone showed real interest. That was fine, but the mess he'd made of things reflected poorly not only on Carlos but on Gerry Connors. And since Dax worked with Gerry, there was the risk of contamination. The Blackwell brand could be damaged before he'd had a chance to re-introduce it if Gerry stumbled. You had to be careful who you worked for in this business. *Independent contractors are not immune to the perils of poor management,* his father had told him often.

For a hick insurance investigator, Abby was surprisingly astute. She was also scared, it seemed, which was interesting. Information and fear didn't go together in Dax's mind—knowledge was power, the cliché promised, and so far in his young life, he'd found that to be true. Then why was this woman so nervous?

Probably it was Tara's dead-eyed stare. Abby the investigator kept pushing, though, almost grudgingly, as if she couldn't help herself.

"And one of these," Abby said, and there was a rustling sound, "belongs to him. Unless the salvage guy kept it or sold it already. Neither would surprise me."

"I've wondered about *her* phone," Shannon said.

Dax Blackwell rewound and replayed that portion.

16

Another advantage of the train—beyond the fact that it didn't make her heart thunder or her vision blur white in the corners—was that Abby could work while she traveled.

She typed up the details of the visit with Shannon Beckley (and Tara Beckley, though that felt more like a visitation, a respectful glance into the casket) on her laptop while the Downeaster rattled back north. Or, as befitted its name, back *down east,* a term that referred to prevailing summer winds along Maine's coast. In most places in America, *down* meant "south," but in southern Maine, *down* took you north.

The visit had been as pointless as Abby had promised Hank it would be—nothing that she couldn't have accomplished with a phone call. And yet she found herself more invested in the work because she'd made that pass by the casket, glanced down at the beyond-reach Tara Beckley in her comatose state.

Those eyes. Her eyes looked so damn alert...

But Abby knew they weren't. She'd been through that cruel illusion before.

Luke was famous for his face, but the audience didn't understand that his eyes were what made his face work. They were so alive, penetrating and laughing and *alive.* There was a reason he'd moved so quickly from sending in his head shots to getting auditions to being offered lead roles in blockbuster action films, and, yes, some of it was talent, and, yes, some of it was his physical beauty, but Abby knew the secret was his eyes.

When they made love, he kept his eyes closed. When they made love, she wanted to see him. Finally, one night, when he was on top of her and inside of her but somehow still absent, she'd put her hands in his hair and tugged his head back and said, "Look at me."

He'd opened his eyes then, and even in the darkness she'd felt that strange, powerful energy, the unique sense of *life* that came from within his gaze. They'd finished together, face-to-face, clenching and shuddering and gasping but never breaking eye contact, the best sex of her life by far.

"I like to see you," she'd whispered, and she bit his shoulder gently.

He'd laughed, the sound soft and low in the room, and said, "I'll remember that."

And he had. He always had.

That made those moments in the hospital even crueler.

Her phone rang, pulling her thoughts away from Luke. It was Hank, calling from the office. Abby answered just as a couple seated beside her burst into laughter.

"Where are you?" Hank asked.

"Headed back."

"Who's in the car with you?"

"Nobody." She grimaced and tried to shield the phone from the sound of the voices.

"Then who am I listening to in the background?"

"I'm on the train," Abby admitted.

"The train? Why in the hell would you take the train to Boston?"

"It gives me time to work."

"You turn a six-hour day into ten or twelve hours so you can buy time to work? I know you're a product of Biddeford public schools, Abby, but that is really bad math."

Hank had gone to Thornton Academy in Saco, which was a public school for some local residents but an in-demand private boarding school for the rest of the world, and he liked to wear it as a badge of honor. He rarely mentioned that he'd dropped out of community college shortly after his stint at Thornton.

"Funny," Abby said. "But I've got the report caught up, and I dealt with the sister and saw Tara, so I checked all the boxes you needed."

"Great. But you've got a big one unchecked that is going to stay that way—Carlos Ramirez isn't talking to you."

"Finally got smart enough to hide behind a lawyer?"

"Nope. He's dead."

"What?"

"Yup. Bullet to the brain."

"Suicide," Abby said, less a question than a statement, because it seemed to make so much sad sense—Ramirez knew he was looking at prison time, and he hadn't been able to bear that prospect.

"Nope. Caught two shots down in Brighton in the passenger seat of a stolen car. I just heard the news. Guess they found him yesterday, last night, something. But he was murdered, so whatever trouble we thought he had over that accident might have been only the surface. I wonder if they checked that van for drugs. Just because his blood was clean doesn't mean *he* was, know what I'm saying?"

The train clattered and swayed as Abby held the phone to her ear without speaking.

"Crazy shit, right?" Hank prompted.

"Yeah. Crazy." Abby wasn't sure why the news bothered her so much, why she couldn't view it with the detachment that Hank did.

"Whatever closure Oltamu's family might've felt from watching that guy go to jail is gone now, and that's a problem," Hank said. "Maybe they look elsewhere for it and sue the school. Meanwhile, my trusty investigator is worried that Ramirez didn't get his facts straight when he talked to the police, which will not make the liability folks happy. Can you get yourself in line with his statement?"

"No."

"Excuse me?" Hank sounded stunned.

"I think he lied."

"He took the blame! Why in the hell would he lie to take the blame?"

"I have no idea, Hank, but I'm sure that he didn't tell the truth. I don't care if it was because he lied or because he was confused, but he did not tell the truth. That isn't good news for your client either way."

"No, it sure isn't." Hank groaned. "Are you *positive* his version doesn't hold together?"

"Yes. And somebody is going to notice eventually, so we'd better warn people before that happens."

"Shit. You're ruining this, Abby. It was so damn simple! Wreck, fatality, confession, and then the guilty dude's dead! That's as clean as they come."

That's why this news bothers me, Abby realized as the couple next to her laughed loudly in her ear again. *Ramirez being killed makes it even cleaner.*

"Let's talk it over when I get back," she said. "Something's wrong here."

"You sure know how to spoil a good thing."

"Come on, Hank, you're an investigator! Where's your detective's gusto?"

"Gimme a break. I hold that friggin' PI license only as a necessary credential to support my career as a bullshitter."

"But this could be a break in the case. That should make your day."

"I've never desired to break open any case that wasn't filled with beers."

"Maybe you'll be able to do both for a change."

"Wouldn't that be something," Hank said dismally.

"Chin up," Abby said. "You might be a hero when this is all done. Get the key to the city or something."

"I got plenty of bowling trophies, thanks. Come by the office and we'll talk, all right?"

"It'll be late by the time I'm in."

"Because you took the friggin' train. Meanwhile the Hellcat's sitting out back."

Abby didn't respond, and Hank sighed and said, "We'll catch up in the morning, then. And I'll start looking for a new employee. 'Wanted: slow learner with lack of ambition.'"

When they ended the call, Abby didn't put her phone away. She sat there for a while as the couple beside her laughed again, that wonderful oblivious-to-everything-else laughter that came when you were so locked in with another person that the rest of the world was only peripheral. She wanted to glance at them but didn't want them to catch her staring, didn't want to intrude on that moment. Good for them if they had that connection. Hope-fully they could keep it.

She found Shannon Beckley's number and called.

"This is Abby Kaplan. I'm the one who—"

"I know who you are; I saw you less than two hours ago. What do you need?"

"Have you heard about Carlos Ramirez?"

"Heard *what* about Ramirez?"

"That he's dead. He was murdered."

Abby didn't think it was easy to knock Shannon Beckley off her stride, but this seemed to do it. Abby heard her take a sharp breath before she said, "You're serious."

"Yes. Shot to death in a stolen car. I wanted to let you know."

"Why?" Shannon asked, and it was a damn fine question. Abby hadn't put the answer into words yet, not even in her own mind, but now she had to.

"Whatever Tara saw might be important," she said.

"Dangerous for her," Shannon answered. "That's what you mean."

"I don't know. But I won't rule it out. Listen, I'm not trying to scare you; you've got enough to be scared of right now. But Ramirez lied to the police. I'm sure of it. And now he's been murdered."

"It was just a car wreck," Shannon said, but she wasn't arguing. She said it in the way you did when you wanted to make something big small again.

"Maybe."

There was a moment of silence, and then Shannon Beckley said, "What are you thinking?"

"Nothing. I just wanted to let you know that this had—"

"Bullshit. You're looking at it differently than everyone else. You didn't believe him, and now that he's dead, you think that means something. So let me ask again, please—what are you thinking?"

Her tone was no longer combative or even commanding. It was lonely.

"When she comes out of it," Abby said, "be careful about the people who are around when she's asked about the accident. Be careful who asks her about it."

"*When* she comes out of it," Shannon said softly. "I like your confidence."

"She's in there," Abby said. "I'm almost positive."

"Yeah? The doctors aren't. So how do you know?"

"Because I've seen someone who wasn't. There's a difference."

I'm almost positive, she repeated to herself. But of course she wasn't. Not now when she said Tara was still in there and not back when she'd said Luke no longer was.

17

It wasn't yet five o'clock, but Savage Sam Jones figured you didn't always need to go by the book, certainly not at his age, and so he opened a PBR well before he locked the gates at the salvage yard. It was a quarter past four and he was hungry as well as thirsty and he wanted a slice or two of pizza from the corner store, but right now it would be the old, dried-out shit left over from lunch. For the good pizza, he'd have to wait until five.

Might as well wait there as here, he thought.

He'd closed the door to his office and turned to lock it, and he was standing with his keys in one hand and a beer in the other when he heard the car pull in.

Son of a bitch. There was business after all.

He left the keys in the door, set the beer down on the step, and walked toward the gate as a young guy stepped out of a Jeep and gazed at the place. That wasn't uncommon; teenagers were always coming around. They were young enough to still have an interest in working on their own cars, and they didn't have the money for new parts.

"Come on in, but don't forget it's gettin' on toward closing time," Sam hollered.

"It's not even four thirty." The kid said this in an amused voice, not confrontational, but still, it riled Sam. Who gave a damn what a kid thought closing time should be?

"Like I said," Sam told him drily as he picked up the PBR can. The kid watched him and then smiled, like he'd just learned something that pleased him.

"I don't want to impose on you, sir. I can tell you've got better things to do." This was smart-ass, but he plowed on past it so fast that Sam didn't have a chance to retort. "I'm just doing my job, which requires hassling you about a couple of cars that you towed in here from up by Hammel College a few days ago."

"Shit." Sam drank more of the beer. He was tired of those cars from the college. They were costing him more in headaches than they were worth in dollars. "They send you to take the pictures?"

The kid cocked his head. "Did who send me?"

"The gal I gave the phones to, she said she was coming back for pictures."

The kid didn't move his head, didn't change expression, didn't so much as blink, and yet Sam felt a strangeness come off him like an electric pulse.

"Who was this?"

"I don't remember," Sam said, and that wasn't a lie. He was always awful with names and even worse when he wasn't interested.

"Police?"

"Insurance, I think. She gave me a card."

Sam drained the beer and shook the empty can with regret, and he was just about to tell the kid that he had an appointment with a slice of pepperoni pizza when the kid said, "You like whiskey?"

Did Savage Sam Jones like whiskey? He almost laughed aloud. It had been a number of years since he'd heard that question. He was about to shout back, *Does Hugh Hefner like big tits?* but then he recalled his business decorum. That and the fact that Hugh was dead and this kid might not have the faintest idea who the man was or why glossy magazines had ever been needed. The damned internet had spoiled these kids.

"Does the pope shit in a funny hat?" Sam asked instead, figuring even a youngster could follow that old gem, and the kid grinned as he approached. He had a backpack slung over one shoulder and he didn't look like any trouble. Just lazy, that was all. You could tell that by the way he dressed, way he moved, everything. All these damned kids were lazy now, though. If he was here looking for car parts and asking about whiskey, why, he couldn't be as bad as most of them.

"I've got a bottle I might share with you, then," he said, and Sam squinted at him. This was more intriguing—and concerning. Was he some sort of street preacher? Was the whiskey a ruse entirely? If the kid got to carrying on about the spirit and the soul, that was not going to go well. It would go even worse if he was trying to sell some homebrew small-batch bullshit.

What he produced, though, was good old-fashioned American Jack Daniel's. It was hard to argue with that. Granted, it was a higher-dollar version, something called Gentleman Jack, but Sam had seen it at Walmart and so he knew it could be trusted.

"What do you want, son?" he said. He didn't mind the kid, and he surely wouldn't mind the whiskey, but he also didn't drink with strangers who showed up at five—well, close to five, anyhow—on a workday.

"Just a bit of your time. I can pour you a drink if you listen to me for a few minutes."

Sam looked at him and then at the bottle, and then he pictured the pizza slices spinning their slow dance in the warming oven on the corner store's counter. It would be twenty minutes at least until there were fresh slices in there.

"Who'd you say you worked for?" he asked.

"I didn't," the kid said, and smiled. "But I promise I'll be less trouble than any of the rest of them."

"Rest of who?"

"The people who are asking about those cars and the phones."

"Son, I only towed 'em in here. I didn't witness the damn wreck, and I don't have the damn phone."

"But there was a phone in the car?"

Sam wasn't sure whether he liked this kid or not. He smiled an awful lot, but the smile seemed to belong to an inside joke, which was strange considering it was only the two of them here and Sam didn't get the joke. "I don't know," Sam said. "Go call the cop who called me and ask him—"

"I don't think we should call the cops," the kid said. "I think we should have a drink and talk. Because you made a mistake, Mr. Jones. You shouldn't have given that phone away to anyone who didn't have a badge. She had to have been aware of the trouble she was getting you into, and you're telling me she didn't warn you?"

"Shit, no!" Sam was uneasy now, thinking of the number of phones he'd entrusted to the blond gal.

The kid made a disappointed sound and shook his head. "I know her type, all friendly talk, winking at you and then somehow leaving with property she doesn't have any right to, and when the cops show—and they will—the cops will have heard an entirely different story than the one you were told. There'll be petty charges, maybe, but what's petty when it's your own life and your business?"

Shit, shit, shit, Sam thought. Sam did *not* want to appear in court, and he said as much now.

The kid nodded sympathetically and said, "I think we can keep it from going that way."

"You can? What're you, my Boy Scout representative?"

The kid smiled. "You know, that's not far off, really. I was raised to know what to do in the woods, that's for sure. I can still start a fire in the rain."

"All due respect, but I wouldn't mind seeing your boss. Just to talk to somebody at the top, you know?"

"I've been involved in my father's business since I was very young," the kid said. "It's a tricky line of work, and training starts early. I worked with my father, worked with my uncle. I know I look young, sir, but I assure you I know how to handle a situation like this."

Sam thought he'd probably just heard gospel. Immature and lazy as the kid looked, he talked a mighty fine game, said the right things and said them firmly. And, hell, he was a worker. That mattered. Most kids these days didn't show any ambition at all.

"More I listen to you, and the more I think on it, you're right, it could get pretty bad," Sam said. "Got one dead and one with no more brain activity than a head of lettuce, and you just know there's going to be lawsuits coming out of that. Don't matter that the Mexican hit them, he ain't got no money, so they'll find—"

"The Mexican—" the kid began, and Sam interrupted hastily.

"I don't want you thinking I'm racist or nothing, it's just, my understanding was that he was some kind of Mexican."

"Correct," the kid said with the barest hint of a smile, most of it lost to the shadows his black baseball cap cast over his face. "He was indeed some kind of Mexican, and now he's the dead kind. He was murdered outside of Boston, I'm told."

Sam gaped. *Murdered.* That was not a word Savage Sam wanted to hear in connection to any of the cars he towed, even when they were for the police. Murder cases were unholy messes. His sister-in-law over in York County had to serve on the jury of a murder trial once, and it lasted most of a month. Now, she did say the lunches were pretty decent, and the case was interesting, kind of like TV, but Sam had no desire to get wrapped up with anything that could get him on the witness stand. Once he got to explaining those phones…

"It'll be a damned turkey shoot," he grumbled aloud. "I shouldn't have given the phones to that gal. If she was a cop, maybe. But she promised she'd get them to the police. That ain't gonna sound real good when I say it, though, is it?"

The kid gave him a sympathetic look and didn't answer. Sam lifted the PBR to his lips and then remembered it was already empty.

"What if I could get them back for you?" the kid asked. He'd walked right up to the front porch steps now. Just a child, and yet he talked with such authority that Sam might've believed *he* was a cop. "Once I understand the details of the situation, I can make sure that your property is returned and that the woman who pulled this fast one on you won't bother you anymore. By the end, she'll be more afraid of the police than you will. As she should be."

"Hell, yes, as she should be," Sam said, beginning to think it was a damned good thing that this kid had pulled in when he did. Just ten minutes later, and Sam would've been settled at his booth down at the store, a couple pieces of old pizza on paper plates in front of him.

"Let's have a drink," the kid said, "and you can talk me through it. Unless, of course, you don't drink on the job?"

Sam answered with a snort and crushed the empty PBR can beneath his dusty work boot. "I expect I can get a couple fingers of that sippin' whiskey down just fine."

The kid grinned. "I'm glad to hear it."

Sam turned to the door. The keys were still in the lock. He took them out and then swung the door open and held it so the kid could pass through.

"A few more minutes and I'd have missed you," he said. "Now I've got help *and* whiskey."

"Lucky break."

"So which side of the show are you working for? The girl's family or the dead Mexican fella's? Or the first dead guy's? Shit, almost forgot about him. Lot of death around that wreck."

"There sure was," the kid said. "Say, do you have any glasses?"

Sam got so distracted by searching for clean glasses that he forgot the kid hadn't answered the question about who he was working for. He found glasses and sat down behind the desk. The old chair wheezed beneath him, and dust rose, but the cushions were crushed down to the shape of his frame now, still plenty comfortable. Customized, you might say.

"There you go," he said, sliding the glasses across the desk. The kid poured him a nice healthy shot, three fingers, maybe four. Sam almost told him to stop, but what the hell. He didn't want to come across as a doddering old-timer who couldn't handle his liquor.

The kid sat back and capped the bottle. Sam frowned. "Ain't gonna have any?"

"Drinking on the job is high-risk, according to my father."

"Well, hell, now I feel like you're getting me drunk just to get me talkin'," Sam said, and he was only half joking.

The kid must've seen that because he said, "Tell you what—I'd do a beer if you've got any more of those around."

"Sure." Sam fetched him a tallboy can of PBR, and the kid drank this without hesitation, which put Sam at ease.

The whiskey went down with a smooth burn and a faint tang. Sam pulled the bottle closer and tilted it one way and his head the other so they aligned in a fashion that allowed him to read without his bifocals.

"Gentleman Jack," he said. "Not bad, but what was wrong with just the good old stuff? Why's it always gotta be changing?"

The kid bowed his head and said, "Ah, that's a sentimental thing, really. My father's name was Jack. He was a gentleman too. A charmer, sir. People who made it through a whole day or a whole night with him, they always loved him."

Now, this was something Savage Sam Jones could embrace, a kid who cared about his father. For all the bullshit you heard about these kids and their cell phone addictions and electric cigarettes and liberal notions, it was reassuring to know there were still some good ones.

"That's real nice," Sam said, and that's when it hit him—the kid had said his father's name *was* Jack. "Oh, man. He's gone, isn't he?"

The kid nodded.

"I'm truly sorry to hear it. I lost my old man too young too. What happened to yours?"

The kid lifted his head and stared at Sam with flat eyes. "He burned up in a forest fire in Montana."

"Shit," Sam breathed. "A real damned hero. I'm sorry for your loss, but at least you know he went down doing righteous work. I hope you think about that."

"Oh, I do, sir. I think about that often. Matter of fact…" He rose, uncapped the whiskey, and refilled Sam's glass. "Maybe a toast to him, if you don't mind? Fire season's done here, but out in California and Arizona, they've still got men on the lines."

Sam lifted his glass. "To heroes," he said. "To men like your father."

"To my father," the kid said, and he clinked his PBR can off Sam's glass and drank.

The whiskey tasted fine, but, boy, it snuck up on you too. After just two shots of the stuff—well, two pretty stiff pours—Savage Sam Jones was fighting to keep his vision clear and his words from slurring.

"So what can you tell me about this woman who came to get the phone from you?" the kid said.

Sam told him everything there was to tell. He explained his habit of scouring cars for items of potential value and his immediate quest to notify the owner when such a thing was found. He explained how if nobody claimed their shit within thirty days, then you could hardly be expected to imagine they cared about its fate, and so he'd been known to take it down to his brother's pawnshop a time or two. This kid listened respectfully and didn't give any of the wry smiles like the blond gal.

As his whiskey glass was refilled and went back down, he decided to give this polite kid with the dead-hero father a little more of the truth.

"It was actually in the glove compartment," he said. "But like I said, I always give a careful look. Situation like that, where people get hurt, people *die*? Those sentimental things sometimes really matter to people." He leaned back and waved his glass at the kid. "Hell, you know all about that, with what your dad did. You got anything like that left from him?"

The kid hesitated, and Sam wondered if it was too fresh, if he'd touched a wound that hadn't yet healed. But finally the kid nodded. "More than a few things," he said. "Most of them, I keep here." He touched his temple, then tapped his heart, and Sam nodded sagely.

"Well, sure. Of course. I just mean some people like to have a tangible…"

He stopped talking when the kid brought the gun out.

It was a revolver, a Ruger maybe, with black grips and a blackened muzzle and bore but chrome cylinders for the bullets. It was a beautiful gun, and a mean one. Any fine-looking weapon was a frightening one. People hadn't fallen in love with those friggin' AR-15s because they were ugly guns. They looked the part. Hold one and look in the mirror and you felt the part. Problem was, that got in some people's heads. Some children's heads, for that matter.

"You just carry that with you, do you?" Sam said, and he didn't like how unsteady his voice sounded. He'd been around guns all his life. Why did this one scare him?

"Yeah, I guess." The kid pocketed it again, and while Sam was glad it was out of sight, he was aware of how natural it fit in the kid's hand.

"Where are you from?" Sam asked.

"All over. Moved around a lot, growing up."

"Because of the fires," Sam said, thinking of the kid's dead father. "They don't stay in one place, nice and tidy, do they?"

The kid smiled. "No," he said. "Fires tend to move around." He started to pour again, and Sam waved him off, because at this point if he tried to drive even as far as the corner store for pizza, he'd be taking a hell of a chance. His vision was blurring in a way it usually didn't from whiskey.

"Aw, come on," the kid said. "Just one more, for my dad. His burned bones are on some mountain out there I've never seen. Right now, they're probably already under a blanket of snow. Have a drink for him, would you, sir?"

How could you say no to that? A kid asking you to toast to his dead father's bones, burned black by fire and now buried by snow, and the kid was offering his own whiskey, and you were going to say no? That didn't seem right.

"Pour it," Sam said.

The kid poured it tall again, but what the hell. If Sam needed to doze off here in the chair for an hour or two until he was ready to get behind the wheel, that was fine. He'd done it before. He saw no reason to be troubled by his heavy eyelids.

"The card?" the kid asked loudly.

"Huh?" Sam jerked upright. He realized he'd actually been on the way to sleep, and he'd let his eyes close.

"You said you couldn't remember the woman's name, the one you gave all of the phones to, but that she left a card."

"Oh, shit. Yes. Yes, she did." Sam tried to stand, but he was woozy. Damn, that new Jack Daniel's had a different kind of kick to it. Sneaky as a snake in the grass. He'd stick to the old classic in the future. He fumbled around on the shelf behind the desk and then he turned around, triumphant, the card held high.

"Here ya go." He tossed it on the desk so the kid could read it. No way Sam could pick the words out of that blur, not now.

"'Hank Bauer, Coastal Claims and Investigations,'" the kid read. "Hank was a woman?"

"No, but that's the card she left. She must work for him. She wasn't as young as you, but not very far from it either. Maybe thirty. Tiny little thing, with blond hair. She was decent, I suppose, but she might be a smart-ass. And like you said, she should've left the…the…uh…" Sam couldn't keep his thoughts steady, and he was beginning to sweat. "It should've been the police that came, is what I mean."

"Sure. Well, Mr. Jones, consider your problems solved. I'll take care of this whole matter, and I'll do it discreetly."

Sam tried to nod. Tried to say thank you. Instead he felt his eyes close, and this time he didn't fight them.

"That's some damn strong liquor," he said, and the words were hard to form and seemed to echo in his own ears.

"It's a proprietary blend," the kid said. "I add a little custom touch to it."

Wish you'd mentioned that earlier, Savage Sam Jones thought but didn't say, couldn't say. His eyes were still closed, and he felt his head lolling forward on a suddenly slackening neck.

I need some water, he thought. *I need some help.*

When Savage Sam Jones slumped forward in his chair, Dax Blackwell didn't move. He waited a few minutes, calm and patient, before pulling on thin gloves and checking for a pulse.

Nothing. The old man's flesh was already cooling. His heart had stopped.

Long after he was certain of this, Dax Blackwell kept his hand on the man's wrist and his gaze on the man's closed eyes. He studied the tableau of death where life had flourished just minutes ago, until Dax's arrival on the doorstep of this man now turned corpse.

Finally, reluctantly, he released him.

There was business to do, and time was wasting.

He kept the gloves on while he wiped down the whiskey glass and the PBR can and the desk. Sam's old chair swiveled under his weight, turning the dead man away from the door. Dax carefully turned the chair back so that his face would greet the next visitor.

When he left, he took the bottle.

18

The neurologist's last name is Pine, and if he has a first name, he doesn't offer it to Tara. He is Dr. Pine, period. He has a pleasant smile and smart, penetrating eyes and the kind of self-assured bearing that gives you confidence.

It gives Tara confidence, at least, until he asks her to blink.

"Twice for no, once for yes," he says in his deep, warm voice. They are alone in the room; Shannon objected to that, but Dr. Pine insisted, and Dr. Pine won.

He is the first medical staffer to introduce himself to Tara and explain who he is. *Hello, Tara, I'm Dr. Pine, your neurologist. We're going to need to work together to get your show back on the road, okay? This will be a team effort. But I promise you I'm going to do my part.*

All of this is so nice to hear. So encouraging. But then...

"Blink for me," he says again. "Please, Tara."

And she wants to. She has never wanted anything more in her life than to blink for this man.

She can't do it, though. She tries so hard that tears form in her eyes, but tears are always forming in her eyes, and she doubts this means anything to him. It's not crying so much as leaking, and nobody seems to notice it except Shannon and the black nurse whose name Tara still doesn't know. Sometimes they will dab her tears off her cheeks.

My sister used to call me Twitch, she thinks. *I was that jumpy. If you showed me a scary movie or slammed a door when the house was dark, I'd jerk like I'd been electrocuted. Now I can't even blink.*

Dr. Pine stares at her, says, "If you're comfortable, give me one blink. If you're not comfortable, give me two," and Tara begins to feel exhausted from the strain of effort, an exhaustion that's only heightened by the outrage that there's no evidence of her effort, no sign that she's fighting her ass off in here. She doubles down on the effort of the blink, every ounce of her energy going toward her eyelids. *Come on, come on...*

And that's when her thumb twitches.

She feels a wave of elation; Dr. Pine shows nothing. He didn't see her thumb. He's watching her eyes, and so he missed the motion in her hand.

"That's okay, Tara," he says, and he pats her arm and stands up and turns his attention to his notepad.

But my thumb moved! It moved, how could you miss that, I need you to see that I can move!

Twitchy Tara the scaredy-cat girl is back and better than ever. Twitch is no longer a shame name; it's a lifeline.

Pine looks up, smiles at her, and then says, "Let's bring your family back in, shall we?"

Damn it, Doc, where were your eyes when I needed them!

But he's gone, and her thumb is still again. The lifeline lifeless. He opens the door and they all file in, Shannon in front, then Mom, then Rick with his hand on Mom's arm. Always the reassuring touch.

"Remember," he tells Mom, "the truth is always progress."

He keeps talking, his voice rising and falling with the softly melodic tone that Shannon always claims is attempted hypnosis. When she and Tara were kids, that was one of the inside jokes about Rick that kept them laughing and made his endless optimism and stream of life-lesson-inspiration bullshit tolerable. That and the way he kept Mom away from the pills. She'd been in her fourth stint at rehab when she met Rick, and nobody expected this one to work any better than the first three had. It would buy a few weeks maybe, but then Tara would come home and find her mother hadn't gotten out of bed, or Shannon would open a DVD case and Vicodin tablets would pour out.

Rick, with his relentless *What is your intention for this day?* mantras, his vegan diet, and his awful taste in music—lyrics were an unfortunate interruption of melody, he always said—connected with Martha Beckley in a way no one else had been able to, and that was enough to make him tolerable to her daughters. Because while Mom's obvious vulnerability was to medications, not men, there were always plenty of the latter. The construction accident that had claimed her husband's life, taking from Tara a father that she scarcely remembers, left Martha Beckley both a psychological wreck and a wealthy woman.

Rick has been a good influence for Mom, an absolute relief in some ways, but Tara has never completely trusted him, and she certainly doesn't like the sound of the statement *The truth is always progress.* He's preparing her mother to hear a truth that will be hard to take, and he wants her to believe that it's progress.

"Why don't we let the doctor tell us what progress is," Shannon snaps.

Get him, Shannon, Tara thinks.

Sometimes Mom will joke about her "guard daughters." Mom thinks of it as a joke, at least, but Shannon and Tara take it literally. When Dad died, their lives became a revolving door of people offering help and people seeking to take advantage. Shannon, the older and the alpha, led most of the battles. Now, voiceless, motionless, helpless, Tara can only hope that her sister redirects that same fury to fight on her behalf. *You are a redheaded Dober-man,* she'd told Shannon once. It was a joke then. Now, though, she needs the guard dog.

Do not listen, Shannon. Do not let anyone convince you that I'm just a body, mindless and soulless in here. Please, oh, please do not let them convince you of that.

Dr. Pine studies the three of them and then says, "I really wish she could blink."

Tara's heart drops. Why did he have to start there? Why did he have to start with what she can't do and not with what she might be able to do—listen, watch, think! And twitch her damn thumb every now and then.

"Based on my reading, that can often take time," Shannon says. "We're not even a week into this."

"Correct. I didn't say it was cause to lose hope; I simply said that I wish she demonstrated a blink response. She's so far ahead in so many ways, you know. Breathing without assistance is, on its own, unusual in these circumstances, and encouraging. The question of awareness, however, would be helped by a blink response." Dr. Pine shrugs. "But it hardly means the battle is lost. Tara's brain was banged around the inside of her skull, quite literally pulled from its moorings. That caused bruising and swelling; blood vessels were torn and axons stretched. Critical communication regions were damaged. As you know, this is what the induced coma was designed to mitigate—it decreases the amount of work the brain has to do, which keeps the swelling down, and we have a better chance at restoring these processing areas."

"But it didn't work," Rick says, and Tara wishes that it was her middle finger that could twitch instead of her thumb.

"We don't know if it worked *yet*," Shannon corrects, and Dr. Pine nods.

"Yes and yes. This is, of course, going to be a possibly long and certainly painful process. Each coma patient is different. Some make remarkable recoveries and fairly swiftly. Others make less complete recoveries and over much longer periods." Pause. "Others do not recover at all."

Shannon looks at Tara, and Tara does her damnedest to call up a sister-to-sister radio signal. She is certain that such a thing exists. There are some people who hear you without words. Shannon has always heard her, and Tara needs her now. Oh, how she needs her now.

"There's a coma researcher at the university hospital eleven miles from here," Shannon says. "A doctor named—"

"Michelle Carlisle," Dr. Pine finishes. "Yes. I know her well. An excellent research doctor."

It feels like there's something slightly diminishing in the way he says *research doctor,* as if he's indicating the difference between practice and theory with a mild shift in tone.

"I'd like to take Tara to see her," Shannon says.

Rick says, "I think we need to let Dr. Pine make those decisions, Shannon."

Shannon doesn't so much as glance at him. "Of course I want to consult with Dr. Pine while *we* make these decisions."

Dr. Pine adjusts his glasses and then closes his notebook. The gestures seem designed to delay the inevitable—he's going to say there's no point.

"I'm a fan of Dr. Carlisle's work," he says at last.

"It's another opinion," Mom says, "and that's good, but we haven't heard *yours* yet."

Her voice trembles, but Tara is almost painfully proud of her for speaking up.

"Every case is different," Dr. Pine says again, a hedge that no one, even Tara, wants to hear.

"Scale of one to ten," Rick says.

"Pardon?"

"On a scale of one to ten, how…how close to dead is she?"

"Rick, you *asshole,*" Shannon says, whirling on him. "What kind of question is that?"

"A fair one," he replies, standing firm. "Dr. Pine has treated hundreds of patients in similar conditions. He has an opinion, and I'd like to hear it. We all *need* to hear it."

No, we do not, Tara thinks.

Dr. Pine looks at each of them individually. Tara is last. His eyes are on hers when he says, "On a scale of one to ten, if one is the most alive, then physically she's probably a two or three. She needs assistance, of course, but her body is healthy and it will continue to survive, though obviously not to thrive, for the foreseeable future."

"And what about the soul?" Rick says, and Shannon rolls her eyes on cue.

"I think he means her mind, Doctor. Is she with us?"

More than any of you want to know, Tara thinks, because they've all had moments in front of her that she is sure they wouldn't have wanted her to witness. Moments when their love was buried beneath fatigue and frustration. She doesn't blame them for this, but it doesn't make those moments any less hurtful.

"I'd encourage more tests."

"But right now? What would you say based on the tests you've already done?" Rick presses.

"Eight," Dr. Pine answers without hesitation. "Based on what we've already done."

Eight. On a scale of one to ten, he is rating Tara's brain as far closer to dead than alive.

"Then we'll do more," Shannon says, but there's a hitch in her voice.

Everyone's faith is beginning to waver.

Not fair, Tara thinks. *I was just giving a ride to a stranger. Why isn't he trapped like this instead of me?*

But Oltamu is worse off than her, of course. Oltamu is dead; she's heard them say this.

Maybe the wolf got him.

If she could shake her head, she'd do it just to get rid of that strange recurring image of the wolf with raised hackles and narrowed eyes and pinned-back ears and exposed fangs. That wasn't real, and Tara can't afford to have any distractions in a brain that's already failing to do its job. She's got tests to take, and if she can't pass them, she's going to end up just like Oltamu.

Don't think that way. Once you start that, you're done.

A voice whispers that she is already done, that it is time to give up, give in, quit. She fights it off.

Oltamu is dead; Tara Beckley is not. Tara Beckley is alive and not only that, her thumb has twitched.

She thinks again of the cellar in 1804 London Street, where she once stood in the blackness, gasping, cobwebs on her face, tears in her eyes. She remembers that in that moment of panic, she turned her head to face that darkness directly, and she found the faintest glimmer of light. It was a long way off, and she wasn't sure that she could make it there or if freedom existed beyond it, but she had seen it, and she had tried.

There's a glimmer of light inside this vacant house too. Among all the dark hallways and unknown corridors and treacherous stairs, there are cracks and gaps. The doors might be locked, the windows sealed and shuttered, but there are always gaps.

Find one and force it open. Then someone will notice. Someone will hear.

Tara retreats into the blackness, imagining the corridor between her brain and her thumb, and she gets to work.

Part Three

ON THE BACK ROADS

19

Hank Bauer lived in what had once been a hunting camp. He'd purchased the cabin intending to keep the property's purpose intact, but then his wife learned of his affair with a waitress at Applebee's, and the hunting camp rapidly became his home. He often told this story as a cautionary tale of the risks of marriage—but never of the risks of having an affair with a waitress, Applebee's or otherwise.

Those hunting-camp days seemed long ago and far away. He felt some shame over the way his marriage had ended but no real regret for how his life had gone. He was good on his own, always had been, and the marriage and the mortgages had been the real mistakes, the steps out of character. That had been trying on a suit he knew he'd never care for even though it sure looked nice and comfortable on other men. Margaret had called him an arrested adolescent during the divorce, and he didn't disagree. His life had been mostly games and gambling, drinking and storytelling, hard rock and hangovers. It wasn't an adulthood anybody should really take pride in, but he'd learned to lose his shame over it all the same. At sixty-one, he was too old to be embarrassed. He'd had fun.

And he'd done well too. Not well enough for the mortgage in Cape Elizabeth that had scared him right into the welcoming arms of Applebee's, but well enough that it had been a long time since he'd worried about money. He'd found himself in the insurance business by accident—didn't everyone get there that way?—but the money was steady, you got to meet plenty of people, and sometimes you actually had the sense that you'd helped to ease a person's mind.

On the day that he returned to his home on twenty-seven acres of woodland and trout-brook frontage and found the kid in the black baseball cap waiting on him, Hank was largely content with his life. The only thing nagging at him that afternoon was Abby Kaplan.

He'd met Abby when she was just thirteen. Her mother had bolted after determining that raising a child was less enjoyable than being one, and so it had been just Abby and her father, who was a good man with a bad booze habit. He was also the most talented natural mechanic Hank had ever seen, probably capable of building a functioning engine out of duct tape and toothpicks if you spotted him the gasoline. Hank's first encounter with Jake Kaplan's daughter didn't have the makings of a lifelong friendship: she had stolen his car.

Hank had a ridiculous, souped-up '85 Trans Am back then, and he'd trusted Jake Kaplan to retool it. Then one day the police called to tell him they'd recovered his stolen car and had the thirteen-year-old thief in custody. The cops said she'd been doing ninety-four when they clocked her, and Hank's first question was "How was she handling it?"

He'd told the cops not to press charges, which hadn't pleased them, as they believed he was aiding and abetting the development of a local delinquent. And maybe he had been. But Abby was honest and apologetic when they spoke, ready for consequences, and Hank was struck by both the sadness of her demeanor—a good kid expecting bad things, as if that were preordained for her—and her infatuation with his old muscle car.

Jake Kaplan, a good ol' boy's good ol' boy with a worldview shaped by drunks and dropouts, didn't often mention Abby's missing mother, but that day he did.

"Abby wants to race," Jake told Hank mournfully.

"So let her race. Don't need to have a driver's license on the oval. Ed Traylor's boy was racing when he was no older than Abby."

"I can't let her do that. I'm supposed to raise a daughter to be a woman."

"Ever heard of Sarah Fisher?" Hank asked.

And so it came to pass that Hank Bauer sponsored Abby Kaplan's first foray into racing. It was curiosity and amusement at first, and it made for a damn good story; the boys at the poker games *loved* hearing about how Hank had become the sponsor for his own car thief.

Nobody chuckled after the first races, though. Hank watched her beat older men night after night, and then she went on to the bigger speedways, and when she lost, it was not to better drivers but to better cars. Hank saw that this game, like all of them, had a ceiling that could be cracked only with cash.

Coastal Claims and Investigations became a more serious sponsor then. It wasn't just because Hank liked the girl and felt bad for her; it was also because he was damn curious to see what she could do with the right machine.

What she did was win. Early, often, and then always. She smoked the drag-racing circuit through northern New England and then got onto the oval and kicked even more ass, and everybody's bet was on NASCAR or Indy when she'd fooled them all and gone into stunt driving instead. Hank had seen some version of that coming when Abby fell in love with the drift. Even winning a race didn't put the same light in her eyes that a controlled drift did—a floating test of traction and throttle that looked wildly out of control to the average spectator. If you could control it, though…well, Hank supposed it was a special kind of high.

She'd gone to a couple stunt schools, caught the right people's eyes, and ended up in Hollywood and then Europe. For a while she'd been shooting commercials in friggin' Dubai or someplace, bouncing some bastardized supercar turned SUV around a desert. She'd been all over the world driving the finest cars known to man and making good money doing it, and Hank was awfully proud of her.

And now awfully worried about what was keeping her in Maine.

The crack-up she'd had out on the West Coast would have been bad enough if the boyfriend with her had been anonymous. But he was a rising star, his face was on magazine covers, and that crush of attention had made a bad deal worse for Abby. She'd come back to Maine to clear her head, she claimed, but Hank knew better.

Abby was hiding.

Hank had practically begged his way into the Hammel College job when he learned about the girl in the coma. He thought this might be useful for Abby, if for no other reason than it would get her to open up a little, tell him what exactly was wrong so he could go about helping her. That hadn't worked out, though, and so on the day when Hank arrived at his home to find an unfamiliar white Jeep in his driveway, he was thinking that he needed to get out of this case before it became a real mess.

The white Jeep pushed those thoughts from his mind. Hank didn't have many visitors.

The rain splattered over the windshield made it look empty, but then the door opened and a kid in a black baseball cap stepped out and waited with a weird half smile. Hank got out of the car into the misting rain.

"Can I help you, fella?"

"Mr. Bauer?"

"That's right."

"My name's Matt Norris."

"Okay." Hank waited, but the kid was quiet, hands still in his pockets, odd smile still on his face.

"So you dropped by just to practice introducing yourself?" Hank said. "You did real well on the part with your name. The rest needs work."

Norris laughed softly. "No. Sorry, my mind wandered. I'm not real sure I should've come by at all." He took one hand from his pockets and adjusted the black baseball cap. "I couldn't get the cops to listen to me, though."

Hank straightened. "Cops?"

Matt Norris nodded without changing expression, as if it were perfectly normal to be standing in the rain on a stranger's property talking about the cops.

"I go to Hammel College."

Aw, shit. "Yeah? That's terrific. But Matt, buddy, I don't step in front of police, okay?"

"You're a private investigator."

"No. I'm in the insurance business."

"You have a private investigator's license."

Hank sighed and rubbed his face with a damp palm. "That's marketing crap. I'm no detective, I don't want to play one on TV or in my yard in the rain. You got something to say on that wreck, it should be to the cops, not me."

"Carlos Ramirez wasn't driving the car," the kid said. "How 'bout *that?*"

I almost went bowling, Hank thought. *It was a coin-toss decision back there at the office—head to the alley or head home. Why in the hell didn't I go to the bowling alley?*

Something told him the kid would've waited, though.

"Come on in out of the rain," Hank said with a sigh. "You're going to cause me enough trouble without giving me pneumonia too."

The kid laughed too loudly. As Hank unlocked his door and held it open for Matt Norris to pass through, he was frowning. It hadn't been that funny of a line, but from that laugh, you'd have thought the kid was at a comedy club.

Something's off with him, Hank thought, and then he closed the door to shut out the rain and the darkening sky.

20

Abby was in the shower when her phone began to ring. She let it go, but then it rang again and again, and so she shut off the water, knotted a towel above her breasts, and went out to the living room, leaving wet footprints behind.

It was Hank.

"Can't leave a message?" Abby said, the phone held against her damp cheek. "I was in the shower."

"Sorry, kid." Hank's voice was strained, as if he were calling in the middle of a workout. "Think you can stop by here?"

Abby cocked her head, shedding a spray of water from her hair to the floor. "Now? What's up?"

"I, uh... I guess that Ramirez story might have some issues. You were right, I think. Anyhow, uh, Meredith is coming by with some cop from Brighton, and they want the phones."

"They're coming by your house?"

"Yeah." There was a rustling sound, and Hank gave a quick, harsh intake of breath before he said, "And he's going to want the phones."

"Sure thing," Abby said. "Give me twenty minutes, maybe half an hour."

"Yeah. Faster the better. Thanks, Abs." Hank hung up.

Abby lowered the phone, frowning. Hank had sounded tense, worried. Cops coming to your house could do that, though, especially when one of them was from out of state and working on a murder case.

She thought about that as she toweled off and dressed in jeans, a light base layer, and a fleece. She had the window cracked to let the steam bleed out of the bathroom, and she could hear the laughter of patrons at Run of the Mill, a brewery that shared a portion of her apartment building, all of it the reimagined and re-purposed site of what had once been the Pepperell Mill, a textile mill that had at one time employed what seemed like half of Bid-deford. Now it was a mixture of condos and businesses, and the roof was lined with solar panels—but the Saco River remained, and Abby enjoyed listening to the water as the town found new ways to thrive around it. The river was the constant, and the river ran steady. She appreciated that.

As she tugged a brush through towel-dried hair, she thought of the police waiting at Hank's, and when she picked up the decaying shoe box of phones and chargers, some of the cardboard flaked off in her hands. She didn't relish the idea of explaining to police from Boston that she'd transported evidence in a homicide investigation back and forth through the rain in a shoe box. She found some plastic bags and separated the phones and chargers. Savage Sam had been nearly positive that what he'd taken out of the car was an iPhone, so she separated those too, then put the iPhone chargers in with the iPhones, figuring anything that made it look more official couldn't hurt. For all of Hank's jokes about his PI license, it carried legal liability, and Abby didn't want to put him at risk.

Should've just called Meredith to begin with, she thought. But it had been Hank's idea for her to take the phones to Shannon Beckley, and back then there'd been no questions of guilt and no bullets in Carlos Ramirez's brain. Or at least nobody had known about them.

Abby found a Sharpie and wrote the date and her name and *Beckley case* on the three plastic bags. Hardly a proper evidence folder, but better than a soggy shoe box.

She left her apartment and drove away from the mill toward Hank's house, the bagged phones and chargers on the passenger seat. Usually she avoided the short stretch of turnpike that was the fastest route, but Hank had asked her to hurry, so tonight she took it. Driving was easier for her at night, regardless of traffic. She didn't feel as crowded in the dark or as exposed. There was no horizon line, and your visual range in the mirrors was limited. The blackness obscured both where you'd been and where you were going. Somehow, that containment helped dull the anxiety brought on by visible obstacles ahead, and it eased the dread of traffic rising up behind.

It was only seven miles on the turnpike before she exited onto the county roads, and she made it without incident, no dry mouth or racing pulse. Traffic was light, but it probably helped that she was distracted too. She didn't like the idea of sitting down with police on this. David Meredith was fine; Abby knew him a bit, and Hank knew him well. But homicide detectives from Boston? That was different. That brought back memories too. The detectives in California hadn't been homicide cops, but they'd felt close enough.

Clean blood isn't everything, Ms. Kaplan. We're looking at that curve and that guardrail and trying to figure out how exactly you got airborne. And you're a pretty good driver, we understand. Professional.

She turned off the county road and onto the teeth-rattling gravel that wound through the pines and bone-colored birches that surrounded Hank's place. It was beautiful country, but isolated. The deep woods were never far from you in Maine. Abby was a native Mainer, but she wasn't completely comfortable here at night. Her childhood home had had sidewalks and streetlights; this place, deserted except for snowmobile trails and tree stands, had always seemed foreign to her.

As she drove slowly through the ruts, a few untrimmed branches swiped her Chrysler, and even the high beams didn't seem to cut the darkness. There was a single light on in Hank's house, a glow from the kitchen. That was unusual, because Hank spent only as much time in the kitchen as it took him to microwave his dinner. He also didn't use the blinds, but tonight they were closed.

In the narrow driveway, Hank's Tahoe was parked behind a white Jeep. There was no room to pull up alongside or even turn around without driving onto the lawn. Abby parked behind the Tahoe, and she was about to kill the engine and get out when she felt the familiar warm buzz in her veins that had been her early-warning system for so many years, that rapid pulse of adrenaline-laced instinct that was triggered when you were doing a hundred and fifty miles per hour and saw the cars in front of you shift and knew that something was about to go wrong. That silent alarm had been Abby's gift on the track. She'd been able to tell when things were going bad just a fraction of a second ahead of most.

They're positioned wrong, she thought now.

Hank had said the police *were* coming, not that the police were already there. But the Jeep was sitting in front of the Tahoe. Unless Hank had come and gone in the twenty minutes since he'd called Abby, whoever was driving the Jeep had been here first.

She sat with the engine growling and the headlights on and stared at the cars and the house, and her hand drifted back to the gearshift. She almost put it in reverse. But what was she going to do, back out of here and call Hank from the road and say she was scared of the Jeep? Come on. She'd spent too much time thinking paranoid thoughts on the train after seeing Tara Beckley and hearing about Carlos Ramirez. Her mind was built for that now; the docs had told her this. Panic floated; panic drifted like dark smoke and found new places in the brain to call home.

Screw that. Be tough, Abby. Be who you always were.

She released the gearshift and killed the engine. While the headlights dimmed, she grabbed the three plastic bags of cell phones and chargers, and was reaching for the door when the strange fear rose again, and she found herself shoving the bag with the iPhones under the driver's seat.

I'll say I dropped it. When I know that things are legit, I'll come back and get it.

No clean logic to the choice, just a response to that old pulse in the blood, to that fresh dark smoke drifting through her brain. *People have died and someone wants those phones. You don't just carry them through the door.*

She got out of the car with the two bags in hand, the Chrysler parked behind the two SUVs, forming a mini-caravan in the narrow driveway. She looked at the Jeep's plate—Massachusetts. Good. That was as promised. But where was David Meredith?

The rain had stopped but puddles littered the dirt driveway like land mines. Abby dodged them, crossed the yard, went up the front steps, and rapped her knuckles on the wall as she pulled open the screen door. Hank's muted voice floated out from inside.

"Yeah, Abs. Come in."

She pushed open the front door, stepped inside, looked toward the light, and saw Hank tied to a kitchen chair.

It was an old wooden straight-backed chair, and he was bound to it with thin green cord. His right arm was wrapped tight against his side, but his left arm was free, and he lifted it with his palm out, signaling for Abby to stop.

The gesture wasn't required. Abby stood frozen in midstride, staring at the scene in front of her as the screen door slapped shut behind her with a bang.

"Close the other one too," a soft voice from behind her said, and as Abby whirled toward the voice there was the distinctive metallic snap of a cocking revolver.

21

For a moment it was still and silent. The only light was coming from a battery lantern that threw an eerie, too-white glow over the kitchen and couldn't penetrate the shadows in the rest of the house. Whoever was speaking was standing in the hallway, no more than a silhouette against the darkness.

A silhouette and a gun.

"Abby?" the figure in the hall said. "Close the door."

Abby reached out and took the cold metal knob in her left hand and closed the door.

"Good," the man in the hall said. "Now lock it."

Abby moved faster to obey this instruction, turning the dead bolt and dropping her hand quickly to distract from the quarter turn she'd given the lock, enough to move the bolt but not enough to shoot it home. If she made it back to the door, it would open when she twisted the doorknob.

"Go into the kitchen," the man in the darkness said, and Abby obeyed again, shuffling backward, moving off the wooden floor and onto the tile of the kitchen. She glanced at the kitchen counter, expecting to see the block of knives that always sat beneath a years-old calendar that showed Abby being showered with cheap champagne by her father and Hank and Hank's then-girlfriend after Abby had become the youngest driver—and the first woman—to win at the Bald Mountain Speedway.

The calendar was there. The block of knives was gone.

"Stop," the man said, and Abby stopped and then the man walked out of the shadows and into the light and Abby saw him clearly.

He was a child, almost. Eighteen or nineteen, maybe twenty—but probably not. His boyish face was shaded by a black baseball cap with chrome-colored stitching that matched the cylinders on his black revolver, as if he'd coordinated the outfit. The gun was offset by that almost friendly face. He wore the sort of perpetual but false half smile of someone whose job required him to feign interest in the troubles of strangers, like a hotel concierge.

"Hello, Abby," he said.

"Who are you?"

"You think I'm going to give my name in this situation? Come on. Be better than that."

Abby looked at Hank. He seemed unharmed—no blood, no bruises—but absolutely terrified. He searched Abby's eyes but didn't speak and Abby saw something beyond fear in his face—apology.

"Put the bags on the counter," the kid said.

Abby did.

"You have a weapon?" the kid asked.

"No."

"You don't mind if I verify that?"

"No."

"Very gracious, thanks." The kid pressed the muzzle of the revolver to Abby's head as he patted her down with his free hand. He was wearing thin black gloves, and his touch made her skin crawl and her stomach knot, but she tried not to give him the satisfaction of a visible reaction. He took her phone and felt over her car keys but left them in her pocket.

The gun moved away from Abby's skull and then the kid stepped back, looked down at her phone, and tapped the screen. The display filled with the image on the lock screen: Luke sitting on a rock overlooking the Pacific, a smile on his face, his tousled hair blown wild by the wind.

"He was handsome, wasn't he?" the kid said, and then he tossed the phone onto the counter. "A shame what happened to him. I know the expression is 'Live fast, die young, and leave a good-looking corpse,' but he didn't really earn that live-fast idea. I mean, at least James Dean was driving, right?"

Abby's slap came without premeditation. She simply swung.

The kid sidestepped it with ease—damn, he was fast—and laughed.

"I seem to have touched a nerve," he said. "Apologies." He nodded at a chair that was pulled back from the table. "Take a seat."

"What do you want?" Abby asked.

"More original material, for one. You're asking such obvious questions: *Who are you? What do you want?* It gets tedious to be the guy with the gun. Redundant."

The kid looked so unthreatening despite the gun that Abby found herself measuring the distance between them and wondering if she should attack. She just needed to sweep that gun hand away. As long as the bullet went wide when he pulled the trigger, Abby didn't think it would be hard to take the gun from him. He was looking at her and seeing a small woman who couldn't throw a punch. She'd blackened the eyes and bloodied the noses of a few guys who'd thought that same thing.

If he tries to tie you, then do it, she told herself. *Punch, kick, bite—do anything and everything if he tries to tie you up. But not until then. As long as you can move, then just talk through whatever this is.*

"I asked you to sit," the kid said.

Abby sat. The battery lantern was on the table next to two tumbler glasses filled with whiskey, a bottle standing between them. Gentleman Jack.

She was now facing Hank, and her back was to the door. Hank's jowly face was drained of color, and he was breathing in short, audible pants. His eyes flicked away from Abby's, down and to the left, as if he were trying to see behind himself. Abby followed the look and saw that Hank's portable generator was on the floor behind his chair.

What in the hell is that doing in here? It was a gasoline-fueled backup generator, capable of producing enough electricity to run the lights, TV, and a space heater or two for a few days. The rural road wasn't a high priority for the Central Maine Power repair crews. Abby had never seen the generator inside the house, though.

Battery lantern on, generator inside? The power's out, and the kid doesn't know enough to leave the generator outdoors. But if he wants it, then he thinks we're going to be here for a while. He's not just going to take the phones and go. We're waiting on someone else.

"Get comfortable," the kid said, as if confirming Abby's thoughts. "Let's have a drink."

Abby looked at the full whiskey glass, then back at Hank's face, and shook her head. "What's in it?" she asked.

"Nothing," the kid said. "That's a fine-quality whiskey. Not cool enough for the hipsters, you know, it's not small-batch stuff, but it's awfully smooth. And the name is nice. The name is...meaningful to me."

He gave Abby a smile that looked positively warm and kind.

"Gentleman Jack," he said, and his voice went a little wistful at the end, as if they were all sharing in this strange reverie. "And double-mellowed, it says. That's a funny joke if you knew my family. But you don't, unfortunately. Nevertheless, please have a drink, Abby."

She shook her head again. The kid sighed and leveled the pistol so the muzzle was just inches away from Hank's knee.

"We can drink," the kid said, "or we can bleed."

Abby took the glass. The kid nodded in approval and then spoke to Hank without turning to him. "You too, old-timer. We're all celebrating."

Hank took the glass. His hand was shaking, and some of the

whiskey spilled over the top and dripped down the backs of his hairy fingers in golden beads. Abby saw for the first time that one of the cords binding him to the chair was actually an extension cord, and it had been cut and stripped so the bare wires glistened.

What in the hell had happened in here? What had Hank endured before making his call?

"Drink up," the kid said, and both Abby and Hank took a swallow. The whiskey had a mellow burn, but nothing about it tasted unfamiliar or tainted. Abby drank a finger of whiskey and set the glass down. Hank got less of it in, his hand still shaking; some of the whiskey dribbled from the corner of his lip and down his chin.

"Good stuff, isn't it?" the kid said. He was hardly more than a child. But Eric Harris and Dylan Klebold had been children too.

"Take the phones," Abby said. "Take them and go. We don't know what it's about. We can't begin to send anyone after you. We don't know enough to do that."

"Who else knows about the phones?"

"Nobody."

"No? Then who bagged them? They were in a shoe box before." He smiled at Abby's reaction. "Don't like that I know that, do you?"

She shrugged. "Don't care. *I* bagged them. I labeled them too."

"If I need an assistant, I'll keep you in mind. Now, again, who else has seen them?"

Abby almost answered honestly. She was afraid, both for herself and for Hank, and she had no stake in whatever insanity was transpiring around that car wreck and the lies Carlos Ramirez had told before he was murdered. *So tell the truth,* her brain commanded. But instead she said, "Nobody else has seen them."

"And how many people know you have them?"

"One. The guy I took them from."

The kid studied her intently. "You understand how imperative it is for us to be honest with each other? How badly this night might go if you make one poor decision?"

"Yes."

"Then let's try that question again. You seem to struggle with even basic addition. I didn't realize your academic record was as poor as your driving record." Whatever he saw in Abby's face then made him smile. "Yes, I've acquainted myself with your history. Mr. Bauer here has been helpful in that regard."

Abby looked at Hank, who gazed back with apology, his face sickly white.

"One more time," the kid said. "How many people know you have them?"

Again, Abby thought about telling the truth. Again, she decided against it. "Well, it would be two people, I guess," she said. She nodded at Hank. "He makes two."

"Will two become four if you think on it a little longer?"

"No. That's all."

"You sound convincing. And yet my friend Hank here said you took them to Boston. Which means you're lying to me now."

Hank's exhale whistled between his teeth. "I didn't say—"

The kid moved the gun to Hank's temple without turning his head or body, the gun landing on its target point with the accuracy and fluid speed that came only with practice or natural talent. Or—far worse for Abby—both.

"Hank?" the kid said. "I've still got the floor."

Hank was quiet. Abby tried to remember what exactly they'd said in the phone conversation they'd had when she was on the train. Did she tell him that Shannon Beckley had seen the phones? Did she say that she'd called Meredith? For that matter, *had* she called Meredith? No, Hank had called him. Right? Why couldn't she remember something so simple? She was having more trouble thinking than she should have. Her mind felt foggy and slow.

She looked at the whiskey bottle. The kid followed her eyes.

"Let's finish those drinks, shall we?" he said.

"No," Abby said.

The kid lowered the muzzle of the revolver so it nestled in Hank's eye socket.

"All right," Hank said, and he reached for the glass. His one visible eye was wide and white with panic. "Come on, Abs," he said. "Please. Just do as he says."

"Those are the words of a man who wants to see the morning," the kid said, and he smiled as Hank gulped the whiskey, sloshing more of it down his chin. "But this can't be a one-man party. Abby? It will be that glass or this gun. You pick."

Abby took the glass and drank more of the whiskey. It put a high and tight feeling in the back of her skull. It would not have been an unpleasant sensation in other circumstances. But now it was terrifying.

It's going to slow you down. Even if he didn't put anything else in it, the booze alone will slow you down if you don't do something in a hurry.

There *was* something else in it, though. She could feel that already. This was the steroid-injected version of the fear that haunted any woman who was handed a drink made by a stranger—the taste was just right, nothing there to warn you of what was on the way, of oncoming blackness and horrors that you might not remember even if you lived to see morning.

"Nothing like a little whiskey on a cool dark night," the kid said. "Tell you what, though. Let's do something about that chill in the air."

Still keeping the gun in his right hand, he reached into his back pocket with his left and pulled out a length of coiled parachute cord. The same kind that bound Hank to his chair. Abby tensed, but the kid just smiled and tossed the cord onto the counter.

"We won't need that, right? You're not running?"

"No."

"Good. It's getting cold in here. I'm going to run the space heater if you don't mind." He walked behind Hank, knelt by the generator, and flicked the battery on. Red lights glowed. He switched the revolver from his right hand to his left and jerked the starter cord. The motor growled but choked out. The cord demanded more of his attention than he wanted to give, and when his eyes darted away, Abby slipped her right hand into the pocket of her fleece and closed it around the key fob to the Chrysler. Its surface was smooth, but she was familiar with the four buttons on its face and knew which one operated the remote start. All she had to do was press it twice. The car was parked facing the house, and it would throw its lights toward the door, but, more important, the engine would turn over. She thought that would make the kid look in that direction. It would probably be a very fast look, but it would happen.

That would likely be the last chance Abby would have to move.

The generator caught on the second pull and clattered to life, belching out a cloud of exhaust. The kid plugged in a space heater, and the ceramic coils inside glowed red.

"Damn power outages," he said. "They're a bitch out here in the woods."

He straightened, reached in his back pocket, withdrew a plastic mask, and pulled it over his face. It looked like the masks the fire crews wore at the speedway when they knew the fumes and smoke might threaten their lungs.

Abby understood things then. The kid intended to get plenty of booze in their bloodstream and let exhaust fumes fill the room; when it was over, he'd untie them. They'd look like a couple of clueless dead drunks.

"It's not worth this," Abby said. "Whatever you think we understand...we don't."

"I agree," the kid said, voice muffled by the mask. "Want to stop me? Tell me the truth about who has seen those phones."

Abby said, "This was why he didn't roll the van."

"Pardon?"

"I wasn't wrong. Ramirez was attempting to hit them the whole time."

"Remarkable detective work," the kid said. "Keep this one around, Hank. She's brilliant. She walks into your house, sees you tied up by a man with a gun, and suddenly realizes that there's trouble afoot."

He took a step closer to Abby and lowered himself so he was eye level with her. "Tell me who knows about the phones."

"I already did."

The kid shrugged and adjusted the generator's choke until the engine was fighting between firing and flooding. The exhaust smoked blue in the white light of the lantern.

Her thumb tightened on the key fob, but she didn't press it yet. If the kid intended to use the gun, he wouldn't have gone through the effort of hauling the generator in here. The carbon monoxide from the generator wouldn't knock them out for a while yet, even in a small space. Abby had time. Not much; it was going to be an awfully small window of opportunity and she'd have to move awfully fast, but she still had time.

"This is a stupid idea," she said. "It won't fool anyone. You want police to believe we just got drunk and passed out with the generator running? You'll get caught. You'll go to jail."

The mask muffled his laugh. "You'd be surprised how many friends I've got around jails," he said. "Some in cells, some in uniforms."

Who the hell is this kid? "They'll be able to tell that Hank had been tied up," Abby said. "It'll be obvious." Her words came slowly and thickly, but the kid seemed to give them careful consideration. Then he spoke in a gentle voice, as if breaking news that it pained him to share.

"I don't think you two are important enough to warrant intense scrutiny from a medical examiner." He lifted his free hand, palm out, to make it clear that he'd meant no offense. "Now, I might be wrong. But…two hill-jack insurance investigators sitting in a shitty cabin, power out, heater cooking, and their blood full of alcohol? No, I don't think it's going to get the level of forensic study that you're hoping for."

"There's a generator plug on the back deck," Abby said. "Hank installed it. Nobody will believe we sat here with it inside."

The mask nodded up and down. The voice from behind it said: "Your critique is duly noted."

"It won't work," Abby said. Her tongue felt thick against the roof of her mouth. Too thick for just the whiskey.

Time's running out. The window's closing, your fuel is low, your tires are bad, and all these other assholes have more money under the hoods, but that doesn't matter because you've got reflexes, you've got instinct, you've got…

She came back to awareness with a jerk, her subconscious kicking her awake.

The kid smiled. "Getting tired, Abby?"

"No." And she wasn't anymore; that last jolt of adrenaline had cleared some of the fog, but she knew she was running out of time fast. "I'm just telling you that this won't work."

"It seems I'll have to try it simply to settle this debate."

The foggy feeling from the whiskey was blending with the acrid fumes. She stared at the bottle and wondered whether she could grab it and slam it into the kid's skull without getting shot. Wondered whether her motor skills were deteriorating as fast as her speech.

Going to have to try soon.

"How much did you already have, Hank?" Abby said, and Hank blinked sleepily at her and then refocused.

"It's a bad deal," Hank said thickly. "Shouldn't have called you. Knew better. I'm sorry."

"Don't give up yet, champ," the kid said, and his eyes flicked toward Hank.

Abby thought it was the best chance she'd get.

She punched the remote start on the key fob twice, taking care not to move the rest of her body. There was a slight lag, and then the motor growled and the running lights blinked on.

When it happened, Abby turned toward the sound with surprise, even though she'd been counting on it. It was this that sold the trick. The kid originally turned toward her, but when he saw Abby's surprise, he, too, looked toward the yard. Then he leaned across the table to push back the window blinds.

Abby rose and grabbed the neck of the whiskey bottle. She didn't pause to draw the bottle back or change its position, knowing that time was short; she simply swung it up in one continuous motion, aiming for the kid's face. She moved well despite the fogginess in her brain, and she was sure the strike was going to work.

The kid's speed was incredible.

Where his head had offered a clear shot, nothing but air waited.

Abby's momentum carried her forward. The bottle flew from her hand and shattered off the wall in a cloud of glass and whiskey, and then she fell to the floor beside Hank's chair. The kid had somehow pivoted and leaped in a single fluid motion, avoiding the contact and also maintaining his balance. He pointed the gun at Abby's face. Above the mask, his eyes were bright with amusement.

"You're quick," he said. "Better than I'd have guessed."

All of their attention was on each other, so when Hank moved, it surprised Abby as much as the kid. Hank's chair lurched sideways and the hand that had been left untied so he could drink suddenly locked over the kid's forearm.

The revolver fired; the shot went wide, the bullet sparking off the generator's engine block. Hank overbalanced and fell, but he kept his hand on the kid's arm and so they both went down while Abby tried to rise. Hank hit the floor with a splintering crack that

Abby hoped was the chair and not his arm. The kid landed on the other side of Abby, twisting while he fell, composed and nimble. He would've made a clean landing if Abby hadn't gotten in the way by sheer accident.

Her rising shoulder caught the kid's knee and knocked him off balance, and when he fell, his gun hand landed squarely on the glowing grill of the space heater.

The burn achieved what neither Abby nor Hank had been able to—it made the kid finally drop the gun. Even as he howled in pain, though, he was already reaching for the weapon with the other hand, absolutely relentless.

Hank just beat him, managing to roll onto his side and over the gun. He was still bound to the chair, his free arm dangling uselessly now, clearly broken. He couldn't have picked the gun up and fired it even if it had landed in his fingers. But he'd covered it with his body, and he looked up at Abby, his eyes wide and white, and said, "Run."

Abby scrambled to her feet and started toward Hank, but he repeated his command, and this time it was a scream.

"Run!"

Abby ran.

22

She reached the front door and turned the knob and then the door was open and she fell onto the screen door and tore it half off the hinges as she surged through it and into the cold night air.

If she'd been thinking clearly, she would have left the driveway and angled toward the trees, seeking cover immediately, but she wasn't thinking, just moving, and so she ran ten yards straight out of the door and down the wide-open drive, and it was only the sound of the growling engine on the Chrysler that brought her out of the fog.

Don't run. Drive, dummy. Driving is faster.

She had her hand on the door when a gunshot cracked and the driver's window exploded. Glass needled across her hands, and a thin line of blood ran down her index finger as she slid into the driver's seat, jammed her foot on the brake, and punched the starter button to engage the transmission of the idling car. She kept her head under the dash as she shifted into reverse and pounded the gas, focused on two things—she had to stay down to avoid a bullet, and she had to keep the wheel steady and the accelerator pinned to the floor. Hank's driveway was a straight shot through the pines and back to the rutted road; she didn't need to lift her head to drive, not yet.

She kept her foot on the gas and her bloody hands tight on the wheel, driving blind but straight.

You'll know when you hit the road. And then you'd better get your foot on the brake fast.

It seemed to take longer than it should have—driving blind

ruined distance perception—but finally she felt a thunk under the back wheels as the Chrysler left the driveway. She slammed on the brake, sending the tires slaloming through the wet dirt and gravel of the camp road, and managed to bring the car to a stop without sliding into the trees. Now she *had* to risk looking up.

No bullets came for her, and she didn't wait to give them a chance, just cut the wheel hard to the left, shifted into drive, and hit the gas again. The decision to go left was simple—the trees were thick to that side, and the right was wide open, making her an easy target. She was expecting more shots. No one fired, though. Even when she passed through a gap between the pines, no bullets came.

She should have understood that the lack of gunfire meant she'd made a mistake.

Instead, all she felt was relief. She was free. Out of sight of the house, out of pistol range, and moving under her own power.

Or the car was moving under its own power at least. Abby, maybe less so. The adrenaline was losing the battle with whatever was in her bloodstream—*That's not just whiskey; what else was in there?*—and the windshield was a mess of milky cracks that blurred the road in front of her. The combination was disorienting, and she wanted to stop, get out of the car, and put her feet on the ground.

An engine roared to life behind her.

That sound kept her foot away from the brake.

Just keep going fast, she told herself, *go far and go fast, that's all you need to do.*

But she didn't know where she was going. She'd been on the road to Hank's a thousand times, but she'd never turned this way coming out of the driveway. What was ahead of her? An intersection? There had to be. She needed a paved road; please, *please,* let there be a paved road. Give her pavement and nobody would catch her; the devil himself would not catch Abby Kaplan if she had four good tires and a paved surface.

No pavement appeared. The hard-packed dirt road got tighter and rougher. The Chrysler shimmied and shook like it was crossing cobblestones. The trees crept in, branches slapping off both sides of the car. Abby wanted to slow down. Wanted to stop.

No. Hank said to run. You've got to run.

But she couldn't remember what she was running from anymore. Her brain spun, out of sync with her eyes and her hands, and all she could hear was Hank's voice—or was that Luke's? Was that Luke telling her to go…

Faster. Faster.

Sure thing. Abby could always go faster.

She remembered her father's lullaby, the one from the old Robert Mitchum movie about an Appalachian bootlegger with a hot rod, the mountain boy who had G-men on his taillights and roadblocks up ahead. Being the motherless daughter of Jake Kaplan meant that such songs became lullabies. "The Ballad of Thunder Road" had been Abby's favorite. Her father's voice, off-key, his breath tinged with beer, singing, *"Moonshine, moonshine, to quench the devil's thirst…"* had eased her to sleep many times, the two of them alone in the trailer.

All these years later, the song could resurface clearly when she edged toward sleep.

"He left the road at ninety," her dead father crooned softly, *"that's all there is to say."*

When the Chrysler left the road, Abby had no idea if she'd missed a curve or simply driven right through a dead end. All she knew was that suddenly she was awake and the car was bouncing over uneven ground and now it wasn't branches whipping at the windows but whole trees, saplings that cracked with *whip-snap* sounds. Before she could move her foot to the brake, she hit a tree that did the stopping for her, an oak that slammed the car sideways. The airbag caught her rising body at stomach level, a gut punch that stole her breath but kept her from striking the windshield.

She sat gasping for breath and trying to clear her vision, desperate for just a little time to get her bearings.

Headlights appeared in the rearview mirror.

There was no time.

Abby got the door open and hauled herself out of the car, but her legs were wobbly and uncooperative, her vision spinning. She stumbled forward, trying to fight through the branches with her hands held up to protect her face. Her feet hit wet soil and went out from under her and suddenly she was down on her ass in the muck.

She might've stayed there, disoriented and exhausted and near the point of collapse, but she could still see the glow from the headlights, and they triggered whatever primal impulses the brain stem held on to until the very end.

Run. Flee.

She fought ahead on hands and knees, and this was a blessing in disguise because she crawled faster than she could have run. The boggy soil yielded to actual water, cold and deep enough to cover her arms to the elbows. She'd splashed into a creek, and she couldn't make sense of that. What creek? Where did it lead? She tried to remember and couldn't. Hadn't she hiked out here once with Hank and her father? Yes, absolutely. The winter before her father's heart attack. There'd been snow that day and the iced-over creek had turned into a beautiful white boulevard through the pines and birches, leading down past an ancient stone wall and on toward...

Toward nothing. There was nothing out here but trees and rocks and water. That was the point; Hank had never wanted neighbors. Abby needed a neighbor now, though. She needed anyone who could help, because something was behind her. Who or what was no longer clear. Her flight was now instinctual, not logical. Her body was working better than her brain.

That's fine, because all I need to do is keep running, she thought just before she slid over a moss-covered rock and bounced into the sinkhole below, where she lay covered in mud and decaying leaves and dampness. There, her body started to quit on her too.

She knew that she needed to get up and get moving, but this hole with its pillow of old leaves and cool moss felt comfortable, almost safe, except for the dampness. There was something about being tucked into the earth like this that felt right.

Like a grave. You are in your grave, Abby.

She thought she could still see the headlights, but it was hard to tell with the fog gliding through the trees. It was a low, crawling mist that seemed to be searching for her. She wasn't sure if the lights behind the mist were moving or stationary or if they were even out there at all. Her eyelids were heavy and her blood felt thick and slow.

She wondered how long it would take the kid to find her.

The kid. Yes, that's who you're running from. He's a killer.

And he was quick. The way he had ducked that punch? That was more than quick. So it would not take the kid long to find Abby now.

What was his name? Had he said a name? Sure, he had. Gentleman Jack.

Abby burrowed into the soft embrace of the leaves that smelled like death and waited on the arrival of Gentleman Jack.

23

Her first awareness was of the cold.

She opened her eyes and saw a moss-covered rock, beads of water working slowly but resolutely over it, following the terrain like bands of determined pioneers. Then they reached the edge and fell, manifest destiny gone awry.

Plink. Plink. Plink.

She stared at the rock and the puddle for a while without recognition of anything else. Except for the cold. That was still there, and it was intensifying. Uncomfortable but also necessary, because it was pounding clarity into her brain.

Get up. Get up and move before you freeze to death.

She struggled upright, and the motion made her dizzy and nauseated. She rested on her hands and knees, head hanging, waiting for the vomit to come, but the nausea passed and she didn't get sick. She worked a wooden tongue around a mouth so dry and swollen, it felt carpeted.

What the hell happened?

The kid.

That was what had happened. The night chase came back to her, and she was suddenly convinced that she wasn't alone here, that the kid had to be right behind her, the kid with his baby face and his grown-up gun.

There was nothing in sight but the woods, though. Abby was in a gully below a forested ridge; above, white birches and emerald pines were packed in tight, and a stream there split and ran down swales on either side of her. No sound but the running water.

She tried to walk up the hill but her feet tangled and she fell heavily and painfully onto her side. She rolled over and breathed for a while and then tried again, slower this time. Each motion required caution because her head spun and her stomach swirled. She tasted bitter bile and her throat was sore, as if she'd been retching. She didn't remember doing that, though.

The sky was bright enough to show some of the world, but not much of it. Predawn light. That meant she'd been down here for hours.

What had happened to Hank in that time?

She hobbled up the slope. Her left side and left hip hurt the worst, and she wasn't sure why. She didn't remember much about the drive, the run through the woods, or her fall. She just remembered that she'd been trying to get out in front of the kid and of whatever the whiskey had put in her bloodstream. They'd both been closing in on her fast.

And Hank had been well behind them, tied to the chair. Had he gotten loose? He'd had some time alone while the kid pursued Abby. He'd had a window for escape, if he'd been able to free himself.

She got to the top of the hill, but even from there, the Chrysler wasn't visible. Just the trees. In her running and crawling through the night woods, she'd made it farther than she'd thought. The smell of rain was heavy in the air. She could find no clear track to show her how to get back to where she'd started, and she decided that following the stream made as much sense as anything. She started along it, walking uphill, breathing hard and fighting for each step, thinking, *Maybe when I got out, that evil kid got scared and ran, and Hank's still back there, tied to the chair and hurt, maybe, but alive. Waiting for help. For me.*

When she crested the next rise, struggling to keep her footing on the slick leaves, she finally saw her car.

It was punched into an oak's trunk and wedged between pines, and she was bizarrely pleased by how far she'd made it into such dense trees before getting hung up. When she stepped closer, she could see the dangling airbag visible through the shattered glass. Everything about the car was as she remembered.

Then she saw Hank's body in the passenger seat.

Abby froze, then took a wavering step forward, knees going weak, and cried, "Hank!" Her voice was broken and hoarse. *"Hank!"*

Hank Bauer wasn't going to answer. His head lay unnaturally on his left shoulder, and the right side of his face was swollen and bruised, his eyes open but unseeing. Abby wrenched open the passenger door, and Hank's head dropped bonelessly forward, chin down on his chest, eyes still open, his neck obviously broken.

Abby stepped back and sat down in the wet grass. She rubbed a filthy hand over her face. She breathed with her eyes closed, then opened them and looked at Hank once more.

"What happened?" she said aloud.

Hank offered no insight.

The way he sat there, slumped in the passenger seat with the wound on the right side of his head and the broken neck, made it look as if he'd been in the car when it hit the tree and died on impact, when in reality he'd been dead before he was brought here.

Or maybe not.

Maybe he'd been alive and trying to stay alive by obeying orders, the kid saying, *Get in the car,* holding a gun to his head. Abby could picture him climbing into the wrecked car, hoping for mercy, only to have his skull smacked off the windshield, his neck snapped.

Abby looked up the road then, searching for either help or threat, finding neither. It was peaceful and quiet and lonely. When the wind gusted, raindrops fell from the trees like a fresh shower. Hank's house was the last one on the isolated camp road. Nobody would have heard the crash. The kid would have had time to go back and bring Hank down here and not be rushed, but still, it seemed a reckless choice because Abby had been out there in the darkness, free.

He knew you were going to be down for a while, though. He was sure of that. He wasn't rushing because he knew he didn't need to.

Thanks to whatever was in the whiskey, the kid knew he had time. Maybe he even thought Abby was dead. Plenty of time, then.

Why move Hank's body, though? Why bring him down here and put him in the passenger seat? Even if he'd thought Abby was dead, that arrangement didn't make any sense, because there was no driver.

Abby looked at the empty driver's seat, and suddenly she understood.

I didn't realize your academic record was as poor as your driving record, the kid had said.

It was Abby's car, and Abby had wrecked it. The physical evidence would say that, because it was the truth.

Hank hadn't been riding shotgun when the Chrysler went into the trees, and he hadn't broken his neck in the crash, but if the police found this scene and then found Abby dead in the woods, uninjured but with drugs and alcohol in her bloodstream, what would they think?

The kid was panicked and tried to rig the scene. A bad plan, but he needed something.

Was it that bad, though? When Abby called this in, she was going to have to tell the police that she'd been poisoned and that while she was sleeping it off in the woods, a teenager with a gun had killed Hank Bauer and belted him into the passenger seat. That was the truth, but it was going to be an awfully strange story to tell and an awfully hard story for a detective to believe. And if the detectives who heard it happened to know that Abby had ended up back in Maine working for Hank Bauer because of another night that went a lot like this one...

Just call them. Let them figure it out.

The man had been murdered, and Abby knew who'd killed him. In that case, you called the police. Period.

When she stood up and reached for her phone, she realized it was gone, and only then did she remember the kid taking it and tossing it onto the kitchen counter after he'd looked at the photograph of Luke on the home screen.

He'd known Luke was dead. He'd known what had happened. So this scenario, this scene he'd built with Hank, was maybe a little bit better than Abby wanted to imagine.

I can tell the police the truth. They'll need time to verify it, but they'll believe it.

Hank's dead eyes stared through the shattered windshield. *California isn't the only problem,* those eyes seemed to say.

True. Police would learn quickly that Abby had also been arrested in Maine, and for stealing a car from Hank Bauer, no less. Never mind that Hank hadn't pressed charges; whatever police records still existed from that, either on paper or in memory, would show yet another night very similar to this one—Hank Bauer had a fast car, Abby Kaplan had a thirst for speed, and it had ended badly.

It's easier to believe than the truth, she realized. *Either Abby Kaplan fucked up for the third time behind the wheel or a hit man disguised as a Boy Scout killed an insurance investigator in rural Maine. Which would you pick?*

She needed evidence. At least one shot had connected with the car, and it went through the driver's window. That would prove she wasn't crazy, maybe even indicate the caliber of the bullet and the distance of the shot.

She walked around the front of the car, stepping over a torn tree with white-pulped flesh protruding from shredded bark like an open fracture.

The driver's window was gone. Not just cracked with a clean hole through the center, but completely shattered. The sunroof was also demolished. So was the passenger window. Wherever the bullet might have left its mark, the kid had seen it and taken care of it.

That doesn't matter. It's a weak-ass attempt to cover things up, but it won't stick, and the faster you get the police out here, the faster you'll be done.

But she could imagine the cops' faces as she told them about the kid with the gun and the bottle of Gentleman Jack. What would they look like when she got to the part about how she'd started the Chrysler with the remote and Hank had fallen on the gun, still tied to the chair, and from there it was all question marks and darkness…

That was the truth, yes. And the truth should always be enough, yes.

But she wasn't so sure that it would be.

What does the house look like? she wondered. *If it looks like the place I left, then my story is fine. If he took the time to clean it up, though…*

She looked back at Hank. There was no need to rush for him. They didn't use sirens and flashers when they were taking you to the morgue.

Abby closed the door on her friend's corpse and walked up the road. She followed the rain-filled ruts left by her own tires until Hank's house came into view, and then she stopped and stared.

The kitchen blinds were open again. The way they always were, or always had been until last night.

Bad sign. If he took that much time to set things right…

She crossed the yard like an inmate walking to her execution. Went to the window and looked in at the kitchen.

The chairs were tucked under the table, which was bare except for a newspaper, open to the sports section. No whiskey, no tumbler glasses, no lantern. The generator was gone, and so was the space heater. The block of knives was back on the counter.

You'll have to tell them that this sociopath did all this while you were passed out in the woods. You will have to convince them of that, and you don't even know anything about him.

No, that wasn't true. Looking in at the kitchen, all traces of chaos eradicated from it, Abby felt like she knew plenty about that kid.

And all of it was terrifying.

Could she describe him? Not in much more than general terms. And the kid did not fit the story, because the story seemed to be a professional killing, and baby-faced teenagers did not carry out professional hits.

I'll need to be able to tell them who he is, but I don't know who he is. All I know is that he's fucking scary, and he wanted the phone.

He'd wanted it, yes. But did he have it? The bags of phones Abby had carried in were gone, but what about the one she'd jammed under the driver's seat? Had the kid searched the car?

Abby left the house and started back down the road, moving at a jog this time, but it was a long distance and she was hurting, so she quickly fell back to a labored walk. She opened the driver's door, avoided staring at Hank's face, and reached below the seat.

The bag was there. Three iPhones inside.

She took it out and stepped away from the car and looked up at the lightening sky—the day was moving along, and she needed to do the same. One way or the other, she had to make a decision.

It was a memory that sealed the choice. When she'd been sitting at that table trying to reason her way out of the situation, she'd told the kid that he would end up in jail. The response had been immediate, and chilling: *You'd be surprised how many friends I've got around jails. Some in cells, some in uniforms.*

Abby didn't think he'd been lying.

She looked at the dead man who'd backed her time and again throughout her life. "I'm sorry, Hank," she said. She wanted to re-member some other version of Hank's face, not this death pallor and endless stare, not the broken-stem look of his neck. All she could see was that, though—that and the image of Hank's face, sweaty and scared in the lantern light, as he screamed at Abby to run.

Backing her one last time.

"Thank you," Abby told the dead man, and then she closed the door. She walked back up the lonely road to Hank's house and up the steps. The screen was damaged from where she'd blasted through it—the only physical evidence that supported her story. The knob turned freely. Once inside, she didn't waste much time looking for things the kid might've missed in his cleanup effort. She had a feeling there wouldn't be any, and she needed to move quickly.

Hank's guns were stored in a glass-doored cabinet in the living room, impossible to miss. Some people were proud of guns and wanted them as conversation pieces. The cabinet had a lock, which was better than nothing, but a lock didn't mean much when it secured thin glass doors. Abby wrapped her fist in a blanket that was draped over the back of the couch and then punched each door once, without much force. The glass shattered and she swept it away with the blanket. She took one shotgun, a black Remington over/under; one rifle, a scoped .308; and both handguns, a Glock .45 and a SIG Sauer nine-millimeter. The ammunition was stored on a shelf below the guns. She took all of it, boxes and boxes of shells and bullets, and wrapped them in the blanket with the guns.

She stepped back and looked at what she'd done and tried to find the voice in her head that would say this was a mistake. Before it could so much as whisper, though, she glanced into the kitchen and saw the tidy arrangement of chairs and tables, no trace of violence.

Friends in cells and friends in uniforms, the kid had said.

Abby picked up the blanket with the guns and the ammunition and walked out of the living room. She crossed to the kitchen counter and picked up her phone. It had a charge and a signal, but she put it in her pocket without pause. She'd make the call to police, but not from here.

She carried the guns to the door, found the basket where Hank kept odds and ends, and fished out his car keys. She was moving quickly and purposefully now, not wanting to slow down long enough to consider the reality of what she was doing. Driving away in a murdered man's car was obviously a dangerous choice.

Staying, though, seemed worse.

24

In another life, Gerry Connors had been a bomb maker, but that was long ago. For the past two decades, he'd been a networker, a middleman. He was not a fixer, although people often thought of him as one. In reality, he put the players together, and he kept silent when silence needed to be kept. He asked only the necessary questions, and he shared only the minimum of information. He handled contacts and he handled money. For the German, he'd handled the hiring of Carlos Ramirez, but he had not told the German of the hiring of Dax Blackwell. That had been his own decision.

This now had the potential to cause real problems for Gerry.

The kid sat across from him in the dark-paneled office with his customary slouch, eyes alert but body loose, and if he was at all aware of the trouble that he'd caused, he didn't show it. If he was at all concerned about what this trouble meant to him, he certainly didn't show that. If not for the kid's lineage, Gerry might've had to view this as stone-cold stupidity, but Dax's bearing was so similar to his father's that in the midst of the frustration, there was a strange reassurance. Gerry dearly missed the kid's dad and uncle. Right now, Jack and Patrick Blackwell would have kept his pulse down. He needed Dax to do the same. Because the German had paid a lot of money for killing Oltamu and recovering the phone and doing it all quietly. Efficiently. Gerry had managed to accomplish only a third of that.

Now it was growing exponentially worse, Dax Blackwell seemed indifferent to the problem, and the German was due in town in forty-eight hours.

"There was no iPhone except her own," Dax said. "You've got what she brought in. I checked her phone. I chose to leave it behind because if she manages to make it out of those woods alive, it's going to hurt her story when they find the house clean and her phone inside. But it was not Oltamu's phone."

"Then where *is* Oltamu's phone?"

"That question would be easier for me to answer if I knew something about the situation. Like who wants it, why they want it, and who else might want it."

"That's not your fucking role!"

A shrug. "Then it'll be harder."

"You're not even sure she's dead! She saw you, and she might be able to talk!"

"Correct."

Gerry took blood pressure medication daily, and he thought that was the only thing saving him now. He breathed through his teeth and said, "You want to tell me how you're going to deal with that? If she walks out of those woods, we'll have some sketch artist's rendering of your face on every news broadcast in North America."

The kid said, "I don't think so."

"*Pardon?* You poisoned her, shot at her, and killed her boss, but you expect her to go quietly into the night?"

Dax nodded calmly. Gerry was incredulous. Every time he wanted to kill the kid, he found himself asking questions instead. He did that again now.

"Want to explain why she'd stay quiet?"

"Her personal history. She's been involved in a car wreck that left a movie star in a coma and, eventually, dead. People hate her for that. It's always amusing to me just how much people care about some asshole in a movie, but they do. Her boss, Bauer, thought the Tara Beckley case might make Abby confront those demons." He smiled at that, then said, "Sorry. That one kind of broke me up. I mean, how's it going to *help*? But Hank Bauer, may he rest in peace, didn't strike me as a particularly skilled psychotherapist. It was an effort, though. You have to appreciate friends who make an effort."

Gerry could hardly speak. The kid's attitude was that astonishing. "You talked through all this with them?" he managed finally. "You got their life stories but no phone?"

"I really only had the chance to speak with Mr. Bauer at length."

Gerry needed a drink. Needed to lie down. Hell, both. Lying down and drinking at the same time, that was what this called for. "Abby Kaplan is going to bring cops down all over this."

"I disagree. You've got to think about the story she has to tell them. You really think the police are going to buy that? I had this same conversation with her, and my guess is that it lingered. She'll think about it before she calls, at least. I'm sure of that."

He hadn't gotten the phone, he'd killed a man, and he'd left a witness alive, and if any of this bothered him in the slightest, it didn't show.

"The phone, however, remains a concern," he said.

"No shit, it remains a concern!" Gerry shouted. "*That's* what I need. I didn't ask you to kill some hick in Maine, I asked you to get the phone!"

"Well, things come up."

Things come up. Holy shit, this kid. Gerry rubbed his temples and forced himself not to shout. "You said Abby Kaplan had the phone."

"That's what I was told. She showed up in good faith for the boss with phones and chargers, like the salvage guy said she should have. They weren't in a box. When I broke into her apartment, I found the box. Empty. There were no phones in the apartment either. But it's not a lost cause. You can help me with that."

Gerry lowered his hands and stared. "*I* can help *you* with that."

Another nod.

"How might I be of service to you, Dax?"

The kid ignored the sarcasm and said, "I could talk to your client."

You didn't ask to speak to the client. Ever. You pretended there *wasn't* a client.

Gerry said, "Are you out of your fucking mind?"

"I understand it's not protocol, but—"

"You *understand it's not protocol*. Well, that's reassuring. Why would you possibly need to speak to—"

"But I think it's time to consider that someone else has the phone," Dax finished. "It's difficult for me to locate that person if I don't understand the value of the phone, do you see? I've come up with an alternative, though, if you don't want me to have an open dialogue with your client."

"I do *not* want you to have an open dialogue."

"Then in lieu of that, we'll have to settle for a lesser option. Suggest to your client that he give me the phone that Carlos grabbed by mistake. Let me work off that. Oltamu's personal phone gives me a starting point."

The client did not have Oltamu's personal phone. Gerry still did. It was in the drawer just below his right hand.

"Could you do that much?" Dax asked, and there was something about his eyes that gave Gerry the uncomfortable sense that the kid knew Gerry had the phone. He was sniffing around the edges, asking questions that he shouldn't, questions that he knew better than to ask.

"You're not your father or your uncle," Gerry said.

Dax's face darkened. Barely perceptibly, but it was the first anger Gerry had ever seen him display.

"No," he said. "I'm not. I'm better than them."

Gerry snorted. "You think?"

"Unquestionably," Dax said. "They're dead."

He was giving Gerry that flat stare again, the one that sent spiders crawling into your brain.

"Think it over," he said. "I'll get back to work regardless. I will get the right phone, and I will kill Abby Kaplan if she's still alive. These things will happen, but they'll go slower if I don't have some insight into the situation. And speed's important at the moment."

He stood up, and Gerry almost told him to sit his ass back down, but what was the point? He wasn't wrong; speed was important now.

The German was coming.

25

Abby made the call from a service plaza off the turnpike where there was always plenty of traffic. She was in Hank's car, and she knew she'd have to dump that soon, but for now it was the best of bad options. She thought about calling 911, decided against it, and called David Meredith directly.

"What's up, Abby? I gather you heard about our boy Carlos. Neat twist, eh?" He was cheerful, and the disconnect was so jarring that for a moment Abby couldn't speak. David had to prompt her. "Hello? Did I lose you?"

"No, sorry. Yes, I heard about Carlos Ramirez. I've also got a lot more detail on that than you can imagine, and it's all bad. I'm going to tell it to you once, so you're going to want to take notes or record it. Recording it would be better. I won't be able to call back and go through it again, at least not right away."

Silence. Then: "Abby, what in the hell are you talking about?"

"Can you record me?"

"No. Not here. But I can call you back from—"

"Take notes, then."

"Abby—"

"Hank is dead," Abby said, and her throat tightened, but she swallowed and kept talking. "He's in the passenger seat of my car, which is wrecked in the trees at the end of his road. It looks like he died in the wreck, but he didn't. He was murdered, and I nearly was, and it's all got something to do with that accident at Hammel College. I don't know what, but it—"

"Abby, whoa, slow down here. He was *murdered*? You need to—"

"I need to talk, and you need to listen and write it down," Abby said. "I'd love to trust you, but I'm not sure that I can right now. I was pretty well set up. The story I'm about to tell you sounds crazy, but it's the truth. You need to hear it. Can you just listen?"

Another pause, and then Meredith, sounding dazed, said, "I'll listen."

"Write it down too."

She told him about the call from Hank, and her arrival at the house, and the way things had gone from there. Told him about the generator and the Gentleman Jack and how she'd started the car and, with an assist from Hank, made it out the door. Told him how many hours had passed while she lay unconscious in the woods and what she'd found upon waking.

Meredith didn't interrupt, which was a relief. Abby wasn't sure how she'd respond if the man started asking questions, if his voice held any doubt or disbelief.

"You'll find him there, and you'll think that I'm out of my mind, but do me the favor of taking a good, hard look for physical evidence that shows I'm wrong," she said. "Maybe it'll be in Hank's blood. Maybe you'll find a bullet. Maybe the kid screwed up something at the house…but I kind of doubt that. Just promise me you'll look."

"Of course we will," David said, the first time he'd spoken in several minutes. "But you've *got* to come in. You know that, Abby. Running from this thing…it's the worst choice. Nobody will believe you if you run, no matter what we find."

"I don't think that's true," Abby said. "Hank's dead, and I sound like a lunatic, telling this story. Today you'll tell me that it will all work out, but tomorrow? Then the charges come. And you'll promise me that it's still not a threat because a good attorney will work it out, but I'm not sure. Hank Bauer of Coastal Claims and Investigations was murdered over a car accident involving a girl from Hammel College and a guy from Brighton who is already dead? That's going to keep me out of jail?"

"If it's the truth, it will," Meredith said, and Abby smiled grimly. She was watching the side-view mirror, looking for police cars; her scratched and bruised face stared back at her. She reached up and pulled a pine needle from her hair.

"Get started on proving it," she said, "and then I'll consider coming in. Talk to Shannon Beckley, talk to Sam at that salvage yard, and you can verify my movements through the day. That's worth something. Then work that scene right. Look for bullets, look for damage to the generator, get them to run toxicology tests on Hank's blood that will find *anything* unusual. Get some forensics expert to see if he can tell whether he was tied up. Most important? Find out whose phone matters so much that people will kill over it."

She didn't say that she had the phone. All Abby understood so far about the phone was that if she'd given it to the kid last night, she'd certainly be dead by now. She wasn't inclined to hand it off to anyone else just yet.

"When I call you next," Abby said, "you can tell me what progress you've made. Then we'll talk about me coming in."

"This is a suicide move, Abby," Meredith said, and he was angry now. Fine. Let him be angry. Abby just needed him to do the work.

"Two people have been murdered over that accident already," Abby said. "I was supposed to be the third. I'm not inclined to make my location known to the world right now."

"Even if you *did* get charged, which shouldn't happen if you're telling me a legit story, then you're safer with us than on the run, hiding from killers *and* cops."

"He said he has friends in jail."

"We'll have you in protective custody."

"He said some of those friends are in uniforms."

"This is insane. If there is anything to what you're saying, then we'll find plenty of evidence to support it, and we'll do that fast."

"See, I don't like the way you phrased that. *If* there's anything to what I'm saying. Already, you're skeptical."

"That's my job."

"And that's why I called you," Abby said. "To give you a head start doing your job. I'll be in touch."

"Abby, damn it, if you—"

She disconnected, powered down her phone, and stepped out of the Tahoe. She put the phone just beneath the front tire, backed up over it, pulled out of the service plaza, and got back onto the Maine turnpike. She drove north, toward where the towns were smaller and the woods were darker.

26

Blinks are coming.

They're not all the way there yet, but not far off either. Not impossible, certainly. Tara has worked on them with ferocious intensity, and while she hasn't succeeded, something about her eye motion feels different. It's promising, at least, a sensation like a door being forced open, just like when she was in the basement of that house on London Street.

She thinks it's an upward motion. She tries to blink, she demands that her eyelids lower…and while they do not obey, her focus seems to shift. A small difference, and a dizzying sensation, but she's almost certain she's looking upward. Her eyes are so damn dry that it's hard to tell, though. They're dry even though they constantly leak with tears at the corners. People dab the tears away from time to time, but people also avoid the kind of direct, hard stare that could tell her if indeed she's making any progress here. The motion she thinks she's achieving is so slight that thorough scrutiny would be required to observe it. In the early hours, people would look hard into her eyes, searching for her as if she were submerged in dark water. Shannon. Dr. Pine. The strange boy in the black baseball cap—his scrutiny might have been the most intense of all, actually.

Those deep stares are rare now, though. Everyone has become more evasive, as if they're fearful of Tara's gaze, as if a coma is contagious. Or embarrassed by it, as if her eyes are a mirror offering an unflattering image.

If anyone would look hard now, though, they would see that

she is close to blinking. As close as you can be without succeeding, and she feels like that should be noticeable. If Shannon would just pay attention, she would notice. Tara is almost certain of this. But Shannon is immersed in a phone call, and she seems concerned.

She's holding her cell phone to her ear with her left hand and a ballpoint pen hovering above a notepad in her right, and her all-business attitude just crumbled with whatever has been said. Tara watches her face and feels a cold and certain assurance that this is the inevitable call that means the decision has been made. They are going to end her life. If life was what you called this frozen purgatory. Then Shannon speaks, and Tara realizes that it has nothing to do with her at all.

"She might have *killed* someone? The same woman I spoke to? Abby Kaplan, yes, that was her name, but what in the world…" She stops, clearly interrupted.

Tara is trying to follow the conversation, but it's confusing—Abby Kaplan was one of the two strangers who'd visited her. Older than the second one, the one who pretended to be Justin Loveless and stared into Tara's eyes like a hunter looking through a scope. That man seems right for a murderer; Abby Kaplan does not. Abby Kaplan is supposed to be part of her team, someone to help. The college hired her.

Top-notch recruiting, Hammel, Tara thinks, *put that one in your brochures.* She wants to laugh, and even though she can't, it is still a pleasant sensation. Terror is often present, and frustration is constant, but humor is beginning to appear now and then to leaven these, as if her brain has tired of the relentless sorrow. She sometimes thinks that if she could simply communicate her mere existence, the rest could be endured. She could learn to have a life with some pleasure, then. Not the life she'd imagined, of course, but still one worth living. If they just knew that she was in here. But without that…

"Her own boss?" Shannon says into the phone. "Are you kidding me? I just…no, listen, I don't give a damn about how Hammel is going to find a better firm, what does that even mean? Your first hire just killed her boss, and now you'll admit that you could have done better?"

Bless you, Shannon, Tara thinks.

The pen descends to the notepad, but no words are written, and Shannon's mouth screws tight. Then she says, "I *know* I'm not a police officer, that's not a revelatory bit of information, but I still possess common sense, and maybe I should *talk* to the police, don't you think?"

Shannon lifts the ballpoint pen away from the pad and clicks it rapidly while she listens. The sound seems large to Tara; something about that small click embeds in her brain in a different way than other, louder things. Why was that?

Suddenly, Tara's thumb twitches.

Stunned, she tries to do it again, without success. But…it just moved. She is positive of that. Now that her attention is on it and she can't replicate the feat, though, the sensation begins to feel false, a phantom movement, a cruel illusion. And yet, for an instant, she'd been *certain*. It came from the sound, almost, from watching Shannon click that pen and hearing the accompanying sound and then it was as if her muscle memory had fired and Tara had mimicked the gesture.

But she tries again and again, and her thumb rests limply against her index finger.

She's lost track of Shannon's words, but now hears her say, "Listen, I might have been one of the last people to talk to her. I sure think it would be useful if I could talk directly to the police instead of through a handler from the college."

Pause, and Tara hopes she'll begin clicking the pen again, but the pause is brief and then Shannon says, "Fine, just please give me a call back so I can explain this to my family."

Shannon disconnects, lowers the phone, and stares at the wall with an expression that Tara hasn't seen many times on her sister's face: helplessness. The only memories Tara has of this look come from early childhood, in the days after her father's death, when her mother's depression was the darkest, the battle with medications the worst; even big sister Shannon had no idea what to do.

Put down that phone, Shannon had told Tara one terrible day after Tara had picked up the phone to call 911 for their unconscious mother. Shannon's helplessness was gone from her face, replaced by fury. *If you call, they'll take us away, don't you understand that?*

Tara had put down the phone. Shannon sat with their mother until dawn, washing her face with a damp cloth and making sure that her head was tilted to the side so she couldn't choke on her own vomit. Then she made Tara breakfast and sent her to school with instructions to keep her mouth shut about the situation at home; Shannon was handling it.

She had, too. Somehow, she had handled it.

Shannon turns to her, one eyebrow cocked, and Tara could swear that they've bridged the void somehow. This happens with people occasionally, with Shannon more than anyone else and most frequently when they are alone in the room. Now Shannon looks at her and says, "I think you should have gone to a state school, *mi hermana.* You could've saved a lot of money in student loans for the same level of incompetence."

Tara laughs. She doesn't move or make a sound, of course, but she laughs, and some part of her believes that Shannon knows it.

"The college hired an investigator for your case," Shannon says, "who then apparently *killed her boss* and ran away. Talk about bringing in the best and the brightest."

She's smiling; she always seems happiest when she's being sarcastic or cutting, a trait that makes relationships a struggle for her. Then the smile fades, her focus shifts away from Tara, and it is evident that she feels like she is alone in the room again.

Which breaks Tara's heart.

"Abby seemed like she cared," Shannon says softly, clearly speaking to herself now. Then she gives a little snap-out-of-it head shake, pulls a chair to the side of the bed, sits, and looks hard at Tara's face.

"Regardless, she gave me a good idea, T. I did some reading last night, and I made some calls this morning, and I have good news—you get to watch a movie."

Watch a movie? The television is always on. Mostly, Tara hates that. If she were able to change the channel, it wouldn't be so bad, but when they leave it on just for *background noise,* like she's a nervous puppy, it's infuriating.

"Dr. Pine himself approved it," Shannon says. "Even Rick and Mom say it's worth a try. Not just a movie, though, T.—you get a field trip." She takes Tara's limp hand. Her touch is warm and wonderful. So few people are willing to let their touches linger.

My thumb can move, Tara thinks. *Do it again, damn it, do it now, you stupid thumb, while someone has the chance to notice.*

But her thumb lies motionless against Shannon's palm.

"They're going to put you in an ambulance and take you to a lab about an hour away, at a university hospital where there's a coma research program, and then they'll hook you up to even more of these..." She lifts one of the many wires that lead from Tara's body to the monitors beside the bed. "And then they're going to show you a movie and wait to see if the computers can tell whether you respond to it. Whether you can track it, whether you *feel* anything watching it." Shannon's voice wavers, and she bites her lower lip and looks away.

Tara realizes just how important this test must be. If she doesn't pass this one, if she can't somehow let these computers know that she is in here...big decisions are going to be made soon.

This may be her last chance to have a voice in them.

"I did win one battle," Shannon says, turning back to her with a sniff and that forced smile. "They usually use some crappy black-and-white film. I told them that my sister *hates* black-and-white. They didn't like the idea of changing, but I can be persuasive."

An understatement for the ages. *She could* still *sell tickets for the* Titanic, Rick had once said of Shannon.

"So I got to pick the film," she continues, squeezing Tara's hand. "And I'll give you one guess what I picked."

Something scary, Tara thinks. Shannon loves Tara's fear of horror movies, the way even the cheesy ones can make her jump, how she covers her eyes and watches them through her fingers.

"That's right," Shannon says, "your test will be a familiar one. You get to watch *Jaws.*"

Well, now. Tara has long proclaimed *Jaws* to be the most re-watchable movie in history. She hasn't anticipated that being put to a coma test, though.

"You'll respond," Shannon whispers. "I know you will. When Quint starts talking about the *Indianapolis* sinking or when Chief Brody realizes his own son is on the sailboat by the shark, you'll respond. Just to the dumb music, you'll respond." She's imploring now, a hint of desperation to her words that scares Tara. This test is going to be *very* important.

"The people at the lab were encouraging," Shannon says, seemingly more to reassure herself than anything else. "They've had good results." She pauses. "Maybe I won't mention where I got the idea."

27

As Abby drove Hank's Tahoe along the turnpike, she remembered that she'd already spent some time considering life as a fugitive, thanks to Luke. One of his first leads in anything that wasn't a purely over-the-top action film where spiders fought robots was in a movie about a husband-and-wife team on the run, a Hitchcock knockoff that bombed at the box office. While he was reading the script and rehearsing, though, he enjoyed pondering the scenario.

"It's so much harder now than it would have been fifty years ago," he'd said, stretched out on the chaise longue on their cramped balcony during one of the rare hours that sunlight fell on it. "Think about it—you could pay cash for hotel rooms and rental cars and plane tickets, there were pay phones everywhere and no surveillance cameras, and you could hot-wire a car with a screwdriver."

Abby interrupted and asked him to explain that process, to tell her just how he'd go about hot-wiring a car with a screwdriver in the good old days. Luke smiled. "That was the golden age of hot-wiring! Simple! But the newer cars are tougher."

"Oh?"

"Yes." He'd nodded emphatically. "Just trust me on this."

"Certainly."

"The first thing you'd have to do if you were running from the law or people who were trying to kill you is ditch the cell phone, obviously," he went on. "They can always track those. But it's easy to get a burner phone—if you have cash. Credit cards are no good, right? And how many people have enough cash to go on the run? How much cash do you have in your wallet right now?"

Abby had four bills crumpled in her purse—and she was pleasantly surprised to discover one of them was a ten. She'd thought they were all singles.

"So there you go, thirteen dollars," Luke said. "I couldn't get far on that. They'd find me before I hit the state line. I'd run out of gas—"

"Is this in the car you hot-wired with a screwdriver?" Abby asked, and he grinned. For all of his physical beauty—and he was stunning, no question about that—he had a kid's smile, awkward and shy, and his off-the-set laugh was the same, a little too big, too high, far too likely to end with a helpless snort. Abby loved that about him. All the surprising touches that turned the movie star into a human being were reassuring. The more human he became, the more she loved him. That first day, when he'd joked to her about the grief his friends were giving him for having a woman perform his stunt driving, she'd thought he was exactly what she'd expected: good-looking and charming and arrogant and false. The first date, she'd asked herself why she was wasting her time. But soon she realized that her initial wariness about him was understandable, but it was not the truth. The truth was complicated, as it usually is, and the truth of Luke London made him easier to love than Abby wanted. Her truth was that she wanted to stay far away from actors. Her truth was that she was breaking rules for him.

"Sure it's the car I hot-wired," he said of his escape vehicle. "Because I'd have found an old car, right? As we discussed."

"Ah, of course."

"But then I run out of gas, and I've got no cash. What then? Pretend to be a homeless person?"

"It doesn't sound like it would be pretending by then."

Her pointed at her, sculpted triceps flexing under his T-shirt. "Good point! It would be method acting at its finest."

"And you suck at that."

He nodded thoughtfully. "Indeed. I'd stand out, and they'd find me."

"Who?"

"The people who are trying to kill me! So what do I do?"

"You steal," she said.

"I'd get caught. I guarantee it. I have a naturally guilty disposition when it comes to crime. One try at shoplifting, and I'm getting caught and going to jail. Which means, obviously, another inmate will be paid to kill me. Or maybe a guard. But going to jail is not hiding."

"You steal carefully, then," Abby had said. "Maybe break into a house. Just a matter of finding the right place."

Now, two years after that conversation and months after they'd taken Luke off life support, Abby drove along the turnpike and wondered where the right place was.

She had some cash—a hundred and thirty bucks, enough for a hotel room somewhere, but hotels were dangerous. Her face was going to be on the news, and this was off-season in Maine, which meant that the employees of hotels that took cash were going to have time to pay attention to their guests, learn their faces.

That was when she got it.

Off-season. The right places, she realized, were plentiful. They didn't call the state Vacationland for nothing—most people who owned property in Maine didn't stay there year-round. There were thousands of vacant houses, cabins, and cottages out there for her, and plenty of them were isolated.

She left the interstate in Augusta and moved on to the back roads. She realized only after taking the exit that the other cars hadn't made her uneasy, nor had the speed. Her mind was too busy with a real crisis to let the imaginary threats creep in. When you were fleeing a murder scene and a murderer, a traffic accident suddenly didn't seem too bad.

As she followed one of the winding country roads east toward the coast, it began to rain again. That felt good, like protective cover. She was driving east because most of the summer people clung to the coast. There were exceptions at every lake and pond, of course, but nowhere was the population of seasonal houses higher than the Midcoast. When the patio furniture was moved into storage and the lobster shacks folded up their bright umbrellas, the population of those towns fell by at least half.

How to pick the right house, though? Driving around some little coastal village and staring at houses would allow her to identify a few vacant ones, but it would also get her noticed by a year-round resident.

She stopped at a gas station with a lunch counter, a place busy enough for her to feel like she wouldn't stand out and big enough for her to suspect they'd have what she needed. Her clothes had dried but were still covered with mud, and she didn't want many people to get a look at her. She waited until an older couple got out of their car and headed toward the door, and then she got out of the Tahoe, crossed the parking lot swiftly, and walked in on their heels. They turned toward the deli counter, and Abby stepped behind one of the merchandise racks and pretended to be looking at candy while she looked around the store. Just beside the door, she saw what she wanted—a rack of real estate guides, free of charge.

She grabbed one, exited, and tried to keep her pace slow while her heart thundered and her every impulse screamed at her to run.

Nobody gave her so much as a passing glance.

She drove to Rockland and pulled off the road at a busy Dunkin' Donuts where the Tahoe wasn't likely to stand out. She'd have to change plates if she intended to keep the car, but right now her priority was finding a place where she could buy some time.

The real estate guide offered plenty of them. Abby knew what she was looking for; the keywords were *seasonal*, which meant they'd likely be empty now, and *motivated*, which meant they'd been on the market for a long time, and the neighbors were used to seeing strange cars pull in for a look.

She found both of those packaged with an even more golden word: *isolated.*

There was a seasonal property in St. George, a rural stretch of peninsula about twenty minutes from Rockland, that boasted a reduced price, motivated seller, and fifteen isolated acres.

A private oasis, perfect for artists, nature lovers, or anyone seeking beauty and seclusion!

The Realtor didn't spell it out, but the place certainly appealed to fugitives too.

Abby drove south on Route 1, then turned in South Thomaston and followed 131 through winding curves that led out of the hills and down the peninsula, the sea on one side and the St. George River on the other. Past an old dairy truck that stood on the top of a hill like it was waiting to be used for a calendar photograph, past a few houses with tall stacks of lobster traps in the yard, and then through the little fishing and tourist town of Tenants Harbor. More fishing town than tourist spot now; this was far enough out of the woods to be unappealing to the leaf peepers, so it probably ran on a short season, Memorial Day to Labor Day, for most everyone but the locals. Just before Port Clyde, the road to the *private oasis* appeared. She followed it into an expanse of ever-thickening pines and then spotted a FOR SALE sign beside a stone post onto which the house number had been carved: 117.

She followed a dirt driveway up a slope and around a curve and then the house came into view, a tall structure of shake shingles and glass that made her think of a lighthouse, everything designed vertically, with each floor a little smaller than the one below it, so it looked as if the levels had been stacked on one another. On one side of the home was a garage and on the other a small outbuilding that had probably been a studio.

She got out of the Tahoe and stood in the silent yard. A light breeze carried the smell of the nearby sea, and the scent mingled with the pines. The place did feel like an oasis, and that was good, because her adrenaline was fading and exhaustion was creeping in. She needed rest. Hopefully, David Meredith was making good on his pledge to do righteous work down at Hank's house, and when Abby woke, it would all be done, nothing left to endure but a lecture from the cops for running and then listening to news of the kid's arrest and identifying him in a photo lineup, maybe.

Sure. It would be that easy.

She tried the garage door first, and it was locked. The house was the same, but there was a Realtor's lockbox on each door. She left the one on the front door intact and hammered the cover off the one on the side door with the butt of the SIG Sauer. There was a Red Sox key ring with three keys—house, garage, and studio, all helpfully labeled.

Abby put the Tahoe in the garage, lowered the door, sealing it out of sight, and went in the house. It was a beautiful place, with gleaming wood floors and fresh white paint on the walls, so even on a gray day it seemed filled with light. There wasn't any furniture. It had been a long time since anyone lived here. From the third-floor master bedroom, you had a view of overgrown gardens that would once have been spectacular, and, just visible over the treetops, a glimmer of blue ocean. You could also see almost the entire length of the road. There were only four other homes on it, and trees screened them out.

The house was mostly empty, but in a closet she found some old drapes and a throw pillow that featured Snoopy flying a biplane. She picked a second-floor bedroom that faced away from the road and offered easy access to a porch roof. She opened the window, removed the screen, then closed it again, leaving it unlocked. If anyone showed up, at least she'd have a chance to run.

Run where?

Abby didn't have the answer to that. She was out of answers and needed sleep in the worst way. She went back out to the garage and got the bag with the phones and carried that into the house and tucked it in one of the bathroom cabinets. Then she returned to the Tahoe and got the guns. She put the shotgun in the closet near the front door, brought the scoped rifle up to the third-floor master bedroom, and kept the handguns with her as she walked back down to the second floor. She felt nauseated and dizzy and weary. Adrenaline was an amazing thing. There was a certain gift to panic, to terror. As long as you could control it and channel it, there were fuel reserves in fear that most people didn't know existed.

She'd burned through the last of hers, though.

She lay down on the cold hardwood floor, set the guns near her hand, put her head on the Snoopy pillow, covered herself with the old drapes, and slept.

28

For as long as Tara has been awake, the hospital has seemed horrible, and yet as soon as they begin to move her, she's afraid to leave. Fortunately, she has Shannon in her ear, Shannon who, bless her, would talk to a mannequin if that was the only audience she had.

"Dr. Pine says there's no risk in moving you because your spine is stable and your heart and breathing are good, but if there's trouble, have no fear, we'll handle it—that's the best part about traveling by ambulance."

Mom shuffles numbly alongside, and now Tara is certain that they've given her mother tranquilizers. She's surprised—and angry—that Rick has agreed to it. Or does he not know? Is Tara the only one who's picking up on this because everyone else's attention is on her, not Mom? Possible.

A few people give her kind smiles as they pass, and it's both in-teresting and overwhelming to see the sheer size of the hospital. It occurs to her that she has no idea where this hospital is or how she got here. Ambulance, helicopter? She's always wanted to fly in a helicopter. If you're going to be airlifted to a hospital, you might as well get the view.

They descend in an oversize elevator, big enough to accom-modate the gurney, and exit out onto a loading dock, and, sure enough, there's the ambulance, ready and waiting.

The fifty feet between the hospital and the ambulance are the most terrifying part of the journey. Open air isn't a relief to Tara; it's shocking and intimidating, and she misses the con-

fines of the hospital room. *Just leave me in there and I'll get better!*
But then they have her up and into the back of the ambulance
and Shannon is at her side, Rick and Mom apparently driving
separately. There's a young paramedic in the ambulance, an impossibly good-looking guy, and Tara would love to exchange a
glance with Shannon over this.

"Tara, I'm Ron," he says as he pats her leg, and now she likes
him even more—an introduction *and* a kind touch. She listens
to Shannon and Ron talk for the remainder of the ride. Ron
is encouraging; he's heard of the lab they're headed for, and he
knows they've had great results. Dr. Carlisle is the best. Tara is
in great hands with Dr. Pine and Dr. Carlisle. Shannon agrees,
but mostly she's just proud of the way she convinced them to use
Jaws for the test.

"She hates black-and-white film," Shannon tells Ron. "Even the
classics. If they show her anything in black-and-white, she's not
going to be more alert, trust me. She fell asleep in the first five
minutes of *Casablanca*."

Not entirely true—Tara closed her eyes during the first five
minutes of *Casablanca*. She didn't fall asleep until at least fifteen
minutes in.

She's grateful for the conversation swirling around her, since it
helps distract her from the swaying motion of the ambulance. Being inside a moving vehicle is a memory trigger—she can see Dr.
Oltamu's face in the rearview mirror again and hear the urgent
tension in his voice when he insisted that he needed to get out and
walk.

Transition from ambulance to the university lab is quick and
smooth and everyone here is friendly and smiling, far more eye
contact than what she's used to at the hospital. Dr. Michelle
Carlisle is leading the way. She's a tall, striking woman. She kneels
to Tara's level, looks her in the eye, and introduces herself politely
but formally, as if this is just a standard doctor-patient interaction.

Tara is instantly a fan of Dr. Carlisle.

"What we're going to do," the doctor explains, "is both cutting-edge and quite simple, Tara. We're going to give you the chance to watch your beloved *Jaws*"—she looks at Shannon when she says this with an expression that isn't entirely pleased—"and while you watch it, we watch you. You'll be inside an MRI scanner. I don't know if you've ever had an MRI before, but it might feel a little claustrophobic at first. Just be patient and let that pass."

Speaking as if Tara has a choice in that matter is absurd, and yet it is deeply appreciated.

"The movie plays on a scanner above you and is reflected on a mirror that you can see comfortably. While you watch, the MRI will be recording your responses in various brain areas—auditory cortex, visual cortex, parahippocampal, frontal, and parietal lobes. We'll compare your activation results to that of baseline tests, which will help us say definitively that you're alert and aware, that you're watching and engaging with the film and the story." All of this is for the benefit of Shannon, Mom, and Rick, of course, but Dr. Carlisle addresses Tara. "Well…are we ready?"

I don't know, Tara thinks. *Because there's one big question nobody has answered yet: What if your tests don't show any activation?*

Dr. Carlisle smiles as if Tara has given consent and stands. "Then let's get to it."

The doctor lied about the MRI scanner. It doesn't make Tara feel merely *a little claustrophobic*. It's petrifying.

The machine looks big enough from a distance, but when they slide Tara into it and the rest of the room vanishes from view, the rounded walls close in on her, and it's like being in a coffin. When the hatch behind her is sealed, she's instantly convinced that there's not enough air in this thing, and the panic that overtakes her is the worst since her return to awareness. Maybe worse. What if she can't breathe in here, what if she begins to hyperventilate? She can't bang on the walls or scream or thrash; she can't do anything to let them know that she needs out.

She's Twitchy Tara again, worthy of her big sister's snarky nickname, anxiety swelling to panic when she knows it's irrational.

She's certain each inhalation is using up her oxygen supply in this coffin-like enclosure, and now she's worse than paralyzed—she's paralyzed and entombed.

Be brave, damn it!

She tries to think of 1804 London Street again, of the long journey down dark halls. She can't conjure up the image, though. And that was so long ago; that happened to a child! She doesn't need a child's courage, she needs a woman's warrior heart.

The Allagash.

The name rises unbidden in her mind, and suddenly she sees the Allagash River, the big, beautiful, dangerous river that bisects northern Maine's roadless, townless wilderness. The river flows south to north, an unusual path in North America. In her freshman year at Hammel, when she was afraid she couldn't hack it at school, couldn't make friends, couldn't survive so far away from home, Tara went alone to kayak on the Allagash. Imprudent; reckless, even. But necessary. She would make her decision there—whether to stay through the semester or go back to Cleveland and enroll somewhere local, somewhere familiar. Or maybe head west, find a school near Stanford, near Shannon.

But first, she wanted to see this river.

She was afraid that day. She saw no one. She was alone in the wilderness. But gradually, the fear faded enough that she found the beauty of the place. She paddled south against the current and then rode it back to the north, and she took the kayak out of the river as the day faded and the last of the sunlight was filtered through the pines and cast a gorgeous green-gold sparkle over the water. She knew in that moment, bone-weary but renewed, that she could take whatever challenges Hammel sent her way.

She thinks of the river now, remembering the fragrance of pine needles and the feel of the cool water and the soft cry of a loon. Remembering the green and gold light on the bejeweled surface of the river, the river that flowed north instead of south. This river that she had conquered alone.

She blinks. Not a full blink, but a Tara blink, a flick of the eyes.

The tube fills with blue light. The MRI chamber darkens, and this actually helps, because she's less aware of the squeeze of the tight space now, and she can see the movie playing on the screen.

The scene shifts to a woman running across sand dunes and alongside a battered wooden fence. A young man behind her, breathless, calling out, "What's your name again?"

Chrissie, Tara thinks before the answer comes.

She knows it all. The most re-watchable movie of all time—all due respect to *Shawshank,* but the prize has to go to *Jaws*—and the only thing Tara has to do now is watch it once more while lighting up the correct areas of her brain.

No pressure.

Chrissie and the boy keep up their stumbling run along the darkened ocean, peeling their clothes off awkwardly, and he yells at her to slow down, then tumbles drunkenly onto the dune as Chrissie dives into the lapping sea and swims out into the dark water.

Tara tracks the action, but her mind is on the first time she saw the movie, at their house in Shaker Heights back when Dad was still alive. They'd sent her to bed, saying she was too young, but Shannon had crept in and told her she could see the screen from the back of the hallway.

Just don't make any noise, Shannon had commanded. *If you make any noise, they'll know you're here.*

They hadn't known. Tara had passed that test. Now it's the same test, and she needs to fail it. *Make some noise, T.,* she tells herself. *Let them know you're here.*

Chrissie is swimming toward the buoy, alone in the sea. Smiling, tossing her blond hair. Then the camera angle changes and shows her from below. Legs dangling.

And the music starts.

The first soft notes, growing louder as the camera closes in, Chrissie floating in graceful, blissful ignorance and then—

Tara's heart thumps with Chrissie's first scream.

She's seen the damn movie a hundred times, and still she cringes, no different than that night back in the dark hallway when she was seven years old.

Chrissie thrashes, screams, cries for help. Her drunk boyfriend is passed out on the shore, waves teasing the soles of his bare feet. Out in the blue-black sea, Chrissie grabs the buoy and clings to it, a moment's safety, a last desperate chance.

Then the unseen attacker has her again, tugging her toward deep, dark water, while the only one who can save her is sprawled on his back in the sand, oblivious.

"Please help!" Chrissie screams. Her last words before she vanishes from the screen, pulled into the depths.

Good-bye, Chrissie, Tara thinks. *I heard you.*

But did her auditory cortex activate? Did Tara put out a glimmer of light for poor Chrissie?

She will know soon.

29

Abby woke before dawn, stiff and aching but rested. Reality crept back, terrible memories of the previous day, and when she sat up, her hand brushed the stock of the SIG Sauer. The touch of the gun removed the last vestiges of hope that this might have been a vivid nightmare.

A nightmare, yes. But not the kind you woke up from.

She rose and stretched, the sound of her popping joints loud in the empty house. Her throat throbbed and there was pressure behind her eyes and under her jaw that promised the arrival of a cold. Hardly a surprise; she'd spent one night bedded down in wet leaves and the next on the wood floor of an empty house. She went into the bathroom and splashed her face with water, then cupped her hands and drank. The water had a mineral taste to it, but that was fine, and the cold of it soothed her throat. She walked back out and stood on the second-floor landing. Moonlight filtered down from above, and she followed it up the stairs and into the third-floor master suite. She sat on the floor there and stared at the shadowed trees as the moonlight gave way to gray and then to rose hues and then the world was back, though it didn't feel like the world she knew. Abby was alone in a strange house in a strange town, sitting in a bedroom that contained absolutely nothing but a scoped rifle she'd stolen from a murdered friend.

How many hours had it been since she'd grudgingly boarded the train to Boston to meet with Shannon Beckley?

A different lifetime. But she'd been in this situation before, in a way. More than a few times.

The first time she'd flipped a car, it had been in New Hampshire. She'd known her tires were thin, but there were seven laps left and she was sitting in third and although her engine was overmatched by the two cars in front, she was sure she could beat them. She'd gotten outside on turn two and the car in front moved to block her while the leader shifted inside to attack the straight-away, and Abby saw a gap opening like a mistake in a chess game. It was going to be tight, and it was going to test what was left of her tires, but she could do it.

She'd made the cut to the inside and then the back wheels drifted and she knew it was trouble but she tried to ride it out, punching the accelerator, eyes locked on that closing gap. When the contact came from the back of the driver's side, she wasn't ready for it. It knocked her car to the right and then the tires were shrieking as they tried to hold on to the asphalt like clawing fingernails. Then she was airborne. And dead.

Or that's how it had felt. A detached sense of foolishness—*You had third, and third was fine*—paired with the certainty of death.

The car had flipped twice before it hit the wall, but somehow she was upright when it was done, and people were reaching for her and shouting and a stream of fire extinguisher foam was pounding against her.

She was sitting on the gurney in the back of the ambulance, the doors still open, offering a view of the track, when she thought: *This was my last race.*

She'd been wrong about that too.

Either you quit or you picked yourself up and moved on. For a long time, Abby's greatest asset had been her ability to get back behind the wheel after a wreck and feel right at home. You wrecked again; of course you did. You expected death again; of course you did.

But you kept on moving. Up until Luke, she'd always been able to do that.

Up until Luke, she'd also always been alone in the car.

She was alone again now, and there was wreckage behind her, but she knew these feelings. There were similarities between what had happened to her yesterday and what had happened to her on the track; anyone who said otherwise had never flipped a car at 187 miles per hour, never walked out of a cloud of flame.

You survived only when you kept moving. Yesterday, Abby had done that. She'd been all instinct and motion. That had felt right to her. She'd felt more right, in fact, than she had in a long time, which was a damned unsettling realization.

Today she did not feel right. She was frozen and indecisive. Did she call David Meredith to learn what they'd made of the scene, see if she could trust him? Maybe they'd found enough to back up her story already. Maybe she'd slept on the floor in a vacant house for no reason. She needed the internet, but she'd crushed her phone back at the service plaza. She'd have to risk taking the Tahoe out so she could find a Walmart and pick up a burner phone with cash.

"You're an idiot," she said aloud, voice echoing off the hardwood floors and empty walls. She shook her head, got to her feet, and went down the steps to the bathroom where she'd stowed the bag of iPhones from Savage Sam. She took them back upstairs, where she figured the signal would be best, sat down in front of a wall outlet, separated the phones and paired them with chargers. Three phones and only two chargers. She plugged two in and waited for them to power on. Only one was protected by a PIN code, but it had no signal, as if it were old and forgotten or maybe its owner had suspended service on it. It would still work if connected to Wi-Fi, though, and the PIN code would be easy enough to defeat; you just reset the phone to factory settings.

One problem there—people were being murdered over whatever was on these phones, and deleting that material didn't seem wise.

The other phone was functional but had absolutely no personal data. Maybe Savage Sam had wiped it clean in preparation for selling it? Or maybe Oltamu had wiped it clean for other reasons?

She picked up the third phone, and something felt wrong about it immediately. The weight was off. It was in a simple black case with a screen protector, and it looked for all the world like the others, but it was too heavy.

She brought the charger to the base of the phone but couldn't find the port. She turned it over, looking to see how she'd missed the charging port on a phone that looked like a twin of her own.

It wasn't there.

An electric tingle rode up her spine.

The top of the phone had a power button that looked standard. When she pressed it, the screen lit up, and the display filled with what appeared to be the factory-setting background of a new iPhone. She hit the home button, expecting to be denied access, but she was greeted with a close-up image of Tara Beckley's face. Tara was smiling uncertainly, almost warily, into the camera, and behind her was a dark sky broken by a few lights from distant buildings.

Below the photo were the words Access authentication: Enter the name of the individual pictured above.

When Abby tapped the screen, a keyboard appeared. She moved her thumb toward the *T* on it, then stopped. She wasn't sure what she was opening here. If this phone actually belonged to Tara Beckley, it was a strange and poor security feature—a selfie asking for your own name? Then there was the question of the weight, which was decidedly different from a standard iPhone's. She pulled off the case and checked the back and found no Apple logo and no serial number. If it was a phone, it was a clone, a knockoff. But if it wasn't a phone...what did it do?

It had one hell of a battery, that was for sure. It had been at the salvage yard for a week and had no charging port, and still it ran without trouble. Definitely not the iPhone of Abby's experience. But it looked like one. Would it act like one? Would it ring?

She picked up the phone that actually functioned and plugged it back into the charger. Then she went downstairs, out of the house, and into the crisp autumn day. The wind was coming in off the sea, and the smell of salt was heavy in the air. She could hear waves breaking on rocks. Down there, beyond the trees, it would be violent, but up here it sounded soothing.

She found the Hammel College case file in the backseat of the Tahoe and scanned through the loose pages and old photographs, all of it feeling surreal and distant—the idea that this had once been merely a job for Hank and her seemed impossible, laughable. It was the whole world to her now.

College administrators had provided the paperwork that had been given to the conference coordinator; it included two phone numbers for Oltamu, helpfully labeled *office* and *mobile,* and a note saying that the doctor preferred to be called before nine or after three.

Abby didn't think Oltamu would mind the disturbance anymore.

She took the contact sheet, went back upstairs, punched the mobile number into her one working phone, and called, staring at the bizarre clone phone with Tara Beckley's face on the display.

It won't ring, she thought, but then she heard ringing.

She was so surprised that it took her a moment to realize it was from the phone at her ear.

She was about to disconnect the call when the voice came on.

"Hello?" A man, speaking softly and with a trace of confusion. Or fear.

Abby looked at the phone as if she'd imagined the voice. The call was connected. She had someone on the line.

"Hello?" the man said again.

Abby brought the phone back to her ear and said, "I was looking for Dr. Oltamu."

There was a pause, and then the voice said, "Dr. Oltamu is unavailable. May I ask who's calling?"

Abby hesitated and then decided to test him. "My name is Hank Bauer."

Pause.

"Hank Bauer," the man echoed finally, and Abby thought, *He knows. The name means something to him.*

"That's right," she said.

"And what can I do for you, Hank?" A bad impression of friendly and casual.

"Dr. Oltamu is dead," Abby said. "So who are you and why are you answering a dead man's phone?"

The silence went on so long that Abby checked to see whether the call was still connected. It was. As she started to speak again, the man finally answered.

"Would this be Abby Kaplan?"

"Good guess. Now, what's your name?"

"That's not important."

"Of course not." Abby got to her feet and started pacing the empty bedroom, the phone held tightly. "Give me another name, then—give me the kid's name."

"The kid."

"That's right. Tell me who he was and I won't need your name. I want him."

Another silence. Abby glanced at the display again—she'd been on the phone for thirty-seven seconds. How long was too long to stay connected?

"Do it fast," she said.

"I've got no idea what *kid* you're asking about. Or why you called this number."

"Then why did you answer?" Abby knelt and punched the home button on the clone phone, which brought up the picture of Tara Beckley. She was ready to tell the man on the other end of the line what she had, ready to try a bargain, but she stopped herself.

She thought she understood now, understood the whole damn thing—or at least a much larger portion than she had before.

I've been there, she thought, looking at the photo. The background over Tara's shoulder showed spindled shadows looming just past her pensive, awkward smile. Shadows from an old bridge. Abby had paced that same spot with a camera. That place was where this photo had been taken. Hammel College's campus was just across the river.

"You got the wrong phone," Abby said.

"What does that mean?" the man said, but his voice had changed, and he hadn't asked the question out of confusion—he was intrigued. Wary, maybe, but intrigued.

"The one you just answered doesn't matter," Abby said. "The one I've got does. It might not even be a phone, but it's what you wanted. It's what you need now."

When the man didn't speak, Abby felt a cold smile slide over her face. "You took two of them," she said. "You took Tara Beckley's phone and Oltamu's. That was the job. Other than killing him, of course. The job was to kill him and take the phones. I don't know why, but I know that's what you were trying to do. But there were three phones, and you didn't know that. That's the problem, isn't it?"

"Why don't you explain—"

"You missed one," Abby said. "And if you want it, you're going to need to give me the kid who killed Hank. Think we can make that trade?"

"I bet if we meet in person, we can work this out. Quickly. How about that, Abby? You're in some trouble, and I can ensure that it ends. You need some serious help."

"And you need that phone. So make a gesture of good faith. Tell me his name."

Pause. "I'd be lying if I told it to you. There's my gesture of good faith. Whatever name he's going by now, I don't know it."

For the first time, Abby believed him. "I need to come out of this alive," she said.

"You will."

"I'll believe that when you tell me where to find him."

No response. Abby looked at the phone again. What if the call was being traced? How long was too long? "Make a choice," she said.

"Okay. All right. But it will take me some time. And I'll need to know you've got the phone and where you are. You tell me that, I'll put him in the same place. How you handle it then is up to you."

"What do you call him?" Abby said.

"Huh?"

"Forget his real name. What do *you* call him?"

Another pause, and then: "Dax."

"Dax."

"Yes. But it won't help you. Trust me, he's not going to be located under that name."

"That's fine. You want the phone, you'll put him where I can find him. Agreed?"

"Tell me something about the phone."

"It's a fake, for one."

She could hear the man on the other end of the line exhale. "A fake?"

"Yes. It's built to look like an iPhone, but it's not one. Now— ready to make a deal on giving me your boy Dax?"

"Yes."

"Great. Then I'll call back. From a different number."

"Hang on. Tell me where you—"

Abby cut him off. "End of round one. Answer when I call again."

"Hang on, hang on, don't—"

Abby disconnected and stood looking at the phone. Her hand was trembling. She powered the phone down. She didn't want it putting out any sort of signal.

Who the hell was that? Who answered Oltamu's phone?

Not Oltamu, that was for sure. And not a cop.

The options left weren't good.

She sat beside Hank Bauer's rifle and picked up the fake phone, trying to imagine what had made it worth killing for and what Tara Beckley had understood about it when her photo was taken. The smile was uncomfortable, forced, and the man she'd been with had been killed a few minutes—seconds?—later. Tara had been sent spinning into the river below and then rushed to the hospital, where she now lay in a coma. But there was a difference between uncomfortable and afraid, and as Abby looked at her face, she was sure Tara hadn't been scared. Not yet, at least. Maybe after, maybe soon after, but not in the moment of that photograph.

Access authentication: Enter the name of the individual pictured above.

She hesitated, then typed Tara and hit Enter.

The display blinked, refreshed, and said Access denied, two tries remaining.

"Shit," Abby whispered, and she set the phone down as if she were afraid of it.

As if? No. You are afraid of it.

People were being killed over this thing, and for what? Something stored on it made sense, but wasn't everything cloud-based now? What would be on the phone that couldn't be accessed by a hacker? Hacking it seemed easier than leaving a bloody trail of victims up the Atlantic coast. She stared at the device as if it would offer an answer. It couldn't. But who could?

Oltamu.

Right. A dead man.

"Why'd they kill you, Doc?" she whispered.

She couldn't begin to guess because she didn't know the first thing about Oltamu. That was a problem. Abby was out in front, but she didn't know what was coming for her.

Look in the rearview mirror, then. Pause and look in the rearview.

To get answers, she would have to start with the first of the dead men.

30

Whenever the concealed microphones in Gerry Connors's office were activated, Dax Blackwell received an alert on his phone. Generally, he chose not to listen unless Gerry was in the midst of a deal. He was always curious to determine how Gerry valued his efforts, since in Dax's business, it was difficult to get a sense of the going professional rates. There weren't many Glassdoor.com reviews for what he did.

Today he listened, tucking in earbuds. He sat in the car with an energy drink in hand and listened to Gerry Connors give his name to Abby Kaplan.

He was surprised by how disappointed he felt. He'd known Gerry was a risk, because anyone who knew how to find you was a risk, and yet he'd had as much trust in Gerry as anyone on earth since his father and uncle had been killed.

Time to put that away, though. Disappointment wasn't a useful emotion; it did nothing to help your next steps.

And why be surprised? He remembered a day at the shooting range with his uncle and father, Patrick putting round after round into the bull's-eye from two hundred yards, totally focused, eye to the scope, and Dax's father looking on with the sort of pride that Dax wanted to inspire in him. Something about watching that shooting display had made his father reflective. Jack Blackwell tended to be philosophical when guns were in hand.

But that day, as Patrick racked the bolt and breathed and fired and hit, over and over, Jack Blackwell had watched his brother with fierce pride and then looked at his son and said, "Dax, if you find one person on this earth who would never fuck you over for money or women, you'll be a fortunate man. People like that are rare."

There you had it, then. Why feel disappointment in Gerry Connors when he was doing exactly what you'd expect him to? The only question was how to respond.

Dax sipped his energy drink and played the recording once more, then sat in silence, thinking, his eyes straight ahead. At length, he picked up his phone and called Gerry.

"It's me," he said. "I'm struggling here. Our girl Abby has done a good job of hiding. Any ideas?"

3 1

Gerry Connors had a decision to make, and he needed to make it fast. Abby Kaplan was out there doing exactly what Dax Blackwell had predicted—avoiding police and trying to make a play on her own. The German was out there, inbound and impatient, and he didn't even know what a mess this had turned into yet. And now there was Dax Blackwell on the phone asking for guidance, and Gerry had to decide whether to set him up or give him a chance.

It seemed impossible that he'd been put in this situation by some disgraced stunt-car-driving chick turned insurance adjuster.

The most intriguing part of the whole thing was that the kid had been right. Kaplan hadn't gone straight to the cops; she'd gotten scared and run. Gerry couldn't imagine how the kid had been so damned sure of this.

Yes, you can. You have always imagined it. He's one of them.

"Gerry?" Dax said. "Are you there?"

"Yeah. I'm here. And she's not hiding. She's calling people."

"Calling who?" Dax said, and he seemed pleased by the news.

Gerry looked at Amandi Oltamu's silent phone on his desk and wondered how long it would be before it rang again...and what Abby Kaplan would have done in the meantime. Beside the phone was a notepad on which Gerry had scribbled the number she had used to call him. He looked from the phone to the notepad, drumming a pen on the desk.

Trade Dax or trust him?

"Gerry?" Dax prompted.

"She's trying to make her own way out of this," Gerry said. "She might already be with the cops, but it didn't feel like it. She says she's got the phone, although she might be bluffing. But she understands the way it went, at least. She understands what Ramirez did wrong."

Dax was quiet for a moment, then said, "How do you know this?"

There he went again, pushing, fishing.

"My client," Gerry said tightly.

"How did Abby Kaplan reach your client?"

If he'd been in the room, Gerry might've shot him. Instead he squeezed his eyes shut, took a breath, and said, "She's calling Oltamu's phone."

"And your client was dumb enough to answer it?"

"Listen, shut the fuck up and let me talk, all right? She called the phone and spun some bullshit about trading for…safety. I don't know what that means to her exactly and probably neither does she—she just knows she's in trouble."

Dax didn't say anything this time.

"I want to know where she's calling from," Gerry said.

"I'd imagine."

Gerry would have shot him twice for that.

Trade him, then. Give him up.

"How'd you know she'd go this route?" he asked, and the kid must have heard the sincerity in his voice, because for once he wasn't a wiseass when he responded.

"A lot of factors. She likes to be on the move. Has her whole life. From the cradle until I finally put her in the grave, Abby's been about motion and speed. She doesn't have a good history with police either. There are still people in California who are pushing for her to be charged in the wreck that killed the pretty-boy actor. And…" He hesitated, that brief hitch that his father had never shown, or at least had never shown to Gerry, before he said,

"I guess you could call it my own instinct. Abby's not dumb, and I saw that, but I also made sure she knew that *I* wasn't dumb. Everything that's happened since is a reaction to our understanding of each other. That seems simple, but it's not. If someone is close to a mirror, you see it."

"Close to a mirror? What the hell does that mean?"

The kid gave it a few beats before he said, "I understand her. That's all it means."

"She's an insurance investigator. If you feel like she could work with you, then I've sorely underestimated your talents."

With no trace of annoyance, the kid said, "Oh, you haven't underestimated *my* talents, Gerry. Abby Kaplan's, though? She's something more than we'd have expected."

"Because she got away from you. That's all you mean. You don't want to admit that you screwed up with her. Because she got away, we need to pretend she's something special."

Still no inflection change when Dax said, "Didn't you tell me I was right in my prediction about how she'd choose to move, Gerry?"

"*Maybe* you were."

"She's on the run and she's calling you—sorry, calling your *client*. Give me the benefit of the doubt on this one. I was right about Abby."

"After you lost her."

"Once. Yes. After I lost her once." He was unfazed. "It won't happen twice."

Gerry said, "I've got the number she called from, and that's all I've got."

"It's a start."

"You need to work fast. This is going to go in one direction or the other very quickly."

"An object in motion tends to stay in motion," Dax Blackwell said cheerfully, "unless an external force is applied to it. Let's see if we can apply a little force. What's the number?"

Gerry read it off. "See what you can do with that, and let me know in a hurry."

"If Abby calls back, is your client going to answer that phone again?"

"How the fuck do I know?" Gerry snapped.

"I suppose you don't."

"Of course I don't. Just do your job."

"Right," the kid said, and he disconnected.

Gerry looked from his own phone to Oltamu's and found himself wishing Oltamu's would ring. *I'll make that trade, Kaplan. I had high hopes for this kid, but they're vanishing fast. You call back, and I will absolutely make that trade.*

But for now…

He couldn't make the trade until Kaplan called back. In the meantime, he could give the kid a chance to clean up the mess. Keep two plays alive until the right one announced itself and then act decisively. That was how you won.

Gerry would win this yet.

32

When both doctors enter the room together, Tara knows it's bad news. They've decided on an alliance, neither wanting to make the other crush a family's hope. Teamwork, then; they'll break hearts together. At the sight of the doctors, Mom and Rick and Shannon all rise to their feet, their voices loud and chaotic and too cheerful, as if pleasantries can change the outcome. Dr. Carlisle is all warm smiles and soft tones; Dr. Pine looks like a Zen shark, a good-natured predator swimming past potential victims, not yet sure if he'll turn and devour them. He eludes Rick's awful bro-hug-handshake hybrid with grace, then walks to Tara's side and looks her in the eyes.

"When this is all over," he says, "I want you to tell me everything that was said about me behind my back."

The room goes silent, and Dr. Carlisle appears vaguely annoyed. In that expression, Tara sees the results of the test—she passed, and Dr. Carlisle wanted to make the announcement.

She passed. Tara is positive. They know that—

"She's alert," Dr. Carlisle says, the annoyed expression gone and a radiant smile in its place. "Not just alert—fully and completely aware, cognitively and emotionally. Her results are extraordinary. Not unprecedented, but close. Every lobe reacted as it should have; her visual, auditory, and processing responses to the movie were perfect." She turns to Shannon and says, "And she certainly had an emotional response to the girl at the beginning of the movie. You weren't wrong about that."

Chrissie, Tara thinks. *Why can't anyone ever remember her name?*

That's when Mom falls on her knees beside the bed and presses Tara's hand to her face, her tears soaking Tara's palm, and then Shannon is there, saying how she always knew it, but her quavering voice gives her away, and Rick is the only one who holds back, but Tara can't blame him for that, and she's grateful that he's actually pausing to thank the doctors and is touched by the emotion in his voice.

"She's hearing us?" Mom says, staring at Tara with wonder. "You're sure? Right now, she's hearing me?"

"Every word," Dr. Carlisle promises, pulling a chair up beside the bed. Dr. Pine stays on his feet, smiling but pacing. Like any shark, he must keep moving or he will die.

"And she's always heard us?" Shannon asks, and Tara wants to laugh at the poorly suppressed guilt in her voice. Shannon is probably conducting an inventory of everything she let slip in moments when she thought she was alone. No matter what confidence they all professed, none of them were sure that Tara could hear a word. Now they are getting an awareness of that ghost in the room.

"I can't tell you when she came back or whether she's been alert the entire time; all I can tell you is that she is now," Dr. Carlisle says.

"What does that mean for her prognosis?" Shannon asks. Mom looks wounded by the question, as if it's in some way undermining the joy of what they've just been told, but it is also the question Tara would ask if she had a voice.

"Entirely unknown," Dr. Pine says. "But it only helps. One of the greatest challenges in rehabilitating the brain is the constant testing and guessing it requires from the medical team, from the family, everyone. Based on Dr. Carlisle's results, Tara is going to be able to help us enormously there. She may not have her voice, but she should be able to communicate. If we know what she's experiencing, feeling, and requiring, that is a tremendous advantage in treating her successfully." His eyes are locked on Tara with excitement.

I'm an opportunity to him, she realizes. *Something he's been waiting for for maybe his whole career.* It's an odd sensation but not a bad one—he wants to see if he can bring her all the way back. That's a goal Tara can get behind.

"There may be even more reason for celebration," Dr. Carlisle says. "When reviewing the video of Tara's face during the test, Dr. Pine noticed what seems to be some oculomotor progress."

"Oculomotor?" Mom echoes tentatively.

"She can blink?" Rick asks.

"Not quite...or at least not quite *yet,*" Dr. Pine says. "But the progress she's demonstrating since our initial tests may be more useful than even Tara knows."

He's studying Tara's eyes while moving his hand in the air like a conductor. The longer he does it, the more delighted he seems.

"Vertical eye motion," he says. He sits and perches with perfect posture on a stool beside her bed; he looks like a bird of prey. "She's regained that. Consistent with locked-in syndrome."

"Locked-in syndrome?" Rick asks, and he looks at Tara with something between concern and horror. The name seems self-explanatory, and terrifying. They're all learning now what Tara has been living with for days.

"Charming name, isn't it?" Dr. Pine says. "But it's clear, at least. Tara is with us, but Tara is trapped."

Mom murmurs something inaudible and puts her head in her hands.

"Not all bad, though," Dr. Pine continues. "Locked-in syndrome prevents outbound communication, yes, but it also, perhaps, provides some protection. And now that we know she's in there, we can work to bridge the void." He studies her with a slight incline of his head, then smiles. "Excellent."

Tara tracked the motion with her eyes, and he saw it. The rush of euphoria this realization brings is almost overwhelming, and if she could cry, she would. *He sees me. He sees me!*

"Locked-in syndrome is caused by an insult to the ventral pons," he says. "But with vertical eye motion, she's not as trapped as she was before. She should be able to communicate."

An insult to the ventral pons, Tara thinks. That's the term for having your brain knocked around your skull and leaving you unable to move or speak—an *insult*? The word seems woefully insufficient.

"Essentially, her condition has caused paralysis with preservation of consciousness and retention of vertical eye movement. She has some voluntary eyelid motion, but her response to the blink requests, as you saw, showed a lack of control." He leans forward and lifts a pencil with his thumb and index finger. "But there's progress. I think Tara *is* in control of her vertical eye motion now. Aren't you, Tara? Show them."

He lifts the pencil slowly, then lowers it. Mom gasps; Rick puts a hand on her shoulder that seems designed to steady himself as much as her, and Shannon stares at Tara, enthralled.

"Oh, honey," Mom says. "Oh, baby." She's squeezing Tara's hand and blinking away tears. Dr. Pine tolerates the interruption. Behind them, Dr. Carlisle paces and smiles.

Competitive, Tara thinks. *She found me in here first. He wants me now.* That is just fine with her. The more the merrier when it comes to people invested in her return, but she wonders if they'll remember who suggested she watch *Jaws*.

Mom releases her hand, rises, gets her iPad, then rushes back, holding it with the camera lens trained on Tara. She's shaking so badly it seems unlikely she'll be able to keep it in her hands, let alone in focus. Tara wants to laugh. For years, she and Shannon made fun of Mom's insistence on capturing every family moment on film, but even *now*?

Dr. Pine says, "Tara, let's try for yes and no. When you want to indicate a *yes* response, look up once. When you want to say *no*, do it twice." He pauses and wets his lips, and for the first time Tara sees that behind the clinical demeanor, he's nervous. "Okay," he says. "Tara, do you understand what I just said?"

She looks up. Once.

"Tara, does two plus two equal ten?"

She looks up twice.

Dr. Pine lets out a long breath. "We're batting a thousand," he says. "Tara, is Shannon your sister?"

Up once.

"Am I your father?"

Up twice.

Mom is crying now, tears streaming down her face, over those purple rings below her eyes that have darkened with each day in here; her iPad shakes in her hands like a highway sign in hurricane winds.

Shannon pushes in beside Dr. Pine, kneels, and looks at Tara with a trembling smile. "Tara," she says, "did you ever quit?"

Dr. Pine looks annoyed at the intrusion, but when Tara moves her eyes upward twice and they all burst into a clumsy hybrid of tears and laughter, he smiles charitably and lets them have their moment. He keeps watching Tara, though, his focus unbroken.

"Tara," he says, "would you like to try the alphabet board?"

Up once.

He stands. "Okay," he says, "let's see what she can do."

Yes, Tara thinks. *Let's see.* It's the first time she's been given an active role—even the crucial fMRI was passive; she was shoved into a tube and shown a movie—and the opportunity is both exhilarating and exhausting. The joy that comes with being known, with being breathed back into existence in the room, is an injection of adrenaline, but the eye tests were oddly fatiguing, as if simple willpower drains her. Perhaps it does. But she's got willpower reserves they haven't seen yet, and she'll figure out how to replenish them, locked-in or not.

"This is all just a starting point," Dr. Carlisle says. "Yes/no communication is, obviously, an enormous step. But we've got an open road ahead of us now."

Dr. Carlisle begins to talk about a combination of rudimentary alphabet boards and sophisticated computer software, and Dr. Pine chimes in with a discussion of tongue-strengthening exercises—those sound like fun. Mom returns to her chair and focuses on her iPad. Tara watches in astonishment as she taps away, seemingly oblivious to the conversation around her. *Are you bored, Mom? I'm back from the dead, but you've got e-mail to check?* Then Mom rises with a smile and brings the iPad to Tara and turns it to face her.

"You have no idea how badly I've wanted to be able to post this," she says, starting to cry again.

On the screen is the Team Tara Facebook page. Mom has pinned the video of Tara's eye-motion test with a caption: *We have blessed news! Tara is awake!*

33

Back when he'd been rehearsing for the fugitive role, asking Abby countless questions about how she'd handle herself on the run, Luke had given her a simple but memorable piece of advice: "Never underestimate the helpfulness of your local library."

On her first day as a fugitive, Abby headed for the library in Rockland. In Luke's script, there'd been dialogue about big cities being better to hide in than small towns, because nobody paused to look at a stranger in a place where *everyone* was a stranger. She believed that, but big cities were hard to come by in Maine, and so she settled for Rockland, the county seat, home to the courthouse and the jail and the BMV. A regular metropolis by Maine standards, with maybe twenty thousand residents.

She parked several blocks from the library, near the harbor in a busy parking lot that was shared by two seafood restaurants and a YMCA, and she walked along the water for twenty minutes, watching her back, before she moved toward town. No one followed. In the library, she found a computer where she could sit with her back to the wall and her eyes on the door.

When she logged on to the internet, her first instinct was to read about herself. Pragmatic fugitive behavior or clinical narcissism? She wasn't sure, but a cursory review of news sites was reassuring to her invisibility, if not her ego—the reports were that Hank Bauer had died in a car accident whose cause was currently under investigation. Police in Maine were keeping Abby's story quiet for a reason, or possibly they didn't believe it, but in any case, they weren't making a big deal out of her call to David Meredith.

Not yet.

She moved on to Amandi Oltamu. There was plenty to read here, because Amandi Oltamu had been an important man, but Abby was going to need a translator to help her understand half of it.

The obituaries were helpful but vague, capturing his childhood escape from a war-torn Sudan and his education history (Carnegie Mellon and MIT) and revealing that his marriage had ended in divorce and he had no children. He was described as "renowned in his field." *Okay,* Abby thought, *let's find out some more about that field.* A few searches later she landed on a paper written by Oltamu. The title was "Improving the Coupling of Redox Cycles in Sulfur and 2,6-Polyanthraquinone and Impacts on Galvanostatic Cycling."

It wasn't a good sign that Abby was tentative on the pronunciation of two of the words in the title.

She didn't waste time attempting to wade through the entire paper. If there was a clue in that paper, Abby wasn't going to be able to identify it. Instead, she went to the Hammel College site and found a short press release on Dr. Oltamu's scheduled talk. This one was at least a bit more civilian-friendly: He was going to speak on how batteries could combat climate change. The press release didn't mention anything about teenage assassins, though. Less helpful.

Oltamu's bio on the site said that he'd consulted with the International Society for Energy Storage Research. The ISESR page noted that his work was focused on a new paradigm for battery energy storage at atomic and molecular levels.

Terrific. And tragic. He'd been doing vital work, and then he was killed. Maybe the vital work was why he'd been killed. If so, that was going to require more understanding of the topic than Abby could glean from web searches. There was a better chance of her figuring out how to jailbreak the security on that cloned iPhone than of her determining the breakthrough Amandi Oltamu had made with regard to the new paradigm of galvanostatic coupling. Or cycling. Whatever. Understanding the importance of Oltamu's work required an advanced degree, or at least the ability to pronounce *polyanthraquinone* without sounding like Forrest Gump.

Jailbreaking the device Oltamu had left behind seemed like the better option, but Abby had failed once already. She'd tried *Tara* and not *Tara Beckley,* but if *Tara Beckley* was wrong, she was down to one swing of the bat. She still didn't understand the security approach either; shouldn't it be more advanced, a fingerprint or a retina scan or facial recognition?

Maybe it was. Maybe the prompt asking for Tara's name was a ruse, and the only way the device unlocked was with Oltamu's retina. That would be a problem, considering that by now he'd been buried or cremated.

Had Oltamu been trying to protect himself at the end, adding Tara Beckley's photograph as a lock just before Carlos Ramirez drove into him? Or was Abby's instinct wrong, and Oltamu hadn't taken the picture? Even if Abby was right about the location, and she was pretty sure that she was, it didn't mean that she was right about when it had been taken. For all she knew, it was Tara Beckley's Facebook profile picture.

Bullshit it is. Not with that smile. Something was wrong when that picture was taken. She wasn't sure what yet, but she knew something was wrong.

Tara's Facebook profile was private, but Abby found an open Facebook page called Team Tara, the one Shannon Beckley had said kept her mother occupied and away from tranquilizers. Abby opened it without much hope, then froze.

The first post was a video with a caption claiming Tara was awake.

She moved the cursor to the video and clicked Play. The camera was shaking, but Tara was clear, and so were her eyes. As a doctor asked her questions, she looked up. Once for yes, twice for no. The motion was unmistakable.

Her mother wasn't being optimistic; Tara was awake and responsive.

Abby whispered, "Oh, shit," loudly enough to earn an irritated glance from an old man reading a newspaper a few feet away.

Abby lifted a hand in apology and returned her attention to the screen. The video had been posted only a few hours earlier but already it had hundreds of shares, people eager to distribute this good news far and wide.

A blessing, yes. And maybe a terrible invitation.

She logged off the computer, picked up the case file, and left the library, then walked back down to the harbor and stood about five hundred yards from the Tahoe. She pretended to stare at the sea, but she was really looking for people watching the car. There was no obvious sign of interest in the vehicle, but right now everyone felt like a watcher. Paranoia was growing. She forced her eyes away from the parking lot and looked out across the water. The wind was rising, northeasterly breezes throwing up nickel-colored clouds, as if the morning's sunshine had been a mistake and now the wind was working hastily to conceal evidence of the error.

Abby knew that making contact with Tara Beckley's family would be a suicidal move. They'd rush to the police, bring more attention, and, quite possibly, kill whatever faint hope she had of trading the phone in her pocket for evidence that exonerated her in Hank's death and for the chance to send his murderer to prison. It was too early to reach out; she'd be better off walking into the police station.

Unless the family believes you.

Unless that, yes.

She watched the ferry head out from Rockland toward Vinalhaven, and she thought of the way Tara's eyes had flicked up at the doctor's questions, the responsive motion so clear, so undeniable, and then she thought of the countless tests Luke had failed. Then she withdrew the working cell phone from her pocket, the one she'd promised herself she wouldn't use again. Just by turning it on, she was broadcasting her location.

But she had to try.

She opened the case file she'd taken into the library and flipped through it in search of another number. Not Oltamu's this time. Shannon Beckley's. She dialed.

Shannon answered immediately. "Hello?" A single word that conveyed both her confidence in herself and her distrust of others. She wouldn't have recognized the number, so she was probably already suspicious.

"This is Abby Kaplan and it is very important that you do not hang up. You need to listen to me, please. You've got to listen to me for Tara's sake."

She got the words out in a hurry. She had to keep the conversation short on this phone.

"Sure," Shannon said. "Sure, I remember you." Her voice was strained, and Abby heard people talking in the background and then the sound of a door opening and she understood that Shannon was leaving a crowded room. She was at least giving Abby the chance to speak.

"Have they told you I killed Hank Bauer yet?" Abby asked.

"They have." She spoke lightly, as if trying not to draw concern or attention, and Abby heard her footsteps loud on the tiled floor of the hospital. She was walking away from listeners.

"It's a lie. We were both supposed to die and I made it out."

"That's different than what I've heard."

"I'm sure it is. If I could explain it, I'd have gone right to the police. But Hank is dead because whoever killed Oltamu—and Ramirez, there are three of them now, all of them dead..." Her words were running away from her and she stopped and took a breath, forcing herself to slow down. "Whoever did that wants a phone. Not your sister's, and not Oltamu's real phone. One that he had with him, maybe. I'm not sure it's actually a phone; it might just be a camera designed to look like one. But I've got it."

"What does—"

"Hang on, listen to me. I just read a post from your mother's Facebook page that claims Tara is alert. I saw the video. That needs to come down."

"What? Why?"

Abby looked at how long she'd been on the call—twenty-five seconds. "I've got to hurry," she said, "and I don't have all the answers you're going to want, but you have to limit access to Tara. And you have to limit the questions she's asked. Because if she remembers what happened that night, then she's a threat to somebody. Three people are already dead, and that's just the ones I know of. I was supposed to be the fourth."

Shannon Beckley didn't speak. Abby wanted to be patient, but she couldn't. Not on this line.

"If you think I'm crazy, fine, but I'm trying to give you a chance," she said. "Trying to give *her* a chance."

Shannon's voice was low when she said, "I don't think you're crazy."

"Thank you."

"But I can't limit access to her," she said. "There are too many doctors involved, and they're not going to let me call the shots. If you think she's at risk of being…killed, then who am I supposed to tell? Who do I call?"

The wind gusted off the water, peeled leaves off the trees, and scattered them over the pavement, plastering one to Abby's leg. She stared at the bloodred leaf, then looked over to where the Tahoe was parked. A man in an L. L. Bean windbreaker walked by it without giving it so much as a passing glance, but still Abby scrutinized him.

"I don't know who you call," she said finally. "If I knew, I'd call them myself. Maybe *you* can trust the police."

"You're not sure of that, though?"

"I'm..." She'd started to say she was sure, but she couldn't. All she could think of was the way the kid had smiled when he'd spoken of friends in cells and friends in uniforms. "I'm not sure," Abby finished. "Sorry. There has to be someone to call, but I don't know who the right person is, because I don't know who I'm dealing with. I don't know what Tara saw, what she heard."

She faced the hard, cutting wind and paused again, aware that she was letting the call go on too long but no longer caring as much because an idea was forming.

"Can you ask her the first round of questions?" she said. "Without doctors around, or at least without many of them. Can you handle that?"

"Questions about what happened that night?"

"Yes. You need to do that. But they have to be the right questions. They have to...they need to be *my* questions."

"What are those?"

"I'm not positive yet. I mean, I know some, but...let me think."

"You have to tell me what to ask!"

Abby squinted into the cold wind and watched the ferry churn toward the island, its wake foaming white against the gray sea, and then she said, "Ask her if he took a picture of her. I definitely need to know that. And if he did, then ask if she gave him another name."

"Another name? What do you mean, another name?"

"I'm not sure. If she called herself Tara or Miss Beckley or whatever. Ask what he knew her by. That's really important. What would he have called her?"

"She would have been just Tara. That's it," Shannon said, her voice rising, but then she lowered it abruptly, as if she'd realized she might be overheard, and said, "Why does this matter? What do you know?"

"People are killing each other to get to a phone that was in her car," Abby said. "I have it now. It was in the box I brought down to you. I don't know what in the hell is on it, but it looks like he took her picture. It's on the lock screen now, and it wants her name. But her name doesn't—"

The phone beeped in her ear then, and her first thought was the battery was low, but when she glanced at the display, she saw an incoming call, the number blocked.

The wind off the water died down, but the chill within her spread.

"Hang on," she told Shannon Beckley, and then she ignored her objection and switched over to answer the incoming call. "Hello?"

"Hello, Abby."

It was the kid.

34

Abby didn't speak.

She stood with the phone to her ear and her head bowed, eyes focused on the single red leaf fluttering against her dirt-streaked jeans.

The kid seemed amused when he said, "You *do* recognize my voice, right? I'm usually memorable. Apologies for the arrogance of that statement."

Abby reached down and flicked the leaf free from her jeans and watched it ride away on the wind. Finally, she found her voice.

"You didn't have to kill him."

"Kill who?"

"Fuck you."

"Exactly. This is how we can go for as long as you'd like, or you can make progress. The way I understand it, you're in a bit of a bind."

He talks like an imitation of a human, Abby thought. *Like he's not entirely sure how to walk among us, but he's studied it enough to fake his way. He's got the exterior down just enough to pass. What evil is on the inside, though?*

"I'll be needing that phone, Abby," the kid said, and right then someone down on the pier shook the remains from a bag of fast food into the water, and a handful of seagulls rose in wing and full-throated voice. They danced and dived and fought for French fries and the kid said, "On the coast, are we?"

Abby paced away from the water, a pointless effort given the piercing chorus of gulls, and wished death upon the indifferent diner who'd scattered his French fries to the wind.

"Yeah," she said. "Miami. Come south."

The kid's laugh was the only genuine thing about him.

"I like you, Abby," he said. "I mean that. But we really should get down to business."

Abby looked at the phone display. Twenty seconds and running. Shannon Beckley still on the other line. But the kid wasn't wrong. Abby had to get down to business or get to a police station, one or the other, and in a hurry.

"You want the phone, and I want you in jail," she said.

"There's not much to entice me in that scenario."

"I want you in jail," Abby repeated, "but I know I might not get that."

"Wise. So what do you need instead?"

"To keep myself alive *and* out of jail."

"Typical millennial. One thing is never enough. You want free shipping too?"

"The phone keeps me alive," Abby said. "The police will too. The right ones, at least."

"Be very cautious about that. Finding the right ones isn't impossible, but it won't be easy. Not for you. That's not a bluff. That's a promise."

He said it with calm, earned confidence. If Abby weren't already scared of his reach, she'd be with the police now, and they both knew that.

"Give me a number where I can call you back," Abby said.

"Call the German. He'll get me."

The German? The guy who'd answered Oltamu's phone had sounded anything but German. A trace of Boston accent, maybe, or a hint of Irish, but not German.

"You don't know him," the kid said. "Do you?"

"No."

"Interesting. Let me ask you something, Abby—do you need *me* to go to jail or do you just need somebody other than you to go?"

"I need the right person to go."

"Then you don't need me. Not if you care about the food chain."

"You killed him."

"Think I won't be replaced, Abby? You're smarter than that. I know you are."

Abby hesitated. "Hold the line a minute."

"What?"

Abby switched calls and spoke without preamble to Shannon Beckley. "I'm going to be in touch from a different number. Keep people away from Tara. If you see a kid, somebody who looks like he walked out of the high-school yearbook, call the police."

"What are you—"

"I won't blame you if you don't trust me. But you need to." She switched calls again. "Still there?"

"Yes," the kid said. "You have a recorder going now or a helpful witness listening, maybe?"

"No. I'm going to tell you where to find me."

"Oh?"

"Yeah. Listen real close so you don't miss it."

Abby left the call connected when she tossed the phone into the sea.

Before it reached the bottom of the harbor, she was running for her car, keys in hand. Even if she'd stayed on the phone long enough for them to trace it already, she'd be gone when they got here. It was time to get moving. Instinct told her to go farther north, to seek ever-smaller towns and more isolation, but she wanted to see Shannon Beckley. There was risk in that, of course, but maybe less than she thought. And Boston was a city filled with strangers. It would be easier to blend in there. They also had an FBI headquarters, probably even CIA. She could pick her police agency instead of relying on the locals. That's what she would do. Get to Boston, get to Shannon Beckley, and then get to the FBI. When she called Oltamu's phone again, she would be with the professionals. A day ago, she'd had nothing to tell them but the wild story about Hank's house, but now she had the phone that wasn't a phone, evidence of what all this killing was about, and that changed everything. They would believe her now.

She unlocked the Tahoe, slid behind the wheel, and cranked the engine to life. Her hand was on the gearshift when she felt the cold muzzle of a revolver press the base of her neck.

She moved her eyes to the mirror, and from the backseat, the kid in the black baseball cap smiled congenially.

"Found you," he said.

Part Four

EXIT LANES

35

Abby waited on the kill shot. There was no reason for the kid to hold off on it now. Unless he had a sadistic streak, which Abby thought he probably did.

He didn't take the shot. Instead, he said, "Go ahead and put it in drive."

Abby didn't move. Why make it easy on him? If she was going to die either way, she'd make the little prick take the shot in a crowded spot, where people would hear it and respond to the sound, where maybe surveillance cameras would give the police a lead.

"Abby?"

"Do it here," Abby said. She could feel the weight of the SIG Sauer in her jacket pocket, where she'd jammed it awkwardly, more concerned about concealment than access when she'd walked into the library. An amateur playing a pro's game.

"No."

"You're going to have to," Abby said, and as she spoke, her eyes drifted higher on the mirror, and she estimated the distance to the curb and the slope that led over the jogging path and down to the boardwalk and that deep-channel harbor. If she could get it in reverse and keep her foot on the gas, she'd at least be able to take this sociopath down with her.

"You think you're done?" the kid said, sounding surprised. "That's a disappointing attitude from someone with your resilience."

It was less than thirty feet to the curb, and once she cleared that, gravity might handle the rest. If the kid fired, the bullet was going to obliterate Abby's brain and any control she had over the wheel and the gas pedal, but as long as momentum and gravity worked together, the Tahoe might make the water.

"I was thinking we could go back to the house in Tenants Harbor," the kid said, and his smile brightened when Abby's eyes returned to him. "Yes, I knew you were there. Beautiful spot. Love that detached studio too. Made me feel creative. The whole place is nice and peaceful, though, much better than this parking lot. And we'll need to pick up your guns. They're likely to concern the Realtor."

When Abby still didn't move, the kid sighed and said, "If I wanted you dead, you'd be dead by now, get it?"

Abby pulled the gearshift down. She considered reverse, passed it, and put the car into drive.

"How'd you find me?" she asked.

"Bauer's phone is in the glove box, and I enabled tracking. I did the same to yours, but you were smart enough to get rid of that one. You didn't check the Tahoe out fully, though. Poor choice, Abby."

All day and all night, Abby had believed she was off the grid, hidden. In reality, she'd been exposed and at the kid's mercy.

"Why'd you let me live?" Abby asked, pulling out of the parking lot and turning right, then left, putting them back on Route 1, headed south.

"Priorities. You were there for the taking if I needed to do it, but the phone was the bigger problem, and I didn't think you had that. Tell me, where was it?"

"Under the driver's seat. You didn't check the Chrysler out fully. Poor choice, asshole."

The kid laughed, and suddenly the pressure of the gun was gone from Abby's skull. "I like you," the kid said. "I really do."

"It's not mutual."

"I struggle at first impressions. Give me time."

"Okay," Abby said, and then she added, "Dax."

It was the only card she had to play, the only thing she knew about him that might make him pause, but he took it in stride.

"There aren't many people left who call me that, but go right ahead. It's always been my preference. And, Abby? Keep a close eye on your speed, please. You're going pretty slow, and it would be a bad day to be pulled over."

"Where am I driving?"

"I told you."

"We're really going back to the house in Tenants Harbor?"

"I think we should. We could use a private, peaceful place like that to talk."

"Not much to talk about. You've won."

"Plenty to talk about, and if you hadn't polluted Penobscot Bay with that phone, we might already understand each other better. But I've always preferred face-to-face conversations, anyhow. We're going to be together for a while. Gerry is waiting on your call, and you will need to be alive to make that. Good news for you, right?"

"Gerry?"

"That's the name of the man who answered the other phone. Gerry Connors. Crusty old bastard. I liked him. For a long time, I liked Gerry just fine."

"He's the German?"

"No. He's not. But we'll get to the German before we're done, I think. I'm pretty sure we're going to need to do that."

He shifted in the backseat, and Abby looked in the mirror again and saw that he'd hooked his right foot over his left knee, as relaxed as a passenger in a chauffeured car. Which, Abby supposed, was exactly what he was now.

"You don't work for him?"

"I did. But I think the relationship is on the rocks at this point."

"I don't follow."

"Sure you do." He leaned forward. "You've already tested him. You offered him the phone for my life once. You're going to do the same thing again."

How did he know this? He'd known Abby's location; he knew

her movements, her calls, her words. How was he so damned omniscient?

"By the way, Abby, where is the phone now?"

She could lie, but what was the point? "My jeans. Front right pocket."

The kid nodded, satisfied. He leaned back in the seat, slouched and nearly uninterested, although the gun was still pointed at Abby's back. It would be easy to spin the car and throw off his balance, and Abby thought there was a good chance she could do that and buy enough time to get out, but she couldn't imagine she'd buy enough time to get out and find cover. The kid would shoot before then. Abby could flip the car, of course, but then she was as likely to die as he was.

"Do you know what's on it?" the kid asked. "Do you actually have a clue what's on the phone?"

"No."

"It's just a phone?"

Abby hesitated but realized there was no point in holding out. "It's a fake. Looks like an iPhone, but it isn't. As far as I can tell, it's not really a phone at all."

For the first time, the kid showed real interest. He shifted into the middle of the seat, where he could keep the gun trained on Abby's head and watch all of her movements, and said, "Pass it back to me, please. I'm trusting that you won't reach for the gun in your jacket instead. Remember, you're still alive due to my choices and to yours. Make the right ones."

Abby took her right hand off the wheel, slid the phone out of her pocket, and passed it back. The kid accepted it and leaned away. For a while, he didn't so much as glance at the phone; he kept his eyes on Abby, assessing her.

"Keep driving, and you'll keep living," he said. "Can you do that? Keep driving?"

"Yes."

The kid looked away then. Down at the phone. The gun was still in his hand, but his attention was compromised.

Flip the car. Just do it, you coward, flip it and take your chances. You'll have witnesses and people calling 911 and police cars screaming out here...

She kept driving. She couldn't will herself to flip the car, even though she'd walked away from worse before. She tried to tell herself it was because of the gun in the kid's hand.

While Abby drove, the kid alternated between glancing at her and studying the phone. He never lowered the gun, keeping it in his right hand as he turned the phone over carefully in his left. When he finally spoke, it was softly, almost to himself.

"Didn't expect that."

Abby didn't respond. The kid was silent for a moment, and then he looked up and said, "You know who's on the screen, don't you?"

"Yes."

"A picture of Tara. Interesting. Any idea why that would be there?"

"No."

"But you've taken a swing at it, I see. It looks like you tried her name, maybe?"

Abby nodded.

"Do you know why that didn't work?"

"No."

"Guess." The kid slouched back against the seat, the phone in his pocket now, all of his attention on Abby. "Show me some promise, Kaplan. Offer a strong theory."

"It's all fake."

"What does that mean?"

"That the picture is pointless, maybe. A smoke screen. It's not how you unlock the phone." She glanced in the mirror and saw the kid staring intently at her.

"How do you think the phone is unlocked, then?"

"I'm not sure."

"Give me another effort. I think you're close."

"A fingerprint. A PIN number. I really don't know."

"Actually, you're very close. Not bad at all. It's biometrics, but it's not a fingerprint. The camera is real, so I'm betting on facial recognition."

"Do you think it's really Tara's face that has to be recognized, though?" They were on a narrow stretch of the peninsula now, Penobscot Bay looming to their left, the sea gray-green under the massing clouds, a tower of battered lobster traps stacked high on a weathered wharf.

"Smart question," he said, and his voice softened in a way that made her think he hadn't considered the possibility before. "Is Tara the key that opens the lock, or is she a ruse? And if she is…" He let the sentence drift, then said, "I think she's the key. Smart play by Oltamu, if I'm right. Tara Beckley would have been anonymous to anyone who took the phone. She was a stranger. That's quite brilliant, really. The problem is that she stopped being a stranger that night. But he wasn't counting on that."

Abby didn't speak, but that didn't stop the kid from talking. It seemed nothing would stop the kid from talking. He liked conversation, and he liked to watch people. He reminded Abby of some demented dentist, poking and prodding, testing nerves, coaxing a reaction.

"I wonder if he told her what he was doing," the kid mused. "Was she just a face, or does she know something? If he was feeling urgency…maybe Tara knows a lot more than we think."

"Too bad she's gone," Abby said.

"Don't rush to judgment on that. I received an encouraging update on her condition this morning."

Fuck, Abby thought, and she was so defeated by that news that she let the speed fall off. The kid leaned forward and tapped her head with the gun.

"Pick it back up. Speed limit or five miles over, no more."

Abby accelerated to five miles over the limit. She tried to look indifferent to the discussion of Tara, but all she could think about was whether the kid had heard her talking to Shannon, whether he knew what Abby had disclosed to her.

"In fact," the kid said once he was satisfied with Abby's driving, "the news about Tara is particularly encouraging after seeing this. She can move her eyes, Abby. Isn't that wonderful?"

Abby was silent.

"Okay, maybe you're not a member of Team Tara. Rather cold-hearted, but to each her own. As a proud member of Team Tara, though, I'm especially encouraged after seeing the phone, because a lot of facial-recognition systems depend on active eyes. While once she might have been useless, now..."

He let the thought hang unfinished, then said, "Do you get it yet, Abby?"

Abby didn't want to engage with him again. Each time she did, she felt like the kid was seeing more of her brain, learning her heart. It was through his strange dialogue that he opened you up somehow, laid you bare on the table and decided whether there was anything in you worth keeping alive. If he decided the answer was no, that was the end.

"I think you do, but you're in a sullen mood. Understandable. It's been a tough couple of days for you. I'll explain what you already know, then, since you're not willing to play along. If I'm right, Abby, then what we have is a lock..." He lifted Oltamu's phone. "And Tara Beckley, bless her miraculous survivor's will, is the key."

He put the phone back into his pocket, braced his gun hand on his knee, and said, "That makes our next move pretty easy, doesn't it? We'll need to bring the lock to the key. Usually it would work the other way around, but we're in very atypical circumstances. Tell you what, Abby—we're going to detour. Forget the house and turn around. Right up here will work."

He nudged Abby with the gun. They were approaching the

Tenants Harbor village center, which amounted to a general store and the post office on the left, a volunteer fire department up ahead, and the school and the library somewhere off to the right. The street was empty save for one man in a rusted pickup filling plastic gas cans at the general store's pump. He didn't even look up when Abby pulled in behind him and then backed out. She didn't leave the parking lot, though. The clouds had obscured the sun and now the first drops of rain fell, fat and loud as they splattered on the hood.

"Where am I going?" she said.

"Southbound," the kid answered. "Boston or bust."

Abby kept her foot on the brake, and this time the gun muzzle found her ribs, a jab with more force.

"Don't sit here waiting to be noticed. Get on the move."

Abby eased her foot off the brake. She wasn't sitting there hoping to be noticed or expecting to find help in this isolated fishing village.

She was thinking about I-95 southbound in the rain. They'd hit the Boston area around rush hour, although every hour seemed like rush hour in Boston. Cars and trucks squeezing you from all sides, tens of thousands of drivers oblivious to the killing power controlled by their hands and feet.

And a sociopath with a gun in her backseat.

This was the first time she'd shared a car with anyone since Luke. Always, she'd made sure to drive alone in the days after that, making any excuse. No excuse offered itself now.

"Let's go," the kid said, and Abby moved her foot to the gas.

The Tahoe rolled out of the general store's parking lot and passed the post office; the North Atlantic was visible briefly to the right, then gone. Abby drove on through the gathering gray as the coastal fog swept in. She told herself this would be fine, this was the simple part, whatever came next was the trouble.

Faster, Abby, Luke had whispered just before the end. *Faster.*

Or had it been *Slow down*? It was so damned hard to remember.

36

The hospital room is abuzz with joy, yet Shannon seems distant.

Tara doesn't understand this at all. Shannon, her champion, the one who would never quit on her, is somehow the most distracted person there. She's left the room four times now, and each time she returns, the phone in her hand, she seems farther away. She's stopped looking Tara in the eye and she seems, inexplicably, more concerned now than she was before Dr. Pine and Dr. Carlisle arrived with their good news.

What does she know that I don't?

Recovery prognosis. That has to be it. Either the doctors have been more honest with Shannon than they've been with Mom and Rick or Shannon is doing her own research. Maybe Shannon understands already what Tara fears—it would have been better if she'd failed the tests, because there's no return to real life ahead of her. Nothing but this awful limbo, only now they all know she's awake and alert, and that means they feel an even greater burden of responsibility. Endless days of one-way chatter, countless hospital bills, all to sustain an empty existence. This would defeat even Shannon's willpower.

But the doctors are excited, and the disconnect there is confusing. It's also something Tara can't focus on any longer, because Dr. Pine is demanding all of her attention. In his hands he has a plastic board filled with rows of letters, each row a different color. The first row is red, the second yellow, the third blue, then green, then white. At the end of the red row is the phrase *end of word*. At the end of the yellow row is *end of sentence*.

This is Tara's chance to speak.

"It's going to feel laborious," Dr. Pine warns, "and you might get tired. It's more work than people would guess."

He's right about that. Even the yes/no answers were draining. But Tara is a marathon runner. She knows how you keep the finish line from invading your thoughts too early.

"Do you have enough energy to give this a try?" Dr. Pine asks.

She flicks her eyes up once.

"Terrific. What I'm going to do is ask you to spell something. You get to pick what it is. You're in charge now, Tara, do you understand?"

She flicks her eyes up again and feels like she could laugh and cry simultaneously—she's paralyzed, but he's telling her that she is in charge, and right now, that doesn't seem as absurd as it should. The simple possibility of communicating is empowering, almost intoxicatingly so. Her message is within her control. Such power. So easily taken for granted.

"Tell us whatever you want to tell us," Dr. Pine says, "but I'd suggest a short message to begin. The way we get there is simple— we're going to spell it out together. That means I've got to narrow down the first letter of the word. So I'll ask whether it's red or yellow or blue. You will tell me yes or no. Once I have the color, we'll go through the letters. You'll tell me yes or no. If I'm trying to go on too long, you'll tell me that we're at the end of the word or the end of the sentence." He studies her. "It's not easy. But stay patient, and let's give it a try. Do you have a message ready for your family?"

Does she have a message? What a question. She's overflowing with messages, drowning in them. There is so much she wants to tell them that the idea of picking just one thing freezes her momentarily, but then she remembers to flick her eyes upward, because he has asked a question and is waiting on the answer. Yes, she has a message.

"Great," he says. "Now, is the first letter red?"

Two flicks. No.

"Yellow?"

No.

"Blue?"

One flick.

"Is it *I*?" No. "*J*?" No. "*K*?" No. "*L*?"

One flick. Tara is exhausted, but she has her first letter on the board.

Next letter. Not red, yellow, or blue. Green. Then she gets a break—finally, it's the first letter in the column. One flick, and she has her second letter on the board: *O*.

It's harder than any race she's ever run. She's exhausted, and the focus makes her vision gray out at the edges, blurring the columns and letters, but she's not going to quit now. Not until it's out there. Her first words, tottering forth into the world like a newborn. She has to deliver them, even if they're also her last.

L
O
V
E
End of word
Y
O
U

They're all crying now, Mom and Rick and Shannon; even Dr. Pine might have a trace of mist in his eyes, but maybe that's Tara's blurring vision.

"Tara," he says, "you just spoke. And they've heard you."

She wants to cry too. She's so tired, but she has been heard, and it is remarkable. It feels like all she has ever wanted.

"Do you have another message you want to share with us right now?" Dr. Pine asks.

Two flicks. No. She got out the one that mattered most. She can rest now.

She fades out, grateful for the break, as Dr. Carlisle begins to talk excitedly about computer software that should make this a faster process, and Rick asks if there's a more holistic approach, which makes Shannon tell him to shut up and let Dr. Carlisle finish, and Mom tells her not to talk like that. The conversation is a chaotic swirl but Tara is not put off by it because they know she's there now, they know she's hearing it all. She's so relaxed, relieved, and so, so tired. The last thing she hears before she drifts off is Dr. Pine excusing himself from the room. That makes her smile. She thinks he's happy to leave Dr. Carlisle to handle this mess.

"I have to make a phone call," he says.

Yeah, right, Doc. People have used that excuse around my family before.

The last sound she hears before sleep takes her is the soft click of the door closing behind him.

37

Boone's phone began to ring while the plane was still descending, and she caught a reproachful look from one of the flight attendants.

"Airplane mode until we're on the ground, please."

"Right," Boone said. She'd never used airplane mode in her life, preferring to have her phone flood with e-mails and messages while they eased down through the clouds. If this habit were truly dangerous, a lot of planes would be tumbling out of the sky, she thought. But why quibble with the flight attendant—Boone's business cards said Department of Energy, but her expertise wasn't really in that field.

Instead, she simply silenced the phone while pretending to put it in airplane mode. The caller went to voice mail. Boone looked at the number and didn't recognize it, but the area code was Boston's.

It's a big city, she thought, trying to tamp down the swell of hope. *Could be anyone, about anything. Could be the boneheads in the Brighton PD calling to state their unequivocal confidence that Carlos Ramirez was killed in a drug buy gone bad.*

Or it could be her one hope: Dr. Pine.

She held the phone in her lap as the plane made what now felt like an endless descent, and as the signal strengthened, the iPhone offered an awkward attempt at transcribing the voice mail. While some of it was clearly a mistake—she doubted the phrase *jazz trombone* would be involved—the first words were crystal:

Hello, this is Dr. Pine.

Son of a bitch, son of a bitch, son of a bitch. There was hope. Dr. Pine meant there was hope.

The plane finally hit Tampa tarmac, tires shrieking, cabin shuddering. Boone was in the aisle seat, still staring at her phone, and when she didn't rise instantly at the chime indicating they were now free to take off their seat belts and exit the plane, the passenger beside her cleared his throat loudly and made an impatient gesture toward the aisle, where people were attacking the overhead bins in a frenzy, as if they'd all boarded the last flight out of a failed nation-state. Actually, Boone had been on two of those flights, and they weren't all that energetic.

She unclipped her seat belt and rose, ducking her five feet ten inches to avoid the overhead bins but never taking the phone from her ear. Now she could hear what the transcription software had missed.

"Hello, this is Dr. Pine, in Boston. I trust you'll remember me. I just left a pretty jazzed-up room. Tara Beckley is alert. She has what we call locked-in syndrome. This means her ability to move and vocalize her thoughts is lost, at least temporarily, possibly forever, but her mind is intact, and she is aware. I just asked her to spell out a message to the family and she completed this task successfully. She is also capable of answering yes-or-no questions." He paused, and Boone could sense both his pride in the moment and his conflicted feelings about sharing the information.

"I'm not sure if I would have made this call if not for the mother," he continued. "She's making regular updates on social media, broadcasting Tara's condition to the world. Since it seems the news will not be hard to find, I suppose I will take a chance on telling you. If, as you once suggested, her life may be in danger...well, we're going to need to take swift action on that. I didn't know how to keep the mother from sharing this joyful news. Perhaps this is why you should have dealt with the family to begin with. At any rate, this is Tara's status at the moment. If you have any questions that don't involve a deeper invasion of my patient's confidentiality, I would be happy to answer them."

"You stupid bitch," Boone said aloud, and though the sentiment was directed at a joyful mother two thousand miles away, her seatmate clearly thought it was for him as he rushed to pull his bag out of the overhead bin. Boone ignored his umbrage while she called Pine back. *Answer, damn it. Answer.*

She was on the jet bridge being jostled by the crowd when he picked up.

"You've got to shut her down," Boone said without preamble.

"Pardon?"

"Protect that girl. Limit access to her and get the mother to pull that shit off the web."

"Isn't this *your* role?"

"Yes, it is. But I just touched down in Tampa, where I'm not even going to leave the airport, I'll just get the first flight back north. In the meantime, I need your help." She felt a rush of humid Florida air as she crossed the jet bridge and entered the terminal, and then the blast of air-conditioning washed it away and brought harsh reality along with the temperature drop. Boone was in the wrong city and she could not fix what had already happened. She said, "It's too late to pull the news down, isn't it? People will have gotten notifications as soon as she posted. They'll be sharing it. So we don't need to worry about the mother. We just have to limit the people who have access to the girl."

"This simply isn't my role," Dr. Pine said. "You need to get the police to talk with this family if they are—"

"I understand your role, and I understand mine much better than you do. Bringing police off the street and into that hospital will only make things worse. I just need to interview her. That's all. You say she's able to communicate."

"In a limited fashion, yes."

Boone fought through the crowd to a row of flight monitors and looked for the next departure to Boston. It was a three-hour wait. Not great, but not terrible either. She wouldn't be able to charter a plane much faster, and until she knew if Tara Beckley had any memory of the event, nobody was going to approve that budget item.

"Does she remember what happened?" she asked.

"I don't know. That wasn't today's priority. Again, this is simply not within the—"

"A lot of the risk depends on whether she has any memory at all of the moments around Oltamu's death," Boone said. "You need to find out if she remembers the night."

"That's *your* job!"

"And I'm going to do it. But Doctor? You're there. She's there. Her protection and her threat are both still outside the hospital walls. Want to make sure the right one gets there first? Find out if she remembers the night. I don't need you to interrogate her, I need you to assess whether she has any memory of it. It's that simple, and it's that crucial."

Silence. She thought about waiting him out but decided to press instead. "When you do that, make sure the mother is out of the room. Then call me immediately."

She hung up on his protest.

Did it matter that Tara Beckley was back? It was surprising—stunning, actually, based on the initial diagnosis—but it wouldn't mean a damn thing if she couldn't remember her ride with Amandi Oltamu. If she had any memory of that night, she would be of use. Boone was confident of that because of Oltamu's last message.

Ask the girl.

Boone walked toward the nearest Delta gate. If she could get on the next flight to Boston, she would ask the girl. And if the girl remembered?

If she woke and remembered, they'd need the best in the game. If she woke and remembered, they'd need Boone.

38

A bby did fine until they reached Portland.
Driving out of Tenants Harbor and back to Rockland, she
stayed on winding two-lane country roads that were no problem,
and in Rockland she picked up Route 1 heading south, although it
would have been faster to take 17 west all the way to Gardiner,
where she could jump on the interstate.

She was in no hurry to get on the interstate, though. She was
in no hurry, period. She wanted time to think and plan, and if the
kid was bothered by her choice, he didn't voice concern. Didn't
voice anything at all, surprisingly. His focus was undeniable, his
eyes and the muzzle of the gun returning to Abby any time she so
much as shifted position, but at last, finally, he was silent.

He seemed to want this time to think too, although they were
contemplating different goals. Abby wondered if he was any closer
to understanding how to reach his.

Traffic was minimal on Route 1, the occasional chain of stoplights in one coastal village or another breaking things up, and the
road always had a shoulder if she needed it, a place to pull over and
catch her breath and focus her eyes.

They curled through Wiscasset and up the hill where, in the
summer, tourists would gather in long lines outside Red's Eats
waiting for lobster rolls, and then they crossed the Kennebec River
into Bath, where naval destroyers rested in their berths at the
last major shipbuilder in Maine, Bath Iron Works. Once they'd
made five-masted schooners here; now they made Zumwalt-class
destroyers at four billion dollars a ship.

The hills were lit with fire-bright colors, but clouds kept pushing in, and the rain fell in thin, windswept sheets, flapping off the windshield like laundry on a line. The pavement was wet, but the Tahoe's tires were good and the car never slipped. Abby was trying to think about the things that mattered—Tara and Shannon Beckley in Boston, the kid with the gun in the backseat, those vivid, real things—and yet her mind drifted time and again to the feel of the tires on the wet road, to the weight of the car pressing on the curves, and to the fear that she would push too far, too fast. The power of a phobia was extraordinary. *Yes, I know there's a gunman right beside me, but I think I just saw a spider in that corner...*

It was as if the brain couldn't help but yield the battlefield when a phobia appeared, no matter how irrational the fear.

Just drive, she told herself, breathing as steadily as she could. *Just drive, and keep an eye on that shoulder, and know that at these speeds, nothing that bad can happen. You're in a big car, cruising slow.*

She was through Brunswick and her mind was on the upcoming I-295 spur and its increase in speed and traffic when the kid broke the silence for the first time in nearly an hour.

"We'll need to lose the Tahoe before we hit civilization."

For a moment, Abby was ridiculously pleased, as if they were going to take the bus or the train from here while the kid held the gun on her and smiled at the other passengers in his polite but detached fashion. He added, "We should be in my car already, but I had different visions of the way this day was going to play out. An oversight on my part. Oh, well. We've got options. Stealing a car is one, but that has its own risks. The other option is at your office, I believe. The sports car. What kind is it?"

A shudder in her chest, cold and sudden, like a bird shaking water from its wings.

"You know the car I'm talking about," the kid said. "What is it?"

"Hellcat," Abby managed. Then, clearing her throat: "A Dodge Challenger. Hellcat motor."

"Nice ride. The title is in Bauer's name, but the police already searched his office, and I doubt they thought to add that plate to the mix, since the car was still there. It was pretty clear what car of his you stole after you killed him."

To Abby, the idea of shifting to the Hellcat somehow seemed worse than the lies he was telling.

"I also doubt they're waiting for you there," he continued. "Small county with limited resources, and common sense says you're not going to show up at the office. So we will."

"Back roads," Abby blurted.

"Excuse me?" The kid leaned forward, the gun's chrome cylinders bright in Abby's peripheral vision.

"I'll need to take the back roads to get there. Otherwise, we'll go through the toll. The tollbooth cameras will pick up this plate. They're wired in with state police."

She had no idea if this was true, but it sounded good.

It also apparently sounded good to Dax, because he leaned back and said, "Good call, Abby. I knew there was a reason I'd entrusted the driving to you. Take the back roads, then. We're in no hurry."

The approach allowed her to avoid the I-295 spur and stay in the thickening but slow-moving traffic, bouncing from side street to side street, grateful for the stoplights and speed limits. It added at least forty minutes to the journey, and in truth they wouldn't have had to pass through a tollbooth, but Dax evidently wasn't familiar enough with the area to know that.

Abby's focus was entirely on keeping control—of the car and of herself—until they reached the office. Then the memory of Hank's dead face, his head rolling on his broken neck, rose, and she felt sick and shamed. Not only had she been unable to save Hank; she was now chauffeuring around the man who'd killed him.

Dax was sitting tall in the backseat as they approached, head swiveling, scouting the surroundings for any watchers. There were none.

The office of Coastal Claims and Investigations had once been a hair salon, and Hank had kept some of the mirrors and one of the barber's chairs. He'd insisted the chair was comfortable and too expensive to waste, and he liked to sit in it and have a cigar while he read the paper, which always made him look like a man waiting on a ghost to cut his hair.

The building and its oversize detached garage sat alone in a large gravel parking lot surrounded by empty fields. There was a Dunkin' Donuts visible just down the road, and a gas station across from that. They were the only possible places for covert surveillance, but Abby agreed with the kid—the police would have seen no purpose for that.

"Drive past," Dax said.

Abby cruised by, came to the four-way stop with the gas station and the Dunkin' Donuts, and waited for instructions. The kid was leaning close again, the gun in Abby's ribs.

"If you saw something out of place, speak now or forever hold a hollow-point in your heart."

"Looked clear. He has security cameras, but they don't work. Just a deterrent."

"I noticed that in my previous visit, but I appreciate your honesty. Okay. Go on back."

Abby turned around in the Dunkin' Donuts parking lot and drove back to the office where she'd spent countless hours as a child talking tires and engines with Hank and her father, the office to which she'd returned when she couldn't get a job anywhere else.

"Open the garage door," Dax said.

Abby hit the button and the overhead door rolled up, exposing the low-slung Dodge Challenger with the red paint, black trim, and black hood, looking every bit deserving of the Hellcat name.

Her heartbeat quickened at the sight of it.

"Pull in."

Abby parked next to the Challenger and put the garage door

down, sealing out the daylight. She cut the engine on the Tahoe and the kid said, "Do you have keys to the office?"

"Yeah. But I've also got the keys for that car. There's no need to go inside the office."

"Actually, there is. We're going to make a phone call." He got out of the Tahoe and waved the pistol at Abby in a hurry-up gesture.

Abby got out and led the way across the narrow opening to the office. A few stray raindrops splattered off them, and the parking lot was pockmarked with puddles. A relentless gray day. The cars on the road passed quickly, everyone in a hurry to get home. Still, being there was a risk. Locals knew Hank, and locals knew that no one should be at his office.

"Let's go," the kid said, impatient, as if he was thinking the same thing.

Abby opened the side door and stepped in, entering behind a desk facing the windows. Hank's various collections of oddities filled the room—the barber's chair, an antique gas pump, a neon Red Sox sign, a gumball machine filled with gumballs that had to be forty years old.

The kid settled into the barber's chair, swiveled to face Abby, and pointed at the desk. "Pick up the phone."

"If I use that phone, it'll be traced back here."

"The guy you're calling is going to ask me to trace it, so I think we're good."

Abby looked at him, surprised, and Dax nodded. "You're calling my boss. Terms are going to be straightforward, and you're going to set them, just as you promised before. You'll give him Oltamu's phone if he gives me up. Now, you don't trust him, of course, so you'll want a nice public spot. Safety. You'll want me to come to you, not the other way around. Someplace you're familiar with, and I won't be. Someplace with good visual potential, where there might be cops I won't notice. What sounds good to you?"

Abby thought about it. "The pier at Old Orchard Beach. Wide open, plenty of people, and if I got there first, I'd be able to see everyone coming and going."

The kid smiled and pointed at Abby approvingly with the pistol. "That's not bad. It's even better because you thought of it. Now, where are you going to give him Oltamu's phone? Can't be the same place. He'll want it before he gives me up."

He said it without sorrow or anger.

This time Abby didn't have an answer.

"You're going to put it inside the mailbox of a vacant house in Old Orchard," Dax said, "and at eleven forty-five tomorrow morning, you'll text him the address. By noon, I'll need to walk onto the pier. You've got to give him time to pick up the phone. That's only fair."

"He'll think there's a trap in both places," Abby said.

"Yes. But he really needs that phone."

Abby looked at him, sitting there so at ease in the barber's chair, with the dim light filtering through the blinds and painting him in slats.

"You're going to kill him too," she said.

The kid shrugged. "Too early to say."

"No, it isn't. If he's willing to trade you for the phone, you can't overlook that. It's personal to you."

"Nothing is personal. It's a matter of price point, Abby. I feel like mine is moving north."

Abby parted her lips to say more, but the kid stopped her.

"Just make the call. The same number you did before."

Abby reached for the phone, then hesitated. "I don't know it. It's written down, but it's out in the Tahoe."

She moved for the door as she spoke. If she could get to the garage alone, if she could open the door and get behind the wheel while the kid waited in here, then maybe she could—

"Good news," the kid said. "*I* remember it."

He did, too, reciting it without taking his eyes off Abby. The gun muzzle never wavered. Outside, cars passed in the rain, but there were no lights on inside the office, no indication that anyone was inside. If people gave the place a glance, they'd think nothing was amiss. Maybe they'd mourn Hank Bauer and curse Abby Kaplan for killing him, but they would not slow.

She punched in the last of the digits, and the line hummed, and then rang. Once, twice. Then—"Hello?"

It was the same man. For a moment Abby couldn't remember what to say or how to begin. Then Dax left the barber's chair, leaned across the desk, and punched the speakerphone button. He set a digital recorder down beside the phone, then leveled the pistol at Abby's head.

Abby finally spoke. "I don't want this thing," she said to the man Dax had called Gerry. "This phone or camera or whatever. I don't want it, and I never did. It has nothing to do with me. I don't understand what it is, so I'm no threat to you once it's gone. Do you agree?"

The man said, "Yes. That's a smart choice," with enthusiasm that bordered on relief.

"But I need him," Abby said.

"I gave you his name."

"And you said that it wouldn't be worth a damn. I need *him*. Not his name, his address, or even his fucking fingerprints. I want him."

Dax smiled in the darkness. Approving of the performance. His eyes, though, weren't on Abby. They were on the phone. He was waiting to hear whether he was considered expendable.

The silence went on for a long time. Abby watched the recorder on the desk count off the seconds of silence. Eleven of them passed before the man spoke.

"How am I supposed to get the phone?"

Dax stepped away, as if he'd heard enough. He returned to the barber's chair.

Abby followed the script—the phone would be in the mailbox of a vacant house in Old Orchard, and she'd give them fifteen minutes to pick it up and get clear. The kid would need to step onto the pier at noon. Throughout her spiel, the man never interrupted, just listened. Abby could hear the faint scraping of a pen on paper.

"What's your plan for him?" he said when Abby had fallen silent.

Abby hadn't anticipated this question. She hesitated, then said, "That's my business."

"I need to know. Are you coming for him with police or..."

The answer rose forth easily this time.

"I've got something else in mind for him," Abby said. Dax lifted his head to meet Abby's eyes. He smiled at her.

"All right," the man said. "Then if I see a cop, everything's off."

"You won't see one. After what he did, I'm not worried about police. I want him."

Abby held the kid's eyes while she said that, but Dax never lost the smile. Instead, he gave a respectful nod.

It was then that Abby realized that she wasn't lying to the man on the phone. She *didn't* want police. She wanted to kill him. Or try.

"So you'll text the address at eleven forty-five tomorrow morning," the man said, "and you'd better pick a location that's close to the pier."

"Why?"

"Because I'm not going down there myself. Think I trust you? He'll get the phone, then I'll get the phone, and then I'll send him along to you. So choose your spot carefully."

"Don't worry about that," Abby said. "Just make sure he's there."

"He will be."

The kid left the chair, walked to the desk, and killed the connection. Then he set the phone back in the cradle, picked up the recorder, and put it in his pocket. The smile was still on his face, but it seemed to have been painted on and forgotten.

"Well," he said. "That's that. Nicely done, Abby. You're going to survive all of this, I think. You're earning your way out."

Abby didn't say anything. They stood looking at each other in the office that Hank Bauer had worked out of for thirty-three years, and then the quiet was shattered by a shrill ring. Abby looked at the desk phone, but Dax stepped away and reached into his pocket and withdrew his cell. Before he answered it, he lifted the revolver and put it to his lips, instructing Abby to be silent. Then he said, "Yeah?"

Abby could hear the caller's voice faintly, but she couldn't make out most of the words.

Dax said, "Old Orchard is pretty exposed. You couldn't negotiate a better spot than that?"

The voice on the other end rose a bit this time, and Abby heard the phrase *know your role*. Dax's face never changed.

"Right," he said. Then: "So we'll pull her away from the pier beforehand. You're sure that she'll go?" He listened to the caller. "Why don't I pick out the house? I can sit on it all night. Make sure it's clear."

Pause. Then: "All right. We'll ride together. I'll drive."

Pause. Then: "You're the boss. I'll be there. Let's put an end to this one. This bitch has been too much trouble already."

Pause. A smile slid back onto his face, and this time it was genuine, and it was cold. "Yes, I did allow it to happen. I realize that. But trust me—I'll end it, too." He disconnected and put the phone back in his pocket. "Get the gist, Abby?"

"He's lying to you."

Dax nodded. "In his version, *he* will pick the house. I would expect that's where you and I are supposed to die. The pier was never ideal. A vacant house, even if you pick it, is much better—provided there are no police. And you know what? I think he believed you on that. He'll check first, of course, but...he believed you. Do you know why I'm so sure?"

Abby shook her head.

"Because I believed you too," the kid said. "I don't think jail is the fit you want for me anymore. You want me to die."

He seemed to wait for a response. Abby said, "Doesn't matter either way, does it?"

"Actually, it does. You're finally growing into someone I understand."

He walked around the desk and opened the top left-hand drawer. The Challenger keys rested beside a spare set for the Tahoe and one for the office.

"Grab the winners," he said.

Abby picked up the keys. The kid faced her, gun extended, and smiled. "Now we *really* ride," he said. "But keep the race-car-driver instincts in check, okay? No flashing lights in the rearview mirror tonight."

Abby moved woodenly out of the office, across the rain-swept parking lot, and into the garage. The Hellcat sat before her, looking smug, as if it had always known Abby would return.

This time, Dax took the passenger seat and not the back. Abby slid behind the wheel. The interior lights glowed bright, then dimmed down once she closed the driver's door. She felt an immediate claustrophobia when the door was shut. When she turned the engine over, the 6.2-liter engine's growl filled the garage and put a low vibration through the base of her spine. The dash lights glowed red, her mouth went dry, and her pulse trembled.

Beside her, the kid laughed. "This is a beast, isn't it?"

Abby put the garage door up and backed out. In reverse, the car only hinted at its power. Once they were outside, though, when she shifted into drive and tapped the gas, she could feel it immediately. The car seemed to leap rather than accelerate. It was always crouched back on those beautiful Pirelli tires, just begging for the chance to spin off a few layers of rubber. At low idle, the engine offered both a throaty growl and a higher, impatient tone, a whine like a beehive.

"I'll stick to the back roads," Abby said. "Then take Route One down to Old Orchard. That's the safest way."

"We're not going to Old Orchard."

Abby looked at him. He was positioned at an angle, the gun resting on his leg, finger not far from the trigger.

"I thought that was the plan," Abby said. "The pier and the house, all that."

"That's for Gerry. Something for him to chew on while I got a sense of the world through his eyes. The actual plan is a little different. We've got a few stops to make along the way. Starting with Boston. I have to determine whether our girl Tara is really the key to the lock."

Boston. I-95 in the rain. All that traffic. Some of the bees left their hive in the engine and took up buzzing residence in Abby's brain. They brought gray light with them, clouding her vision, and their stingers injected adrenaline that rode through her veins, made her heart rate quicken and her throat tighten and her finger-tips tingle.

Dax studied her and said, "While you're thinking of the chess-board, Abby, you might add this to it: People who see me are likely to die. You've probably noticed that trend by now. I'll get to Tara one way or the other, but you can help pick the path."

"Okay. Back roads are still smarter, though. If anyone is aware of this car, we'll be—"

"I'm not worried about the car. I'm worried about time. Take the interstate. It's faster, and speed's going to count for us tonight. You're just the woman for the job. I need to stay on schedule, and time's wasting, so let's go a little faster."

Faster, Luke's voice agreed from somewhere behind the droning bees.

Abby pulled out of the parking lot and drove into the darkening night.

39

The day of joy has given way to a contentious night. A show-down is brewing, and Tara doesn't understand it. Two people are determined to test her memory, and each one is determined to do it alone.

Tara imagines that Dr. Pine is used to winning these battles. He is also probably not used to having them with the likes of Shannon.

Mom and Rick conceded without argument. The doctor said it was time to see what Tara remembers about her accident, and the doctor must be right. The doctor said this should happen in private, with less "external stimuli," and, again, the doctor must be right. It's his business, after all. Mom and Rick are the type of people who trust doctors.

Shannon, though, is not having it.

"I want to be the one who asks her what happened," she insists, and she waves Rick's objection off before he can gather steam. "I agree with you that there shouldn't be a crowd in the room. So it will just be me."

"We don't have family members conduct medical tests," Dr. Pine says acidly.

"Dr. Carlisle encouraged us to engage with her. She said, in fact, that in most cases of locked-in syndrome, it is a loved one who detects progress. Not a doctor."

Ding—put a point on the board for Shannon.

"My colleague is right," Dr. Pine says, "but I'm not talking about simple engagement, I'm talking about specific memory testing, and with all due respect, I am the primary—"

"This could be traumatic for her," Shannon cuts in. "I think she'd feel less trauma if she were with someone she knows. You have no idea what she's been through in life, what fears she has, what triggers. I do. If she remembers the night, she'll share it with me."

Mom tries a timid "Shannon, let the doctor—"

"No!"

Even Tara is taken aback by the fierceness of Shannon's response. She's always been tenacious, but there's something different here, a humming tension under her skin. Shannon is afraid.

But why? What scares her about leaving Tara alone with a doctor now?

"I'm simply going to have to insist—" Dr. Pine begins, but Shannon cuts him off again.

"Ask her."

"What?"

"Ask Tara. You have a patient who can communicate her own wishes, Doctor. Let's respect those."

They stare at each other like gunslingers, and then Dr. Pine takes a deep breath and says, "Very well. We should know her opinion. I can't argue with that."

He seems disappointed and also to be speaking largely to himself. As with Shannon, there's something different about Dr. Pine's demeanor, something beneath the surface, but Tara doesn't know him well enough to guess what it is.

As he reaches for the alphabet board, Shannon turns and focuses her fierce green eyes on Tara. She doesn't say a word, but she doesn't have to. Tara feels like she's nine years old again, being quizzed by a child protective services worker about Mom's drug use. Shannon would fix that stare on her, and Tara would say what Shannon had prepared her to say. Things were under control. That was Shannon's mantra. Things were always under control. Even when things were absolute chaos, Tara believed that her big sister would wrestle it all back to order.

Dr. Pine swivels his stool to face Tara, slides closer to the bed, and extends the alphabet board. He's moving distractedly, his usual focus lost. There is definitely something else on his mind. What's going on here?

"You don't need the board yet," Shannon says. "Can't we just ask her yes or no?"

A good question, and while he seems disgusted that she's right, he nods grudgingly. "I'll ask her. You can watch. There is no deceit here, Ms. Beckley."

He focuses on Tara. "Tara, are you willing to communicate your memories of the accident with me?"

She's a ghost again; she's the thing on the other side of the Ouija board being summoned into the real world. *Are you willing to communicate?* When she and Shannon were kids, they would sneak up to the attic with a Ouija board and candles and play this game, and inevitably Tara would grow scared, and Shannon would never admit that she was moving the planchette. Mostly, though, Shannon wouldn't use those moments to scare her. The planchette's messages were always positive. *Yes,* the board would say, *Mom will get better. Yes, Daddy can hear you when you talk to him at night, and he loves you. No, they will not break up this family.*

You have to believe it, Shannon would say, *because what reason would a ghost have to lie?*

Tara, now the half-ghost, has no reason to lie. She flicks her eyes up. Yes, she is willing to communicate her memories of the accident.

"Thank you," Dr. Pine says. "Now, Tara, are you willing to be alone with me when—"

"Don't phrase it like that," Shannon snaps. "Ask her if she wants me to stay."

Dr. Pine turns and regards Shannon as if he's considering new uses for his scalpel, but he submits. "Fine. Tara—do you *need* your sister present for this?"

She doesn't need Shannon present for this. Why would she? But she remembers those looks from her big sister across the years, and she remembers the messages the Ouija board carried. She'd known that Shannon was the force that moved the planchette across the board, but she never minded because that force was love. A fierce, protective love that carried Tara through the worst of her life.

She flicks her eyes up once. Yes—she needs her sister to be present for this.

Dr. Pine seems to deflate, and Shannon offers him a tight smile. When he turns away, she gives Tara a wink and a thumbs-up.

"Maybe we all stay, then," Rick says, and Dr. Pine and Shannon answer in unison, both the word and the tone:

"No."

"I think we want to limit the stimuli and the pressure," Dr. Pine says, gentler. "But we can ask Tara again if you'd like."

"I trust your judgment," Rick says, clearly more for Shannon's ears than Dr. Pine's. "We can let you do your job."

Shannon doesn't react. Mom squeezes Tara's hand as she and Rick pass by, and then it is just the three of them: Tara, Dr. Pine on his stool beside the bed, holding the alphabet board, and Shannon standing at the foot of the bed, arms folded across her chest, eyes hard on Tara's.

"Okay," Dr. Pine says. "Let's just begin with some basics, Tara. Yes-or-no questions to start. If there is any trouble with the process or if at any point you feel you wish to stop, I want you to give me three looks upward. Do you—"

He stops abruptly because Tara's thumb twitches. This time, he sees it. Shannon does too. They both stare at her hand, then at each other, and then Dr. Pine says, "Tara, can you do that again?"

Not yet, she thinks, *but soon. I'm getting closer.* Because she knows what triggered it this time, just like with the clicking of the pen—old muscle memory, a delayed response to the thumbs-up Shannon gave her. Tara wanted to return the gesture, and she just did. Or came as close as she could, at least. There's a lag, but there's something opening too, a door between brain and body cracking open, and in time she may be able to push it wider.

She flicks her eyes up twice. No, she can't do it again. She wants to say, *Keep trying me, though,* but there's no way to do that.

"Did you feel it?" Dr. Pine asks.

One flick.

Dr. Pine reaches for a notepad and jots something down. When he turns back, he's frustrated again, running a hand over his face as if to refocus. He's conflicted in some way. Why?

"Okay, back to the memory test. Yes-or-no questions to start. Tara, do you remember anything about the night of your accident?"

One flick.

"Do you remember the man in your car?"

One flick. Oltamu, the doctor from Black Lake. Yes, she remembers.

"Do you remember the moment of the accident?"

One flick.

Dr. Pine wets his lips and shifts forward. The stool slides beneath him, moving soundlessly on the tile, bringing him closer to the bed. He lifts the alphabet board, then hesitates and lowers it again. He glances at Shannon, who is motionless, still standing with folded arms. She hasn't interrupted him yet, a surprise to Tara, so surely a shock to him.

"Tara," he says, "was it an accident?"

This sets Shannon in motion. She takes a step forward, staring at him, and says, "Why would you ask that—"

He lifts a palm. "Let her answer. It's important. Tara—was it an accident?"

She's not sure. There's no way to respond *I don't know,* though. She's supposed to answer yes or no, period, but what she remembers of the night doesn't fit neatly into either of those categories. Those memories are fragments laced with unease and an unidentifiable fear. She remembers the doctor looking behind them, over and over, remembers the way he wanted her to secure the phone, remembers the sound of an engine and terror of...of *something,* no clarity here, just an overwhelming memory of her fight-or-flight response, and she'd tried to flee.

Then there was blackness. The long dark.

Tara recalls Oltamu pressing that phone into her hand, and she thinks of the engine that roared, no lights, black on black, the vehicle seeming as much a creature of the night as the wolf. A predator.

She flicks her eyes up twice. No, it was not an accident.

This is a showstopper. Dr. Pine doesn't ask another question, doesn't really respond. Shannon, who had been advancing toward him as if to physically prevent him from asking anything, is frozen in midstride, halfway around the bed, almost like Tara was halfway around the CRV before the impact—the blackness—came. She's staring down at Tara, but when she finally speaks, the question is for Dr. Pine.

"Why did you ask that?"

"Memory assessment."

"Bullshit," Shannon says.

He turns to her and the two of them gaze at each other in a silence so loaded that it seems to have texture, like an electric fence.

"What do you know?" Shannon asks. "And who told you?"

He doesn't answer. Shannon lets her gunslinger gaze linger, then pivots away, leans close to the bed, and says, "Tara, did Dr. Oltamu take pictures of you?"

"Hang on," Dr. Pine says, but Tara responds immediately, one flick. Yes, there were pictures, the strange and awkward pictures, but how in the world does her sister know this?

"You need to step back and let me do my job," Dr. Pine says, rising from his stool as if to block Tara from Shannon's line of sight. Shannon fires off another question.

"Was there something strange about Oltamu's phone? Something different?"

The camera grid. It wasn't an iPhone camera. Not a normal one, at least.

Tara gives one flick: Yes. How does Shannon know this? How is she inside of Tara's brain, moving through the dark corridors of her memories?

Dr. Pine is now attempting to physically get between them, determined to keep Shannon from making eye contact with Tara, but Shannon evades him, prowling to the other side of the bed like a cougar stalking prey.

"Tara, do you think—"

"Stop this," Dr. Pine says, nearly hissing the words. "We're not interrogating her, that's not my role or yours, and that is *not going to*—"

Shannon speaks over him. "Tara, do you think someone killed Oltamu because of that phone?"

Because of the phone? Tara has no idea. Shannon now has access to something more than Tara's memories. Shannon is capable of passing through the locked doors and joining Tara in her lonely house of memories, and she can also move outside it. Tara can't match that; she's bound to the cellar, with no idea what is happening anywhere else. But the question Shannon posed makes sense to her, though she's never considered it in such precise terms.

Because of the phone? Maybe. Yes, maybe it was all about the phone.

She gives one flick, signaling affirmation, even though she's not sure it's correct. She knows it's possible, at least, and the recognition fills her with hot anger—she is trapped in her own body, paralyzed and mute, all because of a *phone*?

Dr. Pine doesn't lose his focus on Tara even while he's trying to shut Shannon up, and he sees Tara's eyes move, understands her answer and the weight of it. He and Shannon both do. Tara's doing more than passing awareness tests now; she's describing a murder. There is a long silence, and then Dr. Pine speaks in a soft voice.

"I think it's my turn to ask who has been talking to *you,* Ms. Beckley."

"I can't tell you that," Shannon says.

"You're going to have to."

"No." Shannon shakes her head, and Tara sees the fear lurking beneath her frustration. Shannon is scared, and Shannon is never scared. Both she and Dr. Pine seem to know more than Tara, which is infuriating, and when Dr. Pine suggests to Shannon that they step into the hall to speak in private, Tara is so outraged that she wants to scream.

No sound comes—but her thumb twitches again.

I'm building a connection, she thinks. *Restoring one, at least.* That cracked-open cellar door is swinging a little wider, scraping across the damp concrete, the rusty hinges yielding, as if pushed by a relentless wind that is capable of rising in sudden swift gusts.

For the first time, Tara understands the source of that wind: her own willpower. Her willpower is not gone yet, and she is certain it is capable of gathering strength. She will continue to widen the crack, keep pushing until she can slip through the gap.

"You want us to stay," Shannon says to Tara, and though it isn't really a question, Tara flicks her eyes up gratefully.

Dr. Pine is reluctant, but Shannon is firm. "If we talk, we talk in front of her. She's got to be scared in so many ways, scared of things we can't even begin to understand. We can't build more silence around her."

Thank you, sis. Thank you, thank you.

The doctor sighs, rubs his eyes, then nods once and sits heavily on the stool.

"I don't know much," he says. "That's the truth. I have been warned that Tara might have been a witness to something more than an accident. That's all." He looks up at Shannon. "You know it too."

She nods.

"Who told you?" he asks.

Hesitation. Shannon doesn't want to give up her source. She looks at Tara, considering, and Dr. Pine apparently takes her silence as a refusal to cooperate, because he gives up.

"You don't need to tell me," he says. "I probably don't even want to know."

"She's in danger," Shannon says, her voice scarcely more than a whisper. "I have been told that she is in danger. I don't know how to help her. Who to call."

"I can help you with that," Dr. Pine says.

"How?"

He leans forward, elbows on his knees, and studies Tara. When he speaks, his eyes are on her, not Shannon.

"There is an investigator with the Department of Energy who will be very interested to know that Tara has memories of the night. All of this talk about the phone and the pictures—I know nothing about that. But you're going to need someone to trust. Tara, I'm asking you this, doctor to patient—do you want to meet with the investigator?"

Department of Energy? This shouldn't make sense, and yet it touches off a faint chord of familiarity, something that Tara has either forgotten or never really paid attention to, something that once seemed trivial and was quickly shuffled off into the mists of memory.

Tara flicks her eyes up once: Yes, let's meet the investigator.

Dr. Pine says, "Okay." Then, turning to Shannon, he repeats, this time as a question, "Okay?"

Shannon looks from Tara to the doctor and nods, then stops and grabs his arm as he starts to rise.

"Hang on. What does he look like?"

"What?"

"The investigator. How old is he?"

Dr. Pine stares at her, bewildered. "The investigator is a woman. And she is probably around forty."

Shannon releases his arm, but he looks at her with narrowed eyes. "Would you like to be more candid about who's spoken to you?"

Shannon considers. "Is your response going to be any different if we talk about that now? Or are you going to make the same call?"

He acknowledges the point with a slight nod. "I'll make the call," he says. "So I might as well do it sooner than later."

When Shannon doesn't object, he leaves the room, closing the door behind him with a soft click. He forgets to take his alphabet board. Shannon looks at it, then looks at Tara, an unspoken question in her eyes.

Tara flicks her eyes up once.

Yes. Let's chat.

40

The clouds that had begun massing along the coast during the day swept in off the North Atlantic and collided with a warm front as darkness fell, and then the night was illuminated with flickering tongues of lightning as the pressure systems fought for dominance.

Abby drove southbound on I-95, trapped between and beneath the battling weather fronts. Thunder cracked and boomed and rolled to the west, and from the east, the winds continued to buffet the car.

She didn't notice the impact of the wind as much as she had before, though, when she was sitting up high in the Tahoe. She was low now, riding close to the pavement, only a few inches of steel separating her from the asphalt that was buzzing by at seventy-five miles per hour. She had the Challenger in cruise control so she could ignore the speed and focus on keeping her breathing and heart rate steady. She was grateful for the darkness, for the shrinking of the horizon, the tightening of the world.

The lightning, though, was a problem.

With each flash, the highway lit up bold and bright. With each flash, cars that were nothing but taillights in the darkness were suddenly given shape. With each flash, her breathing became harder to control.

The lightning was worse than a high sun and a clear sky. When the road came at her in flashes, unpredictable and unexpected, suddenly she couldn't work saliva into her mouth; her heart was thundering, and the breathing exercises weren't doing a damn thing. Her head felt high and light and dizzy. *Just concentrate on the tires and feel the road,* she told herself, but then a brilliant flash of lightning would paint the road white, the world would shudder with thunder, and dizziness drove through her brain and into her spine.

She was sweating, cool beads on a hot forehead, her shirt clinging damply to her back. Dax watched with curiosity but in silence. As Abby's sweating grew more noticeable and her breathing more ragged, Abby was sure he would speak, but then two things happened nearly at once: The rain began to fall in torrents, clattering off the windshield as loud as coins on a winning slot-machine pull, and the kid's phone gave a shrill chirp. Not a ring, an alert tone.

Abby had no interest in the phone. She was tunnel-vision-focused on the road, hands tight on the wheel—too tight; like an amateur, not a pro—her head forward, her hand shaking as she set the wipers to high. Even at that rate, they didn't seem to achieve much, merely adding a slashing motion across her field of vision, which was already graying out at the edges. The Pirellis held the road, but she was certain that they couldn't continue to, not in this weather. There was too much torque to the Hellcat. If she made a mistake, she'd start to skid.

But that was fine, she told herself, because she could steer out of a skid, she'd done it successfully thousands of times before.

Not always.

You just turned into it, that was all, the only requirement—turn back into it. Counterintuitive, but it worked. You regained equilibrium if you could only teach yourself to go against instinct and trust the physics. The world rewarded you for trusting physics. In time, that trust became instinct.

You'll get that instinct back. You'll get it back, and tonight's a good run, a good trial, because there's nothing to worry about out here, it's just a little rain, that's all.

As if to contradict her, the sheet lightning flashed, revealing what waited ahead—two semis, one in the left lane on its way around the slower-moving one in the right lane, passing even in this weather. There was a truck coming up behind Abby, too, one that looked to be loaded with logs from the north woods. Damn it, damn it, damn it. Why so much traffic? Why couldn't everyone get off the road and home to bed and let Abby drive to Boston with a murderer in peace?

Dax's face was lit by the display of his phone, his attention pulled away from Abby, responding to whatever that chirp had signified. Suddenly, voices filled the car.

It took Abby a moment to recognize Shannon Beckley's voice. There were several in the mix, male and female, but hers rang a clarion note that the others lacked. Shannon was asking about methods for her sister to communicate easier and faster.

Abby chanced a look in the kid's direction. He lifted his eyes immediately. He seemed preternaturally aware of Abby's movements. The gun was in his left hand, on his lap, pointed at Abby. It was always pointed at Abby.

"Checking on our girl's progress," he said cheerfully. "Sounds like it was a big day, and you and I have had our share of distractions, haven't we? I'll need to get caught up."

Shannon Beckley's voice faded, others overtaking it, but they were all discussing the same thing—Tara was awake. Tara could talk.

He bugged the hospital, Abby thought. The realization was almost enough to pull her attention away from the dizzying, sweat-inducing fear of the drive.

Almost.

It didn't last, though, because she had a car on her left now, neither trying to pass nor, evidently, aware that passing was the point in the left lane. Instead, the car just rode alongside, penning her in. She looked over and swore under her breath.

"Everything all right, Abby?"

Abby didn't answer. She accelerated, thinking that she'd pass on the right and get out in front and then maybe this moron would get the idea and shift back into the right lane. As long as she kept some clear space, some avenue of escape, she would be fine. All the way to Boston, she'd be fine.

But these idiots, calm behind their steering wheels, were sealing her in.

As she accelerated, the semi in front slowed and flashed its head-lights, signaling that the truck trying to pass was clear to shift back into the right lane. The truck driver in the left lane, like the driver of the car next to Abby, didn't take the opportunity or the hint. Maybe it was the weather, this pounding rain, scaring them both off from making the simple lane shift. Maybe they were dis-tracted. Maybe they were morons who never should have been issued driver's licenses.

None of that mattered. She was trapped.

She took a harsh breath and sat up straight, then leaned forward quickly, hunching over as if caught by a stomach cramp, because she was suddenly sure that she couldn't get air into her lungs. Or her brain. Her blood was oxygen-free, thickening and slowing, her heart thundering to try to make up for it but pushing nothing but sludge through her veins. Her vision dimmed and then came back and then went again.

The kid said, "Abby," in a warning voice, but it barely pene-trated the fog.

Going to crash. I am going to crash and I'm going to take one of these poor people out with me, because there is nowhere to go, when I black out I am going to hit them or they are going to hit me and then we'll be skidding together through the night on the wet road, glass breaking and blood flowing and screams, someone will be screaming, but there is nothing I can do to stop it, because there is no...

She saw the gap in the guardrail of the median just ahead. It looked freshly cut, probably the result of an accident, some other night when they'd pulled dead bodies out of mangled cars. It was small, a narrow opening, not meant for access, but...

"He left the road at ninety, that's all there is to say," her father sang.

Faster, Luke said.

Abby pounded the accelerator; the Hellcat roared and the Pirellis spun, hunting for traction, then caught and hammered the car forward. As she shifted in front of the car on her left side, a horn blew, piercingly loud, but by then Abby was out in front and angling farther left, the guardrail looming, the gap in it no more than fifteen feet long, maybe just ten, an almost impossibly narrow target to slip through at this speed and in this rain...

She made it without creasing either side of the car. Shot the gap and pounded the brakes and brought the car to a fishtailing stop in the grassy median between northbound and southbound lanes, plowing a furrow of damp sod beneath the tires.

She fell back against the seat, gasping and half smiling, almost oblivious to the horns and the rain, aware of nothing but the victory of having gotten off the road without harming anyone.

Safe, she thought, and only then did she realize the muzzle of the gun was pressed against the side of her head.

"What are you doing?" Dax said.

"I need to breathe."

"What?"

"I just need to—"

"If you get the cops called, a lot of people are dying tonight. You'll be the first but not the last. You better back this thing up and get moving right now or I promise, Abby, you're going to—"

"I just need to breathe!" Abby screamed.

The kid pulled the gun away and stared at her. Abby shoved the gearshift into park and leaned her head back against the seat and sucked in air as sweat trickled down her face in cool rivulets. The sweat was good; the cooling was good; everything needed to cool down, it had gotten too hot in here, it had gotten dangerously hot and—

Faster. Faster! Slow down. Slow down!

It had almost gone very badly.

"You're freaking out," Dax said. "What's going on? Scared of the gun, Abby? You've done so well with it. I can't put it away. I don't think we have the necessary trust for that."

Abby didn't answer. Just closed her eyes and concentrated on that slow, sweet cooling. Tried to listen to the rain, hoping it would drown out Luke's voice. *Faster,* Luke said, then *Slow down!* he screamed.

Shut up, Abby thought. *Please, baby, just shut up for one night so I can do this thing. So I can see morning. Then come back and talk all you want and I'll listen forever, no matter how miserable it is, but for this one night, just please . . . be quiet. Let me drive.*

"So *this* is why Abby Kaplan came back to Maine," Dax said. "You're not hiding from media. You really can't do it anymore, can you? You lost the nerve."

Abby still didn't speak.

"What a sorry shame," Dax said. "End of a good run for you, wasn't it? But that's of no interest to me. And the longer we sit here, the more likely it is that a cop joins us." He shifted around in the darkness and leaned forward and suddenly Abby's hands, which were still on the steering wheel, were bound tight and zipped together by a plastic cord that bit into her skin.

"Get out and trade seats with me. Do it quick and do it calm, or I will shoot. There is no more patience."

Abby fumbled with the door handle, struggling with her bound wrists, then stepped out into the pouring rain. She didn't mind it. The rain was cold, and the rain was clean.

The kid pushed open the passenger door, then slid across into the driver's seat, and he lifted the gun and pointed it at Abby's face as she stood there in the downpour.

"Your choice," he said. "Die there and leave the sweet Beckley sisters to me, or get back in and ride. Good news—you don't have to drive anymore, Anxious Abby."

I got one thousand dollars, Hank Bauer had said on a humid July night at a New Hampshire speedway, *that says that little girl kicks all their asses and wins this thing.*

Abby was fifteen years old and couldn't drive legally on a highway, but she won that night on the track. Hank gave her half the money, and they'd piled into his truck with her father and driven into the night with the windows down and Green Day loud on the radio, and Abby's future was firm.

The world was hers that night, and she understood that all she needed was four good tires to take it.

She looked up the highway now, through the rain and into the blur of oncoming headlights, and then she walked around the car, past those beautiful Pirellis, and toward the passenger seat. The door was open, waiting, rain streaming down the interior panel. Lightning strobed, illuminating the car, and Abby saw the kid's cell phone. It was on the floor mat on the passenger side. He'd dropped it, maybe when he'd slid into the driver's seat or maybe when Abby had shot the gap into the median.

And I made the gap too. Not all bad. It was reaction, not strategy, but I still made it.

"Get in," Dax said, and he cocked the revolver.

Chill rain streamed down Abby's spine in ribbons. She stood there for just a second longer, just enough to make sure that the kid's focus was on her face. Then she made a show of tumbling awkwardly into the passenger seat and fell forward, almost across the gearshift, as she landed.

Dax's attention stayed on her. He did not follow the motion of Abby's right foot, did not see her lower her shoe onto the phone and slide it backward, did not hear it clatter up and over the door frame and out into the rain.

"Get off me!" he snapped.

Abby leaned back, said, "Sorry," then turned her bound wrists toward the door, grasped the handle, and slammed it shut. She moved quickly, but she got a last glimpse of the phone sitting there in the rain.

Did it matter? Probably not. For a moment, though, Abby had taken one thing from him. He wouldn't be able to play Shannon Beckley's voice for a little while. It wasn't much—wasn't anything, maybe—but it felt like a victory. She'd taken something from him.

And I made the gap. Thought I couldn't do it, thought we were going to die in the rain, maybe die with other people too, innocent strangers, all of us burning in the rain because I couldn't hold myself together. But that didn't happen. I saw the gap, and I took it.

I fucking took it.

The kid leaned toward her, shoved the muzzle of the revolver under her chin, and forced her head up. His face was shadowed by the black baseball cap, but you could still see the smile.

"Pretty-boy Luke London did a real number on you, didn't he?"

Abby went for him then. She lunged forward, trying to snap her forehead off the kid's nose, not fearing the gun any longer, scarcely aware of it.

When he hit her behind the ear with the barrel, Abby sagged and her vision went black, but she could still hear the rain.

Then he hit her again, and this time the sound of the rain went away too.

41

Thirty thousand feet in the sky, Boone sat in the bulkhead seat and turned her phone over and over in her hands, compulsively.

Check signal. Nothing. Of course nothing. Even cheating on airplane mode wouldn't help at this altitude.

She turned the phone, turned it, turned it...and checked again. No signal.

She was on Wi-Fi, but it wouldn't let calls through.

Land this bitch already. The thought rose with such intensity that she almost shouted it aloud. Containing frustration was always a struggle for her. Once more, she was passive, Detroit all over again, sitting at the gate and waiting, waiting, waiting. Back then, unknown to her, Amandi Oltamu was already dead, and Boone had been reduced to waiting, clueless.

Tara Beckley wasn't dead, though. She was coming back. But did she know a single thing that might help?

Boone's phone vibrated, and for a glorious second, she was sure that the signal had somehow pierced the clouds.

Wrong. It was just an e-mail slipping through on the wireless network. She knew that it wouldn't matter, but she checked it anyhow, needing something to fill her time. When she saw the sender, she caught her breath.

It was Pine.

I have been trying to call for the past twenty minutes. Your phone goes straight to voice mail. I am assuming and hoping this is because you are in the air and en route. Tara is not only alert, but she has memories of the night. Specific and clear memories. There is also a difficulty with her sister, who appears to have been contacted by someone other than you, someone with knowledge of the danger in this situation. Knowledge that I don't have. She has lots of questions about Dr. Oltamu's phone. She seemed unsurprised to learn of your agency's interest, but she will not tell me why or who has provided her with whatever information she has. It is imperative that we have guidance on this situation. I am going to give you a little time, but then I feel it's essential to contact local authorities.

Boone nearly jammed a thumb in her hurry to respond.

Keep her safe, keep her quiet, I am inbound, almost there.

She hit Send, leaned back in the seat, and stared out the window. Lightning flashed below them, entombed in the clouds, giving an otherworldly quality to the night sky.

Shannon Beckley had lots of questions about Oltamu's phone? Why? If Tara Beckley remembered the phone, that was one thing. But her sister? Who had been in contact with her sister? And if someone had told her sister so much about the situation that she understood things at the level Pine seemed to suspect, then there was a much bigger question: How was she still alive?

The intercom gave a burst of static, and Boone let out a relieved breath, anticipating the message—they were beginning their descent into Boston's Logan Airport, please fasten seat belts and prepare for landing.

"Ladies and gentlemen, you might have noticed the lightning outside your windows," the pilot began, and Boone tensed.

No, no, do not tell me we are being delayed or diverted, not tonight...

"What you're seeing," the pilot continued, "is part of a series of supercell thunderstorms that are moving north-northeast at the moment, and they're delaying operations at Boston Logan until that weather clears."

"No!" Boone said aloud, drawing stares from the flight attendants in front of her. She shook her head, closed her eyes, and clamped her molars together as the pilot kept babbling.

"We're going to be in a holding pattern for just a bit, hopefully not more than fifteen to twenty minutes," he said. "I'll let you know as soon as we get word from the folks at Logan that we are cleared for descent. We don't expect it to be a long wait, so just sit back, relax, and enjoy. The good news is that all the turbulence is below us, and the storm seems to be moving fast."

42

Blue.
Not *I*. Not *J*. Yes, *K*. One flick.

Tara is exhausted, but Shannon is pressing, and Tara won't quit on her. She's answered every question Shannon has thrown at her so far, and she's surprised at how the task is sharpening her memory, bringing images back with clarity and vividness. The growing paranoia she'd felt with Oltamu has more precision now, and she remembers a specific question he'd asked, about whether everyone took the same route from dinner to the auditorium. She'd thought he was worried about being on time, but a man worried about his destination didn't keep looking over his shoulder. He was worried about what was behind him, which meant that the place he'd come from might matter, and she remembers this name and is trying to spell it out, quite literally, for Shannon.

Red? No. Two flicks.

"Yellow?" Shannon asks, and then interrupts herself, a feat only Shannon could achieve. "Hang on, we don't need to waste your time. It's *E,* isn't it? It's Black Lake?"

Tara gives one relieved upward flick of the eyes. *You win Double Jeopardy!* Tara thinks, and she wants to laugh hysterically. She's never been so tired in her life. All she's doing is moving her eyes, and yet it drains her more than any marathon ever has.

"He came from Black Lake," Shannon repeats, and now she has her phone out, tapping into it, probably searching for the town. "Black Lake, New York? Or there's…a ghost town in Idaho. I hope he didn't come from there. Was it New York?"

Tara doesn't know, so she doesn't move her eyes. Shannon waits, then says, "Do you even know where it was?"

Two fatigued flicks.

"Okay." Shannon lowers the phone. "Did he take any other pictures?"

One flick.

"Of you?"

Two flicks.

"Someone else."

Tara hesitates, then looks upward.

"We're going to have to spell, aren't we?"

One flick.

And so they spell.

Yellow—*H*. Green—*O*. Red—*B*.

"Hobbs?" Shannon guesses.

Two flicks, more angry than exhausted now; just let her finish.

"Red?"

No. Finally, they get there. Green—*O*.

"Hobo?" Shannon says, voice heavy with disbelief. "He took pictures of a hobo?"

She looks at Tara as if she's crazy, as if this is the first clear misfiring of memory, and Tara wants nothing more than the power to reach out and strangle her. Her thumb twitches against her palm, but Shannon doesn't notice, because Shannon is watching only her eyes. This is the only window out. For now. Tara has to stay calm, stay patient, and keep working at it. It's 1804 London Street all over again—Tara trapped inside, Shannon waiting to rescue her from the outside, and the two of them working to widen the gap in the steel doors that separate them.

"A hobo," Shannon says, taking a breath. "Can you explain more than that?"

One flick.

"Spell it. Red line?"

One flick.

"A?"

Thank goodness, yes, it's finally the first column and first letter. *A* is a common letter, isn't it? How in the hell is Tara never drawing an *A* in this thing? She's got two of them in her own damned name!

"Red line?" Shannon asks, and again, this is a yes, but Tara has to go all the way to the end of the row now to get to *end of word,* and halfway through she realizes that she didn't need the stupid *A* anyhow—stick to nouns and verbs, damn it!

So over they begin, but good news—it's red again! Not *A,* not *B,* not *C,* but *D, D* for *Damn it, I want my voice back.*

Green—*O.* Yellow—*G.* Thankfully, Shannon doesn't make her indicate *end of word* again, but guesses. "A dog? That's not what you mean. Tell me that's not what you mean?"

If I could kick you, Tara thinks, *you'd have bruises for weeks. What in the hell am I supposed to do with that phrasing? "A dog? That's not what you mean. Tell me that's not what you mean?" How do you answer that with a yes or a no?*

So she doesn't answer. She waits. She's swell at waiting. She's becoming the best there ever was in the game of waiting, a natural, a pure talent.

Shannon gathers herself, finally understanding that her typical flurry of speech is not the way to go about this, and says, "Did Oltamu really take pictures of a dog named Hobo?"

She says it in the tone of voice in which you might ask someone to tell you the details of her alien abduction. Tara gives her one flick of the eyes, a flick with *attitude.*

Yes, it was a dog named Hobo, and kiss my sweet ass if you think I'm crazy.

Shannon sets the alphabet board down flat on her lap and stares at Tara as if she can't decide what to ask next. Tara wants to hold her arms up in a giant *V* for victory. She has achieved the impossible—not in coming back from a coma, not even in proving she's awake despite being paralyzed. This is a truly heroic feat: she has rendered Shannon Beckley speechless.

"You're serious. Do you think the dog matters, or am I going on a wild..." She stops herself, holds a hand up, and walks her words back. Communication with Tara favors the short-winded, which doesn't play to Shannon's strengths.

"Do you think it matters that he took pictures of a dog?"

Tara doesn't know, so she doesn't answer.

"You're not sure?" Shannon says, beginning to understand what a blank stare means.

One flick.

"Did he take any other pictures after the dog?"

Two flicks.

"Did he tell you anything about the phone?"

Tara wishes she could think of a way to communicate the odd camera and its unique grid, but she can't. Or she doesn't think she can, at least, but then Shannon does what only a sister could possibly do: she seems to slip inside Tara's mind.

"Was it a real phone?"

Two flicks.

Dr. Pine enters almost soundlessly.

"Can't you *knock*?" Shannon snaps, startled.

He takes a step forward, brow furrowed, hands clasped behind his back, as if he would have been content to remain a spectator.

"Pictures of a dog?" he says.

"That's none of your business," Shannon says. Still not trusting him. Tara understands this but she disagrees with it. Shannon hasn't trusted many people in her life, having been burned too many times, but for all of Shannon's force of personality and will, she doesn't have the most intuitive reads on people. Extroverts are too busy projecting their opinions and personalities to intuit anything submerged about anyone in their audience, in Tara's opinion. Tara, the introvert—and has there ever been a more undeniable introvert than the current model of Tara Beckley? She's the literal embodiment of the concept now. She does not see herself as superior to her sister in most ways, but she is more intuitive. Tara doesn't distrust Dr. Pine. The very tics that make Shannon nervous are the reasons Tara trusts him. He's genuinely concerned about her, and he's genuinely concerned about his ethical dilemma in this situation.

"Where's your investigator?" Shannon asks.

"En route. I couldn't speak to her, but she e-mailed from the plane. She'll be landing soon and coming directly here." He pauses. "Would you like to wait until she is here before you tell me what you've been asking Tara?"

"Yes."

"Fair enough." He paces, hands still behind his back. Outside the window, lightning strobes in dark clouds, and the wind throws raindrops at the glass like handfuls of pebbles.

"Your parents have gone to the hotel to take a short rest," he says. "I didn't object. If you wish to bring them back, though…"

"No," Shannon says, firm, and Dr. Pine seems unsurprised. He looks at Tara, and this time she answers without needing to hear the question voiced. Two flicks: no, he does not need to summon her parents. Mom is an exhausted mess, and Rick will battle with Shannon. Tara needs to save her energy for the Department of Energy—*ha! Why can't anyone hear these jokes?*—and whatever information this mysterious investigator will have. Tara wants to hear answers, and that will mean providing answers, a task that she now knows is utterly exhausting.

"You could call the local police," Dr. Pine suggests. "But you haven't done that yet. Why not?"

Shannon looks like she doesn't want to answer, but she says, "I'm not sure. I guess because I haven't had time to figure out what I would even tell them. And I've been instructed…I've been warned about trusting the wrong people."

"Warned by whom?" Pine asks gently.

Shannon shakes her head and gives a little laugh. Dr. Pine seems to read it as frustration, but it's more than that—Shannon is unsure of herself. Tara knows. Tara is just as curious as Dr. Pine, though. Where is Shannon's information coming from?

"Who have you told about the Department of Energy investigator?" Shannon asks Dr. Pine.

"Just you."

"Really?" Those dubious Doberman eyes fixed on him.

"Really."

Shannon takes a breath and leans back. "All this for a phone," she says softly. "What in the hell was on that phone?"

Even if they were using the alphabet board, Tara would have no answer for this one.

Outside, lightning strobes again, but it is dimmer, distant. The storm is clearing. Tara hopes she can take some confidence from the symbol, but she doesn't believe that. There are too many things she doesn't know, and most of them are happening outside of these walls.

43

Abby fumbled for her harness. She'd been knocked out, but her helmet was still on, and she was upright, trapped in the seat. That meant she needed to release the harness, but where was the pit crew? She needed them. Needed help.

Something wrong with her arm too. Broken, probably, and it felt like her hands were smashed together. Why couldn't she separate them?

She opened her eyes and stared at her hands as if they were unfamiliar, and only when a lightning flash lit the yellow cord that bound her wrists together did she remember where she was and that there was nobody in the pit coming for her.

But she was too upright, just like if she'd been harnessed into the seat. Why was that?

A cord was around her neck, too, that was why. She was bound against the headrest, the cord just slack enough to let her breathe but not to let her slump sideways or forward. The kid had positioned her well. He'd also put his black baseball cap on Abby's head, pulled low, shading her face. That was what Abby had confused for the helmet. To any passerby who glanced in the car, she was just a woman in a baseball cap, dozing in the dark.

Dax Blackwell looked over. "Morning, Abby."

When Abby turned, the cord chiseled across her throat. She winced, then refocused.

It was the first time she'd ever seen the kid without the baseball cap, and even in the dark, his hair was a startlingly bright blond. It was cropped close to his skull, moon-white and luminescent in the glow from the dash lights.

"Nice touch with the hat," Abby said. Her voice came out in a dry croak.

"I thought it would help. You had a little blood in your hair. Sorry about that."

The road rolled beneath them, the lights of Boston up ahead. They were still on I-95, cruising by the northern suburbs. The hospital wasn't far away.

"You're lucky you're necessary," the kid said. "I'd have very much enjoyed killing you back there, but...priorities. Nice trick with the phone too. I almost missed it."

He took one hand off the wheel and held the phone up.

Abby tried not to show her defeat. It had been the only win, the only thing she could take from the evil prick.

"Interesting developments in Tara's room," the kid said. "Investigator en route, it seems. Department of Energy, no less. Do you understand that?"

"No." Speaking made Abby's skull ache. She closed her eyes and waited out the pain.

"You've done some research on our friend Amandi Oltamu," the kid said. "Where is Black Lake? Seemed to confuse Shannon, and I don't know anything about it either."

"I don't know."

"Tara thinks Oltamu came from Black Lake, but my information said he came from Ohio. There's no Black Lake in—"

"Yes, there is." Abby's eyes opened. Suddenly she understood Oltamu. Something about him, at least. And why the Department of Energy would be interested in him.

"Siri disagrees with you," Dax said. "Surely you don't mean to tell me Siri is confused? She's a voice of reason in a mad world."

"Black Lake is not a town. Or even a lake."

The kid looked at her, interested now. "What is it?"

Abby stared straight ahead, watching taillights pull away. Dax was keeping the Challenger pinned at the speed limit, refusing to tempt police.

"It's the nickname for a place where they run cars through performance and safety tests," she said. "It's fifty acres of blacktop, and from the sky it looks like dark water—that's where the nickname comes from. You can ask a car to do anything in that space. A high-end car, tuned right, can be a lot of fun out there."

It could also be instructional, of course. The Black Lake was all about pushing limits. Sometimes you exceeded them. That was the nature of testing limits, of playing games on the edge of the deep end of the pool. Sooner or later, you slipped into it.

"Oltamu wasn't in the car business," Dax said, and Abby didn't argue, but she believed Oltamu might very well have been in the car business. He was the battery man—and every automaker on the planet was working on electric vehicles now. But if Tara was right, and Oltamu had just come from Black Lake in East Liberty, Ohio, then he'd been watching performance tests. You didn't go to the Black Lake to test a battery-charging station. You went to the Black Lake to push a car to its performance limits—or beyond.

Dax shifted lanes. Despite the late hour and the storm, traffic was thick. Welcome to Boston. Traffic was always thick.

"We've had to reroute, and I've been tempted to drive faster, but if I got pulled over, I'd have a hard time explaining you, wouldn't I?" He laughed, a sound of boyish delight. "It's a waste of the car, though."

He put on the turn signal and then shifted again, gliding left to right in a move that would attract no attention, and yet Abby could feel that he was still learning the throttle of the Hellcat, the bracing amount of torque that even a light touch on the accelerator brought. It was a waste of the car with him behind the wheel. He had no idea how to handle it, how far it could be pushed. Or how quickly control could be lost.

I made that gap in the guardrail, Abby thought dully. *That was one hell of a move. Splitting traffic with the angle and acceleration perfect, then the hard brake and turn without misjudging the tires and rolling, putting it through a gap most people couldn't hit at forty, let alone ninety, and doing it all on wet pavement...dumb, yes, and a product of panic, but...not easy to do.*

Strange and sad, how that still pleased her. It was nothing to be proud of—she'd been melting down, her nerves no longer merely fraying but collapsing like downed power lines, sparking flashes of failure.

But it was also the first time she'd taken anything remotely resembling a test of the old instinct, the old muscle memory.

The old Abby.

For a moment, the woman she'd been had surfaced again. For a moment, she'd seen nothing but that narrow target, had anticipated the speed of the cars crowding in, felt the tires exploring the pavement in a way that was as intimate as skin on skin. She'd executed the intended maneuver perfectly and in circumstances where inches and fractions of seconds mattered.

There weren't many people alive who could have pulled that off without causing a deadly pileup, and she'd landed without even scratching the paint.

And now you're riding shotgun with a killer, tied to the seat, and you didn't even succeed in taking his phone from him. Some victory, Abby.

Victories, though, like phobias, weren't always rational. Sometimes they were very internal, invisible to the outside world. Matters of willpower or control were still wins. The short-term impact didn't matter nearly as much as the fact that you'd held on in the face of adversity. A win was a win, as they said. No matter how small, no matter how private.

She watched the traffic thicken as Dax rolled southeast, and she wondered how she'd feel with the wheel in her hands again. The same old panic? Or would it be diminished by the knowledge that when things went to hell, she'd maintained enough of her old brain and body to execute the escape maneuver? Tough to call it an escape maneuver when there'd been no real external threat, nothing except the irrational dread that soaked her brain like chloroform, but the brain didn't operate strictly on facts; its fuel was emotion.

This much, Abby understood very well.

The exit for the hospital was fast approaching, maybe five miles away. She wondered what the kid's plan was and if he had any concern, any fear. He projected nothing but confidence. He was to killing what Abby had once been to driving—a natural pairing, in total harmony with his craft.

But killing Tara Beckley wasn't his goal. Not tonight, at least. He had to get Oltamu's phone to her, and she would need to be alive for that. How he intended to walk through a hospital and achieve this without attracting attention, Abby couldn't imagine.

She figured she'd be a part of it, though. There was a reason she was still alive, and it wasn't his compassion.

Dax shifted right again, decelerated, and exited. Abby didn't follow this choice; if time was now an issue, then he shouldn't abandon the interstate this far north. Then they were moving into a residential stretch, high-dollar homes on tree-lined streets. Driving farther from the hospital.

The kid pulled into a parking space on the street, tucking in behind a behemoth Lincoln Navigator, and studied the road. His eyes were on the houses, not the cars, but then he paused and checked the mirrors as well. Satisfied by whatever he saw or didn't see, he killed the engine.

"Time to start earning your keep," he said, turning to Abby. The boyish features seemed to fade, and his hard eyes dominated his face, eyes that belonged to a much older man.

"What are we doing?"

"You'll be sitting right there. But you'll be watching too." He picked up his phone from the console, tapped the screen, and then set it back down. The screen displayed a live video image of the interior of the car. Abby twisted her head, searching for the camera, the cord rubbing into her throat. She didn't see a camera, but when she looked back, she realized the video was in motion. When she stopped, it stopped.

Dax smiled. "I'll need my hat back," he said.

He took the hat off Abby's head, and the video display followed the jostling motion. He settled it back on his own head, then turned to Abby, and Abby's face appeared on the cell phone display, a clear, high-definition image. She saw there was dried blood crusted in her blond hair from where he'd hit her with the gun.

"I need to confess something," the kid said. His voice seemed to echo, but it was really coming from the phone's speaker. "Covert audio recording is illegal here in Massachusetts. This is a two-party-consent state."

He sighed, and the sigh echoed on the phone like a distant gust of wind.

"I've had to make my peace with that," he said, "because my uncle was a big fan of recording things. Knowledge is power, right? The more eyes and ears one has, the more one knows. I think my uncle would've liked this hat. I never got the chance to show it to him, but…" He shrugged. "I'm confident of his opinion."

He moved his hand to the ignition and started the engine again.

"You're about to meet the man who's responsible for the unfortunate trouble Hank Bauer encountered," Dax said, pulling away from the curb.

"You killed him," Abby said. "I don't care who paid you."

"Sure you do."

At an intersection, they paused at a stop sign, then they continued along the dark street and pulled into a driveway that was flanked by ornate brick pillars, a gate between them. Dax put the window down, punched four buttons on a keypad mounted in one pillar, and the gates parted. He drove through. The gates closed behind them and locked with a pneumatic hiss followed by a clang.

He pulled down the drive, parked, and cut the engine.

"Just sit tight," he said. "I know it's uncomfortable, but at least you'll have a view."

With that, he stepped out of the car, slammed the driver's door, and locked the car with the key fob, engaging the alarm. If Abby tried to smash the window, it was going to be loud, and the kid would have plenty of time to get outside. There was a slim chance that a neighbor might come to investigate, but probably not. Car alarms were viewed as nuisances, not cries for help. Unless Abby freed herself from the passenger seat, she wasn't going to achieve anything by breaking a window.

Dax walked around the back of the house and disappeared from sight. Abby's eyes went to the cell phone, and now she could see from Dax's point of view: a light came on in the back of the house. Dax went to knock, but the door opened before he could make contact, and a short, wiry man with graying hair and a nose crooked from a bad break stood in front of him, gun in hand.

For an instant, Abby thought this could be good news—she didn't care who this guy was; anyone who shot the kid was on her team.

But the man didn't shoot. He lowered the gun and said, "What in the fuck do you think you're doing?"

"My job," Dax said. If he was in any way troubled by the gun, he didn't show it.

"Your job? You don't come to my fucking home unless I tell you to! That's not your—"

Something moved at the edge of the frame and then came into the center. Dax was holding up Oltamu's phone. "This was my job, Gerry."

The man stared at the phone. He leaned forward, then pulled back, suspicious and confused.

"How'd you get it? Kaplan said—"

"Kaplan's trying to bluff her way back to life," Dax said. "Let me in. I don't want to stand outside and talk about this shit."

Gerry hesitated, then nodded, and stepped aside. Abby followed the bouncing path of the camera as the kid walked through a sunroom with a marble fireplace, opened another door, and stepped into a kitchen that was filled with expanses of white cabinets and stainless-steel appliances.

"You alone?" Dax asked.

"Yeah. And remember, the questions are—"

"The questions are yours to ask, right. I didn't think that one could do much harm."

Gerry paced back into the frame. His body language was tense, like a fighter's before the bell. The kid worked for him, but he didn't seem to have his employer's trust.

Maybe that was because Gerry had just arranged to kill him.

"How in the hell did you get that?" he asked.

"Kaplan's been bullshitting you the whole time. She never had it. The salvage-yard guy gave it to his brother. It was in his pawnshop. I bought it for ninety bucks. I assume I'll be reimbursed?"

"Let me see it."

Dax passed it over. Gerry set his gun down on the counter to study the phone.

Unwise, Abby thought, watching in the car. She was captivated by the scene playing out on the phone's screen, but it was time to worry about more important things—she was *literally* captive within the car, and that wasn't going to change unless she could free her neck.

She reached for the cord with her clumsy, bound hands. There was just barely enough room between skin and cord to get a grasp, and when she did, the cord had no give. She leaned forward, straining painfully, and twisted until she got her hands over her shoulder. It was an awkward movement that put pressure on her rotator cuff as well as her throat, but she was able to feel the way the cord had been looped around the headrest and knotted. The knot was a pro's work; Abby wasn't going to be able to untie it from this angle, working blind and unable to separate her hands.

There was, however, another option. She was tied to the headrest, which was a perfectly effective approach when the headrest was in place, but the headrest could be removed. It would be awkward, and it would be painful, but if she could lift the headrest out, the cord would slide off it.

She arched her back, wincing at the pain, stretched her shoulders until the tendons howled in protest, and began to hunt for the headrest release with her fingers.

44

When he'd seen the kid arrive at his back door—his *back* door, he didn't even walk up the front steps like a normal human—Gerry was tempted to shoot him. It had been years since he'd killed anyone, but he intended to do it in the next twelve hours regardless, and the sight of Dax seemed to portend trouble. Gerry didn't want to kill him on his own property and in a quiet neighborhood with an unsilenced weapon unless it was necessary, though.

Then he saw the phone, and killing Dax Blackwell became less of a concern. The phone was the whole point, and somehow the kid already had it.

Standing in his kitchen, Gerry was no longer thinking about the arrangements he'd made in Old Orchard or the suppressed handgun that was under his driver's seat, the one that already had a bullet chambered for Dax. The phone had all his attention.

It was the right phone—no signal, a clone, and with a lock screen featuring a picture of the girl. Everything about this was good news except for the last.

"How do you unlock it?" Gerry said.

"Either with facial recognition or a code name." Dax leaned laconically against the counter. "But does it matter?"

"Of course it matters!"

"Why?"

Gerry lifted his head and stared at the kid. He was standing there in the shadows, slouching and wearing his hoodie and the dumb friggin' baseball cap, same as always.

"If you can't open it, then it's not worth a shit."

"Were you hired to open it?" Dax said. "Or just provide it to your client? My understanding was that he wouldn't even want you to wonder too much about it."

Gerry's angry rebuttal died on his lips. It was a fair point. He could do more harm than good if he even told the German about the lock screen. Let the German deal with it.

"I do think it could change your price point, perhaps," the kid said.

"Change my price point."

"Sure. The girl is alive. If your client wants us to bring that phone to her, I can do it. We can unlock it, which I'd assume is your client's desire. But that's above and beyond the initial job, isn't it? Value added should not be free." He shrugged. "At least, not in my opinion. But it's your show."

Damn right it was Gerry's show. However, the kid was spot-on. The German was inevitably going to want to get the phone to the girl if this was indeed a biometric lock, and Gerry wasn't doing that shit for free. He wasn't sure that he wanted to do it at all, though. This job had been sliding sideways from the beginning.

"Maybe he wants this thing to disappear, period," Gerry said, turning the phone over on the counter. It was a perfect replica of an iPhone. "That's all he wanted for Oltamu."

"He wanted Oltamu dead. The phone, he wanted in his possession. If he'd planned on having it destroyed, he could have asked you to do it. But he didn't."

Gerry had made it his business not to ask questions that he didn't need the answers to, but the German had wanted the phone, and Gerry was curious just what was on this thing that made it so valuable. Already, the German had been willing to go to two million for the job. Gerry hadn't even had to push to get that much. How much could he get for an unlocked version?

"Call him and ask," Dax said, as if Gerry had voiced the question aloud.

Gerry looked from the phone to the gun and then up at the kid. He couldn't see his eyes because of the shadow from the black baseball cap, but his posture was the same as it always was, the slouch of a bored delinquent. In this way, he was different from both his uncle, who had a military bearing, and his father, who was always in a state of physical calm but had *presence,* a means of commanding attention and respect without any alpha-male posturing. The kid would need to grow into that or learn the hard way that he came across as more sullen than sinister. Hard men would look him over and feel like they could test him. The more that happened, the more likely it was that one of them would succeed, and Dax Blackwell would be in a coffin before he was twenty.

His mind and his hands worked fast, though. He'd killed Carlos and walked away clean; he'd eliminated a pair of difficulties in Maine; he'd called Kaplan's bluff and found the phone. While Gerry had been scrambling to deal with Kaplan, Dax had been solving problems. Maybe he was right. Maybe this was worth making a call.

"We'd have to be sure we can get to her," Gerry said.

"I can."

"Yeah? How? She's in intensive care, she's got doctors and nurses and family all over her, and there are cameras everywhere in a hospital."

"I'll get to her," Dax said, unfazed. "I look the part. A visiting friend from good old Hammel College. I don't need to stay long— I can just pass through, say a prayer, take a picture."

Gerry grinned. The kid could probably play that role just fine. He was young enough to get away with it. "Okay," Gerry said, straightening. "I'll make the call. But keep your mouth shut. He's going to need to think I'm alone."

"Sure."

It was two in the morning in Germany, but Gerry figured he'd get an answer. He wasn't even sure if his man was still in Germany.

He was supposed to be in the States by tomorrow, so maybe he was on a plane or already on the ground.

Wherever he was, he answered the phone. They used an end-to-end encryption app that allowed for texting, voice, and video calls. Virtually untraceable, and the messages vanished. The German also used a voice-distortion device, though Gerry had never wasted time on that.

"Do not tell me there is trouble," the German said. Through the distortion, he sounded cartoonish, a Bond villain.

"None on my end," Gerry said. "Maybe some on yours."

"Explain."

Gerry did. Told him that Oltamu had put a facial-recognition lock on the phone before he died, and the face wasn't his but the girl's. He could get to the girl, he said, or he could hand the device off and let other people deal with it. He didn't care; his work was done.

There was some swearing, and then some silence. Gerry was beginning to think he'd made a mistake by allowing the kid to goad him into this when the German said, "Do you know it will work? She is in a coma. Will it work with someone who is in a coma?"

Gerry looked at Dax, who nodded, pointed at his eyes with two fingers, then moved his fingers up and down.

"It should," Gerry said. "She's got eye movement."

Dax gave him a thumbs-up. The kid was so damned cocky. He was also awfully good. In fact, after Dax's work on this job, Gerry's faith in him was renewed. The kid was more than a beta-Blackwell; he was the real deal.

And to think, Gerry had planned to kill him. What a waste that would have been.

"If it can be done safely," the German said, "then do it. Otherwise, back off."

"Fine," Gerry said. "And how much is that worth to you?"

Another pause. Then: "Half."

Half was a million. If Dax Blackwell could walk into that hospital, hold the phone up to Tara Beckley's face, and unlock it, Gerry was three million dollars richer.

"Fine," he said again, but he saw Dax shake his head and gesture upward with his thumb. He wanted Gerry to go higher. The *balls* on this kid. Gerry didn't respond, just glared at him, and Dax shrugged and jammed his hands back into the pockets of his hoodie.

"Has to happen fast," the German said.

"It will. Or if it isn't doable, I'll back off."

"We meet at the same place and same time, no matter what. Don't risk anything that compromises that. I won't wait."

"You won't have to."

They disconnected. Gerry put his phone in his pocket, looked at Dax Blackwell, and smiled. He was feeling warm toward the kid, and why not? He'd just made Gerry an extra million bucks. "It's on," he said. "Think you can get to Tara Beckley without trouble?"

"Yes."

"Don't push it."

"Of course not. What about Kaplan? She's still out there. She doesn't have the phone, but she's still a threat. Somebody ought to meet her in Old Orchard, right?"

"Ought to be you. You're the one she's seen, the one she wants."

"It's personal to her, huh?"

Gerry was still riding the buzz of an extra million, and problems seemed to be solving themselves, so he nodded. "Yeah, her bullshit was that she'd trade the phone for you."

Dax said, "I don't recall you mentioning that."

Gerry hesitated, realizing that he hadn't brought that up before, then shrugged. "Wouldn't have mattered much. We'd have taken her tomorrow and gotten the phone. Now it's even easier. Cleaner."

"Because we have the phone." Dax was watching him intently.

"Right," Gerry said. "So tomorrow, it can be quick. No need to waste time. Just clip her and move on."

"Where will you be?"

Gerry frowned. "Taking the phone in."

"Where?"

"The hell business is that of yours?"

"Abby Kaplan wants to see you. Maybe we should both be there."

No, Abby Kaplan wanted to see the kid. The kid would go there and kill her. Or possibly he'd go there and fail, but Gerry had trouble believing that. If the bitch actually appeared, the kid would handle her. And if Abby Kaplan was somehow leagues better than anticipated and had arranged for cops all over the pier, well, Gerry still wasn't overly concerned about that. Dax didn't seem like the talking-to-cops type, and if it turned out he was, Gerry had silenced people in prisons before.

"Let me handle my shit," Gerry said, "and you handle yours."

He didn't like the way the kid was looking at him. It was that clinical, under-the-microscope stare, penetrating and yet distant, the look that his father and uncle wore so naturally. The look they'd given those hard boys in Belfast all those years ago.

As if reading his thoughts, Dax said, "I've cleaned it all up pretty well so far. Things had the potential to get out of hand, and now they're back in my control. Do you still think my father and uncle would have done it better?"

"They couldn't have done it any better than this," Gerry said, "and there were two of them."

Dax's face split into a wide smile beneath the shadow cast by his baseball cap.

"You're right," he said. "Since there's just me, I've got to be twice as good, don't I? Nobody in my corner. They were good, but there were two of them. I'm solo. I have to reach their level and then push beyond it."

"You're on your way," Gerry told him, unsettled by the conversation, by the way the kid happily measured himself against dead men. He nodded at Oltamu's cloned phone, which was still sitting on the counter. "But you got some work left to do. Let's not waste time."

"They liked you," Dax said, as if he hadn't heard the instruction. "They didn't like many people either. But my father once told me that there were only two things I could trust. One of them was Gerry Connors."

This was oddly flattering. Gerry had looked out for the kid. Giving him chances, bringing him along in the business. And now, he'd decided to let him live. He'd extend their relationship; grow it, even. It wasn't too late for that.

"Glad to hear I earned their trust," Gerry said. "Who was the second man?"

"What?"

"You said he told you to put your trust in two things."

"Oh." Dax laughed. "I confused you, sorry. The second one wasn't a person."

Gerry cocked his head and frowned. A question was rising to his lips when Dax Blackwell said, "It was this," and then there was a clap and a spark of light that seemed to come from within the kid's black hoodie, and suddenly Gerry was down on the floor, hot blood pumping out of his stomach. He put a hand to the wound and let out a high moan that brought the taste of blood into his throat and mouth. He looked at the counter and saw his gun sitting there, out of reach.

Dax took a black revolver with gleaming chrome cylinders out of his hoodie pocket and waved it in the air like a taunt. Or a reminder.

It was this. Gerry saw that gun and remembered where he'd seen it before: Jack Blackwell's hand.

Of course, he thought, the pain not yet rising, the panic not rising, nothing rising but the taste of blood and the sense of inevitability. *Of course Jack would have told the boy to trust the gun above all else.*

Dax knelt beside him and brought his face down low. This close, Gerry could finally see his eyes beneath the shadows of the baseball cap. They were a light blue, and the expression in them could almost pass for compassionate. Gerry needed some compassion now. Just a trace of it. He needed the kid to understand that they could make this right. They could get Gerry patched up, could save his life, and if that happened, he would never turn the kid in, would never try to get revenge for this. He'd never even speak of it. If the kid just gave him life, there would be no end to Gerry's kindness.

He opened his mouth to speak, to convey his promise, but all that left his lips was a warm stream of blood.

Dax Blackwell looked down at him sadly, and then he leaned even closer, his eyes still on Gerry's, his gaze unblinking.

"I want you to know," he said, "how much I've appreciated the opportunities."

When Gerry opened his mouth to beg for his life, Dax shoved the gun between his lips and pulled the trigger once more.

Gerry Connors died on his kitchen floor, three thousand miles and thirty years from the place where he'd first met the Blackwell family.

Part Five

THE LONG WAY HOME

45

Abby had succeeded in lifting the headrest to its fully extended position, which required bracing her feet on the front of the seat and arching and twisting her back like an Olympic diver attempting a half gainer. She could feel the release buttons, but removing the headrest entirely required more pressure and a lifting motion, a feat that was not easy to execute when you were tied to the damned thing and each lift strangled you and each push at the release buttons numbed already clumsy fingers.

She was close, though. She was very close, and she was so intent on the task that she'd almost forgotten about the scene playing out on Dax's phone.

Then came the gunshot.

She spun at the sound and slipped, and the headrest slid back into place. She could hear it clinking down, level by level, lock by lock, like an extension ladder closing.

"Shit!" she cried, the cord tight against her throat, her swollen fingers numb, all of her gains lost. She could see the display of the phone again, though, and so she was looking at it when a man's horrified face came into view, the man Dax had called Gerry. Gerry's lips parted, and blood ran over them and down his chin. Abby stared at the image in horror, and when the revolver appeared from offscreen and slipped between the man's bloodied lips, she closed her eyes, a reflex action.

"I want you to know," Dax said, "how much I've appreciated the opportunities."

She didn't see the second shot, but she heard it. The sound was loud on the phone, but out here in the driveway, beyond the walls of the brick house, it was softer, swift and insignificant.

That was how a human life could end. Neither with a whimper nor a bang—just a muffled pop that wouldn't turn any heads in the neighborhood. The night didn't pause for the kill shot. The night carried on.

The night always would.

Abby sat in the passenger seat, breathing hard, eyes squeezed shut, sweat on her brow from the exertion of her work on the headrest. She'd been so close. A fraction of an inch away, a few more seconds, that was all she'd needed, but now she would have to start over, and without even opening her eyes to check the phone display, she knew that time was short.

It was. She opened her eyes in time to see the kid moving for the door, and then she didn't require the display anymore, because she could see Dax emerging from the shadows. He was walking at a leisurely pace, no sign of panic or even concern. There was a brown paper bag in his hand. The gun he'd just killed with was nowhere to be seen.

He used the key fob to unlock the Challenger, and too late Abby wondered whether there was any sign of her nearly successful effort to free herself. Dax opened the door, dropped into the driver's seat, and looked her over quickly but carefully, but if he saw anything that troubled him, he didn't show it.

"Sorry you had to watch that," he said, apparently attributing Abby's sweat to fear over what she'd seen play out on the phone. "Remember, the man was going to kill you too."

When Abby didn't answer, Dax lifted a hand in an *It's all right* gesture and said, "No thanks needed. Happy to help."

He tossed the brown paper bag into the backseat. It landed heavily, and Dax registered Abby's response to the sound.

"There's a wallet, a watch, a gun, a phone, and two hundred thousand dollars cash in there," he said. "I'm afraid Gerry was robbed. But good news—if anything happens to me, all of that is yours."

He picked up the phone from the center console and closed out of the concealed-camera application. The video disappeared, and audio replaced it—the feed from Tara Beckley's hospital room. Abby recognized Shannon's voice and a lower, male voice that she thought was the doctor who'd been with them previously. They were making small talk now, long pauses between comments.

Dax listened thoughtfully, then said, "Killing time."

It was a common expression, and yet when it left his mouth, Abby thought he meant that the hour of murder was upon them again.

"They're waiting on the cavalry to arrive," Dax said. "Which means we can get there first."

With that, he backed out of the driveway. This time, the gates opened automatically. Abby still hadn't spoken. She stared at the gates as they closed again.

"Onward!" Dax said jauntily, and he pulled onto the street. "It's your time now, Abby. Are you ready to own the moment? A lot of people will be counting on you."

He had a heavy foot on the gas pedal, was doing forty-five in a thirty-miles-per-hour zone and gaining speed. The Hellcat's power could sneak up on you if you were distracted, and the kid was distracted. The cheerful mask was a false front, and his voice was no longer his natural taunt but something he was ginning up because he needed to feel that old confidence. Abby was confused. She had no sense that killing bothered Dax, and yet something about this one had rattled him.

"Who was he?" Abby said.

"No one of significance to you."

"But he knew your father." This much Abby had heard while she strained at the cord around her throat. Talk of a father and an uncle. That had mattered to him in a real way, one that his masks could not fully conceal. The car was still gaining speed, roaring down the residential street at more than fifty, and he had no idea.

"You're going too fast," Abby said.

He registered the speed with surprise and eased off the accelerator.

"Good eye," he said, the forced cheerful demeanor back. "You're a fine partner, Abby. Don't ever let me forget to acknowledge that."

The weakness is family, Abby thought, watching him, and then: *One of them was named Jack. That person matters to him. And this last murder wasn't like the rest. For a reason involving family, it was different.*

Had he killed a family member back there? It seemed possible; with him, any horror seemed possible. But Abby didn't believe that was it. The dead man had been important to him, but he wasn't family.

The kid hooked a left turn and then they were on a four-lane street, leaving the neighborhood, and up ahead, the lights of the interstate showed.

Abby leaned back against the headrest to let the cord loosen as much as possible and felt the thrum of the big engine work into her spine. Only hours ago, that had driven panic through her, but now she felt the connection again.

She knew that the headrest would come off. She'd been close to getting it, and she would be faster the next time.

If she survived until the next time.

"Where are we going?" she asked. "Or have you killed enough people for one day?"

"We're not done," the kid said. His voice was a monotone, as if he couldn't muster the energy to do his typical upbeat act. "You're going to see Tara. If things go well, you might live a little longer. So might Tara."

When Dax shifted onto the interstate ramp, the Pirellis spun on the wet pavement, and the Challenger fishtailed briefly. He got it under control fast, and he didn't react with fear or even surprise. He might not understand the car, but he understood power, and he learned quickly.

46

Boone wanted her own car, but asking for assistance from her employers would break the silence around Tara Beckley, and adding more actors to the mix, even a simple driver/bodyguard who understood rank and wouldn't ask questions, felt risky right now. The operations protocol around Oltamu had been silence, and though he was dead, she didn't think that protocol should be.

The rental counter would waste time, and Uber would not, so when she made it to the ground, she went against her strongest instincts and sacrificed control for speed. The plane had circled for twenty-five minutes while the storm lashed the New England coast beneath it, but it had finally landed, and now all that was left between her and Tara Beckley was fifteen miles. She summoned the Uber, and when it arrived, she stepped off the curb, got into the car, handed the driver—a too-friendly chick with dyed-pink hair—a hundred-dollar bill, and told her to start moving fast and keep moving fast.

"I don't want to get a ticket," the girl protested. She had approximately twenty piercings and fifty tattoos, but she didn't want to challenge a speed limit?

"If you get a ticket, I'll pay it," Boone said.

"It still affects my Uber status! They'll know if I—"

"Then you won't get a ticket," Boone snapped. "I can make it disappear. Trust me on this, would you? Any cop who stops us will let us go in a hurry." The girl, mouth open, looked at her in the mirror, and Boone said, "Keep your eyes on the damned road."

Boone texted Pine while they pulled away from Logan. She told him she was en route and asked if anything had changed. Pine said no. Boone asked where the family was. Pine said the sister was present but the mom and stepdad were in their hotel room; did she want them? Boone said no. She just wanted the girl. Tara might or might not have the answers, but the parents definitely didn't.

Get rid of the sister, Boone texted.

Can't be done, Pine replied.

What do you mean, it can't be done? Boone wrote.

You'll learn, Pine responded.

47

Tara rests while Dr. Pine and Shannon talk about inconse-
quential things; everyone is waiting on the arrival of the
investigator who will make sense of it all. Tara knows that will require conversation again, the exhausting process on the alphabet
board. Dr. Carlisle has promised they'll experiment with computer
software soon, but that's not going to help Tara now. She's got to
rely on her eyes, nothing else, and she's got to call up the stamina to
make it through. Last mile, running uphill. She's been here before.

But she hasn't, of course. She has never had to face that last mile
suffering the relentless pain of tubes jammed into various orifices
or the maddening cruelty of paralysis. There is no analogy in the
world that applies here. She's not invisible any longer, but she's also
no closer to leaving this bed or even making a sound than she was
when she woke up.

Don't let yourself think that way. Be strong.

She's tired of being strong, though. Tired of how much everyone cares about Oltamu and his fucking phone. He's dead, but
Tara isn't, and maybe she's worse off than him. Endless days like
this, endless expenses...what if there's no finish line? What if this
is it?

Remember your thumb.

Yes. Her thumb. Capable of spasmodic twitching. What a win!

You take your wins where you can find them, though. Water
could erode rock, drop by drop.

She tunes out the conversation around her and focuses on the
channel between brain and thumb. Visualizes it, imagines it like

a river, sees her force of will like a skilled rower pulling against the current, forcing her way upstream. Brain to thumb, no turning back, and no portages around treacherous water. You had to beat the current.

The visual takes clearer shape, and she can see a woman who is like her but who is not her, a different version of Tara, more dream than memory, but so tenacious. The rowboat becomes a kayak, and though real Tara is awkward with a kayak paddle, dream Tara is not. She's strong and graceful, fighting a current that flashes with green-gold light just beneath the surface. As she paddles, the river widens, and the current pushes against her, and then, impossibly, it reverses direction and begins guiding her downstream, an aid rather than an enemy now.

Make it to the thumb. Make it there, and once you know the way, you will make it again. Once you know you can go that far whenever you like, then try another river in another direction. We'll explore them all, run them to the end. We have nothing but time.

She could swear she feels a tightening in her thumb, a faint pulse of muscle tension.

Yes, it can be done. It's long and hard but it can be done. Keep riding the current, keep steering, keep—

"She's on her way," Dr. Pine says, and at first Tara is convinced that he's speaking about her, that he's somehow aware of her journey downriver. Then she sees that his eyes are on his phone.

"Fifteen minutes," he reports. Then he looks at Tara. "Do you want your parents here?"

The two eye flicks are necessary, but they also take her away from the river, and she feels a loosening of tension in her hand. She was so close. Why did he have to interrupt?

No matter. She's found the way once, and she will find it again. Over and over, however long it takes. The water was not so bad. Eventually the current had shifted to help her, and whatever produced that green-gold hue beneath the surface was good. She's not sure why she's so sure of that, but she knows beyond any doubt that it is a good sign.

I'll be back, Tara promises herself, and then she gives Pine her attention again. He smiles in what is supposed to be a reassuring fashion, but she can tell that he's nervous. Who can blame him? It's not enough to be tasked with bringing a patient back from the dead; now he's supposed to see that the patient provides witness testimony to some sort of government agent? Even for a neurologist, this can't feel like another day at the office.

She'd like to smile back at him and let him know that she's grateful for all he's done and that she felt better the moment he walked into the room, looked at her with those curious but hopeful eyes, and introduced himself. And used her name. Sometime soon, when she has the computer software that makes all of this less of a chore, she will let him know how much that mattered. Small things, quiet things, but he gave her dignity when others did not.

Shannon isn't offering any smiles. She's not even offering her attention. She's glued to her own phone and seems distressed. Tara watches Shannon tap out a text message and send it, but she can't read the message because Shannon is shielding the phone with her free hand. It's an unsubtle way of making it clear that she doesn't want Pine to see it. Once the message is sent, she stands up, her chair making a harsh squeak on the tile.

"I'll be right back."

Pine turns and stares at her. "Where are you going?"

Shannon gives him an icy look. "Is that your business?"

"Right now, I feel that it is, yes. We're fifteen minutes away from—"

"I know! Trust me, I am aware. I just need to…breathe for a few seconds. Okay?"

Pine doesn't like it, but he decides not to fight it. He seems to think Shannon is on the verge of a panic attack, which would be a logical assumption if he were dealing with anyone other than

Shannon. Tara knows better. Shannon has no fight-or-flight response, it's only fight with her. If she were flooded with adrenaline, she'd refuse to leave the room. So what in the hell is going on, and why won't she meet Tara's eyes?

Then she's gone. Without a look back.

48

Inside the Challenger, Dax and Abby listened to the exchange in the hospital room. Dax nodded, pleased, and said, "Attagirl. Way to stand your ground."

Abby, still bound to the passenger seat of her dead friend's car, said nothing. They were parked on the fourth floor of a five-floor garage attached to the hospital, and most of the spaces around them were empty, as were many on the third level, which connected to the hospital through a walkway. There should be little if any traffic up here.

When Dax had parked, he'd sent a text message to Shannon Beckley, making sure that Abby saw each word. He identified himself as Abby, and from there the text was simple: he told her the car he was in and where it was parked in the hospital garage, then said he would give Shannon Oltamu's phone provided she came alone.

It was, Abby had to admit, a smart choice. Shannon wanted the phone, and she knew Abby had it. Any other tactic—threatening her, for example—might not have rung true. But the promise of the phone was tempting, particularly with the DOE agent on the way, and the situation made sense. As far as Shannon knew, Abby was doing what she'd said she would: reaching out to her from another phone number and offering what help she could from her own perilous position in the world.

Shannon should have no reason to doubt her.

"You're going to have the opportunity to make some noise, I suppose," Dax said, pocketing the phone and turning to Abby.

"You could scream, kick the horn. I don't know what all has run through your head, but I'm sure you've had ideas, and I can promise you that all of them are bad. Right now, she's got the chance to walk in and out of this garage alive and unhurt. Don't ruin that for her, Abby."

He studied Abby's eyes for a moment, then nodded once, opened the driver's door, and slipped out. They were parked beside a large panel van with a cleaning company's logo, and he vanished on the other side of that. Abby watched him go and then turned to her right, where the stairwell was.

Shannon Beckley should come from that direction. Maybe alone, maybe not. If she walked through the door with a cop in tow, Abby didn't think it would take long for the shooting to start.

Shannon came alone. She'd moved fast too, because the wait hadn't been long. The stairwell door opened and there she was, tall and defiant, or at least trying to look defiant, though you could see her nerves in the way she scanned the garage even after she'd observed the Challenger parked where she'd been told it would be. She hesitated, and Abby saw her glance back at the stairwell door as it clanged shut behind her, but then she steeled herself and started toward the Challenger with long, purposeful strides.

She made it halfway there before the kid got her.

Abby hadn't seen him move. She'd thought he was still waiting on the other side of that van, but he must have crawled under it or around it, because he emerged from behind a pickup truck that was parked four empty spaces from the Challenger, now on Abby's right instead of her left. Shannon Beckley was walking fast, her eyes on the Challenger, and she might have glimpsed Abby's face through the darkly tinted glass because she seemed to squint just before Dax rose up beside her.

She had time to scream, but she didn't. Instead, she tried to fight and run at the same time, stumbling backward while throwing a wild right hook. If she'd stepped into the punch, she might've landed it; she had a fast hand. But because she was trying to both attack and flee, she missed the punch, and then Dax had her. He caught her right wrist, spun her, twisted her arm up behind her back, and clapped his gloved left hand over her mouth.

Abby jerked forward instinctively as if to help. The cord bit into her throat and forced her back. She reached for the headrest release, but before she could even find it, they were walking her way, Dax whispering into Shannon's ear with each step. When they arrived beside the car, he released her and drew the gun. He did this so quickly that it was pressed against the back of Shannon's skull before she had time to react to being free. She stood still, staring through the window at Abby, close enough now to see the cord around her throat.

"Open the driver's door," Dax said to Shannon. His voice was soft but menacing, like early snowflakes with a blizzard behind them.

Shannon walked around the back of the car and opened the driver's door, and then she and Abby were briefly face-to-face with no glass between them.

"I'm sorry," Abby said. The words sounded as hollow to her as Shannon's expression told her they felt.

"Backseat," Dax said, folding the driver's seat forward and allowing access to the back. Shannon hesitated, and he cocked the revolver. She crawled into the backseat, scrambled across the leather, and crouched in the far corner. Dax followed, swinging the door shut behind him and sealing them all inside, Abby tied to the front passenger seat, Shannon and Dax and the gun in the back.

"All together now," he said. "Terrific. This thing is close to done, Shannon. Closer than you think. You've got a big job to do, though. You've got to get our beloved little phone to your sister and unlock it and bring it back. You've got to do that quickly and without anyone else seeing it. Otherwise, the killing starts fast."

Shannon had been staring at Abby, but now she looked back at Dax and seemed to be sizing him up. Other than having the gun, he didn't appear all that imposing. Abby remembered the night she'd made the same mistake.

"You need to listen to him," Abby said. "And not for me. I'm not worried about myself anymore. But you need to listen to him because you need him to go away fast."

"That's excellent advice," Dax said. "Abby's been along for the ride for a while now. She's seen some things. I'd trust her wisdom if I were you."

Shannon Beckley looked at Abby and then back at Dax, and Abby knew her mind was whirling, and she was almost positive she knew what she was thinking.

"When the Department of Energy agent gets to the room, she isn't going to be able to help," she said, and Shannon's eyes widened. "Nobody in that room can help, because he can hear you. He's listening to the hospital room. Has been."

She'd taken this chance expecting retribution from Dax, expecting maybe even a bullet, but instead she received a smile.

"That's right," Dax said. "But we won't need to worry about ears anymore. Shannon's going to give us eyes too."

He took off the black baseball cap and extended it to her. She recoiled and smacked against the door. But she had nowhere to run, and it was far too late for that anyhow.

"The agent is en route," Dax said. "My understanding is that she's very close. That puts some added pressure on you, Shannon. I'm sorry about that, but…" He shrugged. "I'm not the one who sent for her. It's your turn to wear the black hat."

Abby watched in the mirror. Shannon took the hat from his hand like she was accepting a snake, then put it on. She pushed her hair behind her ears and settled it down. It looked natural enough. Looked good, even. But it wouldn't look right to the doctor who was in that room.

"Why'd she leave and put on a hat?" Abby said.

"Good question," the kid answered, not looking at her. "Why'd you do that, Shannon?"

Silence for a moment, then Shannon said, "I don't know."

"I think you do. I think you get migraines from the lights in the hospital. Stress and bright light? That can definitely bring on a headache. You took some Excedrin, you put on a hat, and now you want everyone to just shut the hell up about you and focus on your sister. I think everyone is ready to focus on Tara."

He reached into his pocket and withdrew Oltamu's phone. When he tapped the display, Abby watched Shannon's face change. She understood the picture. Or at least, she wasn't confused by it.

"You're going to need to hold this up to her eyes," Dax said, "and hope that it unlocks. It asks for a name, but I think that's bullshit. It just needs her eyes. If I'm wrong, though...there'll be a lot riding on Tara figuring out what to do then. Because I know your mother and stepfather are in room four eighty-one in the hotel next door, and they'll die fast if you make a bad choice."

He pressed the phone into her hand. Her hand was trembling, but only a little.

"You can save a lot of lives tonight," Dax told her.

"They'll be watching me," Shannon said. "At least, Pine will be. The doctor. How do you expect me to explain this to him?"

"Convincingly," Dax said. "That's how I expect you to do it. I'm not a fan of scripts. People get hung up on them, they forget their lines, and then things go to hell fast. I like quick thinkers with room to be creative. Maybe you want a word in private with your sister. Maybe you're angry with Dr. Pine. I don't know. But I think you'll figure it out. And Shannon? Make it believable. Because if that phone finds its way back to my hand, your family stays alive. If it doesn't..." He inclined his head toward the front seat. "Ask Abby what happened to the last person who disappointed me today."

Shannon didn't look at Abby. She put Oltamu's phone in her pocket and said, "May I go now?"

"You in a hurry?"

"Yes. I don't want any strangers around. Let me go now, before the detective or agent or whoever gets here."

"Wise," Dax said, and then he moved back, keeping the gun pointed at her, opened the door, and stepped outside. He lowered the gun and kept it down against his leg as she climbed out. He actually offered her a hand, looking like a high-school kid with his prom date. She ignored it and climbed out alone. She ignored the gun too. She ignored everything and just started walking toward the stairwell.

"He sees and hears you," Abby called after her. She knew how pathetic the warning sounded, but she was terrified for Shannon. She was going to try something. Abby was sure of that. She might not have a plan yet, but this woman was absolutely going to try something.

Dax leaned on the roof of the car and sang, "'He sees you when you're sleeping. He knows when you're awake. He knows if you've been bad or good, so be good, for goodness' sake!'"

The stairwell door opened and clanged shut, and Shannon Beckley was gone.

49

Pine wasn't as helpless over the sister as he'd claimed because when Boone arrived, he came down to meet her and said that the sister was gone and it was just Tara now.

"Shannon will come back," he said. "I'd be stunned if she didn't. Maybe we should wait."

"We are not waiting," Boone said. "Less is more, Doctor, when it comes to time and witnesses in this scenario."

She didn't give him a chance to consider that, just walked in front of him and down the corridor as if she knew where she was going. Using motion to push past hesitation was one of her favorite techniques, and it worked. Pine reacted as most men in positions of authority did and quickened his pace in an attempt to not only catch up to her but make it seem as if he were actually leading the way, that the rush had been his idea all along.

The corridor ended in a T, and Pine turned left and exchanged quick greetings with two nurses in the hall. If they had any interest in Boone, they didn't show it. She was just another stranger here to look at the brain-dead girl, evidently. Pine had done a good job of shutting down the chatter about Tara Beckley's return to consciousness in his own hospital, at least. The girl's mother had carried news outside the walls, but inside, it was business as usual. For the first time, Boone was pleased that she'd gotten here so late; the hospital was quieter at this hour.

"The process will seem simple to you," Pine said. "It will seem easy, even. She moves her eyes to give you answers—what could be less taxing, right? But I warn you that it is a laborious process for her. We've pushed her hard already today. At some point, the fatigue will catch up to her. Remember that as you phrase your questions."

"I tend to be concise," Boone said, which was certainly not a lie.

"It's not about being concise. You can talk all you want. What you need to consider is how many words are required for her to respond. You want to cut that down, down, down. As much as possible, use yes-or-no questions. When she has to spell out a word, make that word count."

They had reached room 373.

"Omit needless words," he admonished her, and then he opened the door.

50

O"*mit needless words.*" *Dr. Strunk is here!* Damn it, if Tara could only speak, she would say that to see whether Dr. Pine is enough of a writing geek to laugh. She expects that he is. Aren't all doctors well read? Their patients hope so, certainly.

As Dr. Pine ushers the new woman in, Tara finds herself thinking that she looks forward to having a real conversation with him at some point. She likes him and trusts him, and she suspects that he has good stories. In a business like his, how could you not? Tara wants to become one of his best stories.

A success story.

"Hello, Tara," he says, "your guest has arrived." He pauses, and then, as if reading her thoughts, he adds, "I'm sure Shannon will be here in a moment. But would you like to wait for her?"

Tara has no idea what bug crawled up Shannon's ass to send her rushing out of here, but she's comfortable with Dr. Pine and certain that Shannon will return soon. Then they will all get the lecture on how they shouldn't have started without her. But in the meantime, why not get to it?

She flicks her eyes up twice. No need to wait.

The woman with Dr. Pine is tall and lean, well muscled. A workout junkie, probably. Not a runner, though. Or at least, not just a runner. She likes free weights. Her shoulder muscles are defined under her tight-fitting black top, and Tara is surprised and somewhat disappointed that she's not wearing a jacket. She'd expected a jacket that might conceal a gun. Having never met a Department of Energy agent before, she allowed her imagination to go wild, and she should have known better. This is a notepad-and-laptop kind of law enforcement agent, not a gun-belt type. But, hey, she's clearly strong.

"Tara, it's very nice to meet you," the woman says, walking closer, every movement balanced and her focus on Tara total. "Dr. Pine was explaining how I can make this as easy as possible for you. I'll respect his guidance on that. I understand that yes-or-no questions are best, and I am going to stick to those as much as I can, but occasionally, I might need to ask you to spell. Do you understand all of that?"

Tara flicks her eyes up once, thinking, *Say your name, damn it.* At some point, she's going to have to take the time to get that sentence out so Dr. Pine knows how important it is to her. Common courtesies like introductions make her feel more human, less like a spectacle, some tourist attraction or circus freak, the Amazing Locked-in Woman, five dollars for five minutes of her incredible nonverbal communication.

The woman sits on the stool that Dr. Pine usually claims, and for some reason this bothers Tara. *Let the medical professional run the show, lady.* But there's no one in the room who matters to the woman except Tara.

Until the door swings open, and there is Shannon, dressed like a hostage negotiator. What in the world is she doing in that dumb black baseball cap?

"Sorry I'm late," she says in an odd, too-loud voice. "I was getting a bad headache. The stress and the lights…" She waves her hand at the overhead fluorescents. "I was afraid it would become a migraine."

The agent seems less than delighted to have Shannon join the party but accepts it with a thin smile and nod. "No problem. I was just about to ask Tara a few simple questions, and then I hope I can bring an end to your stress. At least this additional aspect of it." She rises from the stool and offers her hand, and Tara thinks, *Sure, the walking-talking girl gets an introduction.*

"Shannon Beckley," Shannon says, still too loud, as if she wants to be heard three rooms away. Her eyes are skittering all around the room, like someone taking inventory after a burglary.

"Nice to meet you, Shannon. I'm Andrea Carter, with the Department of Energy."

Well, Tara thinks, *at least we now have a name.*

And then, as Tara stares at her sister, something troubling overtakes her: She has seen that hat before. She's seen that hat in this room, when the Justin Loveless impostor showed up with the flowers.

What in the hell is happening?

51

I nside the Challenger, Dax and Abby sat side by side, like partners, and watched the video feed on the phone. It had been a disorienting show so far, with Shannon Beckley's head creating the effect of a Steadicam in a horror movie. Now things finally slowed down, and room 373 took on clarity: Tara in the bed, the doctor named Pine standing in the corner, and the DOE agent sitting on a stool at the bedside. Abby couldn't see her face, just the back of her head, blond hair against a black shirt, but then she turned to the door, and Abby waited with the sensation of a trapped scream for Shannon Beckley to say the wrong thing, to doubt the killing capacity of the kid who'd sent her in there. She might think calling 911 would be the right move, and then she would learn swiftly and painfully that such a mistake would be measured in lost lives.

Instead, she nailed it—voice too loud and a little unnatural, but the rest was right. The bit about the stress and the migraine worked well enough. Abby exhaled, feeling like the first step was a good one, but Dax went rigid.

What did he see that I didn't? Abby wondered.

Dax picked up the phone and used his fingers to change the zoom. The agent's face filled the screen.

"Well, now," he said, and other than during the initial moments after his last murder, it was the first time he'd sounded unsteady to Abby.

"What is it?" Abby said. She wasn't expecting an answer, but she got one.

"That's not a DOE agent," Dax said. "That's Lisa Boone."

"Who is Lisa Boone?"

"She worked with my father a few times. He thought she was very good." Dax finally looked away from the screen, met Abby's eyes, and realized the message meant nothing to her. His gaze was steady when he said, "That means she's a professional killer."

52

Shannon stands there wearing the black hat, the hat that Tara hasn't thought about on this day of developments, her future opening in front, her attention being directed to the past, pulling her in opposite directions. The young man with the hunter's eyes and the black hat seemed a forgotten player to her.

Now he is back. Tara knows this, and Shannon must too.

I could have warned her, Tara thinks.

Shannon says, "I don't want to interrupt this. I really don't. Trust me, I understand the importance. But I would like to have a few words alone with my sister before we begin any interviews."

Agent Andrea Carter is not happy with this. She rises, and for the first time Tara can see the intimidation evident in that lean, well-muscled frame. She moves with a menacing grace, like the instructor in the one self-defense class Shannon made Tara take before she went off to college. *For frat parties,* Shannon explained. *And pay attention to the groin shots.*

"We're not stopping now," Agent Carter says. "This is a lot bigger than this room, Ms. Beckley. This is more crucial to more people than you can possibly fathom."

"I'm not asking anyone to stop, just to give me a minute alone with my sister," Shannon says, and if she's intimidated by Carter, she doesn't show it. In fact, her bearing seems oddly helped by the strange hat, all that flat black beneath the lighter silver thread that draws the eye above the brim.

"You've had plenty of time to discuss this," Agent Carter says. "Tara just gave me consent in front of her doctor. I will not waste her time or put her at risk, but I will also not be interrupted. If you'd like to—"

"Hang on." This is from Dr. Pine, and Shannon and Agent Carter seem surprised that he is still in the room. He and Shannon have clashed from the start, but he's looking at her intently, seeing the insistence in her eyes, and when he looks back at Tara, he takes a protective step in her direction.

"This isn't your jurisdiction," he says, pointing at Agent Carter with his right index finger. "And it isn't your decision." He points at Shannon with his left. "This is my hospital, Tara is my patient, and she and I will make these decisions together. Tara gave consent to an interview, yes, Agent Carter. She also has the right to have a few private words with her sister beforehand."

"I'm not trying to stop you," Shannon says again. "But the private words…I need them." She looks at Tara, trying to convey how badly she needs these words, but the look is unnecessary, because Tara knows the hat.

Dr. Pine pivots, looks at Tara. "It's your call, Tara. I'm going to ask you two yes-or-no questions. First: Would you like a private word with your sister at this point?"

One flick. Yes. Very much so. Because that hat…

"I'm going to—" Agent Carter starts, but Dr. Pine cuts her off with a wave of his hand.

"Second: Once you've concluded that exchange with Shannon, are you willing to continue the interview with Agent Carter?"

One flick.

Andrea Carter's chest rises and falls with a frustrated breath. She's been overruled by the locked-in girl, and she doesn't like that at all. Tara finds a strange pleasure in this. She can't move or speak, but she can control the room. It's a sense of power she hasn't felt in a long time.

"Make it quick, Ms. Beckley," Agent Carter snaps. "There's a lot riding on this."

Commands like this usually don't sit well with Shannon, but tonight she barely seems to register the tone, just gives a half nod and keeps her eyes straight ahead. As Dr. Pine passes by Shannon on his way out, she whispers, "Thank you, Doc." He almost stumbles, he's so surprised.

"Of course," he answers, and then he and Agent Carter are out the door. It closes behind them with a soft click, and the Beckley sisters are alone. With their respective questions. Tara knows hers— *Where did the hat come from, and what does it mean, and did he hurt you?* but she can't voice any of those, so she has to trust her sister. She's back in that basement at 1804 London Street again, steel doors between them, a thin band of light, and a lifetime of trust.

The doors are heavier here, the band of light narrower, but the trust has only deepened.

"Tara," Shannon whispers, "I need your help right now. For both of us. And for Mom and Rick. I need you to understand that without me saying much more. I need you to trust me."

Tara gives her one flick.

Shannon smiles awkwardly. Her grateful smile, the least natural, the most heartbreaking.

"Everything that you've been through," she says, "and I need you to save us all. No pressure, T."

Then she reaches into her pocket and pulls out her phone.

No, wait. It's not her phone. It's a black iPhone without a case. Tara understands immediately: It is Oltamu's phone. Somehow, Shannon has come into possession of this oddly desired item, and it has something to do with the reason she's wearing the black hat and is afraid.

Tara's pulse begins to hammer. Not since they sealed her in the tube so she could demonstrate proof of life has she felt an adrenaline rush like this.

"Do you know what this is?" Shannon whispers, her voice so low it's scarcely audible.

One flick.

"Okay. I don't know if this will work, but I need you to try." She taps the screen with her finger and then turns the display to Tara. The blackness has been replaced with an image: Tara standing uneasily beside Dr. Amandi Oltamu above the Willow River, the spindly shadows of the railroad bridge visible just beyond them.

The last memory Tara has of when her body was her own.

For a moment, her vision grays out, and she's afraid she's doing something that would seem impossible—can a paralyzed patient faint? She's about to. But then there's gold-green beneath the gray, and she sees the girl in the kayak, sees the river wide and rushing and the girl riding it out, riding the current into that shimmering gold-green mist, and Tara knows the mist this time—it is spray from a waterfall. There's a waterfall up ahead, but the girl in the water is paddling straight for it, and she is unafraid.

Suddenly all of that is gone and the room is back and the phone is before Tara once more. Shannon's face is hovering just behind it, her eyes darkened by the terrible black baseball cap.

"I'm going to turn this around now and try to capture your face. Just like a camera. It's locked, and you...you might be able to open it. You understand what I mean?"

One flick. Tara grasps the idea, and, bizarre as it sounds, she thinks she even understands it. The odd photos, the way Oltamu gave her the phone...nothing was accidental. Not those choices, and not the choices of the man who drove into the two of them just seconds later.

All part of competing plans. Tara is the pawn in the middle. She has been turned into a human key.

Shannon wets her lips, breathes, and turns the phone around. Tara wants to adjust her head to face the small camera lens, but of course she can't do that. She has to trust that Shannon will get it right.

It takes longer than it should, and Tara is sure it's a failure, but then Shannon arches up a little and changes the angle, pointing the camera down at Tara's eyes from above, and Tara can tell from the way her body relaxes that she has the result she wanted.

"Okay," she says. "That's good, and bad. Take a look."

She turns the phone back to Tara. It says FRS verified and there is a green check mark. But just below that, there's a red X and a white box beside the command Enter name of FRS-verified individual to complete authentication.

FRS. Facial-recognition scan? That seems right, but it wasn't enough to unlock the device. The name prompt remains.

"Do I just try yours? First and last? First only?" Shannon's voice is rising now, and her attention is totally on the phone, and that can't happen, because Tara knows what she needs to enter, Tara knows this and has to speak it and—

The gray-out comes again, and then the green-gold mist, and Tara is riding the waterfall, tumbling and falling to an endless depth, spiraling down through the green-gold liquid light...

When she comes back, it's with a vengeance—her thumb twitches, yes, but so do two of her fingers. A rapid twitch, a plucking gesture, like a child's frantic grab at a firefly.

She's not immediately sure that it was real, but then she sees Shannon staring at her right hand in shock, and the shock confirms the sensation.

Tara is opening the channel. Tara is forcing her way back into the world.

"Did you feel that?" Shannon asks.

One flick.

"Can you do it again?"

She can't. Not yet. But maybe soon... Tara opts not to respond to that question. She doesn't know the answer yet. Her control of her own body no longer belongs to the land of yes-or-no answers. What an amazing thing that was. She wishes Dr. Pine had seen it. And Mom, Rick, all of them. But at least Shannon was here. At least Shannon saw.

"I tried your name," Shannon says then, and Tara remembers the phone, the reason for all of this. "It says 'access denied.' I've got only one try left." Her voice quavers. "T., do you have any idea what he called you?"

One flick.

"You're sure?" Shannon says.

One flick.

"Can you spell it?"

One flick.

Shannon reaches for the alphabet board with a trembling hand.

53

Her hand moved. Abby thought it was an optical illusion, some disruption of the camera's feed, but then Shannon Beckley's questions turned it into reality.

Tara can move. Maybe not consistently, but she can move.

"The name matters," Dax said. "Shit. That slows us down. That might derail the whole thing, actually. Because if Tara doesn't know what he put in there..."

He rubs his thumb over the stock of the revolver distractedly, a circular motion. Abby watches him and thinks about Tara's hand, that sudden twitch. She's coming back. Maybe. Or was it just a spasm? Regardless, it was something more than Luke had ever managed. Tara has vertical eye motion, and one of her hands can move. She's not only still alert in there, she's progressing.

"Boone is in play," Dax said, uninterested in everything else, his attention lost to the blond woman who'd left the room. "But who put her in play? Not Gerry. I'm sure of that."

Abby didn't respond. Her attention was focused on the screen. All the things that had mattered just seconds ago seemed less consequential.

Tara can make it back, she thought. And then: *If nobody kills her first.*

54

Pine wanted privacy. He took Boone down the empty corridor that smelled of a disinfectant tinged with juniper and then turned into a small office. A desk took up all of one wall, and the other walls were lined with filing cabinets and bookshelves. The only chair was the one facing the desk, but he offered it to her. She sat, although she didn't want to. She was buzzing with anger and energy, too close to be wasting more time now.

"If that sister tries to talk Tara out of cooperating, I'm not going anywhere. I hope you understand that. It matters—"

"Too much," Pine finished for her with a weary nod as he closed the door. "I get it, I get it. I also think I'm going about this wrong."

Boone cocked her head. "Meaning?"

"Something's wrong with Shannon."

"The sister. You're worried about her?"

"Yes." He looked at her defiantly. "I am worried about them all. But as I tried to explain to you, she knows a lot. She knows more than I do. She won't tell me how, but she knows more than I do, and I have no idea who is giving her that information. Her behavior has changed since you arrived, but it's not about you. I think she's hearing something."

Boone started to rise. "You believe all this, but you let her sit in there alone?"

Pine blocked her. "Yes! She deserves that. And I deserve a hell of a lot more than I've been given. You tell me how much is at risk here, but not what. I *understand* confidentiality, trust me. It has been my business and my life. I respect it. But this is..." He searched for the words. "Already operating at a level of secrecy that I'm not comfortable with. That I never should have allowed."

"Dr. Pine?" Boone's voice snapped like a whip. "Do not make a mistake at this stage. I will talk to that girl tonight. I don't care if I have to get a DOJ order to make it happen, I will—"

"That's exactly what *should* happen!" he fired back. "I want the damned order! I want the right security. I want the administrators of this hospital to be made aware of all possible risks. There are many patients here besides Tara Beckley. You're acting as if they're not a concern. I can't do that."

Boone was sitting on the edge of the chair, muscles tensed, eyes on Pine's. She made a show of slackening. Easing back into the chair. Giving him a posture of thoughtful consideration that bordered on the verge of concession.

"I have an acquaintance with the special agent in charge of the FBI field office in Boston," he said. "Her name is Roxanne Donovan. You know her, I assume. Or of her?"

"Yes," Boone lied.

"Perfect. Then let me call her. Let me bring someone into this building whom we both know, whom we both trust, and proceed from there. I can't let all this"—he waved a hand toward the closed door that led to the hallway—"continue in silence. Tara Beckley has experienced enough damage from silence. I won't let the same thing happen to others. Or let any more of it happen to her."

Boone steepled her fingers and rested her chin on them. Thoughtful. Then, with a sigh, she said, "I'll make the call," and she reached into her pocket as if going for a cell phone. She stopped before withdrawing anything, paused as if reconsidering, and looked at his desk phone, which was just past her left shoulder.

She said, "No, actually, you should make the call. From the hospital, and on speaker, so I can hear it. You can call Donovan. No one else. And no details should be shared before I have clearance to share them. Can you get her here with that much? Is your relationship that strong?"

"Roxanne Donovan will be here immediately when she understands the stakes," Pine said confidently. "Can I at least share your name?"

"By all means."

"Thank you," he said, an exhale of relief following his words. He leaned forward and reached past her shoulder for the desk phone. He had his hand on the receiver and his focus on the keypad when Boone withdrew the syringe from her pocket, flicked the cap off with one snap of her thumbnail, and drove the stainless-steel needle into the hollow at the base of Pine's throat.

His eyes went wide and white and he reached for his throat, but the needle was already gone, and Boone was up and had her hand over his mouth. He tried a punch then, but she blocked it easily with her left arm. She held him upright as he stumbled backward, kept him from falling, from making any noise. He looked at her with a cocktail of horror, accusation, and shame before his eyes dimmed completely. She watched him see his mistake and consider its ramifications just before his heart stopped.

Then she eased him into the desk chair. His head slumped forward onto the desk, his cheek on the keyboard, depressing keys, but they made no sound. It looked natural enough for a man who'd suffered a massive coronary, so she didn't adjust his position. A standard autopsy would show a heart attack, and only if the coroners had reason to look very, very carefully would they find any evidence to suggest otherwise.

If that happened, Boone would be long gone.

She was pleased to find that the office door had a push-button lock. It wasn't much of a security feature, but it would delay the discovery. She doubted any of the night nurses would want to disturb a doctor of Pine's stature if he'd closed and locked the door.

He had big things to work on, after all; he'd brought a woman back from the beyond.

Boone locked the door behind her and walked briskly back to room 373. The clock was speeding up now, and the time for games and lies was gone.

55

Twitch? You told him your nickname was Twitch?"

Shannon seems either disbelieving or disturbed. Tara—fighting for patience because Shannon doesn't understand how hard it is to keep battling this current, to keep the channel open, commanding her eyes to answer properly even while her own mind races with unanswered questions that she can't voice—gives one flick of the eyes. Yes, Twitch.

"If the facial recognition worked," Shannon says, "maybe this will too."

Her voice is doubtful but she turns her attention to the phone and taps the name into the display. She's holding her breath.

"It worked," Shannon says, and Tara adds this to her growing collection of points of light. Everything is progress right now. Everything is trending the right way.

Tara and Shannon are so focused on each other that neither one notices she's no longer alone in the room.

Then Andrea Carter says, "I'll need to see that."

How long she's been standing there, Tara has no idea, but it can't have been long. Shannon has her back to the door, but Tara thinks she would have glanced right eventually. Carter's face is a hostile mask. Apparently she feels Shannon has held her at bay long enough. Dr. Pine isn't with her.

Shannon rises from the stool, lowering Oltamu's phone and pressing it against her leg.

"Do you mind?" Shannon says. "I'd asked for just a little bit of privacy. If you could just give me a few more…"

Tara is watching Shannon, so she doesn't understand why her voice trails off, why her eyes go wide. Then Tara looks back at Andrea Carter and sees the knife.

It's a small knife but it seems to be all blade, a curved piece of metal with a razor edge, a crescent-moon-shaped killing tool. She's holding it in her right hand, down against her leg, in a posture that mirrors Shannon's with the phone.

"You need to be very quiet," Carter says, "and you need to give me that."

She advances with her eyes on Shannon, her movements sleek as a panther. Tara wants to scream but can't; Shannon could and won't. In fact, Shannon's face seems oddly unsurprised, as if she's been anticipating something like this. "What's your real name?" she says.

Carter is only a stride from her now, and she moves the knife out and to the side, the curved blade glistening, and extends her left hand, palm up. "The phone."

Shannon doesn't hesitate, and Tara is relieved. There's something in this woman's eyes that promises violence. Her eyes remind Tara of the eyes of the boy in the black hat. The hat that is now on Shannon's head. They must belong together, this woman and the boy. But why, oh, why is Shannon wearing the hat?

56

Dax was very still, his thumb on the revolver's cylinder, his eyes unblinkingly focused on the video display, even his breathing so restrained that it was scarcely noticeable.

That's Lisa Boone. She worked with my father. She's a professional killer.

In those short sentences, he told Abby more about himself than he had in all the terrible hours they'd spent together. It explained the bizarre pairing of youth and skill, emptiness and professionalism, brutality and calculation. Abby knew his world now, and his world explained him. An assassin's son was just right. Nature and nurture.

She found a strange comfort in this idea, as if there might be a rationality to him where before she'd seen only a sociopath.

Then again, she was still bound to the passenger seat, and less than an hour had passed since Dax had committed a murder. You took your reassurances where you could find them, but this one was a hell of a stretch.

When Lisa Boone stepped back into the frame, alone this time, no doctor at her side, Dax tensed and reached for the door handle, then stopped himself, lowered his hand, and relaxed back into the seat.

He knows it will be easier to take it from her once she's outside, Abby thought. Entering the hospital was a risk that Dax clearly intended to avoid—he'd gotten Shannon to make the actual room call, and that was, Abby realized with dismay, a smart move. Right now, however capable a killer Lisa Boone was, she was a full step behind him, and he was patient enough to realize that as long as he had the upper hand, forcing the action was unnecessary. He saw more of the board than she did.

None of that was reassuring.

Abby watched the camera shift and weave as Boone approached and took Oltamu's phone from Shannon Beckley's hand. Then she walked backward, sure-footed and graceful, to the door. Only when she was there, with plenty of distance between herself and Shannon, did she glance at the phone.

For all of Abby's horror, some small part of her just wanted to know—what was on it?

Whatever it was, it didn't please Boone. Her face twisted in anger, and she said, "What is this?"

Offscreen, speaking from behind—and below—the camera, Shannon Beckley said, "How do I know?"

"Because you just said *it worked*. The facial recognition and then you put in her nickname and said that it worked. I heard you and watched you."

"It did work. I thought it did. It changed screens, at least. The old screen was her. Once I held it up to her eyes and put in that nickname, it reloaded and the screen changed."

She was speaking too loud, as if trying to draw people's attention. Lisa Boone said, "Keep your voice down."

Shannon went silent. Boone looked at the phone once more, studied it, then said, "It changed from her face to *this*?"

"Yes."

Beside Abby, Dax sighed and said, "I'd like to know what *this* is."

An instant later, Boone said, "Then what in the fuck is this?"

Dax spread his hands and gave a theatrical nod, like *Thank you!*

"I don't know," Shannon said, voice softer now.

"Does she?" Boone asked.

Shannon didn't respond. Boone advanced, phone in one hand, knife in the other.

57

Tara hasn't seen the image yet, but she has an idea of what the woman with the knife is looking at. In fact, she's pretty sure she knows exactly what it is.

Andrea Carter is moving toward her, and Shannon steps protectively between them, and then the knife is nearly at her throat, the movement so swift and sudden that Tara scarcely registers the fact that her hand twitches again.

Carter speaks with the blade pressed against Shannon's neck.

"There's a way to do this without your sister dying," Carter says. "But you need to cooperate."

Shannon gives a strange, high laugh that surprises Tara as much as it apparently surprises Carter.

"Step back," Carter says, "and shut up."

Please listen, Tara urges silently. *Do what she says, because I can answer her next question, I already did, I told you what he took pictures of, and then he was dead, so I know he didn't take any more. I can answer her questions, and she will leave.*

But will she leave? As Shannon moves away, taking two steps toward the foot of the bed, Tara watches Carter and is not so sure. If Tara doesn't answer her questions, then they both have to die. But if she does...what changes? Is there really any way this woman is leaving them alive?

"Show Tara the phone," Shannon says, and she looks at Tara for the first time, and there's a knowingness to the gaze. Tara thinks, *I am right about what's there, and Shannon remembers what I said.*

The woman turns the phone display to her then, and, sure enough, there he is: Hobo.

"What is the dog's name?" the woman asks.

Tara looks at Shannon. Flicks her eyes up once. Yes, tell her. What is the point in protecting this? *Saving our lives, that's the point.* But Tara's instinct says that talking is better. It's a strange instinct for a woman who can't speak, and yet there it is.

"What does that mean?" Carter asks. "The way she looked at you. Her eyes moved up. That's a yes. What is she saying yes to?"

Her voice tightens with anger, and Tara is terrified of what will happen if Shannon lies or resists, but for once, she doesn't.

"She's saying yes to me because she wants me to tell you who the dog is," Shannon says.

"You know?"

Shannon nods.

"Say it."

"Hobo," Shannon says, once again in a loud voice, but this time the woman doesn't tell her to lower it. She just stares at her as if she's making a very dangerous joke.

"Hobo."

Shannon nods again.

"How do you know that?"

"Because she told me. Earlier. When the doctor and I were asking her about her memories of the accident. Before it happened, Oltamu took a picture of her and a picture of Hobo."

Andrea Carter eyes Shannon, then Tara. She sees either no indication of a lie or no reason for them to lie. She flips the phone over in her hand, and taps on it with her thumb.

"Doesn't work," she says, but her voice is troubled and she keeps staring at the screen.

"I think," Shannon says cautiously, "that's because you'll need the dog's eyes."

The woman looks at Shannon as if she wouldn't mind gutting

her with that knife right here. Suddenly, Tara has a terrible fear for Dr. Pine. Surely she wouldn't have killed him in a hospital.

But where is he?

Dead, she thinks. The fear turns into a certainty, and that grows into a certainty over how this will end. She and Shannon will die too. All for something Tara will never understand, all for whatever is on this stranger's phone. Damn it, don't they at least deserve to know what they're dying for?

"That's how it worked with her," Shannon says. "Facial recognition first, then name."

The woman looks at the display again, and Tara thinks she must be seeing a message that confirms this, because she seems even more frustrated by the device than by Shannon.

"That's insane," she says. "For a dog? It won't work. The technology doesn't exist."

"Actually," Shannon says, "they use it on pet doors. I saw an ad for one."

"I don't have time for this bullshit. *You* don't have time to do this."

"Google it," Shannon says. "You can buy pet doors that open with facial recognition. I don't know why. To keep out raccoons or whatever, I have no idea. But I am telling you, the way it worked with her was to get the facial-recognition lock first, then put in the name. The dog is named Hobo. I am positive."

They stare each other down for a moment. Finally Andrea Carter says, "Where is the dog?"

"He was up there by the bridge. Where Oltamu died. She says he is a stray."

"You're lying," Carter says, but it's more hopeful than forceful.

"Ask her," Shannon says.

Carter turns to Tara. "Is she lying?"

Tara flicks her eyes twice. No, Shannon isn't lying.

Carter pauses, seems to fight down building rage, and then says, "Will the dog be up there? Is he easy to find?"

Hobo is not particularly easy to find, and he certainly won't be for a stranger, but Tara sees more hope for them in that lie than in the truth, so she gives one flick—yes.

"He took a picture of you and asked for a nickname," Carter says. "And then he took a picture of the dog and asked for the dog's name?"

One flick. Yes. Growing more certain with each answer that she's sealing their fates, but not seeing any way out. The world is an extension of her body now—a trap with no escape.

"Was that the last picture he took?" Carter asks.

Tara's thumb jerks. Carter and Shannon both see this.

"What does that mean?" Carter asks warily.

"Nothing. It's a spasm."

But Shannon is wrong. That thumb twitch means everything. It means the girl fighting against the current has found the green-gold waters again, the secret channel where the water rotates and then the current becomes friend and not foe. It is so much more than a spasm. It is Tara coming back. Finding her way through dark halls and riding dark waters, chasing thin bands of light.

"Just use your eyes this time. *Was that the last picture he took?*" Carter repeats.

Tara sees it then, as if the last twitch of her thumb were a courier arriving with critical news, a message Tara should have understood already: She has power here. She has control of the situation in a way none of them suspect she does.

Yes, she is motionless and mute, locked in. But now she recognizes the strength in this. The only move that can save them will come because of her condition. She can buy Shannon time, at least. She can do that much.

She flicks her eyes twice, telling this awful woman, *No, it was not the last picture he took.*

Tara can't do many things, but she can still think, and she understands the dilemma she's placing the woman with the knife in now—the lie is worth the risk, because Tara knows what's coming.

Sure enough, the question arrives like a hanging curveball, belt-high.

"Did he take another one of you?" Carter says.

One flick, and Tara swats it out of the park.

Yes, she lies, *he took one more of me. And you know what that means, bitch? You can't kill me yet. You'll need my eyes again. Think about it. Won't work with a dead face. Or at least, you're not sure that it will. And you can't take me to Hammel with you, so that means you've got to come back to find me, dead or alive. I'll be harder to find if I'm dead, and you'll have to trust that the phone will recognize my face if I am. I don't think it will.*

There's a pause that seems endless but that can't be more than five seconds. Those seconds feel like the countdown before an explosion, though. The crescent-moon blade glimmers, Andrea Carter stands with every muscle taut, and Shannon looks as paralyzed as Tara.

"Here's how we're going to handle this," Carter says at last. "Shannon and I are going for a ride. Together. We will find the dog and test your story, Tara. If it works, and no one follows us, then Shannon will drive back to you. If it doesn't, or if you somehow send someone after us? Well, I suppose you'll have plenty of time to think about that in the days to come."

Shannon is looking at Tara with an expression that Tara remembers well—quiet and restrained, thoughtful. A quiet Shannon is something to worry about, because on the rare occasions that she swallows her anger and retreats, she is lost to thoughts of settling the score. This is good, because it means she knows that Tara lied and that the phone will prove that. Tara bought her time, but Shannon will be alone when the lie is discovered.

"All right," Andrea Carter says, and the blade disappears into a black handle that vanishes into her hand. "Then we'll ride,

Shannon. You'd better hope your sister understands the stakes. People will ask her questions about me. Her answers are going to decide your life."

Shannon doesn't respond to that. She just looks at Tara.

"You know how much I love you?" she says.

Almost too late, Tara remembers to look upward once.

Shannon nods and turns away. She opens the door and steps out with Andrea Carter walking just behind her, the knife not visible but not far away.

58

"Brilliant play!" Dax shouted at the video like a color commentator breaking down a playoff game. "She's caught lovely Lisa, do you see that, Abby? Do you understand? Lisa *can't* kill Tara now. Not if she's going to need her again. That's ingenious. It might even be true that she'll need Tara again, but I doubt it. Boone probably doubts it too. What can you do, though? You can't pick the girl up and take her with you. So you take the sister and hope that keeps her quiet. But Tara called the shot on that one. Good for her."

He spoke with true admiration, although Abby had no doubt that he would still kill Tara himself without hesitation or pity.

No one had passed them in the garage since they arrived, and only two cars had pulled out from the floors below. A hospital never shut down, but it had quiet hours, and they had arrived in the midst of them. When Shannon Beckley exited room 373 and began her walk out of the hospital with Lisa Boone alongside her, the camera showed a quiet hallway ahead. They avoided the main lobby and entered a side stairwell.

Dax started the car.

He backed out of the parking space and started down toward the garage exit, driving slowly, unhurried as always and seemingly sure of his choice. His treasured phone, the item worthy of all this bloodshed, was in the hands of an apparent rival, but he seemed unbothered.

They passed an elderly couple walking to a Buick, and if the pair had looked into the Challenger, they might have noticed the cord around Abby's neck, but they did not look.

"Are you following them?" Abby asked. Once she'd hated listening to the kid's incessant talk, but now she wanted to know. It felt, surreally, as if a part of her were rooting for Dax now. Shannon Beckley seemed more likely to die at Lisa Boone's hands than his at this moment, and he was the only person who knew enough to intercede. Other than Tara, of course, mute and trapped.

"That wouldn't be smart," Dax said.

"You're giving up? Just letting her take it?" Abby had a horrible thought: What if this Lisa Boone worked with Dax? What if his surprise at her presence was simply because she'd been unannounced, not because he viewed her as a rival?

Then he said, "Oh, we're certainly not going to do that. Come on, Abby! We've come too far to give up now."

"Then what are you doing?"

If the questions bothered him, he didn't show it. He put his window down, fed a ticket and a credit card into the automated garage booth, and the gate rose. He took the credit card back, put the window up, and pulled away, out of the lights of the garage and back into darkness.

"It would be a mistake to follow her," he said. "Boone is too good. At least, that's my understanding. It's a long drive, and she'd see us, and she would have the advantage then. Right now we have the advantage, Abby, don't you see? We know where they're going. And we can watch them."

On the cell phone's display, the camera was bobbing along, Shannon Beckley still on foot, walking across the street and toward a parking lot on the other side of the hospital. Lisa Boone was not in the frame.

"Correct me if I'm wrong," Dax said, "but haven't you been to the accident site?"

Abby didn't answer right away. She was seeing the idea coalesce. It was a very simple trap, but a trap set for an assassin. She couldn't imagine how anyone was going to make it out of this night alive. Dax might. Or Boone might. One or the other had to win. But as for Abby and Shannon Beckley?

He'll get out of the car, she thought. *He'll have to, down there. And when he does, he's going to leave you here. You'll need to be a lot faster with that headrest than you were last time.*

"Haven't you?" Dax repeated, an edge to his voice now.

"Yes," Abby said. "I've been there."

"Then you'll guide me and tell me what to expect when I get there. It's important that you remember it accurately. If I lose my advantage, well, that could become an ugly situation for everyone." He caught a green light and turned left, heading for the interstate. "We'll need to drive a bit faster too. Boone won't want to take risks, but I don't think she's inclined to waste much time."

Once they were all on the highway, the camera's livestream began to fade in and out, but they weren't missing much. Just the open road in front of Shannon Beckley, the same open road that was in front of Abby. Dax paid the video feed no mind, but Abby watched, trying to identify mile markers and signs that would show her how far behind Boone and Shannon were. She guessed they were maybe ten minutes behind when Dax exited the interstate and began following the winding county roads that led to Hammel.

They were in the hills now, and a low fog crept through bare-limbed trees and settled beneath those that still had their leaves. A few houses had Halloween decorations up, and jack-o'-lanterns with rictus smiles sat on porches or beside mailboxes. The wind shivered dead leaves off skeletal branches. Autumn charm was dying; winter was on its way.

Dax drove with his right hand only, the gun in the door panel, close to his left hand, which rested on his thigh. Abby watched him bring that left hand up time and again on curves. Usually he didn't bring it all the way to the wheel, but Abby knew that the Hellcat was still foreign to him, and even though he wasn't driving recklessly, he was uneasy about that power and handling. Didn't trust himself with the car yet.

Watching his weakness gave Abby a feeling of strength that would have seemed absurd to any spectator—one person had the gun and the wheel, and the other was tied to the passenger seat. And yet, as a passenger, able to watch the way Dax handled the car and the uncertainty he brought to it, she felt her confidence grow. That uncertainty was a small thing, but it was a weakness. If Abby could get the wheel back, he'd be gone. The gap she'd found in her panic on the rain-swept highway when she'd sliced through the semis and cars and glided through the break in the guardrail seemed to have carried some of her old brain back into her body. A door had opened in that moment. If she got behind the wheel, she could find it again. She could kick that door down if it didn't open willingly.

All she needed was the chance.

She looked back down at the phone's display. They'd lost the signal, and Shannon Beckley's camera was gone. No surprise, not in these hills. Dax wasn't pushing the speed too much, and Abby expected that the women behind them wouldn't be either. They were clones—one killer, one hostage, nobody looking to attract police attention. That would give Dax his five- or maybe ten-minute lead at Hammel. What would he do with it? Abby thought he would leave the car. He would expect the car to attract attention that a man on foot in the darkness would not.

If I get five minutes alone, I'll get that headrest off. I know how it's done now. Feet on the dash, back arched, start with the left side...

She just needed those minutes.

"Turn left here," Abby said.

Dax seemed surprised by the instruction, but he slowed.

"The signs say the college is to the right."

"We'll save a few minutes this way. Minutes matter now, don't they?"

Dax turned to her, looking even younger and less hostile without the hat. Just a boy out for a ride in a muscle car.

"Yes," he said. "Minutes matter."

He turned left.

They wound through a residential stretch with Abby calling out directions, and then they turned on Ames Road and started a steep descent. The darkness was lifting in that barely perceptible way of predawn, not so much a brightening as a fading of the blackness.

"The railroad bridge is at the bottom of the hill," Abby said. "Parking is on the left. There won't be any cars down there now, probably."

She thought about saying more, adding something about how they'd stand out to Lisa Boone if they parked down there, but she caught herself. Let him reach that conclusion on his own. He'd be suspicious if Abby offered too much help.

The transmission downshifted on the steep grade, an automatic adjustment that took the driver out of the equation and that Abby had always hated but that Dax seemed to prefer. You could switch the Challenger to a bastardized version of a manual transmission, no clutch pedal but paddle shifters. He hadn't done that once, though.

Scared of the power, Abby thought, and again the ludicrous confidence rose. *I can beat him if he just gets out of the car.*

The headlights pinned the railroad bridge below them, the angled steel beams throwing shadows onto the dark river. Abby looked at the place and tried to remember what it had felt like when she'd paced this pavement with a camera in hand and confusion rising. That's all it had been then—confusion. Carlos Ramirez's story, so clean and simple, wasn't accurate. Carlos, the second person to die. Hank, who'd wanted nothing but easy money and a chance for Abby to face down her demons, was the third. Gerry, the man who'd died on his kitchen floor, the fourth.

Will I be the fifth? Shannon Beckley the sixth? How many more die before it's done?

"Do you know what's on Oltamu's phone?" Abby asked.

Again, Dax seemed startled by the sound of her voice. He hesitated, then said, "I don't. Should be interesting, don't you think? A lot of people seem willing to go to extreme lengths just to have it in their hands."

"What if it's nothing?"

Dax laughed. "I hardly think that's an option."

"It may be. He could have wiped the data. You don't know."

"No. All those locks on an empty phone? There's something there."

"It will involve batteries," Abby said. "And I think it might involve cars. He came from the Black Lake. He watched testing."

Dax seemed more intrigued now, but he was also in the place where he had to set the trap, and he wasn't going to divide his focus.

"When I find out," he said, pulling into one of the angled spaces in the spot where Amandi Oltamu had died and Tara Beckley had nearly been erased from existence, "you'll be the first to know. You've earned that much, Abby. I'll tell you before I kill you. That's a promise."

He was surveying the area, taking rapid inventory, his mind no longer on Abby but on the possibilities waiting here in the darkness above the river. The possibilities, and the pitfalls.

"Did you see the dog when you were here?" he asked.

"I did not."

"But our girl Tara believes he will appear. Hobo. There's a lot riding on a stray dog named Hobo." He went silent, drumming his fingers on the steering wheel and staring into the dark woods where birches swayed and creaked.

"Boone needs the phone to be opened," he said at length. "Interesting. Gerry's German friend seemed to think it was worth trying to open it, but it wasn't a priority. So our buyer wants to kill the phone, and hers wants to see it."

He looked at Abby again. "You're right—I'm awfully curious about what's on it."

He dropped his right hand onto the gearshift, put the car in reverse, backed out, whipped the car around, and drove up the hill again. Abby tried to stay expressionless, tried not to let her relief show.

Dax was going to park the Challenger where it wouldn't stand out, and that meant he would need to leave the car. The options, then, were to keep Abby in the car or bring her along. The latter carried more risk.

There's a third option. He kills you here. He doesn't need you anymore.

At the crest of the hill on Ames Road, where more houses began to appear, Dax turned the car and parallel-parked in a spot between streetlights where the Challenger would be obscured by shadows. He cut the engine and the lights. Paused and assessed. Nodded, satisfied. He took the cell phone, its screen filled with the image of the weaving night road that Shannon Beckley was driving just behind them, and slipped it into his pocket.

"Now, Abby, I'm afraid we're going to have to separate for a time. I'll miss you, but it's for the best. You'll have nefarious ideas in my absence, I'm sure. Things you could do to hurt me and, in your noble if dim-witted mind, help Shannon." He plucked the gun from inside the door panel, and for an instant Abby could see the barrel being shoved through the lips of the man named Gerry just before the kill shot was fired and thought the same was coming for her.

Then Dax switched the gun to his right hand and reached for the door handle with his left.

"Before you make any choices," he said, "I want you to consider this—I've kept you alive, and Lisa Boone is unlikely to do the same. You want me dead, and that's fine. If I'm dead, though? She's the last one left. I'm not sure I'd choose that if I were you."

With that, he opened the door and stepped out into the chill night. He'd disabled the interior lights, and when he closed the door, he did it softly. Then he started down the hill at a jog, moving swiftly and silently.

Abby watched until he vanished into the woods. Then she braced her feet on the dashboard, took a deep breath, and arched her aching back to extend the reach of her bound hands as far as possible. She found the headrest releases quicker this time, and she set to work.

59

Boone hadn't been planning on a hostage, but that didn't mean she was unprepared for one. She was always prepared for such a contingency.

She used plastic zip-tie cuffs on Shannon Beckley's wrists and a single piece of duct tape over her mouth, things that could be removed quickly in the event of trouble, but she used real cuffs to bind Shannon's left ankle to a bar beneath the passenger seat. There would be no runaways on Boone's watch.

Satisfied, she drove away in the girl's rented Jeep. In the back-seat, Beckley seemed composed enough; she was avoiding hysteria, at least, which was a help. Boone would have no trouble silencing her if it came to that, but she also needed to keep her alive until all sequences of locks had been defeated. Tara Beckley had managed to claim an infuriating amount of control. For a quadriplegic who couldn't speak, an astounding amount of control, actually. Even if they found the fucking dog and the lock actually opened, Boone would still have to make her way back to Tara once more and deal with the challenges of the hospital without her helpful aide Dr. Pine. Shannon Beckley could be key to gaining access during the daylight hours, when the hospital was more active and the parents would be in the room, and Boone feared that the waking vegetable that was Tara Beckley could cause more trouble if she didn't see proof of life of her sister. She could hold out. In fact, Boone sus-pected that she would, and she understood why—Tara didn't have much left to lose.

Then again, there were the parents to consider.

Maybe Shannon wasn't so vital after all.

All this would be decided after they left Hammel. For now the task was dictated by the image on the phone. Her current pursuit was ludicrous—this was a multimillion-dollar job in service of billions, and Boone was chasing a stray dog named Hobo. In her varied and diverse career, leaving corpses in more than a dozen countries, she'd never felt more absurd, and yet a part of her admired Oltamu. Somehow he'd felt the hellhounds closing in, and his response had been as resourceful as anyone's could be in that moment. Nobody was going to get the intelligence he'd collected simply by picking up his phone. He'd played a risky game and lost it, but he'd made a fine effort all the way to the end.

Ask the girl, he'd instructed Boone, presumably having no idea just how difficult that would be. The doctor had come through, the girl had come through, and now the locks were turning, albeit slowly.

The drive ate away at hours Boone couldn't afford to lose, and with the night edging toward dawn, she had to will herself to keep her speed down and use the time to consider what lay ahead. Pine was going to be a problem. People would find him soon enough, and while it would take a first-rate medical examiner to determine that he hadn't died of natural causes, it would also inevitably cause chaos in the hospital. The place wouldn't be nearly so quiet when Boone returned.

Chaos, though, could be used as a shield. It was all a matter of timing. The dog had to be dealt with, then Tara Beckley. Step by step. Unless, of course, Tara Beckley was lying, and there was no third lock. In that case, Boone could leave her sister's body behind and be out of the country before Tara blinked her way through the alphabet board with any message that police might believe.

They reached the outskirts of Hammel, passed signs for the college, and then the winding New England road crested and dropped abruptly, a steep hill descending toward the river.

This was the place.

She slowed and checked the mirrors. No one had been behind them for long throughout the drive, and no one was now. To the right and to the left were peaceful houses with tree-lined lawns, windows dark, a porch light or outdoor floodlight on here and there. The streetlights were designed for form rather than function, and they cast only a dim glow over the sidewalks, where dead leaves swirled in the wind. Three cars on the curb to her right, one car and one truck to the left. None of them looked like police vehicles, but there was one that didn't fit the neighborhood—a souped-up Challenger with a vented hood and wide racing tires. It was parked at the end of the street and in the shadows. Boone gave it a careful look as she passed, but the windows were deeply tinted and she couldn't make out anything. Some professor's midlife-crisis car, she decided, and drove on.

At the bottom of the hill, angled parking spaces lined the left-hand side, all of them empty, and then there was an ancient railroad bridge. Beneath it, the river was a dark ribbon, swollen from recent rains. The current would be strong. If Tara Beckley had gone in the water today, she likely wouldn't have been rescued. That would have cost Boone some serious money. Tara's miraculous recovery to waking-vegetable status had the potential to be very, very lucrative. Instant-retirement money, vanish-to-your-own-island money, though Boone had no intention of retiring. When you loved your work, why stop? And hers wasn't a profession you left easily. Those who remained alert to every motion in the shadows stayed alive; those who didn't died. There was no retreat. This was the journey of any apex predator.

She pulled into one of the angled parking spaces on the river's eastern shore, cut the engine, and said, "It's going to be very unfortunate for your family if the dog isn't here."

The threat had nothing behind it, though. The dog was Boone's problem and one that couldn't readily be solved with or without the Beckleys. Either the girl was right or she was wrong. The dog would be here or he wouldn't be.

"Sit tight, Shannon," she said. She popped the door open and stepped out into the night.

For a few seconds, she just stood there, surveying the scene. The lonely lamps in the area, too dim, cast the only light on either side of the bridge. The next street lamp was all the way at the top of the hill, where the houses began. No one had built down here, probably due to flood risk. The river was high and felt close, the low whisper of moving water almost intimate in the darkness.

To her left, a jogging path curled into the trees, went up a small rise, and then vanished, probably running parallel to the river. To her right, the bridge loomed high and cold above the water, the old steel girders giving the wind something to whistle through. It was a long bridge, maybe two hundred feet, spanning a narrow river below. She saw now that there were actually two bridges—the old railroad bridge, set higher, the tracks running on banked gravel when they crossed the river, and slightly below it, a newer pedestrian bridge, connecting the jogging paths on eastern and western shores. On the other side of the river, ornate lamps threw muted light onto the path as it led through a thicket of pines and on toward the campus. She could see the brighter lights of the buildings beyond, maybe a quarter of a mile off.

It was a dark and quiet spot. It suited her.

Satisfied that she was alone, she moved away from the car. She had the knife in her left hand and the gun holstered behind her back. She left Oltamu's phone in the car, unconcerned about that for now. Priority one was ensuring that she was alone and knew the terrain.

She walked toward the pedestrian bridge, thinking of how far a stray dog might have gone in all this time. He could be in a shelter or dead, hit by a car. What were the odds of finding him?

She went farther out onto the bridge, pivoted, and looked back down at the parking lot. Shannon Beckley's rental Jeep was a dark silent shape in the place where her sister had once posed for Amandi Oltamu, clueless to all that was headed her way.

A dog, Boone thought with disgust. *Amandi, you took it a step too far.*

Somewhere to the west, behind the cold, freshening wind, a train horn sounded, soft and mournful, like something out of another time. Maybe the girl hadn't lied. Maybe the dog would appear for the morning train as promised. Maybe—

"Hobo."

The sound of the dog's name came at her so softly that at first she didn't believe it was real, as if the voice had come from within her own mind. Then it came again, clearer now.

"Hobo! Hey, buddy. C'mere. C'mon out."

Someone at the other end of the bridge was calling to the dog. Boone stared in that direction, trying to make out a shape, but it was too far off. Branches cracked, and bushes shook, and somewhere on the western bank of the river, the voice said, "Good boy! Eat up, chief."

A male voice, young and foolish. A Hammel student, probably. Another fan of a stray dog that the kids had adopted like a mascot.

Or a trap? Had Tara managed to communicate quicker than Boone had anticipated?

Boone considered this and dismissed it. If the girl had been able to summon police this quickly, they wouldn't have been the kind of police who would set a trap. They'd have raced up with sirens blaring, county mounties with big guns and small brains, looking for a heroic moment.

"Good boy," the voice said again, and again the bushes rustled, and this time Boone spotted the point of motion.

She drew her gun with her right hand and her knife with her left. Ordinarily she wouldn't have considered this—you fired with two hands unless you had no choice. But she didn't want to make

any more noise than she had to, and then there was the special consideration of the dog.

Oltamu's phone was back in the Jeep. She considered returning
for it but pressed ahead. She wanted to get a clearer view of what
she was dealing with. She crossed the pedestrian bridge silently
and swiftly, walking to the place where the bushes rustled. It was
just below the pines, close to the water's edge. As Boone neared
the end of the bridge, the boy made one of those annoying cluck-
ing/cooing sounds that people used around animals and babies. It
sounded as if he was trying to win the dog's allegiance and hadn't
yet succeeded. This was a bad sign. If the animal was that skit-
tish, Boone might have to risk a gunshot. But then, trying to get
his eyes lined up for the camera presented its own challenges. How
much fight would the dog have left, and how fast would Boone
lose the opportunity to capture the life left in his eyes? Too many
unknowns. Perhaps if she recruited the help of this kid who knew
the dog, she could—

"Put the gun on the ground and then take two steps back, Boone."

She knew better than to whirl at the sound. She was surprised
by the voice, yes, but Boone had been surprised before, and she
knew that you lived when you listened, stayed calm, and waited
for the opportunity to correct your mistake. Clear head, fast hands.
These were her gifts, and they weren't gone yet.

"The gun," he repeated.

Only the gun. This alone was a reassurance. If he hadn't noticed
the knife, then he was already on his way to death.

She knelt, taking care to let her left hand hang naturally, drawing no attention to the knife curled against her palm, and set the
gun on the asphalt in front of her, then straightened and took two
steps back as instructed. The voice had come from behind her and
to the right. She looked that way, finally.

He was standing on one of the iron spans that held up the railroad bridge. That put him above her and shielded by the shadow

from the bridge, his face obscured. She saw him only as a silhouette, framed above the dark rushing water.

"Hi, Boone," he said.

The voice was vaguely familiar, but she couldn't place it. Youthful but with a lilt to it, a thread of taunt, that evoked someone she'd once known.

"Who are you?" she said.

"Call me Hobo." His hand moved in the darkness, and on the west bank of the river, bushes shook. He had some sort of a line attached to them, designed to draw her attention. An amateur's gambit, one that she should have spotted immediately, but she'd been so certain she was out in front that she hadn't feared the trap. How did he know the dog's name? Who was he, and how had he known that she would arrive in this place, on this mission?

"Who's your client?" he said.

Boone didn't respond.

The man shifted, his shadow unspooling like a piece of the bridge coming to life, and the bushes shook once more. He thought that was cute. Boone was pleased to see it. He had one hand busy with that trick. That he would face her down with one hand occupied told her that she didn't need to worry about placing that voice; he was a stranger. He knew her name, but he did not truly know Boone.

"My client is an Israeli," she said, turning her body to him and squaring her shoulders. "But I don't know his name."

He moved farther out on the steel beam, and she saw that there was a gun in his right hand but that it was held down against his leg. How foolish was he? How did one come to know Lisa Boone's name and not know enough to keep one's gun pointed at her heart? She was almost insulted.

He stood there watching her from what he thought was a clever hiding spot but was really just a convenient place for him to die. The dark river below waited to carry his body away when he fell. His left hand still held the cord that he'd tied to the bushes, and his right hand held the gun with its muzzle pointed at the river. He was out on the center of the beam now. It couldn't have been much more than ten inches wide, and yet he never looked down, had moved with smoothness in the night. What he lacked in brains he made up for in composure and balance. It was a dangerous high-wire act out there. Boone's own balance was also perfect, though, and she had a stable platform beneath her. She would have to throw the knife left-handed, but this was why you practiced with your left hand and in the dark. She was not worried about accuracy.

"You'd better remember the client's name," he said, "because Tara Beckley can't blink that one out for me."

Again, the voice sounded familiar, and Boone probably could have made the connection if she'd allowed her focus to drift. But she wouldn't. Not as she slowly, almost motionlessly, thumbed the knife blade open in her cupped left hand.

"I don't have names," she said. "I only have phone numbers."

"You'll have to do better than that."

"Deal," Boone said, and when she threw the knife, she was almost sad that he'd end up in the river, because she wanted to see his face.

She was down on her back before she understood that she'd been shot.

How? How did he beat me? Did I miss? I've never missed.

Her knife was gone, but where was her gun? Somewhere below her and to the left. She told herself to reach for it, but the command couldn't bring strength. She lay there tasting her own blood and watched her killer jump nimbly from the railroad bridge span down to the footbridge, a treacherous leap in the dark but one he made without hesitation. He caught the railing on the footbridge with his left hand, then swung himself up and over.

She saw then that she had not missed with the knife. The blade was embedded in the back of his right hand. His shooting hand. He'd brought the gun up just fast enough. Fraction-of-a-blink speed. That was the separation between life and death. Before this, Boone had always been the winner in this contest.

Who are you? She tried to ask it but couldn't. No words came. She watched him advance, and her vision grayed out, and she hoped that she would last long enough to know who it was.

He'll get the phone, Boone thought numbly, aware that it was no longer a concern to her yet still disappointed. It had been worth so much.

He came on patiently, without firing again even though that would have been the smart play, and Boone had the sense that he wanted her to know him too. When he was close enough to be seen, though, she realized something was wrong. In the confusion brought on by darkness and imminent death, he looked like a child.

He'd shot like a pro, though. Boone's knife was still embedded in the back of his right hand, blood running down his fingers and falling to the pavement in fat drips. He hadn't paused to address the knife yet, and Boone knew that he wouldn't until he was certain that she was dead. There weren't many in her business with that level of focus.

So who had gotten her?

She blinked and studied him. The boyish face was a lie; she knew his voice, knew his motions, knew his pale hair in the moonlight. Knew him because he'd shot fast and straight even with a knife embedded in his gun hand.

"Hello, Boone," he said. He blurred before her eyes, and in the moment of double vision, she seemed to see two of him smiling down at her, and then she knew them. They came in a pair, always. Her brain whispered that this was impossible, but she couldn't remember why. She squinted up at her killer.

"Jack?" she whispered.

"No," the boy said, "but close enough."

Then came the fulfillment of a promise that Boone had understood for many years now: the last thing she saw was the muzzle of a gun.

60

Abby was halfway down the hill, moving quietly but awkwardly, still trying to get her circulation flowing, when she heard the clap of the gunshot.

The sound came from the far side of the bridge, close to the western shore. She had no idea if Dax had killed or been killed.

She also knew that it didn't matter. She'd escaped the car, the headrest coming free with one spine-popping twist, but Shannon Beckley was, presumably, still trapped in hers. Abby stopped in the blackness beneath a twisting oak limb and took gasping breaths of the chilled autumn air. She looked behind her, out to where the woods promised cover and the houses promised help, and then back down at the Jeep, where Shannon waited alone for whoever had survived the shooting on the bridge.

Abby's hands were still bound at the wrists. She could run but not fight. They wouldn't pursue her. Dax wouldn't, at least, and the woman he'd called Lisa Boone was of his breed. They'd calculate risk and reward, and they'd run.

But they wouldn't leave Shannon Beckley behind. The witness who couldn't run or hide was the witness who would be eliminated.

Abby started downhill again, moving quietly, chasing the shadows. The bridge was bathed in blackness, but as she watched, a figure leaped from the upper bridge, beneath the railroad tracks, and landed on the footbridge, catching the rail with his left hand. In that moment when he flickered through the night, Abby knew who'd come out victorious in the showdown between assassins.

Dax hadn't wasted his advantage. Those early minutes in the darkness, all-seeing and all-knowing as he waited for an unprepared adversary, had been put to good use.

His attention was diverted from the car now, though. The bridge crowned above the river, and the shooting had taken place near the opposite shore, which meant his view of the parking lot would be minimal. Abby stayed as low as she could, approaching the Jeep, and just before she reached for the door handle, she felt the overwhelming certainty that it would be locked and she would have come down here for no reason but to guarantee her death.

Right then, there was another clap on the bridge. A second shot.

She knelt and turned her hands palms up, like a beggar, and got her fingertips under the door handle. She pulled, bracing for the interior lights that would come on like a prison guard's searchlight, pinning her escape attempt.

The door opened, and darkness remained.

She's just like him, Abby realized. The woman named Boone had shut off the automatic lights. She was just like him, favoring control at all times.

And she was dead now.

Abby leaned into the car. Shannon Beckley was in the backseat, a strip of duct tape over her mouth. Her hands rested in her lap, bound with zip-ties, similar to Abby.

"We need to run," Abby whispered. "Can you—"

She didn't need to finish the question; Shannon was already shaking her head. She moved her foot and Abby heard a metallic jingle, looked down, and saw that Shannon was cuffed to something beneath the seat. Maybe to the seat itself.

Shit, shit, shit.

Shannon made a jutting motion with her chin, a series of upward nudges, like a cat seeking attention, and Abby understood what she meant. Shannon was telling her to run. To save herself. Just as Hank once had, and back then Abby had listened and lived.

Abby shook her head. She stayed in place, heart skittering, trying to keep her breathing as silent as possible while she looked around the car for any help, any weapon. There was nothing—except for a phone in the cup holder.

She reached for it excitedly, fumbling with her bound hands, and only when she'd secured it in her grasp did she recognize that it wasn't a source of help at all. It wasn't even a phone. It was Oltamu's fake.

She dropped the phone with disgust, then jerked with surprise when Shannon Beckley kicked the back of the passenger seat, hard. Abby looked up into her fierce eyes and watched Shannon look pointedly at the center console.

Abby found the latch, lifted the console cover, and saw Shannon's cell phone resting there.

Beside the phone was a set of car keys with a Hertz keychain.

Abby grabbed them and swung into the driver's seat. She reached for the door handle with her bound hands and eased it shut, not quite latching it for fear of making noise. Just before she put her foot on the brake pedal, which would flash the telltale lights illuminating her escape attempt, she checked the mirror.

Dax was at the top of the bridge and walking their way.

Better hurry, she told herself, but she didn't move. Instead she watched him walking confidently down the center of the bridge, a gun in each hand, and she saw that he was indifferent to the Jeep, indifferent to the darkness, indifferent to everything. In his mind, the threat had been eliminated, and the rest would be easy. Abby could start the Jeep now, well within pistol range, and hope he wouldn't hit the tires. If he did, though...

She looked up the long, steep hill ahead and saw how it would end—the Jeep grinding to a pained halt on shredded rubber. He'd close on them easily enough then. This wasn't like Hank's house, where Abby had been able to get into the pines and be protected from the gunfire. She would be driving down the length of target range for him and counting on him to miss.

He wasn't going to miss.

"Get down below the windows," Abby whispered to Shannon Beckley. "Fast."

Shannon's eyes were wide above the strip of duct tape, but she didn't hesitate in following the instructions. She slid off the seat and into an awkward ball on the floor of the car. She was tall, and the space wasn't large, but she was bound to the car only by one foot, and she was flexible enough to burrow down tightly.

"Good," Abby whispered. "Stay down. No matter what. I'm going to kill him now."

Abby checked the mirror once more, then slid down in the driver's seat, low enough to bring the back of her head almost level with the steering wheel. She lost sight of Dax in the rearview mirror but found him in the side-view.

He was almost off the bridge. From there it was twenty or twenty-five paces to the Jeep. Unprotected ground. For her, and for him.

If she got him, it would be over. If she missed...

The ignition lag will be the moment you lose advantage, she thought. *That half-second hitch between engine cranking and engine catching. He's very fast.*

He'd shoot before he moved. She was almost certain of that. He'd shoot before he moved, and he would expect whoever was driving the Jeep to be in flight mode, not fight mode. He counted on fear.

He wouldn't be getting any more of that from Abby.

He walked on with a fast but controlled stride. Refusing, as always, to be rushed. Abby bit her lip until blood filled her mouth. Her hands trembled just below the push-button ignition; her foot hovered above the brake pedal, calf muscles bunched, threatening to cramp.

Down he came. Stepping off the bridge without pause. He didn't so much as glance up the road at the car from which she'd escaped. His eyes were locked dead ahead, and she was sure that he was looking right into the side-view mirror and seeing her eyes. The guns dangled in his hands, and the second of them was proof of Boone's death, as sure a trophy as if he'd carried her scalp back.

Thirty feet away now. Abby almost pressed on the brake but managed to hold off.

Twenty feet. Close enough? No. He would have to be almost to the vehicle. Then, she just had three simple steps—press the brake and the ignition, shift from park to reverse, and hit the gas.

Oh, and duck. That was key.

Fifteen feet, ten…

Abby slammed her foot onto the brake pedal and punched the ignition simultaneously. The dash lights came on, and then, with what felt like excruciating slowness, the engine growled.

She ripped the shifter from park to reverse as the back window imploded, and then she hit the gas. Three shots were fired, maybe more. The Jeep ripped backward, and then there was an impact on the left side, glancing, almost imperceptible, but she knew what it was because there'd been only one thing between her and the bridge.

Got him. Got the bastard!

The gunfire was done, and the bridge and the river beyond had to be avoided, so she switched from gas pedal to brake and jerked the Jeep to a stop.

No more shots. Not a sound except for the engine.

She poked her head up and searched for him. The headlights showed a short expanse of grass and then the trees, the jogging path a ribbon of black between them. Empty.

She looked sideways and found him.

He was down in the grass behind the parking lot, fighting to rise to his feet.

He didn't make it. He got halfway up and then fell to his knees. His hands were empty, and his left arm dangled unnaturally across his body, broken. He patted the grass with his right hand, searching for a gun, and Abby pushed herself all the way up in the driver's seat, thin slivers of glass biting through her jeans. She let go of the wheel and used her bound hands to knock the gearshift into drive.

Kill him.

As if he'd heard the thought, Dax looked up at the Jeep. Before Abby could reach for the steering wheel, he lurched upward again. This time he made it to his feet.

Then he turned and ran.

She was so astonished that she left her foot on the brake. She sat motionless, watching him go. His run was awkward; he was hurting badly. But he moved fast for a wounded man. He was panicked.

You coward, she thought. Somehow, she'd expected he would fight until the end. She was almost disappointed to see him run.

But there he went, laboring up the hill toward the Challenger. Did he think Abby was still inside that car and that Shannon Beckley had driven the Jeep into him, or had he seen Abby's face in the instant before she hit him? She hoped he had. She wanted him to know who'd gotten him. In any case, he'd know soon enough, when he found the Challenger empty. He was covering ground surprisingly fast despite his injuries, running on adrenaline. Running on fear. He was scared of her, and that filled her with a savage delight.

The train whistle shrilled to the west. To the east, at the top of the hill near the Challenger, the sky was edging from black to gray. Dawn almost here. Daylight on the way, and Dax on the run.

She'd won.

Abby twisted and looked into the backseat.

"You okay?"

Shannon nodded. Her cheek was bleeding where a ribbon of glass had opened it up, but she seemed unaware of the wound.

"He's gone," Abby said. "He's running away."

Two flashes of light came from up the hill, and she looked that way to see the Challenger's headlights come on as the Hellcat engine growled to life, started with the remote as Dax limped that way. She watched him reach the car, fumble with the door, and then fall into the driver's seat. He'd have a chance to escape now, and she almost wanted to pursue him.

She knew better, though. Let him run, and let the police catch him. He wouldn't make it far. What Abby needed to do was get help on the way. She would go to one of the houses up the road and call for...

"Oh, shit," she said, in a flat, almost matter-of-fact voice.

The Challenger was in motion, but it wasn't turning around. He was headed down the hill, not up it.

The kid wasn't fleeing. He was coming back to finish the fight.

61

Even as she hammered the accelerator, Abby knew there was no real gain to making the first move. She was backed in against the river, and her options were minimal—she could swerve left or right, trying to evade him, or drive straight at him. The Jeep had the advantage if she chose the latter, but that didn't make her feel confident. A head-to-head crash would do more damage to the Challenger than the Jeep, yes, but there was hardly a guarantee of disabling the driver.

I already hit him, she thought numbly. *I broke the bastard's arm, I won, so why won't he quit?*

Beneath that thought, though, ran a soft, chastising whisper that told her she should have known better.

The cars would meet about halfway up the hill. Abby was bracing for the collision and thinking too late that she needed to yell out some word of warning to Shannon when Dax cut the wheel and brought the Challenger smoking in at an angle, and she realized what he was trying to do—block the road.

Easy enough. She swerved right, and the front end of the Challenger clipped the edge of the Jeep's bumper, an impact that felt barely more solid than when she'd hit Dax. The Jeep chunked off the pavement and back onto it and then she was past him, open road ahead.

But the open road didn't mean much to her. Not in the Jeep, not with him in the Hellcat. Ahead of Abby, Ames Road climbed up, up, up. It wasn't a long distance, but it was steep, and distance was relative. The Hellcat went from zero to sixty in a breathtaking

3.6 seconds, absurd for a factory car, and the opening acceleration wasn't even its strongest point. The Hellcat was truly special when it was already rolling. It could go from thirty to fifty or fifty to seventy in a heartbeat. The quarter-mile stretch ahead would take the Challenger maybe twelve or thirteen seconds.

She chanced a look in the mirror and saw the door open. Watched as he leaned out and picked up a handgun from the pavement.

"Fuck," Abby said. Her voice was too calm; disembodied. She couldn't see Shannon Beckley in the mirror. Shannon was still wedged down on the floor, where Abby had told her to hide back when she thought she could win this thing, a minute before that felt like a decade ago now. The rest of the race invited no such illusions. She'd hit him, yes; hurt him, yes; but he hadn't stopped, and now he was outthinking her. Now he was in the superior car *and* he was armed, and whatever injuries he'd sustained suddenly seemed insignificant.

She glanced at Oltamu's phone. What if she threw it out of the car? Would he stop to get it just as he had the gun? It was all he wanted, after all.

Not anymore, she thought grimly, remembering the way he'd fought to his feet, his arm dangling broken in front of his body, useless. No, he wouldn't settle for the phone anymore. He'd take it, but he was coming for blood now.

Behind her, the Challenger's huge engine roared, the Pirellis burned blue smoke, and the headlights swerved and then steadied, pinning Abby.

The top of the hill might as well have been five miles out.

The Hellcat roared up with astonishing closing speed.

He can't even drive it, Abby thought. That didn't seem fair, somehow. To lose to him when he couldn't even handle that car was a cruel joke.

Then beat him, Luke said, or maybe it was Hank, or maybe it was Abby's father. Hard to tell, but Abby understood one thing—the voice was right.

In a decade of professional stunt driving, Abby had asked the finest cars in the world to do things that most people thought couldn't be done. Not on that list, though, was a controlled drift uphill with her hands tied together.

She wanted to use the hand brake, but that would require briefly taking her hands off the wheel, and instinct told her that that would end badly no matter how fast she moved. The Jeep sat up high, and if she didn't have full control of the wheel, the jarring counterforce of the hand brake would likely flip the car.

Just fishhook it, then. Nice and easy. Maybe he'd overcompensate, flip his own car, break his own neck.

Sure.

The headlights were filling the Jeep with clean white light, the broken glass glistening and the roar of the Hellcat almost on top of them, and suddenly Abby knew what he would do.

He'll be cautious, Abby thought, and she had the old feeling then, the swelling confidence that came up out of the blood, cool as a Maine river at night. She had watched Dax drive that car for hours now. He didn't understand the car, but he respected its power. So he wouldn't risk flipping it; he'd overshoot instead.

A tenth of a mile from the crest of the hill, Abby said, "Hang on," as if Shannon Beckley could do anything to prepare, and then she jammed her foot on the brake and spun the wheel through her fingers, passing it as rapidly as possible, like paying out rope, left hand to right hand, feeding it, feeding it, feeding it as the world spun around them.

I needed the hand brake, she thought, but she was wrong. They hadn't been going fast enough, and the hill worked in her favor. Physics came to her rescue as she shifted from brake to gas and pounded the pedal again. All around them was the sound of shrieking rubber as the tires negotiated with, pleaded with, and finally begged for mercy from the pavement.

The pavement was benevolent.

It granted the skid. The Jeep didn't roll.

Beside them, the Challenger smoked by in a roaring blur.

Abby was already accelerating back downhill by then.

She chanced a glance in the mirror only when she was sure the Jeep was running straight. The fishhook had been a simple stunt—awkward and lumbering by any pro's standard, actually—but it had been enough. The kid had had a choice: try to match it or ride by and gather himself. He'd opted for the latter.

Dax was executing a three-point turn to counter. In a *Challenger Hellcat,* he was executing a three-point turn to catch up to a Jeep. Abby wanted to laugh. *We can do this once more,* she thought, *or twice more, however long it takes, back and forth, but he's not getting a clear shot. Not as long as I have the wheel.*

She actually might have laughed if she hadn't looked ahead and seen the headlight from the train.

It was running northwest to southeast, cutting through Hammel and across the bridge on its dawn run, out of the night and toward the sunrise.

Up at the top of the hill, where the Challenger was executing its awkward turn, bells were clanging and guard arms lowering to block traffic on Ames Road. The train would soon take over that task. The train would block them above, the river already blocked them below, and Abby and Shannon would be sealed in the middle with Dax and his gun.

Abby brought the Jeep to a stop, twisted, and looked at Shannon Beckley. She'd clambered off the floor and back into the seat. Blood from the cut sheeted down her cheek, but her eyes were bright above it. Abby looked down at the handcuff that chained Shannon to the vehicle. Only one of them could walk away from this.

I'll take the phone, she thought, *I'll take the phone and I'll make him negotiate. Just like with the man named Gerry.*

The man he'd killed.

The negotiating hour was past.

She looked down the hill. Ahead of her, there was only the parking lot, the river, and the railroad bridge.

And, now, the train.

She looked back at Shannon Beckley, expecting to see Shannon staring ahead. But she was staring right at Abby. Scared, yes, but still with a fighter's eyes.

"I have to try," Abby said.

Shannon nodded.

Abby started to say, *It might not work,* but stopped herself. That was obvious.

Behind them, Dax had the Challenger straightened out and was facing her once again.

Abby let her foot off the brake and started downhill. The wheel slipped in her bloody hands and pulled left, but she caught it and brought it back. Behind, the Hellcat roared with delight and gained speed effortlessly, a thoroughbred running behind a nag. Abby didn't look in the mirror to see how fast Dax was pushing it. Her eyes were only on the bridge and the train. The train was slowing, navigating the last bend ahead of the bridge, and its whistle cried out a shrill warning, and the bells tolled their monotonous lecture of caution.

She fed the wheel back through her blood-slicked palms, bringing the car to the right when the road curved left, toward the parking lot. She pounded the gas as they banged over the curb and off the road and then headed for the short but steep embankment that led up to the train tracks. The Jeep climbed easily, and at the top of the embankment was the first of Abby's final tests—if she got hung up on the tracks, it was over.

The front end scraped rock and steel as the Jeep clawed up

onto the berm, and she managed to negotiate the turn, praying for clearance. She had just enough. The Jeep was able to straddle the rails, leaving the tires resting on the banked gravel and dirt on either side.

Behind and below her, Dax brought the Hellcat around in a slow, growling circle, like a pacing tiger. She knew what he was assessing—the Jeep sat high, able to clear the rails, and its wheelbase was wide enough to straddle them. The Challenger sat low, a bullet hovering just off the pavement. It would hang up on the tracks, leaving it stranded.

Dax didn't seem inclined to try pursuit. The car idled; the door didn't open; no gunfire came.

He watched and waited.

He thinks I've trapped myself, Abby realized.

And maybe she had. Squeezed from multiple sides now, she could go in only one direction: straight toward the train.

She kept expecting a gunshot but none came, and she realized why—he didn't think she'd try it. His brake lights no longer glowed, which meant he'd put the Challenger in park—he was that confident that Abby was done.

She looked away from him and fixed her eyes ahead, staring down the length of the railroad bridge, where, just on the other side, the huge locomotive was negotiating its last turn and entering the straightaway of the bridge. How far off? A hundred yards? Maybe less. It couldn't be more. If it was more...

I've just got to run it as fast as I can, that's all there is to it, she thought. When it came down to the last lap, when the rubber was worn and the fuel lines were gasping for fumes, there was no math involved, no calculations, no time.

You finished or you didn't. That was all.

Abby put her foot on the gas.

62

S he was doing forty when she reached the bridge and she knew that she had to get up to at least sixty, maybe seventy, to give them any chance. But she also had to hold the car straight, and the gravel banks were built to keep the rails in place, not provide tire traction. It was a bone-rattling ride and one that made acceleration painfully slow.

The train was some thirty yards away from the bridge now. Thirty yards of opportunity remained for her to decide if it was a mistake and bail out. Ditch the Jeep, and then Abby could run, even if Shannon could not. With the diesel locomotive's headlight piercing the fractured windshield and the train's whistle screaming, it was easy to believe bailing was the right move.

Behind and below them, though, Dax waited.

He thinks I'm choosing my own way to die, Abby realized.

She kept her foot on the gas.

In front of her, the train straightened out until the diesel locomotive was facing her head-on. In the backseat, Shannon Beckley moaned from behind the tape. Abby was aware of a flicker of open grass to her right, a place where she could ditch the Jeep without falling into the river below.

Last chance to get out ... take it.

She tightened her grip on the wheel. The last chance fell behind. Then they were on the bridge, and out of options.

A brightening sky above and a dark river below. A whistle shrilling, a headlight pounding into her eyes. The bridge seemed to evaporate into a tunnel, and though she wanted to check the speedometer to see whether she'd gotten up to seventy, she couldn't take her eyes off that light.

She would never remember the last swerve.

There was no plan, no target, nothing but white light and speed and the question of whether she could make it. Then, suddenly, the gap appeared, and instinct answered.

Daylight.

Chase it.

She slid the wheel across blood-soaked palms, and the daylight was there, and then the daylight was gone, and then came the impact.

A bang and a bounce and blackness. *I thought it would feel worse than that. That wasn't bad at all, for being hit by a train,* she thought, and then the furious scream of the whistle brought her back to reality. She was facing a wall of grass. It took her a moment to realize that it was the bank on the far side of the river.

The engineer was trying to slow the train, but with that much mass and momentum, it didn't happen fast. The locomotive was across the bridge and headed uphill before the cars behind it began to slow. A timber train, flatbed cars loaded with massive white pine logs from the deep northern woods.

Abby looked in the mirror. The Challenger was in the parking lot, facing her, idling. It no longer looked so smug. In fact, it looked impotent.

She knocked the gearshift into park, then reached out her bloody fingers, gripped the edge of the tape covering Shannon Beckley's mouth, and peeled it away. "You okay?"

Shannon nodded, as if unaware that she could speak now, then said, "Yes." Paused and repeated it. "Yes. I think so."

Abby opened the driver's door and stumbled out into the morning air. The train was still easing to a stop beside them, each car clicking by slower than the last. In the pale gray light, she could see the Challenger's door swing open, and she thought, *After all that, he's still going to shoot me.*

The kid limped around the front of the idling car. He eyed the pedestrian bridge below the train. Abby looked in the same direction, and for the first time, she saw Boone's body. Dax started to limp ahead.

He's still coming, she realized with numb astonishment. He would cross that bridge once more, even after all of this. All for a...

She turned back to the car and reached for Oltamu's phone. Her hands hovered just above it, then drifted left, and she popped the center console open and found Shannon Beckley's phone.

It took her two tries to grasp it in her bloody fingers, and by the time she had it and stepped away from the car, the kid was at the foot of the bridge.

"Dax!" she screamed.

He looked up. He was limping badly, and his left arm hung awkwardly, obviously broken but disregarded, like a dragging muffler. The gun was in his right hand, but she was too far away to fear being shot.

"Go get it!" Abby shouted, and then she pivoted back and whirled forward and sent Shannon Beckley's phone spinning into the air. It sailed in a smooth arc out above the river and then down into it.

Dax watched it splash and sink.

He stood there and looked at the water, and then, finally, he lifted his head to face Abby.

Duck, she commanded herself, but her body didn't obey. She just stood there on the other side of the river, hands bound in front of her, blood running down her arms.

The kid raised his gun. Abby waited for the shot.

None came. Instead, he held it across his forehead, and for a bizarre moment she thought he was going to take a suicide shot. Then she realized that he was offering a salute. He held the pose for a moment, then turned and limped back to the car. As the train whistle shrieked again, he backed the Challenger out and pulled up the hill. The train had stopped before blocking the road, granting him an escape route.

Abby stood where she was until the car crested the hill and vanished, then she sank down into the grass.

She looked back at the bridge, at that narrow window between train and steel girder, and wondered how wide it had been when she slipped the Jeep through. She stared at that for a long moment, and then she struggled upright and went to Shannon Beckley. Abby extended her wrists.

"Can you untie me?"

Shannon looked at Abby's face, then down to her hands. "Yes," she said simply, and she went to work on the knots with nimble fingers. It didn't take her long. Abby watched the cord fall away, and she remembered the strangling cord at her throat, her feet on the dash and her back arched. She flexed her fingers, then reached out and plucked the black baseball cap off Shannon Beckley's head. She studied it and found the pinhole-size camera hidden just beneath the bill, beneath the odd silver stitching that drew the eye of the observer toward the top of the hat. Was he watching? No. But he would go back. He would go back to study what he'd missed.

She was sure of that.

Abby angled the bill of the cap at her face and then lifted her middle finger up beside it. Then she stepped back from the Jeep, turned, and pulled her arm back, prepared to fling the hat as far into the river as she could.

"The police will need it," Shannon Beckley said.

Abby stopped. Sighed and nodded. Yes, they would. But *damn,* how much she wanted to watch it drown.

She tossed the hat on the driver's seat. Sirens were approaching from somewhere on the campus and somewhere on the other side of the river. She ignored them, studying the plastic zip ties that held Shannon's wrists together.

"I'll need to cut that. You have anything that will work?"

"Get the phone," Shannon said.

Abby was puzzled. Shannon had seemed so composed, but maybe she was delirious. Abby wasn't cutting those ties with a phone. "No," Abby told her patiently and began to root around in the console in search of a better tool.

"Get the phone," Shannon said, each word firm as a slap, and when Abby looked up, she saw that Shannon was staring over her shoulder. Abby turned and saw the dog crouched at the tree line, head up, ears back, wary but intrigued.

She picked up Oltamu's phone and walked away from the car. The sirens were growing louder, and someone was screaming at her from across the river, but she didn't look away and neither did the dog. Abby went as close as she dared and then sat in the grass and extended a bloody hand.

"Hobo," she said. "Come see me."

63

Tara has been many things and is becoming many more. Each day seems to bring a new identity.

First she was the vegetable, the brain-dead girl, and then she was the locked-in girl, and then, within hours of learning that Shannon was alive, Tara was the Coma Crime Stopper.

This is because of the story Shannon told, giving credit to her sister's nonverbal lie.

People look at her and think she's helpless. But from that bed, she saved me without speaking a word.

The media loved that quote. They directed feature coverage to Tara on every network. Their attention, as is its way, swells and breaks. A van with bombs is found in DC, and a hurricane is howling toward Texas. The Coma Crime Stopper is forgotten.

Then the contents of the phone are revealed.

Photos, files, videos of an electric vehicle produced by a company called Zonda, which is the name of an Argentinean wind that blows over the Andes Mountains. Most of the files are complex equations or sets of computer algorithms, an FBI agent from Boston named Roxanne Donovan tells Tara and her family. The photos and videos are mostly of cars on fire. Zonda prototypes.

The product of German design, American manufacturing, and international investing, Zonda is on the verge of being about so much more than cars. The company has already agreed to a multibillion-dollar contract with one of the world's largest airplane builders, military contracts are expanding, and, one week after a woman with a knife arrived to talk to Tara Beckley—and kill her—the company was to have its initial public offering. All has been trending positively for Zonda with the exception of one troublesome engineer who, in the months before the IPO, began to reach out to a handful of select individuals, informing them of rumors and promising documentation. What he could show, he told them, was the equivalent of the Volkswagen diesel-emissions scandal that cost the company billions in fines and led to the criminal indictments of nine executives. One of the world's most exciting young companies had been built on a carefully protected lie, and he was prepared to share evidence of that or remain silent about it—whichever was more profitable.

"I'd love to tell you that Amandi Oltamu was noble," Roxanne Donovan says to Tara. "But our early information suggests that he was only looking for a payday."

This disappoints Tara. Donovan is right; Tara wants him to be noble. She wants to have his death and her own suffering wrapped in righteousness.

She won't get what she wants.

"He made at least three offers," Donovan continues. "Two were to people who had stakes in the company. Extortion efforts, basically. When those demands weren't met, he went in a different direction. He contacted a rival."

The rival, it seemed, had gotten in touch with a woman named Lisa Boone.

The source of the baby-faced kid in the black hat is less clear. He is the son of a killer, seventeen or eighteen or possibly nineteen years old, and Roxanne Donovan will say only that the Bureau is working on leads, many of them generated by interviews with Abby Kaplan. Lisa Boone is dead, shot on the railroad bridge over the Willow River where Tara had once nearly died herself, but the young killer is missing. The best lead there, Donovan tells them, involves a rural airport in Owls Head. An isolated hangar on the Maine coast, it serves as a touchdown point for the private-jet set.

On the morning after the killing on the bridge, a small jet from Germany landed in Owls Head and refueled. Its lone passenger was an attorney from Berlin. The plane took on another passenger at Owls Head, a young man with a limp and one arm in a sling. The aircraft then flew to Halifax, and from Halifax to London, changing flight plans each time. Upon the plane's arrival in London, the young passenger from America disembarked after informing the pilot that the German attorney was sleeping and wasn't to be bothered. By the time the pilot discovered the man wasn't sleeping but dead, the unknown American was gone.

While Tara was a feature story, the death of Dr. Pine received sidebar coverage. She thinks this is a crime, that all the nobility Oltamu lacked, Pine had shown.

She hopes that his family will come to see her. On the day that she lifts her right thumb on command for the first time, she uses Dr. Carlisle's computer software to compose a short letter to Dr. Pine's family. It is the first writing she's done in this condition, and the words don't come as easily as she'd like, but would they ever for a letter like this?

The Coma Crime Stopper isn't sure.

What she is sure about is that the task of calling up the words is good for her. When she closes her eyes after that first bit of strained writing, she sees more of the green and gold light, sparklers and starbursts of it illuminating new rivers and tributaries, uncharted waters.

She writes again the next day.

Dr. Carlisle's prognosis becomes a bit less guarded in the following days. More enthusiasm bleeds through, perhaps more than she'd like to show. Tara exchanges e-mail with a woman who recovered from locked-in syndrome and who has just completed her third marathon since the injury. She is an outlier, of course. But Tara watches videos of her race over and over.

She must become an outlier too. She owes them all this much.

She owes Pine, obviously, but also Shannon, Abby Kaplan, and so many more. People she never met. A man named Hank Bauer. A man at a junkyard where her devastated Honda still rests.

She knows the journey ahead is long, and a good outcome is not promised. But she has so much fuel to carry her through it.

Weary but hopeful, she closes her eyes, flexes her thumb, and searches for those green-gold glimmers in the dark.

64

W e'll find him," the investigator from Scotland Yard promised Abby after three hours of taped interviews and the review of countless photographs taken from surveillance cameras around the city of London, Abby having been asked to search the crowds for a glimpse of Dax.

When she considered Dax's destination, the city that shared Luke's last name, she couldn't help but feel that it was a taunt. His silent response to the raised middle finger she'd offered that black hat. Somehow, she is sure that he saw that.

He was not in any of the photographs.

"How will you find him?" Abby asked the investigator.

"The way it's always done: Patience and hard work. We'll follow his patterns, learn who he trusts, and find him through them or when he makes a mistake. It will happen."

Abby wasn't so sure. She didn't think the kid trusted anyone. And while she knew the kid made mistakes, she felt as if he would make fewer of them by the day, by the hour. Each moment was a learning experience.

Abby remembered the salute he'd given her in the dim dawn light across the river, just before the kid got back into Hank Bauer's Challenger and disappeared. He'd been in three countries since then, and no one had caught him yet.

"He's adaptive," Abby said. "And I think he has big goals."

The man from Scotland Yard didn't seem interested in Abby's opinion. "He's no different from the rest of his family," he said. "Which means that, sooner or later, he'll end up dead or in jail. We'll see to that."

Abby wondered how long it had taken Scotland Yard to see to that for the rest of the kid's family, but she didn't ask. The last question she asked was the one she felt she already knew the answer to.

"What was his father's name?"

"He had a dozen of them."

"The most common one, then. What did most people call him?"

The investigator hesitated, then said, "Jack."

Abby nodded, remembering the bottle of poisoned whiskey that the boy had presented to Abby and Hank on the night they'd met.

"And the last name?"

"Blackwell."

"Blackwell," Abby echoed. It seemed right. It suited the family.

"He's quite dead," the Scotland Yard man said in a nearly chipper voice.

Abby looked at the photographs of the boy contract killer, and again, she wasn't sure the investigator was right. The man named Jack Blackwell might be dead, but his legacy was alive and well, moving through Europe like a ghost.

If he was even still in Europe.

"I'll tell you this," the Brit continued, "you're bloody lucky—and so is Shannon Beckley—that you can drive like that. Put anyone else behind the wheel out there, and you're both in the morgue."

"You're right," Abby said, and for the first time she did not doubt the accuracy of the man's statement.

Abby had needed the wheel for this one.

"Not making light of it," the Brit said, "but it seems to have been rather fortunate for your reputation too, based on what I've seen."

"Excuse me?"

"The Luke London thing."

The Luke London thing. Ah, yes. When she didn't respond, just stared evenly at him, he shifted awkwardly.

"I just mean in the media. Plenty of kindness from the same folks who crucified you before. Changes the narrative, right?"

"No," Abby said. "It doesn't."

The man looked at her curiously. Abby said, "It all happened. Nothing's replaced by anything else. They fit together."

"Sure," the Brit said, but he didn't understand, and Abby didn't try to clarify. The wins were the wins, the wrecks were the wrecks, as Hank Bauer used to say. They all worked together. The only risk was in expecting that one or the other was promised to you. Neither was. When the starting flag was waved, all you ever had was a chance.

"I won't waste it, though," Abby said, and this seemed to please the Brit; this part he thought he followed.

"Good," he said, and he clapped Abby on the shoulder and promised her that they'd be in touch soon. Abby was going to be important when they got the Blackwell lad in a courtroom.

Abby assured him she'd be ready for that moment. Then she left to drive to the hospital, where Shannon Beckley waited with her sister. Tara had therapy today. Tongue-strengthening exercises. Dr. Carlisle thought she was coming along well enough that spoken conversation might be possible sooner rather than later. She wouldn't make any bolder predictions, but she'd offered this much encouragement:

She fights, and so she has a chance.

It was, Abby thought, a patently obvious statement, and yet it mattered.

She drove south to Massachusetts alone.

The coastal Maine sun was brighter than the cold day seemed to allow, an optical illusion, the sky so blue it seemed someone had touched up the color, tweaking it beyond what was natural. The Scotland Yard man had taken longer than expected, and rush-hour traffic was filling in. Abby drove at seventy-five in the middle lane, letting the impatient pass her on the left and the indifferent fall behind to the right.

Her hand was steady on the wheel.

65

The girl in the kayak is testing new waters. There are channels all around her, currents previously unseen that are now opening up, and some are less inviting than others, as dark and ominous as the mouth of a cave. Others show promising glimmers of brightness but are lost quickly behind gray fog. Still, she knows they are out there, and she has the paddle, and she has the will. She knows that she must be both patient and aggressive, traits that seem contradictory only if you have never run a long race.

She pushes east through fogbound channels, and then the current catches her and carries her, turns her east to south, and the fog lifts and gray light brightens, brightens, brightens, until she is flying through it and there are glimmers of green and gold in the spray.

Satisfied, she coasts to a stop. Pauses, savoring the beauty of it all, savoring the chance.

When she's caught her breath, she paddles back upstream. The current spins and guides her, north to south first, then south to north. These are unusual waters, but she's learning them, learning when to fight them, when to trust them. Each day she travels a little farther and a little faster.

She dips the blade of the paddle and holds it against the gentle pressure, bringing the boat around in a graceful arc. Now she faces the dark mouth of one of the many unknown channels looming ahead. So much of the terrain is unknown, but none of it is unknowable.

There is a critical difference in that.

She paddles forward boldly into the blackness, chasing the light.

ACKNOWLEDGMENTS

Let's start off with readers, librarians, and booksellers—who should always be first when it comes to author gratitude.

The team at Little, Brown and Company is the best. Thanks to Joshua Kendall, Michael Pietsch, Reagan Arthur, Sabrina Callahan, Craig Young, Terry Adams, Heather Fain, Nicky Guerreiro, Maggie (Southard) Gladstone, Ashley Marudas, Shannon Hennessey, Karen Torres, Karen Landry, and Tracy Roe. Everyone involved in the process of taking the book into the world is deeply appreciated.

Much gratitude to Richard Pine and the team at InkWell Management, and to Angela Cheng Caplan. Lacy Whitaker has done her best to make me presentable to the social-media world, which is no small task.

Thanks to Dr. Daniel Spitzer for his guidance and expertise.

Early readers who suffered painful drafts are always appreciated—Christine Koryta, Bob Hammel, Pete Yonkman, and Ben Strawn provided invaluable feedback and support. My parents always do, and always have.

And thanks to the Blackwell family. You're the gift that keeps on giving.

ABOUT THE AUTHOR

Michael Koryta is the *New York Times* bestselling author of fourteen novels, most recently *How It Happened*. Several of his previous novels—among them *Last Words, Those Who Wish Me Dead,* and *So Cold the River*—were *New York Times* Notable Books and national bestsellers. His work has been translated into more than twenty languages and has won numerous awards. Koryta is a former private investigator and newspaper reporter. He lives in Bloomington, Indiana, and Camden, Maine.